MOUNTAIN WHISPERS

DAYS WITHOUT SUN

Book I

G. Coleman Alderson

ISBN: 978-0-9821822-7-7

Printed in the United States of America

To all who seek the truth and upon finding it, act accordingly

PART 1

"What have those lonely mountains worth revealing?
More glory and more grief than I can tell."
                                              ~Emily Bronte

Prologue

The haloed moon shone through the drifting clouds softly highlighting the terrain that rippled like waves on an inland sea. The ever-present stars and an effulgent Venus phased in and out of view. The winds blew eastward, gently suffusing summer's exhalation through the balsams on high, the leafy forests on the slopes and into the valleys where tall field grasses wavered. Seen from high above, the rivers glimmered like molten silver; the lakes mirrored the sky. As the vestiges of daylight dimmed, lights appeared on the surface forming earthbound constellations in tandem with the stars.

On a hill overlooking the beautiful Shannon Valley, an old farmhouse stood, clapboard in white, its metal roof glowing and dimming as clouds passed overhead. Nearby, stood several outbuildings and a barn. A dog barked in the distance, a confused rooster crowed, and in the barn, horses chuffed and nickered.

From outside the farmhouse, a ceiling light was visible in one of the second story bedrooms. Shadows darted past the window. A light appeared in a smaller attic window just below the gable. A woman's voice was calling. "Honey? Carl? Hey honey?"

From the room below, a man's voice answered. "Yes, love?"

"Have you seen the gray duffle, the one we took last time?"

"Uhhhh. Have you looked inside the big suitcase?"

"Okay. I'll look."

The woman turned from the top of the stairs and creaked her way over to their stash of travel gear. From behind, the slim form, pony-tailed red hair and lithe movement portrayed a girlish vitality when, in fact, she was a decade into adulthood. The attic still held in the heat from the day, and as she crouched down to retrieve the large suitcase, she pulled her ponytail forward to bare her freckled neck and back. Her light green cotton dress was already starting to cling.

She slid the case out of its nook. Upon unzipping the main section, sure enough, the gray duffle was nestled inside. She grabbed the bag, zipped up the case and was about to shove it back in its spot, but then she noticed something had tumbled into the gap—an oblong shoebox. She barely had enough arms reach, but with an extra stretch, she managed. When it came to light, she saw a faded blue ribbon wrapped around the middle and the penciled letters "S A V E" scribed onto the top. Her head shook as she smiled. "Well, I'll be." She touched the box with her fingertips tracing the little floral flowers done in colored crayon. Tears came from nowhere, a mix of sadness, longing and gratitude. She placed her full hand across the lid. "I miss you so much."

A voice from below. "Hey honey, did you find it?"

She answered, "Yes, I have it. I'll be down in

just a bit."

"Okay. Y'know we have to catch the early train. Can't be up too late packing. Right?"

"Right. I'll be down in a few." She caught a little irritation in her voice.

No response from below likely meant her husband was occupied elsewhere. Her little irritations rarely incited him.

Her attention returned to the shoebox. Temptation, temptation. She'd thought it had disappeared during one of the moves. Like a curious child, she shook the box as if doing so might indicate the contents. Objects slid into each other. Some seemed more solid judging by the way they knocked against the sides and each other. *Hmmm. Well, just a peek. Then I'll tidy up and head downstairs. Just a peek.* Very slowly, ceremoniously, she undid the ribbon and inhaling deeply, she carefully lifted the lid. She found the following:

> Faint fragrance of sandalwood
> Photographs jumbled helter-skelter
> A short piece of frayed rope
> A small angel carved out of coal
> A jade stone heart
> A sealed box labeled "Together Forever"
> (Ashes of V & R)
> An empty brass rifle shell.
> A lock of red hair
> A wall plug with a white cord and. . .

Under everything, there it was–
The vintage iPod Touch, Gen 5

She impulsively picked the device up and
depressed the button on the top. Nada. *Well, at least the
charger is still here. Question is, will a fifty-year-old battery still
work?* Something inside her sparked a burning curiosity
and impatient excitement. *We'll just have to see.* She
quickly put the iPod and the ribbon into the shoebox
and slipped the suitcase back in its nook. She grabbed
the box and had nearly walked out the door when she
remembered the gray duffel bag. She rushed back to
nab it and as she made her way downstairs, she flipped
off the attic light.

She came into the bedroom toting the gray
duffle bag and found her husband bent over the bed as
he'd just finished folding the freshly laundered items he
planned to take along. He was shirtless, not to show off
his well-toned physique, but to make sure his shirts still
suited him. Garments lay on the bed in seven neat
color coordinated stacks. He looked up and smiled. He
raised up to his full six three height and proudly
gestured toward the piles. "Hey! Just in time! I have
them all sorted by each day." He started to enumerate
but saw her raise a hand.

"That's wonderful, dear. Just leave them there
and I'll pack them along with mine. I finished the
children's packing earlier so this is the last of it." She
walked toward him, tossed the gray duffle onto the
unoccupied half of the bed and gave him a beguiling
smile. He caught sight of how the green dress clung to
her alluring form. Though he often possessed an air of
the intellectual observer, his wife's charms still

captivated and excited him to no end.

Having gained his full attention, she began to shimmy out of her clingy cotton dress. The shimmy was what really got to him. She was down to a bra and panties. "Sooo, would you care to see a fashion show of what I plan to take on the trip?" She cocked her hip, swiveled her shoulders and vamped like a model.

A strong surge of passion pulsed through his veins. He wrapped his hands around the small of her back and pulled her to him. "So far, I like it very much," he whispered in her ear. They kissed and fell across the bed. His neatly arranged vacation attire was scattered, the overhead fan strobed the ceiling with light and shadow, and the faint scent of sandalwood infused the air.

#

She sat at a small table near an open window. The moonlight had begun to seep through as the salty air gently rippled the curtains. The sound of the ocean waves caressed and soothed her being. It had taken most of the day traveling from station to station to finally arrive. Everybody, even the kids, had turned in early. It was her time now. She'd made herself a cup of tea and had settled down to read. That was what she'd told her understanding husband. He likely figured she'd engross herself in some tattered mystery. *Well, maybe so.* She held the small device as if handling a delicate flower or fallen bird. Did she really want to delve into what seemed a lifetime ago? Was it mere curiosity or did she hope to touch into something more profound? Lessons yet to learn.

Absently, out of habit, she stroked the scar that furrowed a line of flesh just below her jaw. While it was barely visible now, it still pained her at times, even though the tissue had knitted as well as one could hope, given the circumstances. The circumstances. *Well*, she thought, *how ridiculous to have carried the thing all the way here and not at least have a look. I owe it to them, to their memory, to all they made possible.*

She pressed the top button and watched the tiny screen light up. Her heart beat double-time as the icons popped up in neat little rows. *It's working! Okay, then. Calm down.* She was surprised at her reaction. Her finger lightly touched the familiar inkpot icon. A few flickers later, a blank screen came up. After a few more taps and strokes, the title appeared. "The Story of My Life So Far by Celi Pierce (Me)." On the verge of tapping the little string of words, she hesitated, then kicked herself for being such a flake. *Dammit, girl, just get on with it!* It only took a few seconds for the first page to flash into view. It began with her twelfth birthday.

Chapter 1

Celi's Diary
Septembr 27, 2052

Today is my birthday. I'm 12 years old. YAY! My Gram gave me this writer box that I am learning to use. It says iPod on the back, but Gram calls it iTOUCH. It used to be hers and she was REAL careful to keep it. She showed me how to use the buttons, and what to pick off the picture part. It has a cord that plugs into a thing that sits in the light. That keeps it going but there's not much light, so I don't know how long it will last.

GRAM says I can use it to write my best thoughts. It used to connect to a much bigger machine, a computer and you could get stuff to put inside the screen like games and maps and movies. GRAM says you could even talk and show your face with other people BUT not now. She used to have a computer but says the driver died years ago. That sounds sad, BUT Gram told me I can start a dairy, whoops! DIARY. HA Imagine me starting a dairy, MILK COWS.

Anyway, Gram says I can keep track of what is going on in my life. She says I can use the inkpot thingy to write about anything and then press "save." She took off some of the games and other little pictures to make room. I really don't see how so many words can squeeze into such a small space, but that is okay. We used up every bit of blank paper many years ago and it is hard to get more. She also left some old photos for me to see. I will have a look at those later.

I think she felt sorry for me being alone and all and that's why she gave me this iTOUCH thingy. I was so excited and I can remember her exact words. "Okay Celi. Now, you go and write your heart out, girl."

Thank you GRAM! YOU ARE MY HEart!

Chapter 2

"The Story of MY LIFE-So Far"
By Celi Pierce

First of all, it's so very VERY COLD and we don't see the sun anymore. The skies are as gray as ashes. It even tried to snow last night, just enough to stick white on the ground. It is still September. Oh, and it is the 27th, my birthday. When I walk away from the stoves, I can see my breath inside the cabin.

My name is Celi, by the way. It is really Cecilia, but my baby brother never could say it right so "Celi" just stuck. I can read and write. My Mom and GRAM taught me. I like to write 'cause we don't have much to read and I have to stay indoors a lot anyway.

We live in the mountains, in a cabin back in the Avery Cove. Now it is just my Dad, Gram and me. We live in small places. Like the others. We make out on what we can catch and pick and grow. We keep chickens and goats and sometimes folks have horses and mules. We fish and hunt where we can on what's left of our free land or we have to sneak into the wild lands and not get caught by the spotters.

We get heat from an old potbelly stove that burns wood and chunks of coal we find along the railroad tracks. We cook food on an old Heartland Cooker that also heats our water. It burns wood mostly. Jordy and I used to go out almost every day to pick up wood and coal. It's too dangerous now. My dad does it.

3

There are no trains anymore so there's not much to pick.

It's so cold most of the time now. It's all we can do some days just to keep from freezing to death. The ones who go around wearing Green Hats tell us it's not safe to burn wood or coal. We could buy these special made energy pellets they sell for creds in town, but My Gram says they can go to hell. PA too. Only, he says it more.

Chapter 3

A Day in the Life
October 1, 2052

Ben Pierce felt the chill seeping into him as he trudged along the rusted tracks. Luck had failed him so far. His gunnysack contained scant remnants of his quarry, nothing more than a handful of black nuggets. He knew the pickings would get slimmer, just as the refuse piles had all but disappeared, the chunks of coal cast off the mile-long train cars back in the day diminished in size and number. He'd worked this line for nearly a week and he knew it was about to play out. This forced him to range farther out and he hoped not to cross the blurred boundary into the Burkhart territory. As he considered the prospect of meeting up with Sade Burkhart's clan, he pulled up the right side of his long canvas coat to expose his holstered revolver, a vintage Smith and Wesson eight-shooter.

The wind came straight at him. He cinched his scarf tighter and yanked down the brim of his cap. He was keenly attuned to every sound—a drip, the rustle of leaves, the rattling of branches laid bare by the early passing of the fall season. Only the soft rasp of his breathing and the crunch of his feet on the graveled roadbed stirred the silence as he slowly walked Northward along the tracks, hunting, scanning, spotting, and perhaps, finding a sizable portion of coal to heat the cabin for a night or two.

He walked between the tracks that snaked the curves and contours of the creek. Occasionally, he glanced up at the steely sky rimmed by mountains that had once stood tall as the Rockies. Though worn smooth and covered in forest, the dark slopes rose high and pressed in on him like slumbering giants who might awaken at any moment. Judging by how his long, boney shadow was fading into the dusky ground, he'd soon need to call it a day and head home.

Suddenly, the sound of gunfire erupted, rolled down the mountains and echoed past him. Several shots were fired. It made him flinch slightly, but he knew the prey was up on the mountain, a far piece away. He figured someone had to be pretty desperate to be hunting on the Official Wild Lands. *Desperate times.* He'd regularly resorted to poaching on the Wild Lands himself though mostly with his crossbow. It didn't draw near as much attention.

His throat felt dry and his tongue thick. He stopped to drink some spring water from his canteen. He swished and spit out the first mouthful, and then took some down. He listened hard. He hoped those shots had found their mark. At least one family would have meat on the table that night. Maybe the spotters in the fire tower hadn't heard the gunfire and the hunter would get away scot-free. He remembered the time when hunting in the hills and fishing were like a birthright. They even let out public school during the hunting season. No more.

Despondently, he willed himself to turn around. He'd spent the better part of a day with barely anything to show for it. It was something a kid like his daughter Cecelia could do, but not safely. His mother was still spry enough but this kind of scavenging would

wear her out. He'd taken several long strides and then
something he saw made him stop. He tilted his head,
looking part sideways at something on the ground—a
faint, black luster. He unsheathed his old hunting knife
strapped to his belt, squatted down and pried out the
chunk of coal from under the rail's flat edge. It was
bigger than the span of his hand. While elated that this
would give heat for three days, maybe more if
dampered properly, he now carried a treasure that
anyone he might encounter would surely covet. So, as
he bagged the payload and slung the sack over his left
shoulder, he made sure to keep his right hand free and
his revolver at the ready.

He quickened his pace to a trot and could feel
the stones press hard through the patched soles of his
boots. His feet would hurt like hell later but getting
caught outside, past dark, alone, and with only eight
bullets, invited all kinds of trouble he'd just as soon not
court. At times like this, he wished he still had Rommel.
Part shepherd, part redbone hound, Rommel could run
game, fight off wild animals and sense trouble, but
what remained of Rommel lay buried in a grove of
pines by the cabin. A pang of sadness and loss daisy-
chained through his mind dragging up recollections
that were hard to fend off. He was not one to dwell on
the past or tally his personal miseries, of which there
were many, but there were times they came without
bidding.

Flushed with heat, he opened his long coat so
that it trailed out behind him. The wind was at his back.
He'd done pretty well, all things considered. If he came
across any small game, he might chance a shot at it.
Whoever hunted up on the mountain wouldn't be the

only one who brought home food.

Then he heard the sounds of vehicles coming downslope. By the way they surged, he knew they were ATVs, at least two of them. The spotters up in the tower had heard those shots and were tracking the shooter. If they found Ben along the tracks with a sack of coal, he'd have nearly the same troubles as a hunter. He'd have to pitch his sidearm, since it had no permit. They'd hardly believe he was taking the coal home to use as a doorstop. The law forbade any burning of coal without a special permit. The same went for wood. Collecting either amounted to a cardinal sin. Yet, people needed some form of heat to make it through. Mercy Pickett had died last winter, all froze up in his cabin. No one thought to check on him and he'd gotten to where he couldn't get out. As his Uncle Virgil often said, "They've got us comin' and goin', by the balls."

Good ole Virge. It's a shame he's taken to being a codger, and a damned sot to boot. He's just a shadow of himself, a fading shadow. Any day, Ben expected to hear the news that his uncle had been found dead in that flea trap hovel of his on Muddy Creek or along some track or just plain disappeared forever.

He kept up his pace, only pausing occasionally to listen. The motor sounds came to a crescendo and then faded off in the opposite direction. He sighed in relief—he wouldn't need to waste precious daytime hiding. The gunnysack had begun to weigh heavier across his shoulder. Home was about a two-hour hump. He'd not arrive home by dark after all.

Rounding the bend, a pair of rails split off toward the hulking remains of the old Mingo Coal tipple. The slanted roofs had caved; the conveyers that moved the coal from the mines had wrested from their perch and lay sprawled on the ground. The men who'd worked for Mingo Coal had become relics themselves. Fewer remained with each passing day. Yet, some still hung on. The tipple's main structure still managed to stand erect, without its windows, looking hollow eyed and haunted. Ben pondered the fact that he was of the first generation in the family who'd never set foot in the mines. The last of Mingo's mines had been shut down for twenty years.

Once again, he felt drawn into an abscess of memories. The way things were, the way people used to be. He shifted his thoughts away from the past and thought of his daughter and mother awaiting his return. He knew they'd fret about his lateness. His dark humor kicked in as he thought, *Well, I'll just send 'em a text message to say I'm running late and ask if they need anything from the store. Yep. LMAO.* He laughed sardonically. *Not in my lifetime, not anymore.*

A strange sound came from behind him. He stopped and listened as it grew louder—definitely mechanical, clacking, rhythmic, a metal on metal noise. He reached down and felt the nearest rail. A slight vibration came through his fingertips.

Damn! It had to be! He flung himself down the creek embankment into a thicket of wild raspberries, an action he immediately regretted as a hundred thorns tore into his face, his hands and barbed him through his clothing. If they spotted him, he'd be as stuck as a

fly caught in a web. He managed to extract his weapon
and get his body as flat as possible, pointing the gun
uphill at whoever was coming down the tracks.
Through the maze of briers, he spied the rail cart
rolling down the rails. Two men, facing forward and
seated side by side, one of them worked a large lever
back and forth. The other fanned his AR side to side,
as he swept the approaching perimeter. They were clad
in black and wore forest green watch caps patched with
an all too familiar insignia. The guy pumping the lever
had an AR as well slung from his chest rig.

As they came closer, Ben turned his head down
so that his pale face would not be visible through the
brambles. His acuity focused on what he could hear.
The clackety clack grew louder; the rhythm slowed. The
brakes made the sound of screeching fingernails on a
chalkboard. They'd stopped just above him. His heart
kicked like a mule inside his chest and he forced back
the urge to tear off running. For better or worse, he
had committed to this spot. He could hear them talking
on their comms. "Just the one retro," a voice flatly
stated. "We figure he's at the old tipple. The bank's
covered too thick with briers for anyone to penetrate."
Pause. "Understood."

They must've spotted him from somewhere
high above, he figured. Those were the guys on the
ATVs who'd driven down to their handcart. ATVs
didn't do well on these tracks; the wooden ties shook
the rider to pieces. The rail carts worked best; some
were motorized. Obviously, these guys didn't rate the
motorized type.

He heard some clattering and feet landing on

gravel. "Hold up a minute!" Footsteps from above came closer, then stopped just a few yards above him. A zipping noise, then a sigh of relief as the spotter let loose his bladder. Ben lay there for a seeming eternity listening and half expecting to be soaked by a cascade of piss. Every thorn that had spurred his skin, every scratch that marked his face and hands urged him to distraction. His skin crawled with a fierce impulse to be relieved. He itched all over. He closed his right fist and dug his nails deep into the palm. He tightened the grip on his eight-shooter. If the guy spotted him from above, he'd have precious little advantage, but he'd attempt to take him out no matter.

A voice came from some distance away. "Goddammit, Charlie! Will you hurry the hell up? Geeze!"

The man above him yelled back. "Hey, give me a goddamned break, asshole. I'll be there in a second!" The sound of a zipper, a crunch of gravel and then the grand finale–the Green Hat launched a wad of sputum down the bank. It hung up on a branch to the right of Ben's head. Without moving his head, Ben raised his eyes just so he could barely see the man's feet. If the guy had casually looked down to where he'd spat, he'd surely be spotted. Then. . . ? One thing for certain, there'd be no prison, no capture at all for that matter. He simply had to get back home. The women who remained in his life needed what he had in the bag; they needed someone who'd range far and wide for food and whatever fuel he could find. He *would* get home.

He'd never killed anyone, and he was partial to keeping it that way, but if it came down to it, then all bets were off. He held his breath as the man above just stood there. He had no idea of the guy's intention or direction of gaze. A clicking sound—releasing the AR from his chest rig, the definite metallic rasp of the charger chambering the first round. *Oh shit! Here we go.*

Ben carefully raised his head so he could fix his target. The guy loomed so close that Ben could smell him. He was fiddling with his weapon. He had the butt propped on his thigh and was digging for something on the flat side with a pocketknife. Something must've vibrated loose. "Damned piece of shit! Come on! Get in there!"

Ben moved his weapon hand so that the man's center mass came into range. He'd held his breath as long as possible and fought the impulse to burst into an explosive exhale. As he slowly meted his breath outward, he felt beholden to his uncle for teaching him how to track, how to hunt and how to breathe when the quarry came in close range. If spotted, Ben would shoot the bastard dead, take his weapon and shoot the remaining Green Hat. He took no comfort in the fact that he'd rise in criminal status from everyday poacher to homicidal extremist. Kill now, be killed, or worse. He watched and waited. A voice sounded in the distance.

"Charlie? What the hell? Quit jackin' off and get over here. We ain't got all damned day!"

"Yeah, yeah!" his partner shouted. "I'm comin'! This goddamned rifle's fallin' apart!" He pulled back the charger again. A live round ejected and clinked onto the roadbed. "Sonofabitch!" He crouched low and picked it up. At this point, all he had to do was look down the bank and he'd have a clear view of who was hiding in the brambles. "Piece of shit!" He slipped the bullet into his pocket and walked away. Relieved, Ben sank his head back down and eased his breath out followed by a deep inhale. *Not outta this fix yet.* He made certain the spotters had gone a distance before painfully tearing himself out of the morass of briers and thorns. He belly-crawled up the steep bank, avoiding the pissed-on area.

He got to where he had a clear view of the men as they patrolled the broken building. They did so side by side, a few meters apart, not the SOP for clearing a structure. They didn't stack or cover each other and they fanned their ARs from their hips. Poorly trained, badly equipped and lacking in teamwork, they'd picked these two from the bottom of the heap. Ben figured they were petty criminals who'd chosen community service over prison. Would've probably opted for prison if they'd known where they'd be posted. He hadn't seen their ankles, but he bet they both sported signal boosters for the chips planted in their hands or necks. The authorities wouldn't want any trustees wandering off the reservation.

As he eased up beside the rail cart, he considered stealing it. That would sure make up for the time he'd lost and a relief to his sore feet, but then they'd report in and drones would likely appear. He hated those flying contraptions. So, he improvised. If he couldn't take the rail cart, why should they have the advantage? He grabbed up some stones and shimmied his upper body under the carriage. Using his knife, he pried the gearbox cover partly open allowing him to sift in a handful of gravel. That would slow them down

and they'd likely ascribe the breakdown to bad luck—
something they seemed to court anyway. He backed out
and in a crouch, gun drawn, he crept along the gravel
embankment keeping his head just below the sightline
to the tipple. An occasional peek over the rails told him
the men were still poking around inside the buildings.

When out of sight of the tipple, he scrambled
up to the tracks and resumed his journey homeward at
a fast trot. He tried to pick out the thorns he could
reach and got most of them. Some still stuck in his
back, legs and thighs, but he didn't have time to mess
with them. He needed to make sure the spotters
couldn't close the distance on foot. After a few
minutes, he thought he heard noises behind him—voices
yelling. *Oh, they don't sound too happy.*

He took a measure of bleak satisfaction in
knowing at least he wouldn't be the only one caught out
in the deepening dark of a cold night. Having
dispensed with the immediate threat, the known
danger, he had several miles of track and a mountain
trail yet to cover before reaching home. To enhance the
experience, the breeze kicked up and a curtain of rain
came down with increasing intensity. The recurring
thought had nearly become a mantra—*This is no way to
live.*

Chapter 4

Grave Considerations
October 1, 2052

A haggard old man crossed the memorial bridge spanning the Tug River and trudged up toward the hillside cemetery. On a nice afternoon, the view from up there may have been an inspiring vista of the river, the town of Matewan and the West Virginia hills.

As it was, the clouded sun offered only scant visibility. The town below was mostly buried in debris from past floods and dead kudzu vines, leaving vague shrouded forms punctuated by an occasional church spire or power pole sticking out of the sea of vines like the mast of a sinking ship. The mountains and hills were still there, bearing mute witness to the passing of human generations who lived through the booms and busts and having seen many a coal town wax and wane with the tonnage of black lucre hollowed from the deep and dangerous chambers. The mountains themselves had claimed more than a few souls and it didn't matter if they were young or old, native or foreign. They were as indifferent as any ocean. There may have been some miserable folks still living around there, but the old man didn't know of any.

The tombstones cast blurry shadows. If anyone saw this lone figure from afar, they might surmise he was just another vagrant looking for a spot to rest. A closer examination would reveal a man's face that, for all the crags and creases, would be handsome with deep-set dark eyes, high protruding cheekbones, a long, thin nose and squared jaw that was stubbled with three days' growth—roughly hewn yet oddly dapper. Some with memories of the moving pictures said he looked like a beat up version of a Western movie actor. He liked old Clint, so he never fussed at anyone's mentioning the resemblance.

A bottle of sour mash sloshed in the lower pocket of his frayed company-issued rain slicker. He wore what was once a high-quality fedora cocked to one side. His boots were muddy and the lugs were clogged so traction at times was hard to obtain. He smelled of wood smoke, tobacco, and a cross between spirits and kerosene. His whipsawed mouth was half clinched on what remained of a home-rolled cigarette while the other side was spouting smoke and curses.

Upon arriving at his destination, the old man stopped and threw down the remains of his smoke. His demeanor changed. He doffed his hat and bowed slightly. Then returning his hat to a balding head, he reverently proceeded with what had become a traditional ceremony.

From his pockets, he removed two smoky shot glasses and the bottle of sour mash. Taking one of the glasses and carefully setting it atop the tombstone, he filled it to the brim. Likewise, he did the same with the glass he held in his hand. He held up the glass and said in a gravelly rasp, "Here's to you, Sid," and downed the contents in one swift and practiced motion.

The homemade mash bit hard and he clenched his teeth and squinted. "Damn!" He set his glass down on a nearby grave marker and eyed the one he'd just poured sitting on his host's headstone. "Well, Sid, since you've been dead for well over a hundred years, reckon you won't mind." He picked up the shot, careful not to tremble and quickly downed it. "Wooo!" he exhaled. "Man, that is some flaming blue rotgut! Can't complain much since I made it. I'm a hard case of bad luck." He shook his head slightly and looked up at the sky. "Maybe you're the lucky one, Sid. Wherever the hell you are, maybe hell ain't so bad."

The old man pulled his tobacco pouch and papers out of his pocket and began to fix himself a smoke. He lit it with a kitchen match struck off the dry underside of his slicker's zipper. One thing he knew about was fire and how to work it. The pungent smell of sulfur momentarily filled the air.

He began to talk in earnest, "Sid, I don't know why I'm always ending up here. Hell, I don't know why we, well I, carry on these one-way conversations. You were long gone, dead and buried before I ever came along, but y'know, I grew up hearin' 'bout you and what all you did for the people. What all you did there at Matewan and then to be gunned down like a dog with your wife on your arm. You were a man of principle; you laid it on the line and it cost you your life. Even when you knew there'd be trouble, you still laid it on the line. 'Sides all that," he belched, but it caught in his gullet and burned through his chest, "Shooooeee damn!" He took a big drag of his smoke and it seemed to help. "'Sides all that, Sid, you're a damned good listener and never interrupt, even when I'm talking shit." A course, wheezing laugh ended in a bout of lung wrenching coughs. He spat, respectfully off to the side.

Wiping his lips with the back of his hand, he continued, "Now, if you were alive today, I'm sure you'd come down on our side. They used to call us hillbillies, hicks and rednecks. Now, they call us primitives and retros. They try to gather us up and take us to their new cities. They tell people how much better it is inside and how they don't have to worry about anything."

He switched to a nasal whiney voice. "'Just come and live in the city and we'll take care of everything,'" then in a normal voice he continued, "is what they say. That's how they draw 'em in. When folks leave for the city, we hardly ever see them again, and the ones who do return come back all scattered in their heads and not worth much.

"We're still your people, y'know. Even after all this time. So, that's good enough reason for me to drop by and have these conversations now and then, but I do wish to bring you better news." He suddenly felt tired and beaten. His body swayed as if buffeted by a stiff wind.

"Hey Sid, I better sit down. My legs are startin' to get sore and creaky. This weather ain't helping neither."

With a grunt and a slow groan, he sat down on a footstone a few feet in front of the granite slab. His legs were bent, his ankles crossed and his torso was ramrod vertical. He would've resembled an old Hindu were it not for the incongruous hat cocked on his head and the cigarette drooping out of his mouth.

"Ahh, well, here's what's going on around the valley. Most everyone's gone to one of those new cities. The Jenkins, the Stewarts, Bill and Katy Francis. Can't say as I blame 'em. Those of us staying put are living more by our wits than anything else; hunting, growing stuff, burning wood, fetching water, brewing up shine, and such to survive. Guess we're reliving the eighteen hundreds, 'cept most everything we do is illegal. Remember our state motto? 'Mountaineers are Forever Free'? Well, we're still mountaineers and we're still free, but it all has a price, Sid. Freedom ain't free, never was."

"The more we resist their carrots, the more rules they make to. . . What's the word. . . ? contrive us into moving away from our homes to live in one of their chicken coops they've been building and calling them co-ops. Huh! That still spells 'coop' to me. Buncha bullshit!

"Sid, I surely know what side you'd come down on with all this mess and government bullshit–yeah, you'd come in like you did in Matewan with both fucking guns blazing. Yeah, boy! You'd come in like we did in Guanare and Trujillo, and. . . fuckin Vallera. Kill them Chavista sons a bitches, mow 'em down!" His hands made a spraying motion with an imaginary weapon.

"You shoulda been there, Sid, shoulda seen. . ." He stopped as memories swelled into a wave that threatened to engulf him. He'd not intended to stray so far in his reverie. He drew himself back to the present and peered intently at the granite headstone. "In fact, we could use your help now. Ole' Two-Gun Sid rides again!"

The old man paused and closed his eyes for a moment as if to savor the imagery. His eyes opened to regard the tall granite headstone. The inscription read:

TO THE MEMORY OF
SID HATFIELD
MAY 15, 1893
AUG. 1 1921

Below that, there was a ghostly image of "SMILIN' TWO-GUN" Sid carved into the stone showing a long face, hair slicked back, big nose and ears, hollow cheeks, clean shaven and dressed in a what appeared to be a high-collared uniform. He wasn't smiling and his eyes looked strangely alive and dead cold at the same time.

The inscription continued:

DEFENDER OF THE RIGHTS
OF WORKING PEOPLE
GUNNED DOWN BY FELTS
DETECTIVES ON THE STEPS
OF THE McDOWELL
COUNTY COURTHOUSE IN
WELCH, W. Va DURING
THE GREAT MINE WARS

WE WILL NEVER FORGET
HIS MURDER TRIGGERED
THE MINERS' REBELLION AT THE
BATTLE OF BLAIR MOUNTAIN

If anyone cared to do the math, he was just twenty-eight years old when he died there on the courthouse steps along with his best friend, Ed Chambers, whose bones lay buried ten feet away.

Looking up at the empty glass perched on the peak of the tall headstone, he slurred slightly, "Would y' like 'nother drink?"

He thought what Sid would have answered.

With some effort to steady himself, the old man raised up, got to the headstone and gingerly picked up the shot glass. He pulled out the bottle and, by some miracle, managed to fill the glass without spilling a drop. He repeated the same ritual as before for himself, downing his shot, then Sid's, and carefully reset Sid's empty glass. He pulled out his tobacco pouch, absently built a smoke, lit it and sat back on the ground in a cross-legged position.

Then the ragged old-timer in the tattered raincoat rambled on about the GEEO's, the taggings and the way it used to be—when people could go just about anywhere for any reason. The mines were open and the pay was decent. In fact, the sun shone a lot more. They were sunnier days, after all. His orations were often interrupted by a hacking cough and frequent expectorations.

Sid Hatfield's image on the hard granite seemed to waver at times and the old man thought he caught just the hint of Sid's ghostly presence mingled with creeping tendrils of fog that slowly moved up the river valley and quietly enveloped the hills. The day was drawing to a close. Typically, there would be no sunset, just a slow diminishing from lighter grays to black. He felt like he too was diminishing, running out of steam. He regarded the flat features of the carved image. "Fact is, if it weren't for that little gal and her family, I woulda cashed it in long ago. Too goddamned much rememberin', Sid. I got nowhere to go but down. I used to have a life, y'know. Been around the world, seen a lotta things. Some say it's the drinkin'. Maybe so. Maybe so."

With reluctant resolve, the old man who called himself "Boss" rose up to pay his parting respects. He had one more stop to make and preferred to get there before dark. It wasn't safe to be roaming around by oneself at night. He carried a bit of insurance—a sawed-off twelve-gauge nested in his coat and a favored sidearm. Anyone looking for trouble would find it in him, but before he left, he gave one final toast, this time with just the bottle tilted toward the stone monument. "Here's to you, brother! We need more like you!" He took a swig and felt the burn. "Damn! Flamin' rotgut!" He tipped his hat and spoke, knowing full well the import of his words, "See you sooner or later, Sid. . . . You rest easy now."

He turned and made his way back down the hill and like a wondering wraith, disappeared into the fog below. Whether left behind by accident or as a tribute, the shot glass atop the curved headstone remained, empty as the sockets in Smiling Sid Hatfield's stony countenance.

Chapter 5

CELI'S DIARY
OCTOBER 4, 2052

Last night GRAM and me had a very very big scare. I think it was the worst EVER. It was near dark. PA was still gone hunting and GRAM and I were putting the chickens away for the night and there was one missing. Their holding pen had been dug under. Uh oh! I thought I heard a squawking sound by the big acorn tree at the edge of the yard. When I walked over to look, I saw blood dripped all over the ground and there was a rustle in the bushes. Then there came a low growl noise and when I followed it, there was this big dog with a hen in its mouth. It was Jaycee, my Jaycee. She was still wriggling in that dog's mouth. Still squawking. I got so mad I took several steps forward and shouted for it to let go, but it just squeezed its eyes at me and then gave its head a big shake. After that, Jaycee just hung there all limp. I was really mad then and started yelling really loud. I think I stepped in closer. That was a mistake.

It dropped the poor thing and stood over it while it showed its teeth and growled. I wanted to jump back, but I just stood there like a stone and my heart was beating like crazy. The dog then lowered its head and started coming at me. I have never been so scared and I could not move. I couldn't even yell anymore. Even though my inside voice screamed for GRAM!!!!!

The dog came closer, showing its teeth and moving its head around like it was smelling me. I smelled it too. I heard animals can smell fear. Well, I can tell you I smelled my own fear all over myself. I think I was even shaking by then. It came closer and then started to move beside me. It circled behind me and started to move in. Then, GRAM appeared.

She came at us both swinging a long shovel and shouting like I never heard her shout so. She didn't stop either. The dog must have seen this little, old, mad woman and decided a fight with GRAM just wasn't worth it. He turned back around, and as he did so, he was so close to me, he nipped at my right ankle, then ran off, grabbing Jaycee along the way. GRAM saw all this and kept after him even when he disappeared into the bush.

I could hear her in the laurel. Oh, she sounded so mad. She even yelled out a few words that I will not repeat. After a bit, she came back through the laurel, her hair all tangled up and her face red. She came back to me and walked me over to the front porch where she sat me down and then I saw her shaking so bad I got worried something bad might happen to her like a heart attack. She even held her hand over her heart and took these huge breaths. Her face was so red that all of her freckles had become nearly invisible. She's had these spells that make her really dizzy and sometimes she faints but I'd never seen her this way! I got scared all over again.

"GRAM," I said. "Are you okay?" She looked at me and said she just needed to catch her breath. I said something about the dog and she said no, it was no dog but a wild coyote. I said it looked like a brown dog to me and she said to trust her. It was a coyote. She knew about them years ago.

Of course, I asked her how she knew and she acted like she had not heard me. Instead, she fussed over the spot where the coyote had nipped my ankle. We went inside the cabin, and she made me sit on the sofa with my foot propped up. Then she began what she called an exam using a candle to see with. My thick wooly sock had a tear in it, but my skin wasn't hurt at all. She seemed very glad to know this. It was as if that coyote was telling me who was the boss. I asked her again about her knowing about coyotes. She said, "Okay kiddo," something she says when she gets serious about anything. She left me and went into her bedroom. When she came back, she had her keepsake box with her. She keeps it on her mirror dresser. It had a lot of old photos and some funny things like rocks and empty gun shells. I know this because, being me and curious, I had snuck a peek now and then.

Anyways, we cuddle up on the sofa near the warm stove. She picks out something from her box and shows it to me. It's a gun shell, an empty gun shell. She hands it over so I can feel it and look at it. She says it's time I heard about her and the coyotes. She did the thing where she looks up at the ceiling, takes a real deep breath and starts in talking about those long ago days.

Chapter 6

Gram's Tale-The Perils of Rosie
June19, 2013

It was the fifth day of the march and Rosie was fed up with Mike. Mike had lumbered along constantly complaining and caring little about Rosie or anyone else. He'd not been very social and refused to carry any sign. He said he felt exposed and insisted that there'd be coal company agents taking everyone's picture and names. "Some night there'll be a knock at the door and then we'll wonder whatever happened to Rafe or Amber, or you, Rosie!" Rosie understood how corporations could lobby outright and wield influence under the radar, but she thought the days of assigning hitmen to quell activism were well behind them.

On the final evening of the Blair Mountain March, roughly one hundred fifty marchers–the diehards who'd not wussed out–had been invited to pitch their tents in a farmer's field. Along the way to Boomer Mountain, Rosie and Mike had shared a squat two-person tent. Mike's loud snoring, which he ascribed to an asthmatic condition and his general indifference about taking up the entire bed space whatever way he could, had deprived Rosie of restful sleep for four straight nights.

In the morning, she emerged from the tent blurry eyed and in much need of refreshment. She'd thrown on the handiest garments including a ratty coat belonging to Mike and his size thirteen hiking boots, unlaced. Though it was summer, morning temperatures in the valleys and coves were chilly and Rosie chose warm comfort over looks just to go outside and take her morning toiletries somewhere private.

After walking across the road, she trekked through a large hillside pasture into a strip of woods. She found a secluded spot, relieved herself and cleaned up. She covered the biodegradable TP she'd slipped into Mike's coat pocket with leaves. The air was fresh and she was beginning to feel a lot better. She spied the glint of a small, shallow creek a short distance into the woods gurgling brightly, and she thought to herself, "What a wonderful sound to hear in the morning."

The thought of splashing the cool water over her face and hands spurred her forward. So, she clumped downhill, carefully negotiated the steep bank and landed on a sandbar. She noted that the stream had furrowed the earth so that the banks on either side rose steeply. It also afforded a measure of privacy that she didn't mind at all. Squatting down over the stream, she began to splash her face. The water was colder than she'd expected, but it certainly was refreshing. Taking off Mike's coat and rolling up her sleeves, she knelt by the creek and rinsed off her arms. She then thought to take off Mike's clunky boots, roll up her pants and do some wading. It was cold, but she felt the waters would restore her energy and get her back in tune with reality. She sat down on a nearby rock and started to take off a boot.

Suddenly, a low rumbling growl came from the dense brush on the opposite bank. It was a feral sound, which Rosie immediately thought to be that of a wild dog. Perhaps, just a lost dog defending its turf. The low bushes rustled and then parted revealing the muzzle of what indeed appeared to be a dog with its head slung low, slowly moving back and forth trying to acquire her scent. It stood about twenty feet away from where Rosie was sitting. She'd dealt with street dogs before on bicycle excursions and knew, or at least thought she knew, how to handle them in a non-threatening way. She shoved the boot back on and stood up slowly.

In an even, firm voice she said, "It's okay, boy; it's okay." She tried to calmly reassure the dog that she meant no harm. The animal with its head still low and its gold-brown eyes locked on her, took a tentative step forward and let loose another low growl. It was then Rosie noticed a large broken branch lying on the sandbar just behind her. She figured she could reach it well before the dog came within striking distance, but when three other dogs—the same basic size and shape as the first, emerged from the brush, she realized these weren't just dogs. *Coyotes! Here? I thought they were shy of humans and only came out at night.*

While the lead coyote held his ground and unwavering gaze, the others split up and began to flank her. She knew the worst thing to do would be to turn tail and run—she needed to keep an eye on them or they could easily jump her from different sides. A tangle of fallen trees crisscrossed the channel below, forming both a dam and a barricade. Her only exit was upstream. Stepping into the chilling current, she grabbed the fallen branch and began waving it side to side. She yelled at the top of her voice, "Mike! Mike! Help me! Somebody! Help!" As she was yelling, she lowered her body into a half-crouched position and began slowly stepping backward upstream.

The entire pack kept pace with her as she retreated upstream. The water seeped quickly into her boots, numbing her now frigid feet, the stones rounded and slippery under the soles. Unable to take her eyes from the predators, she backed into a pool of water that went up to her kneecaps, nearly falling. She barely noticed how cold it was. The next step backward and she was now thigh deep in the pool and backed up against a rock ledge, the water on one section just to her right cascading. A quick glance and she realized her mistake: This was part of a series of ledges that formed small waterfalls, but also formed a bridge whereby the coyotes on the other side could cross. By blocking her from behind, they'd close off all means of escape. Well-worn trails cut down the bank on both sides.

She realized they had her.

The pack leader, sensing his prey's quandary, scrambled down the bank and began a slow crouching approach directly toward her. A male—alpha. His head was slung low; his eyes locked on her face, close enough to see his nostrils flaring as they inhaled her fear. He paused momentarily standing more erect. Then he began a crisscross pattern back and forth as he drew closer, stepping into the stream without hesitation. Rosie swooped the branch through the air several times just enough to give the leader pause. By this time, she felt her heart pounding in the center of her head and her ears were throbbing. Frantically, she yelled again as loud as she could, "Mike! Mike! Help! Help!"

She sensed movement behind her and saw that

two more pack members had come down onto the ledge behind her—*I'm surrounded!* It was now six to one. She extended the branch as far as she could and tried to swing it in a wide arc. In doing so, her balance tipped and she landed hard, butt first, on the rock ledge just behind her. Though hardly injured, her defensive position had been greatly compromised. She drew up her booted feet and clutched her knees to her chest. She breathed in short bursts and shivered violently.

The leader was now on a ledge less than three feet from her right leg. He came at her lunging forward and grabbed the toe of Mike's boot, its teeth gleaming, head whipping in a ferocious, powerful shake. It felt like he could yank off her entire leg. The laces dangled untied. With a strong pull and a twist, the boot came right off and she fell backward. In the same instant, she felt a tug on the branch she still had in her right hand to fend off the pack members behind her. She grabbed a handful of creek stones with her free hand and hurled them. No effect. Her entire body trembled. The branch jerked out of her hand.

A splash in front of her. Her head whipped forward. In short order, she'd been rendered defenseless, half-shoed and on her backside. In a horrible flash forward, she imagined how they'd discover her body—half eaten, limbs akimbo, partly submerged, flies buzzing. . . . God! The leader gave the boot a violent shake, dropped it into the water and came at her again aiming for the exposed right foot. With adrenalized effort, she managed to swing her left leg out and around with enough force to give the coyote a hard boot in the snout.

It gave a sharp yelp, more out of surprise than pain, and backed up a step. Seizing the slim opportunity, she tried to raise up to a standing position but couldn't find the stability or the strength to do so and fell back onto her side. The lead coyote was making his move, head low, lips curling in anticipation. She could see the haunches tensing for a powerful, deadly leap. All she could do was curl in her legs and cover her face and neck with her arms. *Oh God. No, No!*

Suddenly, from nowhere and everywhere, she heard and felt a deafening, thunderous clap accompanied by a bright flash. It was something she could identify only as a lightning bolt. The animal in front of her was catapulted into the air and landed in a piteously yelping heap on the side of the bank. She could smell acrid smoke and her ears were ringing. She sensed movement behind her and, in her periphery, thought she saw forms scampering away and up the bank.

She was about to feel relieved but then, terror of terrors, there came her old nemesis. She'd named it "the fog." She knew there'd be only seconds left before she'd lose consciousness, as she stared at the bleeding coyote in front of her. His eyes were still open, still focused on his intended prey even as they began to cloud over, fierceness evaporating. He was still alive and she thought she heard its pitiful whines amid the clanging. Then came another deafening blast. Incredibly, lightning had struck again! The second blast had been louder and sent a wrecking ball crashing around inside her head. The coyote had ceased its awful clamor and was just trying to breathe. Its eyes were still locked on her, but now the eyelids were fluttering. The red tongue lolled onto the ground.

Her hearing was gone as if waxed cotton had been rammed in both ears, but the internal clanging persisted. Then came the acrid smell, the tang of gun smoke, and a sense of someone drawing closer and closer. She and the coyote regarded each other as both slipped into their own dark unconscious worlds.

Rosie awoke to semi-consciousness briefly when she felt both her arms being grabbed. She heard herself let out a string of moans as her body got dragged, lifted and carried somewhere away from the creek. Then came shivers and shaking all over. A face appeared, the stone face of a man. Only the gray eyes seemed alive, eyes neither old nor young. The last thing she remembered before the fog came over her again were words spoken in a male baritone, "You are one lucky little hippie chick."

The next thing Rosie knew, she was being shaken by both shoulders and a man's voice was saying something. It was Mike. "Rosie? Rosie! Rosie? Wake up. We gotta go! They're getting ready to march. Let's go!"

Then another voice, a female's. "Mike, you frigging idiot! Can't you see she's had one of her episodes or something?" She leaned over. "Hey Rosie, Rosie." Her voice was comforting and melodic. She gently palmed the sides of her friend's face. "What's goin' on, girl?"

It was Jill who she first saw when she opened her eyes. Jill's face came closer, strained with worry. "We heard gunfire and, like, we thought the worst when we came running up the field and, like, saw you propped up on this tree all limp and soaking wet, scraped up, and covered in muck under Mike's jacket. Then we saw blood. Like, holy shit! We thought you'd been shot by a goddamned local."

Rosie sat up straight and looked at Mike and Jill and then looking past them, noted that they were on a hillside some distance above the marchers' campsite. As her head cleared and Jill continued her rant, smatterings of memory began to buoy into Rosie's head. The morning walk, the creek, the. . . "Oh my God!" she said aloud, pushing the jacket away. "Help me up! Help me up, now!" Her voice verged on frantic.

Mike picked up the green jacket and peered at it intensely. "Hey, y'know, this is definitely not my jacket. Definitely. Where's my jacket, Rosie?" Jill whacked Mike across the chest with a stiff arm. "Stow it, Mike. Just chill. Rosie needs our help now."

Mike and Jill got Rosie up on her feet. She waved them off. "I'm okay, guys. I'm fine. Just a little woozy, but I'm fine." She scanned the landscape and spotting a strip of trees, took off in that direction picking up speed as she went. She looked down and saw she was still wearing Mike's boots—both of them (he had reverted to his old Nikes). *How can that be? Was this only another of my fogs?* She had to find out. She looked cartoonish as she marched down the slope slinging one giant boot ahead of the other, but she didn't care. Mike and Jill were at her heels wondering if Rosie had somehow gone nuts. He was still complaining about them being late for the march, but Rosie was fixated on finding evidence that her memory coincided with reality.

Upon entering the woods with her worried friends in tow, Rosie began to narrate to herself, speaking softly as she moved from one spot to another. "Okay, here's where I did that, I see the paper. Then I went this way toward the creek." She walked stridently as if hot on the trail of some great mystery. "Then, okay, here's the sandy place where I went into the water, and look, here's Mike's coat right where I laid it." She paused looking at tracks in the sand.

Mike picked up his coat and compared it to the one he was carrying. "Y'see, I was right. Here's my jacket, see? Hey, Rosie. . . where did you. . ."

Rosie pointed at something in the sand. "The stick, the branch! There's the hole where I pulled it out and there's a footprint, the coyote that followed me." She sounded manic. Then she looked upstream and pointed. "This way!" She began wading and rock hopping up the creek to a spot where a little waterfall was flowing over a series of rock ledges. "And here's where I fell and over there. . . Look! See the blood! It *did* happen. It happened and somehow I'm alive. I'm *alive*!"

Throughout this whole scenario, Jill and Mike kept glancing at each other as if becoming convinced Rosie was delirious. Jill began in a supplicating sing-song, "It's okay, Rosie. It's okay. You just had a little, like, episode. So why don't we get you back to the camp and find you some nice warm clothes and some food and—"

Rosie snapped, "I am *not* in need of your patronizing concerns about my well-being–physical *or* mental. I just confirmed that I almost died from an animal attack. By coyotes to be exact, and somehow, don't ask me how, I was rescued by. . ." she closed her eyes trying to visualize, "some guy with a gun and a face. . . a hard face, like, like. . ." She trailed off as a rush of dizzy weakness left her fumbling for words.

Mike stood with his head cocked at her, and Jill glanced around the now still woods where only songbirds interrupted the morning. Then Jill stepped closer and put her hand on Rosie's arm. "Okay honey, I believe you. Like whatever. You look like you've been through a war, so let's get you–"

Rosie jerked away and looked at Jill. She pointed to the bloodied side of the bank. "There, just look there. That's where the lead coyote was. See the blood, and look, over here on the far bank! See the weeds and brush? How they're all mashed down and streaks of blood there too? That must be where the guy dragged the dead coyote," she spied a glint of something in the weeds. She leaned over to discover a spent gun shell. She reached down to retrieve it and squeezed it hard into the palm of her hand. Evidence! She shoved it in the jacket pocket and straightened up feeling blood whooshing around in her head. The memory of those fateful seconds rose up vividly; the deafening blasts, the look of the dying animal, the sense of someone drawing near. "Oh God!" She began to shiver and turn pale feeling her legs give way.

Jill sprang forward to catch her and with a frantic wave, beckoned to Mike, who was scrutinizing the red stuff on the bank. "Mike!" Jill's voice jolted him. "Get over here and help me! She's going wobbly on us again!" By the time he lurched over to assist, Rosie was half draped over Jill's shoulder and getting heavier by the second.

They got Rosie back to the camp area, put her on a mattress pad just outside her tent and covered her with a down sleeping bag. A rally had begun near the roadside where most of the marchers had gathered. Only a few stragglers who were just getting up had noticed the trio returning. They didn't evince any curiosity or interest. Late night partying did not make for bright eyes and bushy tails the next day.

Jill told Mike to find Rafe and bring Amber too. Rafe was their team leader and Amber had EMT training though she hadn't been certified as a full-fledged EMT. They both appeared quickly. Amber immediately began checking Rosie's vitals and examining her for any wounds, rabies being her major concern. She'd heard Mike mention something about a dog. Meanwhile, Rafe was getting briefed by Jill while Mike stood some distance away, uncertain of his role.

Rosie moaned and began to move around. Amber, who was kneeling on the ground, placed a hand on her head and softly spoke. "Hey kiddo, rough morning, eh?" Of all her friends, Amber knew the most about Rosie's blackouts—vasovagal syncope. It wasn't a particularly life endangering or even harmful malaise. The main risk being from falls or situations like driving or operating machinery. Rosie had been tested numerous times. She'd tried medication to no avail. The best prognosis was that she might eventually "get over it." So far, that had not happened.

Rosie smiled bleakly and half parted her eyes. "Yeah, word!"

"Well," Amber spoke with genteel authority, "you need to rest a bit, drink some warm liquid and get your body temp back up. Keep this bag covering you. Okay?"

Rosie nodded.

"Now, try to remember, Rosie. At any time, did an animal bite you or scratch you?"

"I don't think so." Rosie relived the scene in fragments. "It all happened so fast and all I know is that at one point the pack leader grabbed my right foot, well, actually my boot, and it came off. Then-" she paused as the memory returned, "I remember it came for me again and I kicked it in the snout. I don't know if I got sprayed or whatever. Then the loud bang sound and the coyote went sailing over to the other side and. . ." she faltered, squeezed her eyes shut and then relaxed her face. "I don't exactly remember from there, 'cause I sorta passed out." She looked at her friend sheepishly.

"What about the shooter guy? Did you see him?"

"Well, yeah. I felt him carrying me and saw his face. Like a mask, not a real mask, just very hard and set, y'know. He must've put me there under that tree where Jill and Mike found me."

Jill was listening nearby and with an alarmed glance at Amber, asked, "Rosie, do you know if this guy touched you anywhere? Did anything like. . . y'know?"

Rosie got the inference and reacted. "No. Nothing happened. Believe me, I would know."

Jill nodded her head. "Okay, kiddo. Just thought I'd ask."

Rosie gave a wan smile. "Yeah, thanks."

They gave her a warm sponge bath and in so doing, discovered Rosie had emerged relatively unscathed apart from the obvious scratches and a few contusions that were blooming forth in places where she'd landed hard on her flanks and side.

By the time Rafe came over to see Rosie, she was sitting up sipping some herbal tea and honey, feeling much better. "So. . . Rosie," he began with a smile, "what's this about a hunter setting his dogs on you?"

She blinked and cocked her head as if to hear better. "What? Did you say dogs? They were *not* dogs, Rafe. They were wild coyotes and one of them was just about to—"

Rafe interrupted. "Rosie, Rosie, Rosie. We know you've had a bad experience and we heard the gunshots. We've heard them now and then almost every day and it's all about the locals trying to scare us off.

"It's well-known that coyotes are not prone to attack humans, and besides, they're very skittish and secretive. So the logical assumption about what happened to you is that there were dogs, hunting dogs most likely, that some redneck turned loose on you and then shot his gun off in your direction as an act of intimidation and hostility. You know these locals; some of them are violently opposed to us. Right? Right!" He didn't wait for her to answer.

"So, Rosie. You just need to be logical and realize that what we had happen this morning was another instance of violent harassment directed not just toward you but our entire organization of marchers, to our movement.

"And chances are really good that this hick who shot at you works for the coal company and was under orders to do whatever it takes to intimidate us and make us turn around and go home."

He gave her exposed arm a little squeeze. "Really sorry, Rosie, you had to be the target of all this, but just remember such things will only strengthen our resolve that we're doing the right thing for the planet. We gotta go march in a few minutes; this is our last day, the most important one of all! Let's make it count! See you!" With that, he launched a gung-ho fist pump. "Earth first! Right Rosie? Earth first!"

She gave a feeble shake of her own fist and Rafe, seemingly pleased, turned to dash back to the rally.

What in the world was that all about? she

wondered. Her story had apparently been "modified" and embellished. Forgetting, of course, that this violent hunter, who supposedly sicced his dogs on her and shot at her would then scoop up her passed out body, carry it a good distance, and place it carefully beneath a tree where her buddies could easily spot her. *He covered me with his own jacket. Oh, yeah and he even put the boot, the one the coyote (yes, it was a coyote!) had torn off, back on my right foot. That's* not *the MO of a violent hell-bent antagonizing redneck!* She looked over at the green jacket, the one "he" had bestowed upon her. She grabbed the sleeve and dragged it close. She smelled it. It smelled of menthol, and pine sap and something earthy she couldn't quite identify. She felt something in one of the pockets. Her fingers slipped inside and extracted the spent gun cartridge she'd found. She closed her hand around it, feeling its solidity, its hollow lightness, a mere shell, yet it tokened a profound connection with someone out there, a Lone Ranger who'd come to her aid and likely watched at a distance to make sure her friends would find her. Out of nowhere, tears welled and gently flowed. She closed her eyes and from the core of her being sent forth the words: "Thank you."

She could hear the rally getting underway. The leaders were barking through a megaphone. The marchers were shouting and chanting. She thought it odd to hear such commotion in these quiet coves.

Then it hit her: how well the modified saga of her morning perils would be spun into the "movement's" agenda. She knew what was true, but then again didn't care to make waves in front of everyone.

Feeling somewhat recovered, she ate two energy bars, drank a cup of cold herbal tea and then wandered over to the fringe of people gathered for the final marchers' rally. A black woman with a United Mine Workers insignia stamped on her jacket stood on a makeshift platform exhorting everyone to organize and activate their local organizations to take action against the greedy and corrupt corporations, "especially these motherfucking coal companies!"

The speaker had a loud and brassy voice aggravated by the megaphone in her hand. "We see what these bloodsucking capitalists have done and are doing! We know they're doing everything they can through their payoffs to government and to keep us down wallowing in misery and powerless to defend ourselves. Well, let me tell you, we are NOT afraid. They can send their jack-booted thugs to shoot at us and set their attack dogs against us, like they did to one of our own this very morning, but we stand strong, united, organized and unafraid!"

The woman smiled and gazed down at her audience. She saw Rosie standing at the back and beckoned her to step forward. "I want you all to meet somebody special. Come on up here, girl!"

Rosie hunkered down into her shoulders and vigorously shook her head, but before she knew it, hands were jostling her forward. Rafe came up beside her and whispered, "C'mon, Rosie! Make us all proud!" He guided her forward and as she stepped up on the platform, a rousing cheer and applause welcomed her. The speaker embraced her with an enormous hug. After that, Rosie waved and began to step down.

"No, no, sister! You just hang tight." She keyed the megaphone. "Marchers, like I said, we have to stand strong, stand united and be unafraid!" She swooped an open hand toward Rosie.

"Just as this young lady, Rosie Pence, stood her ground this morning. *That's* what we mean. *That's* who we are." Rosie was slightly put off at the bungling of her last name but could see no way to work in a correction. The speaker continued.

"And as for these coal company hooligans who've tried to stop us, who are even now spying on us, we say this." The speaker raised her head toward the high mountains. "We'll face down your bullets and your hell hounds. *We* are mighty! We are strong! We are a legion that you will never again throw under the treads of your capitalist machines. And yes! We may see some of our brothers and sisters go down, but we are many, we are strong and we will see the day when justice will be served cold and with no mercy! I will be proud to march into whatever hell you corporate bastards can throw in our face, especially with brave women like Rosie Pence at my side!"

The speaker gave Rosie a parting hug and a sweeping hand gesture that prompted a cacophony of applause accompanied by a wave of whistles, shouts and chants. One particular chant gathered momentum. "Rosie, Rosie, Rosie!" She stepped offstage just wanting to escape the madness and crawl under a rock somewhere. People were all around her beaming admiration, fist pumping, shouting, reaching out to hug her.

"Rosie!" It was Mike coming over beside her. He slung a proprietary arm around her and began steering her toward the outer ranks of marchers. "Wow Rosie! Did you hear that? You're like a rock star!" She made a mental note to ditch Mike ASAP after they got back to Watauga.

Chapter 7

Celi's Diary
OCTOBER 4 2052

GRAM stopped at the part where she was talking about going back to her college and saying goodbye to her boyfriend.

I was still stuck on who had saved her so I asked, "Who?"

She blinked and looked at me as if I had asked a silly question. "Who what?"

I said, "Who was the man with the gun?" I may have said this a bit too loud and sassy, but I really wanted to know.

"Oh, let's see, Celi." She was playing with me I could tell. "Who do we know that's from Madison?" She waited a moment as I tried to recall. Then she gave me a hint. "Tall, rough, and tough."

"Grandpa!" I shouted, thinking that had to be the answer. 'Cause later she'd go on to marry him and they lived there with Pawpaw Rob. I never knew either of them, but I'd seen old family pictures. Some of those pictures were in her keepsake box.

She smiled and shook her head. "Your grandpa was tall but blond haired and handsome as they come. And his dad, your Pawpaw Rob, was too old at the time to be running around saving young chicks." She laughed, at herself I think.

Well, I thought about it and was about to give up when I remembered seeing an old photo Gram had in that box. It was of four people standing in front of a sign. One of them had to be Grandpa (he was blond haired), the man next to him was older, so that was Pawpaw. There was an older woman–Pawpaw's wife? And another man, younger, but with black hair and not smiling. That had to be. . . Pawpaws brother! I shouted, "Uncle Virgil!"

Gram clapped her hands and patted me on the back. She seemed well pleased but then got real quiet and looked at me for a long time. She said she wished I could have known them all and them know me. She sighed and hugged me saying to get ready for bed.

So, I hugged her neck and went to put on my sleeping gown. I liked her story, but there were things that I had to figure out.

So it was Uncle who saved Gram from the coyotes. Wow. He's like a hero. I always liked him from day one. Don't get me wrong; he is what Gram calls a rough character, but I think everyone has their good and bad nature. I know I do cause Gram sometimes gets cranky and gets onto me about the least little thing. She even lets go on Pa, which is kind of embarrassing hearing your own parent being fussed at by their parent.

Back to Uncle. He has always been nice to me and calls me names like butterfly and honeydoll. When Mom and Jordy went away, Uncle came around and we'd go on long walks together and he'd show me all kinds of things an ordinary person may not see. Don't tell Pa or Gram, but he would let me shoot Pa's crossbow. We almost got into big time trouble trying to get the arrow that had stuck in a paper bark tree that I was aiming at. Pa keeps track of all his arrows. Uncle says I could be a crack shot. What that means is I'm really good at hitting the target.

Other times Uncle and I just try to see how quiet we can be moving through the woods, sometimes not even using the trails. He calls it stalking. When we get back, nine times out of ten there's Gram on the front porch with her hands on her hips saying something like "Where have you two been?" or "Virgil Johnson, don't you know Cecilia has chores to do?" or "Cecilia Pierce, your hair is a mess and your face is filthy" and such as that.

Nowadays, we hardly go on hikes or do our stalking thing as often. Uncle disappears and we don't see him for weeks. When he comes around, he looks tired and sad even though he tries to hide it from us, me especially. He may tease like he used to and be on what Gram calls his best behavior, like no bad words or drinking and smoking, but there's something that's wearing him out and I want to hug his neck and tell him everything will be fine. I did just that once and he acted like it smarted. Gosh. That was the last thing I wanted to happen.

I wish Gram would be nicer. She is hard to figure out. Here's what I do not understand: If Uncle saved Gram from those coyotes way back when, then why does she seem so mad at him? You would think she'd be kind and grateful. After all, she has kept that empty bullet shell for all these years. I guess another mystery is if she acts all mad at him all the time, why does he keep coming around?

Chapter 8

Another Day in Another Life
October 12, 2052

Candler Greaves stood on the shiny black marble floor and swiped his green card through the scanner by the elevator door. He had high hopes the day had arrived for a long awaited and, in his mind, a well-earned promotion. The door hissed open and he stepped into the darkly tinted glass enclosure coming face-to-face with the very last person he wished to see so early in the day—his nemesis, Art Jones. It was too late to turn around and wait for the next lift. So, he curtly nodded at Jones, hoping beyond all reason that the creep would say nothing. He quickly punched in his floor number and turned sideways to avoid Jones' probing eyes.

"Ahhh Greaves. How are you? I see you're still on eleven."

Jones, of course, meant several slights with this comment. He could care less how Candler felt but was gleefully aware that he'd yet to be promoted to a higher station, thus a higher floor. His smirking, smarmy demeanor was just a bonus feature. Candler glanced sideways at Jones.

Everything about the guy was angular—the sharp nose, slanted eyebrows, even his derisive smile was crooked. He wore the uniform of upper management—black suit, black turtleneck and black non-leather loafers. His tall, thin body hung loosely together like a marionette's. A hank of black hair drooped forward just touching his right eyebrow. Whatever aftershave he had on smelled oddly medicinal.

"I say Greaves, you seem at a loss for words. Do you have some sort of ailment that's affecting your voice? Should we be concerned about exposure?" He sensed several fellow passengers shifting uncomfortably at the mention of "exposure."

Candler grunted something barely audible and pressed his lips together trying not to give the bastard any quarter. He turned outward and fixed his gaze through the glass panel that afforded a panoramic view of Progress City. The entire landscape was cheerlessly cast over by a dull gray sky. There were distant mountains crested with a dusting of new snow. The irony of the cold gray skies and snow-capped mountains only strengthened the adamantine doctrine that climate change was happening and soon a dramatic turn in temperatures would seal their doom.

The years had grown colder and the days darker. Yet the anticipated changes had yet to manifest. Still, Candler was bound by his agency to hasten progress according to "the plan." The Global Environmental Ethics Organization was top down all the way. He was just a middle link in a long chain and figured that the people at the top surely knew more than he about the coming changes—surely.

Up close, he caught his own reflection. He studied his face–youngish, pale, a bit thin but not sallow. Light brown hair brushed back and neatly tapered. His daily exercises kept him trim. Maintaining one's basal metabolic rate earned extra points. In his dark suit, white shirt, string tie and non-leather shoes, he typified the midlevel global service bureaucrat. He bore nothing remarkable in his appearance but for two notable exceptions—his eyes.

The right eye happened to be golden brown, the left eye green, an oddity from out of nowhere in his known genealogy. He'd researched the topic. Heterochromia iridium was the scientific term for this condition. It caused no debility, just a fluke that a bit more melanin tinted the brown eye than the green one. At times, Candler felt self-conscious, and weird, especially when people would do a double take, but most of them either didn't detect the oddity or couldn't care less. He had no problem with it going unnoticed.

His job suited him. Just a few major a-holes like Jones, who would riff now and then, but he was getting enough creds to live comfortably and even an occasional upgrade. Even the fieldwork was all right as long as he remembered the first precept and focused on doing his part for the organization. He consciously released his breath feeling the tension ease a bit. He realized he'd been spacing and needed to come back to terra firma.

He took another full breath and released. It sounded like a sigh. His workday had been going well up to the moment he stepped into the lift. Of course, Jones wasn't quite finished: "I hear you're doing a lot of fieldwork."

Candler turned his head just enough to catch a

glimpse of Jones, so grotesquely delighted to have found the first peon of the day to dissect and eviscerate. Jones' galling tenor grated up a notch. "Having fun mixing it up with the retro rabble, are you?"

Candler's face flushed with a warm mixture of embarrassment (there were other workers on the lift) and a hot spike of anger, knowing how Jones obtained his promotions at others' expense. They'd been recruited into the agency about the same time. Jones' parents were higher ups in the academic field and had very close ties with past green movements and developing the basic "Earth First" curricula for all levels of education.

Candler's genealogy wasn't so green-blooded as Jones'; though his parents earned certificates as compliance assessors for a carbon credit exchange. They had recently converted into volunteer workers in exchange for med security—a tradeoff that would see them through their peak demand period for health care and social services. They'd also moved from their apartment into a dormitory-style elder community. Candler felt badly that he didn't see them much, but they'd talk on the internal com-link once or twice a week.

Apart from his social advantages, Jones had the schizoid's ability to lick the boots of his superiors while nimbly shivving his peers. For whatever reason, he'd singled out Candler as a favorite target. Perhaps it was the bully's sense that Candler would never fight back that goaded AJ (as he liked to be called) into taking every opportunity to berate him and more often than not, to do so in front of his peers and underlings.

"Yes, Greaves, you must long for the days when you were just a simple paper runner, but now, look at you! Hobnobbing with the best of society. How many showers do you take to get the stink out? . . . Hmmm? Bet you spend half your creds on the sanI, eh?" Though posed as a rhetorical question, he paused for effect. "Well, I hear your supervisors are sending you on special assignment and you'll have even more fun counting those hicks and retrobates. I can't say I envy you, Greaves, but you will send us a post now and then, won't you?"

An electronic chime signaled the lift's arrival at the eleventh floor. The door opened and Candler, face aglow and lips pressed tight, stepped out. A few others followed. As the doors closed, he heard Jones telling his lift mates. "Such a pity, Greaves. A perfect example of what happens when incompetents get. . ." The doors shut and the lift ascended.

As he walked down the long dimly lit hallway, Candler checked his pocket desk to make sure he'd attended to all messages and that the census data file was on top of his stack. He'd already sent the file to his floor boss, Sara Warnski, but liked having the material close at hand, just in case. With the occasional power surges capable of dropping or incinerating data, he thought it best to be safe and redundant. It sure seemed that the surges were happening more and more frequently, but no one said anything about it.

According to the majority view, including Candler's, energy fluctuations had nothing to do with the weather per se, but the outliers (primitives as the agency called them) in the rural communities. They wanted to lead a life completely on their terms, a very wasteful life in which no one subscribed to the principles of GEEO or cared one whit. Even when afforded credits and privileges, they refused to act responsibly and serve the public good. They poached on the Wildlands, burned carbon-laden wood and coal, and raised livestock and gardens for their own selfish consumption.

Lately, there'd been news reports that bands of roaming retros were attacking infrastructure facilities, like the power plants, the train lines and even the food sources. This was why the power outages and food shortages were happening according to the administrators who'd launched a prominent campaign to ferret out these perpetrators and bring them to justice.

Having received a top-notch government sponsored education, Candler could hardly fathom the depravity, the ignorance and denial these people portrayed in blatant disregard of the science and the practicality of living in harmony with the planet. It must've been like this for the early pioneers of planetary consciousness, trying to lead the ignorant masses into a new way of living in harmony with the earth and each other. Obviously, Candler and his cohorts were dealing with the dregs that stubbornly remained locked in their antiquated ways—not an easy undertaking.

"You can't cull all the bad fruit, Greaves. You must leave it to rot on the vine and move on," his old college mentor used to say. "There'll always be deniers, naysayers and ignoramuses who refuse to accept the science. Why waste resources on trying to convert them? It was far more efficient to reward those who smartly accept the global axioms."

All philosophy aside, the central government decreed that every five years a census be taken to assess and identify members of the primitive population. Thankfully, it didn't involve going door-to-door but setting up shop in some ramshackle town center and sending out G-Corps units to "encourage" the locals to come in and register. The job was about as cheerless as tax collecting, but Candler possessed a remarkable talent for getting the primitives not only to register but, furthermore, to become citizens of Progress City. He had a knack for delivering the right pitch and building rapport with them–all by merely acting sympathetic and expressing an interest in their lives. Though he wouldn't admit it, he had developed a genuine interest and curiosity in the way they lived. His registration and conversion rates ranked among the highest in his sector. His fellow agents yearned to know Candler's secret methodology. When asked, he'd offer an honest, but to them incredulous, answer: "I just treat them like people."

He truly believed that he was doing well. He initiated extra follow-ups with folks who had immigrated to the city. He made sure they were linked up with all the social programs they might need. He also brought new citizens along on field excursions to offer personal testimonials that, peer to peer, had a very positive effect.

He entered his office nook. Gray light sifted through a narrow window offering a marginal view of the city. The gray-green walls described a floor area that barely accommodated his desk and chair. He could envision the day when he'd receive his upgrade and literally ascend to a higher station on the twelfth floor. From there, who knew? Maybe a directorship? Definitely, definitely level blue all the way. He smiled thinking this could be the day. Jones had put a damper on that expectation, but Candler knew his meeting with Warnski was pivotal.

His pocket desk indicated the nine a.m. meeting was still a go. *This might be the one*, he thought, *my next and last assignment before a full level promotion.* He'd have a new larger cube, more creds, and access to level blue perks like holiday trips to the ocean, train rides to the hill resorts, and full benefits like uni-health. He'd also become a very eligible candidate for matching. He was partial to several co-workers—Karen in Data Entry, Justine in Media Admin, and the one in HC Review. *What's her name. . . Erin? Erika?* His reverie was interrupted by an appointment alarm on his pocket desk. Time to go!

His mood brightening at the prospect of receiving his upgrade. Candler felt a bounce in his step as he walked briskly down the hall toward the conference room. It was 8:55 a.m. and he was determined not to be late.

Chapter 9

A Refuge of Sorts
October 12, 2052

By the time the old man reached his intended destination, the rain had set in hard enough to make him think it held a grudge against him personally. There was a light glowing inside. He knocked on the cabin door and it cracked open barely enough for a slice of light and warmth to spill out onto the front porch. A long barrel of blue metal protruded at gut level as a female voice inside demanded, "Who's there? State your business!"

"It's me, Rosie." With this, he broke into a spasm of coughing. He spat off the side of the porch.

As the door opened farther, a neatly coiffed head of gray hair trussed up in braids appeared in the gap just above the twelve-gauge. Crinkled eyes widened and she flung the door open. "My God, Virgil! What in the world? You are a complete mess! What are you doing out in this? Don't you know this weather will kill you? And so late!" She was blocking the door and, though slight in frame, she obviously had the advantage. It was clear that the price of admission would be for her to finish her tirade. "Is that hooch I smell? Are you trying to make us feel sorry for you? You look like hell, Virgil. Where have you been?"

The uninterrupted interrogatories were of a rhetorical and familiar nature. She even knew what was coming next as the old man who she'd always called

Virgil looked at her to say, "Rosie, you were one helluva wildcat back in the day so don't go on too righteously about my ramblings. Meanwhile, I'm out here with my knees knocking and I can't feel my feet anymore. Are you gonna let me in or not?"

Rosie clamped her lips tightly and gave the bedraggled figure a scowl of dire warning. She stepped back into the room still grasping the door with one hand and the shotgun with the other as if she hadn't quite made up her mind. As Virgil shuffled in leaving a trail of wet slop and more than a whiff of foulness, she said, "First thing, you get out of those clothes and clean yourself up. I'll fire up the water stove for a bath. Jesus! You stink!"

She added, "There's a stool over there by the stove. . . and don't come through the house with your muddy boots! Take 'em off here. I'll see to finding some other clothes for you. Just. . ." she paused to scrutinize his slightly bulging and sloshing pocket. "Okay, Virgil, none of that in my house. Give it over!"

He gave an involuntary pout, and reaching into his coat to produce the lean remains of his libation, and slowly, very slowly proffered it to Rosie's outstretched hand, the fingers of which she was impatiently wiggling. That done, she pointed to a red string poking out of his shirt pocket. "And no smoking inside the house, Virgil. It stinks and Celi has coughing spells. You're just killing yourself anyway. Why don't you just take a gun to your head and be done with it?"

Virgil cracked a smile and fitting on the tone of a country lawyer said, "I can't do that 'cause who would be around to bother you, Rosie? Your life would be a miserable bore without you having me to pick on. In't that right?" Apparently, it was Virgil's turn to be rhetorical, as Rosie made no attempt to answer. Her expression was unreadable apart from a brief flash of admission in her eyes that came so fast only someone who knew her well would have caught it. Virgil caught it.

"Enough of this claptrap!" Rosie said. "Once those boots are off, you can strip down to your skivvies and I'll call you when the tub is ready. We'll do your laundry in the tub after you're done. Oh. . . and there're some beans in a pot I'll bring you. Just don't go wandering around. Celi's in bed, but I'll bet this commotion has got her awake now. Virgil, are you listening to me?"

"Hanging on your every word, darlin'."

"Don't you darlin' me, you. . ." She had too many derogatory epithets to choose from. "Just because I married your brother don't give you license to traipse in here at all hours and bring your stinking misery along with you. You should be ready to leave in the morning and if you don't like that you can turn yourself around, proceed back out the door and keep on walking for all I care."

Virgil raised both hands in surrender. "Okay, Rosie. No offense. I'll bunk down here tonight and move on. I am grateful for your. . . umm. . . hospitality. Be gone tomorrow. You won't even know I was here."

Seeming satisfied, Rosie turned toward the back

where they kept the water stove and disappeared with the bottle of sour mash in hand.

"Oh, well. . ." Virgil muttered. Then thought, "Mountaineers are forever free. . . till they run up against the likes of Rosie." Yet deep down, he knew he had deep feelings for her and quite likely, with Jim being dead all these years, she had some affection in her heart for him.

He began by taking off the dripping rain slicker that still bore the trademark "Mingo Coal Co." on the back. He limped over and hung it on a rack by the door.

He had to plop down onto the floor in order to take his muddy boots and soaking socks off. Not easy to do with stiff legs and shaky hands. Still wearing his hat, he creaked back to standing with a grunt, and ambled over to the potbelly stove where he undressed down to his skivvies. Standing there in his soaked through long handles for a long moment, he wondered if he'd finally lost it.

The other night, on his way home from the cemetery, he kept hearing a voice he knew was in his head, but it wasn't his voice at all. It came from somewhere behind him, only there was no one there. The voice had spoken the same words over and over:

"Round 'em up, Virgil Johnson. Round 'em up and get 'em fitted. Time is short, amigo. We got a fight coming!" He got to his place and fell into bed. By next morning, the voice was gone, but the words kept echoing in the hollows of his mind. He thought he'd totally lost it and had tried to quell the madness with slugs of mash. Later that day, he decided to trek over to the old cabin for a little family social. It rained the entire way. Darkness had settled in by the time he'd reached the front porch. He'd felt so relieved not to have heard that infernal voice the entire day.

He stood by the woodstove, the cold passing out of him. His whole body reveled in the sensation of warmth and dry comfort. He was beginning to relax. Steam was evaporating off his union suit. He heard Rosie loading wood into the water stove and running the hot water into the tub.

He was startled when the rasping voice came again, much louder and clearer in the small quiet room. "Now looky here, amigo, we got a war on. You asked me back there in the cemetery 'bout comin' to your aid and I'm obligin' you. Your time has come. Best you get ready!" It was a tenor's voice with a nasal twang–the kind that was most often heard coming from the old-timers in the back woods.

Virgil groaned internally. He was so done with war and death and the horrible memories that scarred his soul. He didn't need another voice to join the crowd of voices, faces and horrific flashbacks that already plagued his sanity. He now wished he hadn't let go of that mash so quickly.

She appeared in the kitchen doorway. "Bath's ready. You comin' or not?"

He recovered his penchant for banter. "Only if you'll scrub my back."

Rosie eyeballed him sternly over her reading glasses. "Mister, that'll be about the time they're selling snowballs in hell!"

In response, Virgil crooned an old Merle Haggard tune.

"Are we rollin' downhill, like a snowball headin' fer hell?

With no kinda chance for the flag or the liberty bell?"

He'd forgotten the next line but remembered the hook.

"Are the good times really over for good?"

He spread his arms wide like a romantic balladeer and gave her what he considered his most fetching smile.

Rosie just stared at him and shook her head. "Virgil Johnson, if you only knew how ridiculous you look standing there in those steaming skivvies acting the fool. . ." She shook her head again and sighed. "The water's getting cold, I don't have all night! Now, get your sorry ass in the tub and clean up!"

"What about Ben?"

"Ben?"

"Your son? That tallish fella who lives here. Where's he got off to?"

"Oh, he's out walking the line. I expected him back by now, but he's a clever one. He'll be in soon." She sounded self-assured, but a slight strain on her face showed she fretted. "Now, will you just get back there and don't leave a mess when you're done. There's a fresh night shirt of Ben's on the chair." She pointed to a wet heap by the stove. "And grab those nasty clothes of yours while you're at it. I'll take care of 'em."

As he walked past her toward the back room, he said. "I really do appreciate this, Rosie. I really do."

She nodded. "Virgil Johnson, you need more than a bath to clean yourself up."

He had to admit she was right, but he wasn't about to say so.

Rosie heard the lightest of footsteps in the hallway. "Celi Pierce! Get back to bed right now!" The pattering of feet diminished and a door creaked shut. A man's singing voice croaked the refrain of the Merle Haggard piece.

"I wish a Ford and a Chevy would still last ten years like they should.

Are the good times really over fer good?"

Chapter 10

Home at Last
Oct 12, 2052

Turning his key in the deadbolt lock, he passed through the backdoor quietly. It was dark inside having lived there for nearly ten years, he knew his way around. It was quiet inside except for the very odd sound of someone, a male, snoring in the den. His right hand automatically slipped to the grip of his holstered S & W. Gingerly, he set his sack of coal casts down on the wood floor. He was in the back area of the kitchen near what they called the "washroom" where clothing and occasional bathing were done in an old claw foot tub. He smelled soap and saw where a towel had been roughly hung on a towel bar near the tub.

Zeroing in on the snoring, he crouched down and came into the den as quietly as the creaking floorboards would allow. Slowly approaching the old sofa from the backside where its occupant slumbered, his focus was divided between keeping a bead on where he figured the sleeper to be while slowly inching across the floor on each floorboard trying his best to plant each step squarely on the joists below where the floor was least likely to creak. So far, so good.

The snoring continued. He neared the point where he could just about see the person on the sofa. The slightest of sounds came from under his left foot. Immediately, he heard the distinctive metallic ka-chunk of a pump action shotgun chambering a round.

"You're one dead Rocko!" a matter-of-fact gruff voice announced. "Y'know, I heard you come in the back way. Just wanted to see how you'd handle it. Sounded like a rhino wearing tap shoes! And I'll bet you're carrying."

He still couldn't see the person who spoke. Still pointing his gun at the back of the sofa, Ben countered, "Well, Virgil, let's just say we're even, 'cause I knew it was you by the wet spot in front of the front door. I saw no sign of forced entry and Ma wouldn't have let just anyone in. You're like a piece of string; you just keep showing up. So, I would not be so charitable to an intruder. I guarantee they'd be jiggin' on hot coals right now."

"Point taken, Rocket, but never assume that just because someone's snoring, they aren't awake—an old trick I learned back in the Spec Ops days."

Silence followed as Ben stood there straining to hear any movement. He caught a whiff of something. Soap! Too late! The arm came from behind and closed around his neck while a hand grabbed his gun barrel and leveraged the trigger guard painfully against his trigger finger. A whisper passed just by his ear. "And, Rocko, never assume your target is fixed or that your ole Uncle Virgil has lost his moves."

Ben had yet to beat his uncle at this game. No violence intended, he'd cleared his weapon before coming into the cabin. He felt pretty pissed, but he could only manage a feeble comeback. "Yeah Virgil, and FYI I don't go by 'Rocko' or 'Rocket.' It's Ben."

Suddenly, a metallic ka-chunk sound filled the room. They both flinched. In the dim light of the doorway to the back rooms, there stood Rosie shouldering a twelve-gauge while aiming it in their general direction. She had a clear view of them. "I say you both stop your nonsense and get your butts to bed. How about that *boys*? It's late!" She lowered her chin as if to take aim. "Or shall I count to three?"

They didn't want to bet on her gun being loaded, so Virgil released Ben and stepped back. Ben glanced over his shoulder and flickered a grin; Virgil cocked a smile and let his eyes drift over to Rosie. "Easy darlin', I was just showing Ben a move."

She stood like a statue, making both men a bit nervy. Ben stroked the area of his neck where Virgil's arm had locked like a vice. "Yeah, we were just, you know, messin' around."

She lowered the twelve-gauge and regarded them balefully. "Uh huh, messin' around. You just let a pint-sized woman get the drop on you. So much for SA, Mr. Spec Ops." She flashed a look at Virgil. He offered a slight shrug of acknowledgment. He had indeed slipped on his situational awareness. She'd appeared out of nowhere.

"Save your pissing matches for when folks aren't trying to sleep. I'm onto bed!" She whipped around and, as she turned, she deftly ejected a single shell from the gun's chamber. She caught it in her hand and held it up for them to see. She looked back over her shoulder to catch them staring at her. "Awww now, boys. I never laid a finger on the trigger and besides, it's just rock salt." They couldn't see the smile on her face as she walked down the hall into her bedroom.

Chapter 11

Celi's Diary
October 13, 2052

The other night, after I'd gone to bed, I heard
Gram talking to someone. It sounded like she was mad
at them and then I knew it was my uncle Virgil who got
an earful. I heard them talking about not waking me
but by then I was awake and standing there in the dark
hallway. Gram tells Uncle to clean himself up just like
she used to tell my little brother and me. When she
stopped talking, she must have heard me and hollered
for me to get back in bed so I did just that.

But it was hard to sleep. I just laid in bed
thinking. I still haven't figured out why Gram has it in
for Uncle. He always tries to be nice and all, but she
just won't let up. Like she wants to drive him away. The
other day, I just up and asked her why she acted the
way she does. She looked down at me and said I
wouldn't understand 'cause it's complicated.

So he saves her life way back when and she has
hardly a kind word to say whenever he comes around?
She says he's not the same person as he was back when.
I say to her it looks to me like she's not the same
person either. She gets huffy and says for the
umpteenth time, "It's complicated," as if I don't know
about such things.

What about Jordy, my little brother? In a way, I
still have a little brother, but he went with Mom to live
in the city so in another way I don't have him or Mom

anymore. That's complicated. I was nine, almost ten, then and old enough to care for things like taking care of Gram and didn't want to be a city person. There were lots of yelling fights then, mostly between Gram and Pa and Mom.

Mom wanted me to go too. She said she'd had enough and needed us to be in a safe place where there was always food and warmth, where you didn't have to work so hard just to get by and live. Madison District was no place to raise a child. She said.

Besides, my little brother had some kind of breathing thing where he couldn't suck in enough air and he'd make this awful whistling sound when he tried to breathe. Gram would give him slippery elm tea and make him breathe spearmint vapors over a steam pot, but Jordy got worse. That's one big reason Mom left. I think there were others. Gram thinks she was just soft. She said some people weren't cut out for our way of living, even if they grow'd up here.

That was three summers ago. I think about them and what they do now and how they like living in a beehive. We heard from them now and then. Letters and cards used to come. Mom promised she'd write. I'd make these pretty cards and when we'd get to the post office in Madison, I'd send them all at once, nut not anymore, not since I became a wanted outlaw.

Seems pretty complicated to me! Oops, gotta go feed wood to the stove.

Okay, more to tell. I became a wanted outlaw the last day Pa and I walked to town to get the mail. It

was our summer, cloudy like usual but warmer. I
begged and begged Pa to take me. He finally caved in. I
wore my blue jeans and a faded flannel shirt. I wound
up my hair and tucked it under an old baseball cap. Pa
said it was best to dress that way and it didn't bother
me 'cause I've got a little tomboy.

Then we go into the PO and Pa has me stand
just inside the door. A man in a gray coat was sitting at
a table filling out papers. He looks up and sees me. As
Pa walks by, he asks if he is my father.

For some reason, Pa says no, he's just a
neighbor's boy who followed along. Pa actually made
me a he! The gray guy gets curious and says he sees a
family resemblance. Pa makes a bad joke about how we
are all related, but the man doesn't smile. He asks for
my name. Pa says Billy or Willy. I forget what name he
made up, just know it was a boy's name. Anyways, that's
not what the gray guy wants to hear. He looks at me
and waves his hand for me to come over. Pa says
something to the man and quickly walks over, grabs my
hand and we leave in a hurry.

We go the back ways that take twice as long and
we barely get home before dark. Of course, Gram was
worried sick.

Both she and Pa say they never want me tagged.
It's a family thing. Lots of folks around here feel the
same way. No one in our family is tagged. Well, no one
who still lives here. I reckon that's just our way, but it
makes for a lonely way for me. Just because I don't
carry around a chip in me, I am a criminal?

Since I am hiding from the law, I am a fugitive. I've been away from Sunday school for over a year. I cannot go to any community get-togethers, including church. I have to keep close to the cabin and hide whenever any stranger comes to the door. Ever since that run in with the post office guy in Madison, my life has changed, and as my uncle has been heard to say, it's a ball buster. Not sure what it means exactly, but the way he says it, that is the way I feel.

Chapter 12

A Change of Plans
October 12, 2052

AT 8:57 a.m., Candler sat waiting in the conference room just as Sara Warnski entered. A high-grade green tag on her lapel signified S. Warnski was Candler's immediate supervisor. She was petite, slim and notably precise in all her movements with never a stray gesture or inflection. She appeared to be thirtyish, wearing the customary dark pantsuit, a green turtleneck with a black and white scarf loosely knotted about her neck. Her skin was like gypsum, pale and smooth. She had auburn hair, and a very alluring set of deep blue eyes that flashed with intelligence and cunning.

She knew how to succeed and had proven herself many times. She'd never compromised herself. She was a strategist who adhered to the workplace code of conduct and had no reticence in lodging a harassment complaint no matter the ranking of the alleged offender. She was also quick to lay claim to promotions and upgrades, lest her superiors be accused of discrimination. She was a hot potato in any department.

Candler was just a year or two younger, and tried his best to like his boss. She always seemed to keep an arid professional distance and when he thought about it, he'd never seen or heard her laugh. Not a hint of any sparks between them either, romantic sparks at least but they were on mutually serviceable professional terms and Candler was confident that Warnski would soon be recommending him for an upgrade. Just one more field census and he'd have exceeded his quota.

Warnski sat down across from Candler just as the super saver fluorescent bulbs began to flicker and then surge back to full intensity. "Well," said Warnski looking up at the ceiling fixture, "I guess that only highlights what we're all about, right Candler?" Her tone was flat and in earnest. "Look, Candler, records show you have one more week of fieldwork and we both know how well you're performing." She looked up from her pocket desk and smiled slightly.

Wow! thought Candler, *she actually smiled at me.* Then he wondered why the smile seemed more sympathetic than congratulatory.

"We *have* to bring in more citizens," she said with professionally implied reference to the retros. Candler nodded his agreement. Warnski continued.

"We're having more and more of these power surges and both GEEO and the energy commission are working night and day to make sure the cities are safely supplied with clean, sustainable energy. But these, shall we say, rural citizens refuse to contribute to our efforts and they choose to remain in their individual, well, we can't really call them homes. . . their hovels, and eke out a meager existence. All the while, they're using more than their fair share of resources." Again, Candler nodded with growing concern about where the one-way conversation was heading.

"So," Warnski looked down at her PD and then raised her eyes to meet Candler's and to assess his reaction to what she was about to say. "We have to raise the quotas, Candler, and that means any sort of pending upgrade will be delayed until further notice. By the way, this applies to all census agents and their supervisors like myself. We're all in this together."

He was still processing Warnski's first statement and was dumbstruck to the point of not really hearing the rest of what she'd said about this affecting everyone. Finally, he picked up her last few words. *So everyone is affected? Is everyone as close to a higher level promotion as I am?*

"Candler, do you have any questions or concerns?"

He shook his head slightly and tried to dispel a mental image of Art Jones in the elevator, with that crooked face smirking and grating voice deriding him. *The sonofabitch knew about this!*

"Well, good!" she said with a tone of finality. "I'm so glad you're taking this like a grade two Kelly green should." She evinced a modicum of relief. "You'll be assigned to the Abington District. You're to arrive tomorrow. So today, you can focus on preparing for a two-week stay. Your job will be to train the intake and recruitment units to maximize their registration rate. Please, be sure to build in tracking modalities so we can monitor their progress. From there, you'll be transferred to Clifton District for two weeks field training, and from there to Pulaski District. Same thing. You'll report in occasionally, in person, to me. I'll do what I can to assist you with personnel and equipment. By early spring, you should finish up in Madison

District. It's tough doing anything during the winter there, so we scheduled that as your last posting."

Candler blinked and tilted his head as if he'd heard something extraordinary. Had she so blithely announced he'd be assigned to fieldwork for what, five months? Externally, he looked mildly quizzical while internally all of his denial systems were abuzz.

"Good luck," Warnski said in a cool, codfish tone. With that final halfhearted valediction, she stood, turned out the door and left Candler sitting. She knew he'd comply.

Shockwaves were crashing inside Candler's head:
Fieldwork for five more months. How in the hell?

Leaving tomorrow? I have to form a team, plot logistics, equipment, no way!

For two weeks? I just came off a two-week stint! I need to rest and recoup!

And ending up in Madison District? What? That's the worst shithole in the region! I'll never make the quota there!

He felt the clammy coils of despair encircling and tightening around his gut. Old voices reminded him he'd never be good enough, that he deserved to fail and be just another miserable vassal lost in the system. He could feel every bit of his energy seeping out as the cold certainty of failure cast a pall on his future. Then, a sudden flash of insight set his sagging body upright. *Jones! This is his doing! I can just see him now, the gloating, sneering bastard!*

The rush of anger brought blood to his head; he could feel his heart pounding. His hands formed fists and his slackened jaw drew taut. He stood up and jerked the wrinkles out of his jacket. With the visage of a jeering Art Jones before him, Greaves resolved he'd not only succeed but also see his nemesis go down in flames. *You sorry bastard!*

Chapter 13

Morning Whispers
OCTOBER 13, 2052

Virgil awoke early, his head pounding with every heartthrob. As usual, it had been a troubled night's sleep–monstrous dreams, people dying. Some he knew, some were strangers. The only times he slept through the night were when he had totally self-medicated to the point of blacking out, and then there'd be hell to pay the very next day. Plus, he never liked being that far down the tubes—too vulnerable, stupid really.

He resolved to leave off the sauce, and he hoped things would settle in his mind. Going on these benders was becoming more of a lifestyle than just an occasional foray into self-annihilation. He'd never planned it that way. He just wanted to be left alone and, yet, the world kept pressing in on him, intruding. After a twelve-year career in military service–government then mercenary–he'd come home expecting to start a new life.

He worked the mines and eventually got into fire bossing, just as his father had back in the 90s, keeping watch for the safety of the miners. Like Rob Johnson, he'd come up against those who sought profit over safety. The twist was the mine he was working in at the time had been acquired by a government entity– the Federal Energy Commission. The FEC had partnered with a select group of mine companies that were facing bankruptcy. As a result, both production and safety suffered. Equipment broke down constantly for lack of maintenance. The discovery of an endangered brown bat in one older mine brought everything to a halt. After numerous assessments, the mine was abandoned with three million dollars' worth of equipment left inside to avoid further stress to the brown bat and its habitat.

As a fire boss at the Mingo 17 Mine, Virgil received orders to use upgraded monitors to gauge the presence of noxious and flammable gasses. He'd cautioned his super that the new equipment appeared to have serious flaws and thought it best to stay with the tried and true older equipment. . . but it was clear that the government inspectors would write them up if they didn't see the new monitors in place. The whole thing reeked of a backroom connection between the FEC and the equipment manufacturer.

One night in May, during the third shift, a ventilator fan shut down, the monitors failed to detect gas, and a static spark ignited the invisible cloud of methane. The explosion blew out the lower section. Fourteen miners lost their lives. Though Virgil worked first shift, he was held responsible for not calibrating the gauges accurately —an assertion that was difficult to refute given that the blast had obliterated all monitors within the zone. He could have lodged a wrongful termination suit, but the union refused to back his allegation that the upgraded equipment was faulty. His super acted as if they'd never had that conversation and advised him to take his severance and go. He'd been lucky not to be prosecuted for negligence. It was like the Army all over again. He'd been blackballed from ever working a mine again.

He'd gone on to dabble in private security but didn't like the clientele or being supervised by idiots. He had no use for politics or the creeping influence of government entities prescribing everything from what he drove to where he chose to live. He shucked civilization and took to living in the remote mountains where he could make his own way on his own terms. He'd be close enough to what remained of his kinfolk, yet far enough to keep to himself. None of these life changes cured the onset of nightmares and daytime mind fucks that eclipsed his sanity. He shunned any psychological help. Spilling his guts to a complete stranger was pointless. He'd get a handle on things himself. Always had, and certainly would—someday.

The windows in the cabin glowed bleakly with the first light of day as he got himself up to get dressed. Looking around the room, he didn't see his clothes, then remembered they were likely hanging up to dry in the washroom. He had on his nephew's long nightshirt and nothing else. He stretched and yawned as he padded in bare feet toward the kitchen then stopped when he heard hushed conversation. Celi was speaking softly, "Why be so mad, Gram? We're all the family he has left."

"Celi, you're not understanding how it is. We don't help him by being charitable. It's called enabling. He has to come to terms with himself; it's not our job to fix him."

"Well, then why do you let him in the cabin and clean his clothes?"

"It's complicated, sweetie. I still owe him a debt

of gratitude."

"What's that mean? You owe him money?"

"No, no." She sighed. "Look, you're getting old enough to be told some things. We'll have us a long sit down and I'll explain, but right now, we have to get some breakfast on the table. Go gather us some eggs and make sure nothing's messed with the hens."

Celi sounded disappointed. "Okay but I just want to say one more thing. Uncle Virgil is just doing what all of us are doing, me included."

"And what is that, Celi?"

"He's hiding, Gram. Just like all of us, he's afraid of something and he's hiding, but I know where to find him."

"Really?" Rosie paused and cleared her throat. "Well, that may be, sweetie, but right now I need you to find those eggs or we'll have a measly breakfast. Get going!"

Upon hearing the conversation, a knot clenched in Virgil's gut. His thoughts turned to self-loathing. *I really don't deserve any kindness or that little girl standing up for me. I'll not be bothering them anymore.*

Coming into the front den, Rosie nearly collided with Virgil. She backed off in surprise. "Well, I see you're up and at it!" She sounded purposely aloof. "Your stuff is dry and folded, laid out on the sideboard. Breakfast will be out in a quarter hour."

She appraised him from head to toe. "And, I don't appreciate your recovering that bottle of hooch. I saw it resting empty on the windowsill. You cannot keep doing this, Virgil Johnson. I won't have it!"

Virgil looked down at a face masked by anger, but her eyes showed something different. "Hey, Rosie, like I said. I really do appreciate your hospitality and I know it's worn thin. I'll be leaving directly, no need for breakfast. I gotta head south for some supplies."

Rosie thought there was a note of finality in the man's voice. She surmised that he'd been listening in on her conversation with Celi. She softened her stance and let the words slip. "We do worry about you, Virgil." She reached out and placed her hand on his arm. "It's just hard to see you making a mess of things."

Virgil looked from the hand on his arm into Rosie's glistening eyes. He spoke past the lump in his throat. "Well Rosie, I know what I have to do. You needn't worry. None of you needs to worry about me. Everything's gonna work out." His tentative smile betrayed the opposite. He turned away and proceeded toward the washroom.

Seeing him walk away, she had the distinct feeling he'd come to some terms with himself but to what end she couldn't say.

#

He stepped out on the front porch just as Celi was turning the corner with a half dozen eggs cradled in her apron. She smiled brightly, but her smile quickly faded seeing that he was fully dressed wearing his hat and slicker. "Uncle! You're not leaving so soon. You just got here! And we're getting up breakfast in just a few. You can't be leaving now. Can you?"

Virgil gently resisted her entreaty. He looked at her and saw Rosie's eyes, her freckled face, the rich auburn hair, and for a moment, had a glimpse of what Rosie looked like as a young woman. The spell was broken when she spoke again. "Uncle? Are you gonna stay for breakfast? I'll make those eggs just the way you like them and I'll bet we have a little honey for the flat bread." She smiled, fanned her blue peepers with her long eyelashes and then raised her eyebrows in rapt anticipation. "Will you?"

At that point, he had no will. She had her wiles and charm, more than her mother and grandmother put together. "Oh, all right, Rubylocks, I'll sit down for breakfast, but I gotta leave right after." She rushed into his arms and gave him a fierce hug with one arm, pressing her face against his chest. *She's really growing up, taller every time I see her.* An egg spilled out and splatted on the porch. "Reckon that's one's mine since I like 'em soft and scrambled."

Celi laughed. "Aww, don't worry, Uncle. I'm sure I can find one more. You just go on back inside and have a seat. I'll take care of this." She stepped back and made her way into the cabin careful not to spill any more eggs. She hollered over her shoulder, "Now come on Uncle, we have a place ready for you. Come on now!"

Virgil had to smile as he thought. *Yep, certainly*

has a measure of her grandmother; no doubt about it. He turned around and headed for the inside.

#

"Well, well. So you were hungry, after all." This Rosie surmised from Virgil taking a seat at the well-worn breakfast table.

"Kinda got lassoed by Lil Red." He cocked a smile and looked over at Celi, who stood at the stove with her back turned. He mentally counted down. *One, two, three and. . .*

Celi whipped around waving a spatula at him. "I am not little or red, Uncle Virgil!"

Virgil glanced quickly at Rosie then back to Celi. "Well, now. Maybe I stand corrected Miss Pierce. Is that what I shall call you? 'Miss Pierce'? 'Miss Cecilia'?"

Celi stamped her foot. "No! I'm just me, Celi. My name is Celi!"

Rosie broke in, "Watch your tone, young lady! You ask your uncle nicely."

Celi stammered, "Will you. . . ? Uncle Virgil, will you please call me Celi?"

Virgil nodded saying, "I'll do that, Celi. Since you asked so nicely." He looked at Rosie and winked. "I forgot how easy you red-headed women get riled. My apologies." He made a courtly gesture of bowing with his right hand on his chest. Rosie and Celi looked at one another and shook their heads in mock disgust.

Ben appeared just as breakfast was set on the table. After Rosie said grace, they talked about the day. Ben announced that he planned to do some hunting and invited Virgil to go along. Virgil declined the offer saying he needed to go down to Fyco to pick up supplies. The adults all knew the town to be a haven for bootleggers, whoremongers, gamblers and other nefarious types. Celi naively asked why anyone would want to go there. "I heard folks down that way are real mean and ornery."

Virgil looked down at his plate and sopped up egg yolk with a piece of flatbread. "Well, lil'. . . I mean Celi, there's things you just can't go out and pick off a tree. Supplies and such, but don't you worry 'bout your old uncle. I'll be just fine." Again, he flashed his best derring-do smile. No one, not even Celi, bought it.

Chapter 14

Distant Relations and Reveille
OCTOBER 13, 2052

They walked from the cabin to the old logging road that ran north and south. "I wish you'd reconsider, Virge. We could hunt a while and then you could take care of your. . . *business*." Ben flavored the last word with a dash of sarcasm.

Virgil caught the drift. "Right. Well, maybe I'll catch up with you later after attending to *my* business." As they parted ways, Ben to the north and Virgil to the south, Virgil offered a familiar bit of parting wisdom, "Keep your head low and your powder dry."

Ben smiled. "I'm using a crossbow." He patted his holster that was under his coat. "The Maggie's just for back up."

"Well, in that case, Rocket, watch your back!"

"You too!" Ben ignored the pet name his uncle fell into using decades ago; he gave a quick nod and turned northward. He had the crossbow strapped to an old camouflaged REI backpack. His long coat flapped against his legs as he strode away. A foggy drizzle began to set in as the barren treetops swayed slightly.

Virgil turned his coat collar up and pulled his hat down low. He hated cold rain running down the back of his neck. He began walking at a fast clip. He hadn't gone ten paces before a voice came from just behind him.

"Well, that were right interestin', amigo." Virgil felt a jolt. Sid was back. At least he'd kept quiet in the presence of others. Whether he lingered during the interim or went on to haunt others remained a mystery. "'Course you got your priorities. Yeah, gotta git you some hooch makins, steady your nerves, make you feel right."

Virgil stopped in mid-stride. "Who the hell are you? What are you?" He knew he'd just crossed a threshold by directly engaging the voice as if it existed separate from his own being. He kept going. "For the record, I don't need any more noise about what I do wrong. So leave me the hell alone!" Strangely, the chatter in his head turned silent. He listened to the dripping of rain, an occasional birdcall, the light wind flowing through the branches. Whatever he'd said seemed to have exorcised the phantom voice.

Then, just one word came into his head. "Trouble!" An instant later, several gunshots rang out behind him, to the north. It sounded like a rifle shot, not a hand piece. There came another gunshot. That time it was a hand piece. *Ben!*

Virgil felt his blood quicken as he reversed course and took off running in the direction of the gunfire. A dark dread shadowed him. He fought to keep his senses sharp and his mind focused on whatever lay ahead. Trouble indeed.

#

As he reached a rock outcropping that overlooked the railroad line, he saw a rail cart parked on the tracks. *Goddamned spotters!* There was a breach in the overgrowth on the downhill side where a trail led to the river and what they called the game lands. Virgil slipped the Desert Warrior forty-five from its holster and crept down the bank toward the rail cart. The sound of voices drifted his way.

"Can ya see 'em, Charlie?" a man shouted.

"Naw. I thought you'd a had 'em pinned down. I never saw 'em."

"Bullshit! He was headed your way and I'm pretty sure I clipped him. He's gotta be in that thicket somewheres."

"Well, okay then." In the next instant, the sound of automatic rifle fire erupted, but seemed to hang up partway through the firing. "Goddamned piece of shit! What the hell?"

"Hold up, Charlie! You dumb shit! I didn't say you needed to strafe the fuckin' thicket! Jeezeus! We want this one alive. He ain't worth much bounty dead. Just wait till I get there!"

Virgil eased over the tracks and quietly down the gravely slope. He needed to reach Ben, but first he had to neutralize the two spotters—obviously amateurs. He pulled up a tattered shemagh, a relic from his Spec Op days, to cover the lower half of his face. He smiled beneath the cover. For the first time in months, maybe years, he felt alive. *Show time!*

Chapter 15

No Turning Back
"Sooner or later, everyone sits down to a banquet of consequences."~R.L. Stevenson

"Hell Charlie! What were you thinkin'? Oh, I get it; you weren't 'cause all you got is shit for brains." Charlie merely stewed and grunted as he gave his partner a blistering glance. The two spotters were crouched behind a fallen sycamore. They peered past a clearing to a cluster of brambles that spanned about forty feet left to right. "All right, here's the thing. You stay here while I try to flush 'em out. Do not shoot to kill, understand? I will shoot you myself if you mess this up. Got that?"

Charlie nodded and gestured to his rifle. "This piece of shit jammed on me again. It won't shoot but one bullet at a time now. Just sayin'."

"Well, in your case, douche, maybe that's a good thing. Just watch and if he flushes out, aim for his legs. His legs, you hear me?"

Charlie nodded. He'd just about had it with his old buddy, his old pal. He tendered the thought of how nice it would be not to have to split any bounty.

The other man turned toward the bottom end of the fallen tree and took several awkward steps trying to keep low. As he did, the alarming sound of a pistol being cocked stopped him in his tracks. He knew Charlie wasn't sporting a sidearm. *How in the world could that poacher have gotten the drop on us?*

A steely voice came from the brush behind them. "Drop 'em, real slow now." Charlie turned to face the masked intruder with his finger still on his gun's trigger. A loud clap of gunfire rang out as a bullet creased his ear, causing him to drop the gun and feel for his wound. Another shot followed and Charlie's partner collapsed forward as a bullet ripped through the meat of his calf. Both men cursed and hollered as Virgil stepped out to face them, his forty-five raised to eye level. The apparent lead man half lay on the ground but still had a hand on his weapon. Whether it was bravado or sheer lizard-brained reaction, he grabbed his weapon and began to swing the business end toward Virgil. From ten feet away, Virgil knew he couldn't physically prevent the guy from getting a shot off.

He'd forgotten how complicated it was to kill a person. Rules of engagement, Geneva Conventions, minimum force protocols and as a Spec Ops soldier, every situation had to be assessed. As a mercenary, assessment simply amounted to serving the mission and consequent paycheck. As he watched the spotter train the weapon on him, he knew this would be a turning point. No matter what transpired in the next second, life was about to get a whole lot more interesting—or not.

A single shot to the apricot, the medulla oblongata, generally induces the quickest loss of motor response. It would be over in just an instant. Then came the old death cheating wish. *Why not give that feller an even chance? Let him draw a bead and then see who's the fastest trigger in the west.* The shooter's weapon was set on full auto, and by the time he'd brought it up and around, he was already firing wildly. Virgil could feel the wake of the lead balls as they came increasingly close. Finally, he'd had enough and his finger eased back on the trigger. Just as the gun discharged its deadly projectile, a streak of black flew past Virgil's right shoulder and struck the spotter through his chest. The cross bolt buried itself up to the notch and with a thud, pinned the upper body against the tree trunk. The man's eyes bulged and froze in dismay. He coughed, sending a spray of bright crimson into the air. Then his head nodded forward onto his chest as more red flowed onto his shirt.

The other spotter, Charlie, kicked his gun away and started blubbering about how he never meant to hurt anyone and that all he did was take orders. He kept feeling his wounded ear and then looking at the blood on his trembling hand. His other arm was extended above his head. The sound of movement came from the nearby brush as Ben emerged, crossbow in hand, and a scarf, similar to Virgil's, covering the lower half of his face. His eyes flashed to Virgil, and then took in the scene before them. Virgil noticed Ben's shoulder had been striped by a bullet, but nothing more.

About that time, radio static crackled, followed by a scratchy voice, "Post 37, Come in. Post 37." The radio was attached to the dead man's chest rig. Virgil strode over to the wide-eyed corpse and removed the device. He tossed it onto Charlie's lap and instructed him on exactly what to say.

#

They had the surviving spotter drag his partner's body down to the edge of the river, at the mouth of a creek where a jumble of logs had lodged against several live trees on the bank. The spotter complied with Virgil's orders without hesitation. The body was placed lengthwise along a dry log and drug out into the current. Almost immediately, the body flipped over to hang from its bindings so that only the hands and feet were visible. Not perfect, but good enough to drift the body downstream a good ways and for the trackers to see the blip on their screens still moving.

As for Charlie, his ultimate fate presented a conundrum. Granted, he did surrender, but keeping him prisoner would be a major hassle. Naturally, Charlie swore he'd just go off and disappear and never say anything about anything or anyone—ever, but could they trust him? Likely not. They trussed up Charlie's hands around a low hanging tree branch and threatened to gag him if he didn't stop squalling. He stopped. As a precaution, Ben and Virgil had kept their scarves pulled up for masks.

Out of earshot, Ben and Virgil went over the pros and cons of what to do with Charlie. Ben's position leaned toward letting him go. Virgil reminded him, "He was all for dragging you in, dead or alive, for bounty. The only problem he had with strafing your hideout with bullets was that his gun jammed."

Ben nodded. Today, he'd experienced two firsts–getting shot at and killing a human being. Even if he'd only been grazed, and it was a tossup as to who actually killed the lead guy, both incidents would leave their mark on his psyche but at the moment, he felt a crash coming off a supercharged adrenaline rush. He rummaged around in his mind until a thought occurred. "Well, this guy's a stooge. Why not play him?"

"Do what?" Virgil's eyebrows rose.

"Look, he doesn't know our faces. They've only seen me at a distance. Why not feed him some bull and send him on down the road?"

"Hmmm, okay. Tell me more."

#

They walked up to Charlie and looked him over, obviously having come to some decision. They kept their faces covered and Ben's eyes shadowed by his hat.

Virgil went first. "Well, Carter. I reckon we can take this feller at his word that he ain't saying anything to anybody."

"Yep, Sade, I reckon the same. Just let him know we'll gut him and feed his innards to the hogs if he goes off and says anything to anybody."

"Yep." Ben gave Charlie a poke in the back. "You hear that? Not a word. Or else. . . "

Charlie stammered. "I wwwon't say nnnothin 'bout nnnobody, Mr. Burk–uh sir. I'll just tell 'em we got lost and separated. That's what I'll do. I swear!"

Virgil and Ben glanced at each other. The ploy to pin the incident on the Burkhart Clan appeared to be working. The spotters were likely quite familiar directly or indirectly with the violent gang headed by the elder Sade and his heir apparent Carter Burkhart. The imposters weren't exactly of the same physical build but close enough to make a bet that good ole Charlie would spill the beans in the wrong direction.

They untied Charlie, walked him up to the tracks, fastened his hands to the rail cart's pump handle, removed his boots and told him to take off before they changed their minds. He looked forlornly at his boots as if he pondered a complaint, but then thought the better of it and started pumping. As he disappeared around a bend, Virgil pulled his scarf down from his face and proffered the man's boots to Ben. "Looks like about your size."

Ben slipped his scarf down and shook his head. "Not any better 'n mine, 'sides, they smell a might bit rank." Virgil chucked them down the bank into the bushes.

Ben stared at Virgil who returned the look for a moment and then said, "What? Do you think I shoulda kept those boots?"

"Nope. It's not about the boots." Ben's gray eyes continued to bore in.

Virgil kept eye contact. "Well, you got something to say? Go on."

Ben leaned toward his uncle. "What the hell

happened back there with you and that lead spotter?"

Virgil smirked. "Uh, lemme think. . . . Oh yeah, I shot him—dead. So?"

Ben countered, "No. I mean why did you wait for him to start shooting before you pulled the trigger?"

Virgil quickly turned his head to the side and spat, never taking his eyes off Ben's. "I knew I had him, no matter. So what're you getting at?"

"Looked to me like you were cutting it mighty close, by a hair. That's when I took the shot. It didn't look like you were gonna."

"So," Virgil parried, "make your point."

Ben had never gotten in this deep with his uncle—another first. Nevertheless, he didn't mince words. "You tryin' to get yourself killed?"

The other man unexpectedly broke into a spasm of laughter, which he struggled to control. Though it sounded like a raucous laugh, it carried a hollow tone of concession. The way someone might laugh having been caught at some mischief.

"'Scuse me, Virgil, but I fail to see what's so goddamned funny!"

Virgil calmed himself and took a deep inhale. "Well, Rocket, it's all about perspective. This weren't my first little shootout, y'know. What seemed to you to be a split-second was an eternity for me. Instead of getting myself killed, it was the exact opposite. When I felt the hot lead brushing past my cheek, I truly never felt more alive in years." He winked at his nephew. "And, for the record, Rocket, I do appreciate your concern and the way you expressed it."

Virgil reached over and clapped Ben on the shoulder. "You did good, Ben, but here's the thing." Ben watched his uncle's smile disappear and his face harden. "What happened today changes everything. It won't be long before that Charlie feller gets his story to the Green Hats and they'll soon find out it wasn't the Burkharts. The other guy's body will wash up somewhere downstream. A few scans of the terrain and they'll spot the cabin and soon they'll find us out. All we did today was delay. How soon they'll catch on and catch up with us, who knows."

Ben tugged at the lapels of his long coat as if making ready to move on somewhere. "So, we go into hiding, find a place that's more remote, somewhere safe."

Virgil pursed his lips and solemnly shook his head. "There is no safe place, Ben. We just dispatched one of their spotters. They're already looking for Celi. It's like the goddamned Jewish persecution! All we've ever done is tried to live our lives. That's all! The Green Hats detest us for being who we are. We've been shoved back, beaten down, baited, trapped, hunted and taken. I thought, after a while, they'd just give up and leave us alone; all we had to do was wait them out but, as of today, this is personal and I'm not gonna run anymore, or hide or kowtow to their bullshit!"

Ben thoughtfully scraped the underside of his beard with the back of his hand. "So, what are you gonna do? Take on the whole establishment?"

Virgil was quick to answer. "We never meet a superior force head on. That's Art of War 101, but there are other ways, at least to begin whittling down the odds."

"Like what?"

"Small units, strategic targets. We outrun them and outthink them."

"You're talking guerrilla warfare, right? If it's just you and me, Virge, we're screwed."

"Never said it'd be just us, Ben. We need to form up some allies."

"How?"

"Well, that's the trick, innit? What kinda thing would draw folks together, 'specially when they're scattered about just makin' ends meet?"

"What thing is that?"

Vigil scratched the back of his head and smiled grimly. "Justice? Liberty? Food? Fuel? I've no notion whatsoever but we have to start somewhere."

The handheld radios in their pockets burst with static. They were tuned to monitor mode to track any communications relative to their situation. The devices would soon be useless without their charging dock. "Post 37 come in. Confirm your location. We have you three clicks south of Clinefeld Crossing and another signal puts you on the rail line 40 clicks north of Fyco. Say your status. Are you in pursuit? Repeat, are you in pursuit?"

Virgil signaled that he would handle the call. Keying the mike, he imitated the lead man. While speaking, he shut the mike off and on to fake poor transmission. "Post. . . Confirm. . . river. . . Pursuit in pro. . . Burkhart. . . will advise. No need for backup. Loose connect. . . thirty-seven out."

"That might stall 'em a bit." He held out his hand. "Here. Hand me that radio. Second thought. There are likely to be locaters too." He placed the plastic devices on a flat rock and, seizing a fist-sized stone, commenced breaking them into little bits.

"So, what now, Virge? Never did find any game. You up for huntin'?"

"Figure we've scared off everything from here to three miles out. Too bad. I'd say pretty soon we'll be the hunted."

Ben solemnly nodded. "Reckon we better get back to the cabin and plan our next moves. Like you say, Virge. This changes everything." He pondered the import of his own words for a moment and then remembered something. "Just a minute. I need to get my pack." Ben scrambled down the slope and out of sight.

As soon as Ben had disappeared into the brush, Sid chimed in. "Well, 'migo. That were a might interestin' little showdown. That boy's right. You did play it pretty close. Kinda casual too. Good shootin' though, but if it were me, I wouldn't have let that Charlie off so easy. Can't trust that sort."

Virgil tried to counter the intruder's presence. "Never asked for your advice. You're just a random fly buzzing inside my head. A nuisance I'd just as soon be shed of!"

"Uh huh!" Virgil felt a tap on his right shoulder and whirled around. No one was there. Another tap. He whirled back. No one. "I can't do this all day, 'migo. Takes a mighty effort to turn even my finger solid but you should get the point. I ain't no figment." This time it was a poke not a tap, and Virgil whirled around again. "You wanna be shed of ole Sid? Well, 'migo, it was you who called me forth and like it or not, it were for a higher cause than rescuin' your sorry ass."

Virgil felt the seams that barely held his sanity together begin to rip apart. He grabbed his lower jaws with both hands and pushed upward as if to wrest his head from his neck. An internal siren screamed in his brain. Every muscle in his body coiled with the intensity. This was it. He'd finally crossed over into certifiable lunacy. Sid's voice softened and he spoke as a rider would to a spooked horse. "Easy there 'migo. Just take 'er easy. I'm here to help. Understand? Help. You need something that'll bring folks together? I can help."

Virgil's panic subsided. He took several deep breaths. His stoic nature had won out over his self-concern. *Well, if going schizoid helps get us through this mess, if that's what it takes, then I'm all ears, whatever or whoever you are.*

"Atta boy, amigo. I knew you'd come through."

He could hear Ben coming back up the hill and wished to conclude the conversation ASAP since Sid so thoughtfully clammed up whenever sane folks came near. *So, "Sid." What've you got that will help?*

"Haint what I got. Hit's what you need to get."

Virgil's patience began slipping. *Well, go on. What is "it" and what do I need to do to get "it"? Just tell me!*

"Somethin' special to give to the people, in a particular place."

Ben was almost to the foot of the gravel embankment and would soon climb up to the tracks. *Enough beating around the goddamned bush, just tell me where I need to go?*

Right as Ben reached the tracks, Sid said two words that echoed like pebbles dropped into a deep well, *"The farm."*

Chapter 16

Next Moves

"Okay. You ready?" Ben looked at him curiously. "Hey, you okay Virge?"

"Beteren you, Rocko. Hey, hold up a sec. Let me see that shoulder." He pointed to where a bullet had ripped through the fabric of Ben's coat leaving a frayed streak of dark brown.

"It's nothing, Virge. Just a scratch is all."

"Well, then drop your pack and let me see it."

Ben halfheartedly unslung the pack from his shoulder, then peeled away his coat and pulled down his shirt to display a bright red stripe running across the beefy swell of his deltoid. It had bled very little, but there were tiny bits of fabric that had been seared into the skin by the bullets' pass-through.

"Damned lucky! You better get some turpentine on that and try to pick out those bits of cloth. I'd say forget doing anything more. Just call it a day."

Ben looked crestfallen. "I'm fine! Really!"

"Well," Virgil tried a different tact, "do what you want, Rocket. I still got business south of here and will likely have to stay there for the night. I'll do a bit of recon to see how ole Charlie made out. That is, if they didn't string 'em up first."

Ben covered himself back up and looked down at his feet. As he hefted the backpack, he sounded resigned. "Well, what do you suppose I oughta say to Ma and Celi? Anything?"

Virgil pursed his lips and scratched his jaw beard. "Nothin' for now. Those Green Hats'll be off track for a while." He thought of the spotter, Charlie, rolling into Fyco whose inhabitants would just as soon shoot him as look at him. The other spotter's body would eventually be found, but maybe not for days. They'd be after the Burkharts anyway. "On second thought, tell them we had a little trouble with some spotters so we need be on the lookout for trouble. Be prepared to leave the cabin and head up to my place. I'll catch up with you at the cabin or there."

Virgil reached out and grabbed him by his good shoulder, giving it a gentle shake. He waited for eye contact and then said, "You done good today, Ben. Remember, they would've taken you down and left Rosie and Celi to fend for themselves—or worse, much worse."

"Hey, thanks, Virge, for coming back and evenin' things up. I woulda had 'em, but I don't know if I coulda done that spotter like I did without. . . Well, you know."

They both nodded, appreciating that which remained unsaid. Ben had shot the spotter to save Virgil. "That's just the way it happens. Seen it a hundred times. Soldiers don't fight for God 'n country.

They fight to save their buddies right next to 'em."

Ben momentarily reflected on his uncle's words. "Well, you take care. I mean it, Virge. Take care." Ben's gray eyes probed deep into Virgil's, seeking some hint of reception. *Hard to tell.* He grabbed his pack and picked up his crossbow, already cocked and loaded with a bolt, just in case.

Virgil cautioned. "Keep a sharp eye out for any spotters or Green Hats, and keep your powder dry." He touched the brim of his hat and turned south to Fyco.

As they parted company and distanced themselves from each other, Ben cast a final glance at his uncle walking down the tracks. The Virgil he'd known back in the day had momentarily resurfaced. Now, it seemed the real man was receding once again into the shadows. Yet, there seemed to be an urgency in the way his uncle looked just before they parted ways. Something had shifted. He saw his uncle glance back several times, not too obviously but enough to know he was checking to see that he wasn't being followed. *What's he up to now?*

He hefted the pack to keep its weight centered on his left shoulder and began taking measured strides, feeling anxious about the future and what they'd gotten themselves into with the spotters and quite likely, the whole damned authority.

Chapter 17

Backtracking and Facing Shadows
OCTOBER 13, 2052

After rounding the first bend and ascertaining that he was out of Ben's sight, Virgil edged downslope to the riverbank and backtracked upstream to what appeared to be a jumble of flood debris laying atop a fallen willow. He found a loop of rope and dragged an upside down, beat-up johnboat from under the cover of leaves and branches. The aluminum hull had deep dents but no holes. He flipped the boat over and was glad to see the oars jammed under the back seat. There was something else he hoped to find. He unlatched the lid to a storage compartment in the bow and fished around with his hand until his fingers came in contact with a jar. He pulled the container out to examine the contents, then spoke aloud, "Ah yes!" As he unscrewed the lid, he felt his throat tighten with an awesome thirst as if he couldn't quench it fast enough.

Just as he was tilting the jar, a powerful spasm jerked his arm causing the jar to fly out of his hand and land at his feet. Nearly every drop spilled onto the sandy ground. Virgil looked at his hand, then at the jar in stunned disbelief. "What the. . . ?" He felt like his right arm had been tazed.

The Sid voice blasted, "Hain't you heard a thing, 'migo? You need that sauce like you need a bullet in your brain. You barely got your shit together as 'tis. Then you wanna get yourself even more messed up?"

Virgil reacted defiantly. "None of your Goddamned business what I do or don't do! Fuck off!" The eerie presence brooded silently. "What is your problem?" Another stretch of silence ensued. Once again, Virgil wondered at his state of sanity. *I'm shouting at the air, arguing with the wind. Like tryin' to punch a hole in water.* He looked at the empty jar and the useless lid he held in his hand. *Now what?*

"Now that you've had your little tantrum, how 'bout we get down to business, 'migo? You need to haul ass to the farm and do so undetected. If you can't figure out why, then 'ole Sid will show you what's what. Yes, sir. That I'll do." A pause ensued. "Oh, and, by the way, I'm not the one with a problem."

#

The river was murky and swollen but not as swift as one might expect.

As he steered the boat downstream, keeping close to the bank, Virgil thought about the challenges of starting a campaign of resistance–a war. His mind reeled with strategic calculations. He knew where to obtain a few ATV gas mobiles, horses, armaments and ammo. He wasn't sure he could muster the patience and political skill that would bring men together. Ben might help there. Ben had always had a way with people. They'd likely have to start small. There were already small militia groups that defended their own turf in much the way he and Ben had justly dealt with the spotters.

Like the clan and chieftain days of Scotland,

bringing those contentious factions together was like stuffing cats and dogs into a gunnysack and asking them to get along, but Sid had it right. You could just feel the big wheels were turning and something dark and dreadful was about to descend upon them all– unless they joined forces and fought. The Green Hats could simply hunt down and pick off the small bands of resistance one community at a time. It would take something of an army to fight an army. Could they get the communities to agree to band together to fight a common enemy? How?

He began to take account of himself. *It's just me and this dead guy's voice inside my head. Who the fuck's gonna pay any attention to a wasted old sot who hears voices? 'Specially when he does what the voices tell him to do?*

As if on cue, Sid broke in. "Naaaaaw. Stop thinkin' like that. You just foller what I tell ya and you'll see I ain't no spook blowin' smoke. You'll see. I'll take you to the one thing that'll make it all happen."

Virgil seemed unconvinced. "And what would that one thing be?"

"Hope, Virgo, hope."

Hearing this, Virgil was assured he'd gone completely bat-shit. He'd never included hope in his skill set of people persuaders. His methods were more direct and often involved pain and/or threat of termination. He never had subscribed to the notion of winning hearts and minds–he'd lost too many comrades to the cause. And to more things, like ROE, and such. As a mercenary, he'd burned that card a long time ago along with the Geneva Conventions.

Hope? For what? For the Green Hats to let the hill folk live without interference, no raids, no tagging, no making people disappear? Hope that life would become more than a hand to mouth, bottom feeding, fear stoked existence—waiting for the sound of a motor, the sight of a Green Hat posse, seeing friends and neighbors caught in the matrix—or turning themselves over in exchange for medicine, food, comfort, or social security?

Sid's voice cut in. "O ye of little faith!"

"Oh, so now you're goin' on with the Bible? Jesus calming the waters and all that?"

"Ahh, Virgo. Good. You remember your Bible. I wished I had. Yes, indeed." The rhythmic sound of the oars splashing the water became hypnotic. The handles creaked softly in their oarlocks. Something apart from Sid's voice slipped slowly into Virgil's mind—a soft sound of a piano, then a voice singing, his mother's voice. The melody floated through with the words. "The Lord has promised good to me. His word my hope secures." She had an abiding faith and an angelic voice to match. He listened in rapture until another sound intervened, that of the boat scraping bottom on the east shore. His mother's singing faded away with the last lines, "He will my shield and portion be. As long as life endures."

He remained in the boat for a spell. The tune still reverberated as if a chord deep inside him had been touched. She had given him life, had tried to lift him to a higher calling and failing that, had always held out hope that he'd one day see his way to a higher power. Hope.

He didn't hear Sid's voice, but he felt his nearness. "Okay, Sid. Let's see what you got."

#

It was all business once he touched shore. After stashing the boat under a patch of laurel, he shouldered his rucksack and slung his Sig 551 over his shoulder. He reflexively drew back the charging handle to chamber the first round of 5.56 ammo he himself had loaded. He pressed a release and the stock folded over to shorten the weapon for quick draw mode. Checking his sidearm—a classic forty-five caliber 1911 Colt, Marine issue—he yanked back the slide, then released it slowly. Satisfied all was sufficiently cocked and locked, he holstered the gun and commenced climbing the steep bank toward the old roadbed.

Knowing the terrain as he did, he easily skirted around the town proper of Madison. On the hills above, misty fog had covered the ramshackle homes and outbuildings. Anyone on watch would be oblivious to the lone figure moving quietly through the haze. The road up to the farm was an easy find even though briers and brambles pinched it on both sides with eight years of overgrowth. It never ceased to amaze him how quickly nature could swallow up the works of men. Lucky for him, the deer and other wildlife had found the road to be the easiest way up the mountain and they'd laid down a passable trail. He just had to crouch down occasionally to avoid the vegetation the four-legged creatures could easily go under. *Good.* He thought. *No one's been up here for ages.*

He saw the old sign first, partially nailed to a fencepost and cocked at an extreme angle. Faded red letters on flaking whitewash: "The Johnsons." He took a deep breath as the onrush of memories began riffling through his mind like a stack of postcards. The good, the bad, the familiar—all gone, all done, buried. His first stop would be to pay his respects at the family plot–where his dad, mother and brother had been laid to rest.

The farm had consisted of over one hundred seventy-five acres of woods and rolling pasture, an even mix. Rumor was that his great-great-great-grandfather had homesteaded the land when it was still known as the frontier of Virginia. They'd had to contend with clearing the land, pulling stumps, laying in supplies for winter and, all the while, fighting off Indians. The pioneer way was the roughest.

Family cemeteries often contained many little gravestones and markers. A testament that a lot of children died back then–often in infancy–sometimes at childbirth taking their mothers with them. Hard times. There were family cemeteries dotted all over these parts, most of which had fallen into neglect.

The Green Hats cared not a whit for family heritage, ties to the land, and legacies. To them, the private ownership of land and other property had led to "earthkind's" troubles. Only a fraction of the district's population, like Virgil and his kin, still retained independent ownership of any property, but it didn't include their farm that'd been the wellspring of eight generations. The GEEO administration had declared domain over the entire region. All areas outlying the town limits were to be managed under the auspices of the Wild Lands Project.

Virgil climbed the hill. What had once been a field was now festooned with young tulip poplars, cedars and pines growing through brambles of wild rose and honeysuckle. He chose to follow the trails cut in by the only creatures officially permitted to roam the land. At the top stood the cemetery–cordoned by a rusting wrought iron fence. His grandfather, whom he'd never known, had hand-forged every iron picket. Virgil muttered to himself, "Seems like I'm always winding up in graveyards."

"Well," Sid opined, "be thankful you're still standin' 'bove ground. . . . Plus, there's almost always a nice view."

When opening the gate, a rusted hinge broke so that he had to heft the entire gate out of the way. He approached solemnly. An all too familiar cloak of weariness draped over him. This branch of the Johnson line had nearly all disappeared. Done. Buried. He remained the last but why had he been the one to survive? He'd acted the black sheep, the thrill-seeking marauder, the rebel who never wrote a single letter home, hardly ever called. Just showed up now and then.

He looked at his brother Jim's headstone

James Henry Johnson

Beloved and Loving Husband and Father
Born June 2nd, 1988
Died February 11th, 2029

Why you, Jimmie? You had so much more going for you.
Rosie, lil Ben, the farm. . .

Then he recalled while he was traipsing around
the globe in jungles deserts, and terror-ridden hotspots
with his Special Ops assignments, Jim was holding it
together against a tide of GEEO regulations, executive
orders and eventual seizures that led him, Rosie, and
Ben with Ben's new wife, Estelle, to a marginally barren
existence on the farm. When they came for his horses,
it was the last straw that broke not just Jimmie's back
but his heart. How he loved those animals. Something
Virgil could never understand was how someone could
grow so attached to a dumb creature like that, but he
knew Jimmie had taken on their mother's aspect of
nurturing all creatures great and small.

He gazed over at the other headstones. His
dad's inscription read "Robert Henry Johnson"; and his
mom's, "Judith Marcel Johnson." More memories,
images, music, happy reunions, sad gatherings. A soft
whisper came to him like a breeze. "Hey Virgil." It was
Sid, again. Only there was a respectful, tentative tone in
his words. "We need ta take this up later 'migo. There'll
be more time for paying your respects and visiting old
memories on down the road."

Sid's kind persuasion was like a windlass
gradually drawing Virgil's consciousness up from a
deep well. He surfaced into the present, gave his
noggin a slight shake and drew in a deep draft of cool

mountain air. As he exhaled, he said aloud, "Okay, Sid. Where's this thing that's gonna give us hope?"

Chapter 18

Charlie Rolls into Fyco
October 13, 2052 (Later in the Day)

The strongest attribute Charles Dwight Harris possessed might have been his ability to wriggle out of situations. He had spent most of his thirty-three years getting into trouble and then finding all sorts of ways to minimize the consequences. As he maneuvered the rail cart into Fyco, he knew he would present himself as a spectacle. Filthy, shoeless, and generally bedraggled, with his hands bound tightly to the pump handle. His gun-shot right ear was a gory mess. He would certainly appear to have a tale to tell.

The main problem was that he still wore the insignia that described him as a GEEO spotter. Not the kind of profession much admired in a town known for its lawlessness and chicanery. Such townsfolk might be as inclined to do, well, who knew what to a spotter already incapacitated like that? He managed to pitch his Green Hat and, with a bit of maneuvering, rip off his green shirt leaving only a bloody undershirt to cover his torso. There was still the issue of the ankle tracker. It would just have to be explained. While he pumped his way toward town, he worked up a story that he hoped would draw forth sympathy rather than ire from the local populace.

A trio of armed men met him on the outskirts of town. They regarded him with both puzzlement and outright hostility. The tallest of the three leveled a double-barreled shotgun at Charlie's chest and demanded to know, "Who the hell are you?" He looked Charlie up and down. "You're a goddamned spotter. That's who you are!"

Charlie came back quickly. "I ain't no spotter! Them boys back at Ford's crossing jumped me, stole my stuff and sent me downriver on this here railcar half-naked." He exaggerated his shivers and chattering teeth.

The lead man regarded Charlie with profound skepticism. "What boys are you referring to?"

"I don't know. They had masks on. They called each other some names. Pretty sure 'Sade' was one."

The three men looked at each other. All recognized the first name of the Burkhart clan leader.

The lead man advanced with his gun and pressed it into Charlie's midsection. "Back to my first question. Who the hell are you? You answer me quick or I will cut you in half right here, right now!"

Charlie thought fast. He tossed up the name of a neighbor from back in the day. "Carson, Ned Carson from Paint Creek, over by the tunnel that—"

"We know where that is," one of the shorter men piped in. "Fact is, I know lots of folks up that way." He stepped closer to get a better look at the man on the rail cart. "And you don't look like any Carson I ever knew." He turned to the tall man. "This son of a bitch is full of shit!"

MOUNTAIN WHISPERS – DAYS WITHOUT SUN

His story was falling apart. Charlie blurted, "I was an orphan. They took me in back when the big move commenced. My whole family was gone!" As some of what he said was actually true, he drew from a reservoir of emotion that made his eyes glisten and his voice waver.

The tall man gestured toward Charlie. "Case, you get up there, pat him down, and cut him loose from the handle but leave his hands tied. Lester, you check out this cart and make sure it's clean. No transmitters, no explosives. Clean! I'll send a man to help you. Case and me are gonna take this little asshole to see Hamer. He'll know what to do for sure."

The man named Case soon discovered Charlie's ankle hardware. "Boss, he's wearin' a tracker. It's blinking too!"

"Well, shit! Gimme your forty-five!" It took only seconds to roll up Charlie's pants leg, a few more to point blank aim, and then with a deafening bang, a bullet slammed into the homing mechanism. Charlie screamed and screamed while he watched his own blood spill out onto the deck of the rail cart until a fist crashed into his face sending him into a black void. If he had any last thought, it likely had to do with how this just hadn't been his day.

The next thing Charlie felt was ice-cold water being dumped on his head. His hands jerked in an attempt to ward off the shock, but he found them bound behind him where he was strapped to a chair. All he could do was shake his head and blubber. He heard someone shout, "Wake up, you lame sonofabitch.

Wake up!"

When he blinked his eyes open, he immediately looked down at his left ankle. The plastic strap remained, but the device itself splayed open with only a few wires dangling. Fragments had cut through his skin, but it seemed the bleeding had stopped. Someone had carelessly wrapped his wounded calf with a dirty rag. He glanced furtively around him. He was in some kind of room, with an old potbelly stove in the corner, and he could see at least three other men in the room. None of their faces bore anything other than malice.

A long-faced, gray-bearded man loomed over him. "You've got some explaining to do and I suggest you start right now." He jerked his head toward the tall man to his right. "Vince here tells me you said you were a Carson from uppit Paint Creek? That's total bullshit!" He narrowed his eyes. "You also said it was somebody the name of Sade that ambushed you and set you on the rail cart. That's bullshit!"

The old man continued. "Fact is, we got every reason to believe you are a spotter working for GO and you're here to spy on us or to mark us in some way that'll bring the troopers down on our heads with drones and agents. That's the way we see it, unless you got an explanation that makes any sense." He drew a large Bowie knife out of his belt and held it up for Charlie to see it gleaming in the candlelight. "Y'know, apart from being the sheriff, I'm also the town butcher. What with your GEEO rules and regs about raising meat stock and hunting, I don't get the business I used to. You Green Hat fucks have seen to that."

Charlie realized he had to change his story. "All right! All right! I can definitely explain everything, but I need to talk to the headman around here. Alone."

Charlie's outburst generated a certain curiosity. The old man smiled indulgently, placed the knifepoint just under Charlie's jawline and spoke in a half-whisper. "Okay. Then let's hear it 'cause I'm also the mayor here. Say what you have to say."

He locked eyes and stated flatly, "Just you and me then. As you can see, I ain't much of a threat hogtied to this chair." He did his best to sound reasonable.

The old man gave the prisoner a look that bordered on newfound respect or perhaps a renewed wariness. "Well, there ain't a man in this room that I wouldn't trust with my life, exceptin' you, of course. So, you say what you have to say now, and by Jehovah, it better be good!" He withdrew the blade and slipped it back into his belt sheath.

"To be sure. To be sure." Charlie kept his voice steady. He shifted slightly in his chair and winced at the pain. "It's kind of hard, though, being all bound up and tied to this chair."

The old man gave his men the sign to untie the prisoner. Charlie pushed his luck a little further by asking for something to drink. They brought him a tin cup filled with water. It tasted like iron filings, but he drank it all. He knew for certain this would be his make or break performance and he needed every swallow to buy ever second of time to figure it out. He began leading his story with a line that grabbed every man in the room.

"Gentlemen, I am here to make each and every one of you rich beyond your wildest dreams!" A long silence followed as the surprise announcement took hold. "I know where old man Burkhart is hanging out and there's a five thousand credit bounty for information that leads to bringing him in. And his older son is with him, that makes ten thousand total."

Again, there ensued a period of stunned silence as if the men Charlie spoke to were in awe of this revelation. He proceeded. "They're just upriver and I know 'cause it's them who actually ambushed me and sent me down the rails. That's ten thousand credits I'm willing to share. Hell, I'll let you split it all if you'll let me go." All of this had a measure of truth. The bounty and the sharing of it. Of course, Charlie would find a way of escaping and turning them all in for an even larger reward. A troubling thought occurred–they might try to torture him and/or kill him after he disclosed his information.

So, he ad-libbed, "Now, I do have a partner who escaped and he'll need a cut. He's my insurance, y'see. You harm me or try to find them on your own and the deal is off. Let me lead you to them and the major part of the big reward will be yours." The men before him eyed each other as if delving into a common understanding. Charlie knew he had them going.

Finally, a different voice barreled out from behind Charlie. "Well, there spotter man, that sounds mighty temptin'.'" A mountain of a man came around and stood in front of Charlie. He was grinning, gapped teeth, from ear to ear. Shocks of long white hair hung from under a battered baseball cap. Bloodshot eyes set amid a face raked with years of hard living regarded him with amusement that was anything but friendly. "Say, you know where them Burkhart boys is?"

A twitch of anxiety joggled Charlie's confidence. He merely nodded. His prospects changed from dim to grim. Something wasn't right.

"I see. I see, says the fly." The man gave a look that signaled another man forward. He stood nearly as tall as the elder and bore a striking resemblance. He carried with him some material, darkly splotched and wet. He stretched it up in front of Charlie's face. It was a spotter's shirt soaked with water and partly dyed in blood around a prominent hole in the middle. "We pulled this off a spotter who came down the Tug tied to a log. After they got a look at the feller, they sent him on down river. Seems he met up with some kinda accident. Like he ran into a bullet and an arrow at the same time and then decided to go for a log ride. Hmmm. Coulda this been your partner? If so, I'd say your insurance has expired."

Charlie felt an icy curtain of dread closing in around him. He started to speak, but the gray-bearded mayor held up his hand, flashed a cold grin and gestured toward the two who stood in front of him. "Well, pardon my bad manners. Let me introduce you, spotter man. This here's Sade Burkhart and his eldest, Carter." Everyone in the room erupted in raucous laughter. Except for the pair in front of him and

Charlie himself. He watched as the elder Burkhart reached forward with both hands and, quick as a blink, snapped his neck.

Sade Burkhart pointed at the broken body draped over the chair. "Put 'em on the rail cart, take the cart down the tracks a good ways, cover it all with pine tar and torch it."

The old mayor of Fyco watched as Burkhart's men did as told. Now the mayor felt all the more secure in the deal he had just cut with Sade Burkhart for a proprietary corner on the white liquor market. The gambling and black market would also fall under the clan's purview. The Burkhart's had essentially gamed the town of Fyco into their pocket. They also proffered the town protection from "interfering elements"– competitive interests and government agencies. It was clear as the spotter's body was dragged out that the Burkhart clan would take care of that part of the arrangement.

"Any idea who did the other spotter?" the man named Vince asked Sade.

"Oh yeah. I know just the feller who'd do this, or at least what's left of 'em. Seems he's done us all a favor of sorts, but then again, I don't take kindly to being blamed for something I didn't do. We'll have to get square on this someday—fair and square."

Chapter 19

Hope is a Thing with Magnets

Sid described the structure and the spot inside the structure where "something" would be found. Virgil recognized the building right away as his father's workshop. He descended down to the farmyard. The old two-story homestead stood resolute but vacant. A few graying clapboards drooped and the front porch sagged. The windows had been boarded up giving the structure a solid appearance. A pantheon of memories were boxed within; every room, every nook and cranny, had a story to tell.

The rectangular structure Sid had identified was smaller than he remembered–about the size of a one-car garage. It too remained standing erect on its mortared stone piers as it had for over three-quarters of a century protected by a metal roof that'd remained intact; he knew the inside would be relatively sound as well. *Gotta love a tin roof.* The entry door was sagging and the glass panes in the upper sash were randomly missing. The glazing had cracked and crumbled away over time. Though there was an old padlock hasp on the weathered gray door and frame, the lock itself was gone.

A rickety ramp led up to the door. The top boards were mostly rotten, so Virgil stepped where the topside was nailed to the lower frame. When he reached down to pull the door open, the outside knob came off in his hand. The rusted square channel that once held it fast had crumbled. He managed to twist the square rod where the knob had been mounted. The latch gave way enough for the door to swing open. A musty, acrid smell rose into his nostrils, as his eyes roved into the dim interior lit only by a small window at the far end.

He spotted a cluster of dark objects dangling from the ceiling in a corner. Bats, about two dozen. Guano covered the floor–which explained the tangy odor. Only a few bats stirred, adjusted their folded wings and then resumed their repose. He made a silent deal with them about leaving each other alone. He equated bats with rabies and rabies with death.

His ghostly guide hadn't piped in for some time. *Okay Sid, I'm in. Now what?* No answer came. Virgil scanned the interior, picking up details as his eyes adjusted. There was the long workbench along the windowless wall where his dad had spent hours applying his skills and imagination. He could fix about everything and at one time, the workshop brimmed with machining and woodworking equipment—all gone. Only the holes in the floor traced the locations where the shop machines had been mounted.

Virgil closed his eyes and remembered seeing his dad bustling back and forth, humming or lightly whistling, completely immersed in his element. He'd made most of their furniture. Even welded together a majority of their tractor attachments out of bar and plate stock. He made a lot of his own tools and took great pains to keep everything in tip-top shape. After his near-deadly mining accident, it seemed his dad's talents were boosted. He'd gotten into electronics, read all he could of the technical magazines, *Popular Science*,

Popular Electronics and such.

He would sit at the dining room table with a little notepad he called his idea book and write things down or draw tiny little diagrams with arrows, lines and labels. He had so many ideas that his collection of little notebooks grew into a mini-library that he kept stacked in a big drawer under the workbench. Hmmmm. Virgil kept mindful of the bats and stepped lightly toward the bench. There was a middle section where a stack of wide drawers was mounted to the underside. He grabbed the two knobs on the largest drawer at the bottom and pulled. Surprisingly, the drawer glided out as if it'd been newly installed. Virgil peered into it. . . . Empty.

He couldn't recollect what had happened to his dad's stuff. He wasn't around during those days. Jim and Rosie had been married for. . . what. . . three or four years and Jim had sold the store and they were trying to make it on the farm alone. His dad, Rob, had a series of strokes that whittled him down bit by bit, until the last one. If one believed in God, one could say that last stroke was a mercy.

On a mission with his team in North Africa at the time, Virgil had received notice of his father's death, but it was nearly two weeks past, the funeral and burial done. Last time he'd seen his dad was just after the second stroke, which put him in a wheelchair. He still worked in his shop and piddled around the house. He even managed to construct his own ramps and hydraulic lifts that gave him access to the house, the truck, the workshop and the farm buildings. He seemed happy and they'd parted on good terms.

Other remembrances swarmed into his mind, which he cared not to recollect, mostly, the wars. Then there was Consuela, her awesome beauty, shining, fading, gone. Then came Rosie, her bright eyes, her smile. There was Jim striding toward him, face aglow, leading his favorite team of Percherons. Fading. . . feeling a lost longing. . . falling. A now familiar voice intruded. "Hey, Virgil. You'll have to lay aside your trip down memory lane, friend. Now's the time to be moving ahead–not going in reverse. Adelante, 'migo."

Virgil gave his head a slight shake. His awareness came back to the moment and he stared into the empty drawer. Nothing there.

"Look on the backside of the drawer cabinet," Sid's voice instructed. "There's a catch at the top on either side. Can you feel them?"

Virgil had squatted down and extended his hands along the upper side of the cabinet. He felt two metal depressions and a lever of sorts in each hollow. "Yes. Okay."

"Then flip them levers up and turn them down and toward you." Virgil had to wonder how the hell Sid would know all this.

"Never you mind, friend. We'll get to that later. Just do those latches and then slide the front part out from under the bench. Easy. . ."

The latches released and the cabinet rolled forward and out. A section behind was revealed. There was a front panel secured with several bent over rusted nails. He turned the nails to where the panel could be removed. When the panel came off, several sheets of yellowed paper slipped out and skittered across to the dusty floor. They looked like some kind of official forms, applications, US Patent Office, 2017. He picked one up to see a big faded red stamp on the diagonal that read "REJECTED." He picked up more sheets; it was the same, only dated 2018 and 2019. Also stamped "REJECTED."

Laying the papers aside, Virgil's eyes probed into the exposed recess. There were shelves and dividers nearly a foot and a half deep. On top sat a burnished metal object that looked like the wheel side of a small sewing machine. When he extracted it from its cubby, it turned out to be a long spindle-like device that was extremely heavy. He struggled to cradle it in his arms and cranked his legs up straight so he could set the thing up on the benchtop. He looked at it closely. It was some kind of rotary device with a series of wire harnesses attached to the front and backside. He'd never seen anything like it. On a whim, he gave the end with the wheel a quick turn.

The wheel spun around several times and then, rather than slowing down, began to pick up speed. As it did so, a vibrant hummm emerged from the machine's core and the wiring harnesses on either side began to send brilliant arcs of energy toward anything metallic.

The bats above his head came to life and dropped from the ceiling, filling the room, some actually smacking against objects including Virgil and even each other in a frantic effort to escape the building. Apparently, the machine had wrecked their internal sonar and they were relying on their poor eyesight to escape. Several crashed hard into the window and fell senseless and fluttering on the floor. Others flew out the open door. There were still a few bats careening from wall to wall, terrified and screeching.

Throughout all the chaos, Virgil never lost his composure. Even when several bats smashed into him, he still kept his cool. He pulled his shemagh up to protect his face and watched the scene unfold. *They just want the hell outta here.* He strode over to the door and threw it wide open. He kicked the dead and ailing bats across the floor and out the door. The rest found their way to the widened portal. His main concern was not getting bitten. Rabies infections could kill.

When he got back to the workbench, the little dynamo was revving higher and higher. "Holy shit!" Virgil saw arcs flickering toward the metal on his weapon, the hasp of his k-bar knife, and onto the back of his holstered pistol, even his belt buckle. The interior of the shed was illuminated with lightning-like arcs randomly hitting every bit of metal in the room. It was like being inside an electrical storm cloud.

Virgil had no idea about the ultimate result of this electrical power surging all around him but knew for certain the mysterious machine was pulling energy out of nothing. Even the old incandescent light bulbs in the ceramic ceiling fixtures were phasing bright and dim. He decided it was best not to allow the engine or machine or whatever it was to cycle up to full power, as it seemed it still had a ways to go.

Knowing he couldn't use his hands to stop the flywheels from spinning, he doffed his coat and laid it over the entire thing. Doing so immediately snuffed out the arcs and he was able to slow the rotations by pressing down on the flywheel with his hands. He could feel the machine fighting to stay alive. The friction was so intense that his coat began to smoke. He doubled it over again and practically stood on his hands. Finally, the spinning subsided. The smell of burned leather and fabric censed the air. "Holy—"

Sid interrupted, "You got that part right!"

He decided to explore further. In one of the cubbyholes, there was a metal file box. Virgil pulled it out, set it on the workbench and flipped open the lid. It was loaded with an assortment of typewritten pages and folded up diagrams including a how-to, step-by-step, illustrated guide to building a kinetic generator from readily available components: magnets, copper wire, old engine parts.

Virgil knew his father had a remarkable knack for inventing things. He grew up with whirly gigs, hand-cranked and automated corn huskers, even a homemade chess set with the chessmen made of welded nuts and bolts. Given their remote location, it wasn't unusual for folks to make do by taking up welding, blacksmithing, wiring, plumbing and such in addition to practicing the rigors of farming.

Rob Johnson's talents went beyond typical. He never excelled in academics per se, except for shop class where the shop teacher noted how easily Rob found his way around every bit of the shop's equipment. The instructor challenged him with increasingly complex projects, one of which culminated in a rock picker that attached to a disk plow and was eventually awarded a utility patent by the US Patent Office.

Virgil knew that his dad's last years as a whiz-bang shade tree inventor involved super magnets, something called "Stirling engines," and a lot of research on Nikola Tesla. As he raked through the old plans and diagrams, he wondered if his dad had ever achieved any recognition.

As if in answer, he found a manila envelope wrapped in twine at the very back of the file box. A small black notebook labeled "Kinetic Gen. Proto. 2018" was bound to the outside envelope with nylon twine. Undoing the twine, he drew out a hard-backed composition book and opened it. His father's small print-like script covered every page up to August of 2018, about the time he'd had his last stroke.

Thumbing through, Virgil read an entry:

July 12, 2016
USGPO returned application for second time. Cover letter read: "No applications accepted for designs yet unproven to function including those claiming to defy laws of physics, e.g. perpetual motion devices."

Resent application with same information.

Explained in my cover letter that kinetic generator is not a perpetual motion device but is 92.3% efficient and requires minimal input to recover heat loss (entropy) noting that only a gram of carbonaceous material (e.g. low-sulfur bituminous coal) will suffice for top end operation over a 48-hour period. Interim inertia, if carbonaceous material is unavailable, can be supplied by a forceful (approximately 12-pound torque) turn of the right flywheel enough to generate at top end for .5 hours under maximum 800 amp load.

Closed by repeating, this is <u>not</u> a perpetual motion device.

It was filled with dated entries in his dad's small hand-written block letters. Virgil flipped pages to read the last entries.

Aug 20 -USGPO rejected application for third time. Maybe not even reading the last two apps. Just sees name and title and stamps "Reject."

Sept 18
Letter from a private company in Richmond. Says they can help get patent. Asking for money up front to cover costs plus 25% share of revenues, should there be revenues. May be a scam. Asked for detailed schematics and photos. They guarantee a patent.

Don't know how they found out about device or got my contact info. Spooky!

Virgil agreed. There was something wrong there.

He heard a slight rustle behind him, then a creak. He cursed his inattentiveness. He quickly turned around while reflexively drawing his sidearm to take dead aim at the intruder. Ben Pierce just stood there. His eyes were wide open and his hands were raised.

"Whoa, Virge!"

It took a few intense seconds for Virgil to slip his finger off the trigger and ease the hammer forward. He holstered the weapon, then let go a string of epithets at his nephew. "Well shit, Virge, I didn't know you're going deaf and couldn't hear me walking in here. I thought you Spec Ops guys were on constant guard. Y'know?"

This did nothing to defuse his uncle's anger. "Not a goddamned thing wrong with my hearing! 'Sides, if it weren't you, you think you'd be standing there right now?"

Ben knew when to back off. "Well, sorry. Didn't mean to cause a situation. Saw you go round the bend and, I don't know, something seemed off somehow. What you said about everything changing and the way you acted kinda reckless. I didn't get far before I figured I better turn around and follow you." He noted his uncle's reproachful look. "Well, you think your boat's the only one stashed along the river? I knew you were up to something. What are you doing here? What's all that commotion I heard coming up the hill? Why all the dead bats? And the burning smell? That is rank!"

Virgil did his best to explain what had happened and what he'd discovered. Of course, there was no mention of any disembodied voices in his head, driving him crazy.

Ben looked around the shop and silently reminisced about his grandfather's inventions and all the time they'd spent together tinkering and dabbling for hours on end. Fond memories with a dash of longing bobbed into his consciousness. "Man, I tell you Virge, I sure do miss him." A tear welled in one eye and escaped. He wiped his face with the back of his hand, a bit embarrassed by the surge of emotion.

Virgil interrupted the bittersweet reverie. "Remember any gadgets that had to do with generating electricity?"

Ben cleared his throat and pondered a moment. "I knew he had notions to make a perpetual kind of machine, and after a fashion he'd succeeded. I heard talk of him sending mail off to DC at the time, but I was just a kid. Knew little to nothing about patents and such. Anyway, he got the electricity shut off and used a couple of the gadgets to run power to the house and outbuildings. Guess they broke down about the same time he did. He had the last stroke and was gone."

Ben's forehead creased as he looked up toward the ceiling. "Wait! I remember that summer. Two men came in suits and wanted to see Gramps and look in his shop. They looked official. I stood outside the window there and listened.

"They asked about his work, in general, then started in with questions about a generator, or maybe they said engine. Anyway, Gramps told them he'd scrapped it, burned the drawings and moved on to other things. He started pulling out other drawings of gizmos and asking if they could get the patents for

135

them. They kept asking about the engine. Then Gramps began to act a little crazy, talking about UFOs he'd seen land on the barn roof and crop circles in his field. The agents soon left. Never saw them after that."

"So he made it sound like he mothballed the thing." They both regarded the little dynamo still partly covered by Virgil's smoldering coat. "Can't say as I blame him. There were many who'd not want a thing like this to reach the public. I know. I used to merc for them. If they'd fight a war over a patch of oil, you know they'd close in on anyone with a real contraption that appears to run on nothin'."

Ben frowned. "Do you mean the government or the big energy corps?"

"Don't you know your history? They're one and the same, welded at the hip."

Ben looked stunned. "Damn! Just think what could've happened if only. . . "

"Can't live with 'if onlys,' Rocket. What we have is now, right here. Your grandfather, my father, has given us a way back from living like cave creatures. If this can be copied and made available to folks, think how our lives will change." As he spoke, he felt a surge of energy coursing through his veins, a leaden heaviness lifted from his heart, and his eyes brimmed with newly stoked determination. A word rose to his lips and quietly slipped out as a whisper.

Ben watched as his uncle seemed to grow taller, taking on the look of a much younger man. It was that younger Virgil who'd seen Ben streaking around the yard and henceforth dubbed him Rocket. "What's that you said, Virge?"

"Hope."

Chapter 20

What Makes Us Green
October 12, 2052

Candler swiped his Kelly Green ID tag as he left the building. He had stayed an hour later than usual getting his next foray lined up. His resolve to embrace the assignment as a challenge had wavered. Too many what ifs were like spoiled children clamoring for immediate attention and assurance. He kept reminding himself that his trove of past field experiences would hold him in good stead and all would be well. It had been a stressed out day. He just wanted to return to his cubicle and sleep, start fresh.

His footsteps echoed in the nearly vacant underground passageway to the tram; it was well past the peak use commute period. He strode by faded poster signs touting catch phrases like "Green for Good," "Retire Now-Earn Extra Credits," and "Good Citizens=Good Earth." The tunnel smelled of mold and urine. Even in Progress City, there were occasional appearances of homeless and hapless persons. Where they came from was something of a mystery because every citizen living in the city was supposed to have all the basics provided to them. Food, shelter, hygiene and health care. *No matter*, thought Candler. *The admin is on top of this.* These wayward denizens seemed to vanish just as quickly as they appeared but their traces, like urine smell, anti-admin graffiti scrawled on the walls and vandalized public use facilities, seemed to persist for longer and longer periods. People who walked the passageways were mildly oblivious. They took little notice of the cracks in the walls, the flickering floro lights, water drips from the ceiling and the tang of bodily excretions in the air.

After a fifteen-minute tram ride, Candler arrived at his port and swiped his card in front of the green scanner by the elevator that whisked up to his third-floor cube. At his level, he'd acquired twenty-five meters of space—nearly three hundred square feet. For a single guy like him, this was huge. The double-sized Murphy bed/sofa combination folded out from the wall. Nearly all appliances were built-ins so that it afforded the impression of space. All lighting was recessed. The light gray walls and ceiling formed a single room. The bath area was tucked behind a partition that also defined a kitchen nook. The floors were of stamped concrete made to resemble tiles and dusted with a greenish patina. He enjoyed a narrow viewing port that looked out on the city proper.

It was a green max building, which meant all energy use was subject to auto allocation programming based on work level status, peak use and, as of late, availability of GP (generated power) which was a euphemism for fossil-fuel-based energy. Even nearing the mid-twenty-first century, the shortfall issues about how modern cultures could be sustained by renewable energy alone had yet to be resolved. No one apparently had found the magic whizz-bang solution of "free" energy.

In grade school, Candler learned how scientists and global organizations had met the challenge of climate change head on. Once the vast arrays of solar collectors and wind turbines were in place fossil fuels had become a relic of the past. The planet had entered into a cooling trend decades before, but those at the vanguard of the Earth First movement said their computer models accounted for such small-scale variations–the crises of climate change would worsen unless modern nations undertook drastic measures.

During Candler's graduation year at the Academy of Earth Sciences, cloud formations began to encompass the entire earth. The specific causes were as obscure as the sky. Rumors of a rogue nation's weapons test, an asteroid impact in some far-flung quarter of the world, a mega volcanic eruption–were singly and collectively cited as instigators. Global temperatures dropped even more. Yet, the climate scientists proclaimed substantial confidence in their computer models, which projected long-term planetary climate disruptions due mainly to the past and persistent use of carbon-based fuels by industries, internal combustion engines and rampant deforestation.

The biggest disappointment for the climate advisors and the admin was the reduction of sunlight over most of the planet, with clouds masking the sun's face more often than not. Meaning cooler temperatures overall. There were stories circulating about people from the north country pulling up stakes and moving south to more temperate climes.

Mysteriously, the north and south arctic regions, however, were not so affected by this constant cloud cover, though they remained mostly uninhabitable due to the extreme frigid conditions. Even with more direct sunlight, the polar icecaps had yet to melt away as predicted previously. Instead, their ice-packed perimeters were growing at a steady pace year to year.

A year ago, a chum from Candler's college days, who worked in the Energy Development Administration confided that the city's brownouts were deliberate attempts to deal with an energy shortage. Wind turbines were failing, conservation measures were becoming draconic and they were relying more and more on fossil fuels, coal and gas to generate enough power to sustain the status quo. He recalled his pal quipping, "If we don't find some breakthrough energy source soon, then coal and gas will be it. We might even have to start burning wood. Can you believe it?"

All mechanisms were subject to entropy. They age; they break. Even with heavy government subsidies, the alternatives couldn't sustain themselves without injection of fossil-fueled energy.

So it came down to burning natural gas or dirty coal. A lot of pretzel-like justifications were used to keep a modicum of gas and gas/coal hybrid electric plants open. An official emergency was declared, but the emergency had gone on now for over thirty years. A rather tortured definition of green energy explained that these plants were, after all, earth-friendly given that they enabled the use of alternative energy and, thus, any carbon footprint was offset by the sustainability of wind power and by the declaration of more forests as off-limit carbon sequestration zones.

A handful of coalmines still functioned under regional government auspices with the typical pattern of cost overruns, safety issues and frequent breakdowns. Candler's Global Region 2 had the good fortune of containing mineable coal reserves within its boundaries. Most other regions had to import coal from South America or far eastern Russia.

Ideally, wind power provided the greater portion of energy generation when the winds were blowing steadily within a range of twenty-five to twenty-seven knots, when eighty percent of the turbines were online, and when energy demand was off-peak. In fact, this would be the case only twenty-five to thirty-seven days of a year, thus, relegating the green city to dependence on fossil fuel as a base load and primary energy source for about ninety percent of the year. *Maybe Bates was right*, Candler thought. *Maybe we are still addicted but I'm sure the admin scientists and engineers are figuring it out. I just need to do my job and let them do theirs.*

As he entered his living cube, the smart energy sensor engaged the cube's energy allocation system. A single LED lit up the center of the room. It had been a long, tiring day so he decided to splurge a few extra credits and treat himself to a flash meal of Rasta Pasta, which actually tasted much like Toni Roni and Delhi Ghetti. No matter, he ate it and then washed it down with a dram of tap water—Progressive City's finest. After a three-minute micro-mist shower set to medium lukewarm, he got into boxer shorts and made ready for sleep. *What a day. What a day.* He connected his PD to the port receiver by his bed. An alert was crawling across the otherwise blank screen.

Body recovered at Tug River Power Dam. Madison

*District. Believed to be that of missing Wildlands Protection
Officer. Illegal poachers suspected. Enforcement team sent to
investigate. Updates on the hour, every. . .*

Candler clicked off the message feed. *Oh great!
Madison District! These retros are getting more and more out of
hand.* He'd circuited through there as a registrar and
recruiter numerous times. Looked like come next
spring he'd have to bring along extra security. He
actually preferred the carrot approach versus the stick,
but those who stubbornly remained in those hills were
the worst and would only heed the stick.

He remembered one instance the year before
where a man appeared at the post office with a lanky
freckle-faced child he claimed was a neighbor's kid—a
boy he said. Candler had never seen such long lashes
on a boy who also happened to lack an Adam's apple.
When he began to question them, they took off. If he
had the resources, he would've tracked them down but
he remembered their faces and at least ID'd the man as
a Benjamin Morgan Pierce whose wife and son had
been processed into the citizenry several years before.
The girl who took off that day was definitely not in the
system, but she bore a strong resemblance to the boy
he'd registered and tagged. She had to be a sister.
Catching and processing an unknown meant double
quota points. *Who knows, I might get lucky and bring in a
whole slew of them. What a capper that would be!*

He pressed an icon on his PD putting his cube's
environment into night/sleep mode. As his head
nestled into the pillow, his mood lightened with the
belief that everything he wanted could be attained. He
shot a vengeful thought toward his nemesis, Art Jones.

Just you wait and see, AJ! I can't wait to see the look on your face when I return with enough quota points to outrank you! Oh, I say, Jones still stuck on the twelfth floor? What a pity!"

Chapter 21

The Game Changer
OCTOBER 15, 2052

Uncle came back, just as he said he would. With
Pa too! Gram was laid up with an ache or pain, in her
left knee. She said it was rooma tiz. I'll have to look it
up. Oh, and by the way, I did look up ache and pain in
the big thick dictionary. They mean the same thing. So
it's like me saying there isn't and there ain't. I know
Gram doesn't like hillbilly talk, but they mean the same
thing.

So here comes my uncle and Pa and they are
carrying these boxes and all excited but wouldn't say
about what. When I asked what's in the boxes, they said
it was a surprise. They'd show Gram and me later. Then
they disappeared into the little building next to the
woodpile. I could've sworn I heard a humming sound
and saw flashes of light. I wondered why would they
start a fire inside like that and what was that noise?

Well, that evening I found out. They got set up
on the kitchen table and convinced Gram she needed
to get her cane and come out of her room to see
something special. They'd covered whatever it was with
Uncle's coat. The coat smelled pretty bad, but I didn't
wish to offend Uncle by saying anything. When we
were all there, Gram was in her chair and I was so
excited about a surprise I couldn't just sit. Uncle told Pa
to pull off the coat and there was this funny looking
wheely thing with a small wheel on one end and some
wires coming from the other. Those wires went to an

old light bulb socket that had a round bulb in it. I'd not seen one of those things in years!

Uncle says for me to come up and on the count of three give the little wheel a spin. He counts and on three, I give the thing a good turn. The little wheel goes around for a few seconds then starts to slow down but the light bulb did flicker a little.

Uncle said, "Shit." Then for some reason, I said "Shit" as if that's what you say when something goes wrong. Uncle laughed. Gram reared back and glared at me and then at Uncle, and said she'd wash my mouth out with soap if I said that word again. Then she got on Pa about teaching me better. I wonder if writing it is as bad as saying it?

Pa and Uncle talked it over and I tried to understand what went wrong. The light bulb did flicker. If we could figure a way to keep that little wheel turning, we could have an electric light, like maybe fix it to our sewing machine that you pump with your foot. That would be amazing!

Pa remembered something about carbon and Uncle gets a small piece of coal that missed going in our stove. He opens a little door at the side of the wheely thing and closes it up. Then, he tells me to give it a spin again. I do. Talk about a surprise! That thing nearly took off from the table. The little wheel was going so fast you couldn't see it and the light bulb got so bright it broke the glowing wires inside but there was light everywhere in the room because these rays started touching anything made of metal. It was WILD! The thing was going faster and faster until

Uncle threw his leather coat over it and squashed it with his hands. It burned a little and stunk a lot, but he got it to stop. Then he took his coat off it.

Gram had her hand covering her mouth just staring at the thing. Her first words were "What in the world?"

It took a while for Uncle to explain about his hunch that Papaw was working on some electrical thing. That he'd gone back to the farm to see if there might be something the Green Hats had overlooked. He found it behind an emptied out cabinet with drawings and a bunch of writing. Gram eyed him for a while. She didn't seem to understand how he found the thing saying she and Gramps had gone through that building. They'd used some kinda of comb is what she said or something similar.

Uncle told her he'd just had a hunch. I think she still didn't believe him.

Pa said it didn't matter who found the thing or how. It was a game changer. He told us he could get all the necessary parts from the local metal crafters and make more machines like it, maybe make them large enough to send electrical power to an entire town. It would mean folks could have light and heat and the old factories might be running again. It could make us all completely free of the city and the Green Hats. I don't think I ever saw him so excited.

Gram was like the fox in sour grapes. She said that as soon as the Green Hats got wind of the thing and what it would do, they'd come and take it away.

Uncle was quick to agree with her, which was unusual. He'd thought the same thing and that was why they had to work a plan so they could band folks together to fight against the Green Hats.

He and Pa were going to set out for the other counties and tell all the clan leaders about the machine and give them a little show just like they did here. Pa could build a few more like the one on the table and stash them away for future use. The thing they kept saying over and over was that it would give our people hope, that it was a game changer.

Uncle clapped me on the back and said, "There's a bright future for you, after all, honey doll."

I saw Gram ease back in her chair. She never took her eyes off that little machine. She was talking to herself like she sometimes does, saying over and over again real quiet like, "We never knew. We never knew."

PART 2

Chapter 22

Seven Months Later–The Taking of Tug River

"To destroy your enemy in head-to-head battle is not the best way to win. Much better to break his spirit and crush his will to fight, even to take your enemy's troops without harming them or yourself." ~*Sun Tzu*

April 1, 2053

The Tug River Power Plant, one of a handful of old-fashioned power plants in the region, was still operating. Emergency measures bypassed GEEO's mandated efficiencies and the minimum emissions requirements. The scrubbers inside the single stack had been installed in the '90s and compared to a spread of wind turbines or solar panels the area footprint was quite small while the net energy production was five to one. The proponents of eradicating the use of fossil fuels saw the white clouds spewing skyward from the stacks and concluded noxious vapors were being released into the atmosphere. It was actually steam, harmless water vapor.

The facility was a hybrid design that burned coal, natural gas and had a separate hydro turbine that made use of the water flow using the same diversion technique as a mill. At the time, the little 400-megawatt plant was state-of-the-art.

TRPP became known as the Trip plant and was

built by a small power company, then assumed under a larger one and eventually taken over by a regional council. The plant provided base load power to Progress City. The council had originally announced that the burning of fossil fuels in the plant would be curtailed and it would run exclusively on hydro, but even the greenest of intentions can be thwarted by nature. Seasonal fluctuations in water level and maintenance issues rendered very sporadic and meager power production. There were also questions about the naturalness of diverting water and what impact it would have on the native species. They quietly reverted to using natural gas and coal as the primary heat source to steam power the turbines.

Access to the "Trip" plant wasn't easy. The King Coal Highway, once a vital corridor, suffered from minimal maintenance. Only a single lane remained open, and it became increasingly pockmarked and crazed by the elements. Asphalt was harder to come by with the prescribed diminishment of fossil fuels, concrete too. Several of the more zealous regional council members questioned why the plant should remain online at all. Others countered that it was vital to keep the minimum of Progress City's life supporting services and technologies running. Yes, it was a blotch on their vision of a world free of horrific fossil-based pollutants, but a necessary compromise nonetheless.

It was a strategic asset, which made it a strategic target.

From atop a high walled ridge, Virgil and Ben scanned the terrain. The air was relatively clear. The valley fog had lifted into the cloud ceiling. The river was running high, and the sluice gates of the hydro dam stood wide open. A collection of wires, transformers and switch boxes could be seen strung along the south side of several large masonry buildings. These buildings were enclosed by a fifteen-foot high fence topped with coils of concertina wire. One large power trunk line ran to the south, toward Progress City. A smaller line ran north toward Madison, the town and the few mining operations that shipped coal downriver in barges to the Trip plant. A transmission tower loomed over the structures. Its companion relay tower sat on the ridgeline above, less than three hundred feet from Virgil and Ben's location. The relay tower was their first target.

Virgil checked his watch. It showed 12:47. "Ready?" Virgil asked. Ben nodded. They crept under the brushy laurel to where they could set up shop. Virgil slipped an elongated pack off his back and set it on the ground. He unzipped the casing and extracted a vintage Macmillan TAC-50 sniper rifle with its long-range scope affixed on top. He cleared the chamber, grabbed his pack, and belly crawled forward to a slight opening in the bushes that allowed a clean view of the target tower and the power plant below it. He lay prone on the ground using the backpack case to support his upper body and elbows. Then, he extended the bipod supports at the business end of the weapon and commenced a rapid series of adjustments–calculations for windage and trajectory, correcting the rifle's position and calibrating his optics.

Meanwhile, Ben had pulled out a spotter's scope and began setting it up on a miniature tripod. He too had belly crawled forward and lay in the prone position beside Virgil. Ben relayed his own calculations, most of which Virgil heeded. Within three minutes, they were set. Their first step was to cut communications. In addition to several antennae and dishes mounted on the high tower, security cameras had been attached to scan the valley and the surrounding hills.

Rather than take each component out one by one, Vigil had aimed at the power cable that fed them. He placed the crosshairs just below a large junction box where the cable was most exposed. Satisfied, he drew the bolt back then pushed it forward chambering the first five and a half inch armor-piercing round. He got a final reading from Ben, adjusted his aim, took several deep breaths and at the bottom of his exhale, squeezed the trigger. A loud cracking explosion echoed over the hills.

"Good one," Ben reported as he gazed through his scope, "but still hanging."

Virgil could have loaded an incendiary round, taken out the entire distribution box, and possibly brought down the tower itself from the get-go, but he always adhered to the art of war philosophy that advised minimal destruction of the enemy's infrastructure. The cable could be cut and later spliced. Not so the box.

"Okay," Virgil said, half to himself. He repeated the firing procedure but took several extra deep breaths. Once again, the muzzle erupted with a loud flash bang. Barrel smoke drifted out in front of them.

Virgil's ears were ringing, but through the clang, he heard his spotter say, "Done!"

Ben flipped over on his back, drew his 1911 sidearm and fired three rapid shots into the air. "Okay, boys," he spoke as if they could hear him, "it's all yours!" He rolled back over to direct his scope down toward the power plant. Virgil was already eyeing potential targets that might offer armed resistance. It was over a quarter mile but well within the TAC-50's range.

They came from all directions: upriver, downriver, across from the hillsides, about two dozen altogether, banded for the common purpose of reclaiming their independence. Some carried long guns, some handguns; some had no real weapons at all, but they crashed through the gates and swarmed around the buildings.

A trio of security personnel emerged from the main building. Virgil could see they had drawn their weapons. The middle guard shouldered a carbine rifle, likely an old M-21, with a thirty-round magazine. The other guards, presumably caught by surprise, held revolvers. It reminded Virgil of a movie, something like the ending of Butch Cassidy and the Sundance Kid. These guards had to know they were toast. Question was, would they go the way of Butch and Sundance or buy themselves a future? Even from his distant perch, Virgil could sense the tension.

The trio stood their ground in front of the building, likely firing off words of dire warning to the aggressors. They were outgunned and, by now, knew they had no way of communicating with the outside. It was all a bluff. *Well,* Virgil thought. *Give 'em credit. They've got some cojones, after all.*

He could've taken out all three guards in rapid succession, but there was something about shooting a man in the back at a distance that just didn't sit right. *Seen it; done it.*

"Well, my boy," an all too familiar voice quipped, "why don't you just part their hair?"

Hey, Sid. You mind piping down? I got this!

"Oooooh, a bit touchy are ya?" Sid's voice grated, doused with mewling sarcasm.

He uttered just under his breath, jaws clenched, "Just shut the fuck up and let me shoot!" Something shifted inside his head as if a window had been closed and the blinds drawn. Pristine silence. *Sid's actually gone and bugged out. Whaddya know!*

Taking a deep breath, his cheek pressed hard on the stock's weld. He squeezed off a shot. It landed just in front of the middle man's feet. There was a little spout of debris where the bullet struck. All three guards reactively jumped. It had to be unnerving, to see a round hit right in front of you and then, three seconds later, hear the gun's thunderous report. It had the intended effect. All three men rapidly dropped their weapons and raised their hands.

Hence, the battle of the Tug River Power Plant involved no battle—just a hostile takeover, in broad daylight. The twenty or so plant workers and the security men were marched out into the courtyard. They'd be detained and well treated. In fact, several workers and one of the security guards, all with local family ties, asked to remain there and become part of the yet to be named uprising. The technicians, who knew the workings of the plant, would prove their value in spades.

According to plan, a detachment of men barricaded the single-lane access road at several choke points and stationed themselves along the way. They'd appropriated handheld communication devices and had the energy available to keep them charged. Marksmen were assigned shifts to take out any drones that might be sent their way. As expected, several flew in during the day and were quickly dispatched. Just one drone made it through during the night; fortunately for the raiders, the aircraft's light frame carried only surveillance equipment and lacked weaponry.

#

It took an entire day for the regional authority to realize what had happened. At first, they presumed equipment failure—a minor glitch with communications, but when the plant's power feed shut off and brownouts riddled the city, they realized the ominous nature of the breakdowns. That's when the drones were deployed to investigate. It didn't occur to them until late in the game that the plant had been taken, hijacked by force.

The single drone that achieved its mission revealed infrared images of personnel scattered about the facility. The GEEO surveillance monitors were alarmed to see many more human heat signatures than the number of plant workers. There were also several rooms populated by tight clusters of human forms, which they correctly presumed to be detainees. A revolutionary takeover of a critical facility had happened right under their noses during daylight hours.

Chapter 23

Troubles and Vexations
April 3, 2053

When Progress City's top leaders heard of the
Tug River hijacking, many of them, including Regional
Minister Jasper Hugo Dirkson, were stunned and
outraged. Dirkson was swift to assign blame. He
released a barrage of scathing internal memos decrying
and disparaging the abilities of his underlings. Every
message conveyed dire warnings to anyone who
blabbed about the incident.

One such memo read:

To All Grade Level Blues

*In the entire history of this region, there
never has been an assault of this nature, much less
a takeover of any power generating facility. I find it
reprehensible that those responsible for
monitoring the outlying population could fail so
miserably in their intelligence operations and, by
doing so, have tacitly permitted terrorists to
occupy a vital part of our infrastructure. As of this
moment, I am ordering a full investigation into the
matter and I can assure you that those who have so
flagrantly neglected their responsibilities will be
dealt with severely.*

*Furthermore, anyone breaking their oath of
confidentiality regarding this matter will be
charged and accorded the harshest consequences*

the law will allow.
— RM Jasper H. Dirkson

\#

Two days had passed since the drone transmissions. The administration was in the throes of assessing how to address the situation when a handful of bedraggled Tug River plant workers appeared at the city gate. They were cleared and taken into Operations Central for extensive debriefings by intelligence officers. Dirkson remotely observed the interrogations from his office via closed circuit cameras. He preferred to keep such matters at arm's length, particularly if they involved any coercion.

Word was that Dirkson had made his mark in the GEEO operation in Colorado, Global Region Ten, where huge swaths of private lands had been seized by the government and dedicated to wilderness zones–all within a phenomenal two-year period. Credit went to Dirkson, who'd hatched the plan of declaring all mountains and foothills watersheds supremely vital to the ecology of the Colorado Basin. Nearly all human impact had to be restricted and, in large part, prohibited. Any large tracts not covered by the provisions were assayed by Fish and Wildlife agents for the sake of endangered species–a kind of bird, a creek chub, a butterfly, or a species of cactus. They all rated special consideration and protection.

Persons and businesses were relocated by either conservation easements (via seductive tax breaks), eminent domain, condemnation, enticements to live in a central city of their choice or failing all that, by government fiat. Dirkson much preferred the latter. At that point, the holdouts could do nothing. Either they would cooperate and receive a token compensation or they'd get nothing at all. There were, however, numerous exceptions and waivers to a select number of ski resorts and their access routes (air and ground), which had been nationalized into "study areas–for the continuing research of human impact on dedicated environmental sectors." Highly restricted access waivers were afforded to the uber-elite who occupied the stratosphere of GEEO. Naturally, J. H. Dirkson counted himself among them.

Additionally, he had ethnic sway, with Jamaican, Portuguese, and Mexican blended into his ethnic profile, giving him a remarkably light Creole complexion, high cheekbones, an aquiline nose set on long face, and startlingly pale agate-green eyes. He could easily pass for a male model. Even with the dusting of gray at his temples, his tall, lean frame exuded grace and confidence. He attracted both men and women and rumors circulated about his dalliances with both. He was actually an asexual narcissist, wielding his looks and charms as they suited his self-centered designs.

His administrative successes and his photogenes had caught the attention of his superiors. He was offered the job as Regional Director of the Eastern District. The current director was struggling to maintain a mere semblance of order. Unlike Colorado, the rural and mountain populations remained backward and even rebellious toward the efforts of GEEO to consolidate the citizenry into sustainable living zones. It was the military equivalent of serving in combat–risks were high but so were the rewards. One of Dirkson's superiors confided, "Jasper, if you can manage this situation like you did Colorado, you will be on the fast track to the World Council."

The move had been a stepping stone in his overall plan though he hated being in the stifling heat and thick air of the Eastern District but, it was his intent to work his way out of it in whatever way he could. He'd been on the job one year, fourteen days, and six interminable hours so far. He had to wonder if he'd been lured into a dead-end trap, that maybe he'd been considered more of a threat due to his supreme talents. In spite of these paranoid tendencies, he knew he would prevail despite being surrounded by idiots. *In fact, some of these idiots will be most useful.*

Chapter 24

The Breakdown

"We lost contact with base, and then all hell broke loose." One of the security guards was being debriefed, sitting at a bare table across from the lead interrogator. He was wide-eyed and waving his hands as he described the scene. "They came out of nowhere, from all directions. Must've been a hundred or more, shooting at us from all angles. We had no choice. We had to surrender."

More debriefings followed. The storyline told by all of the returning crew held together, more or less. The estimated number of attackers was slightly discrepant as was the number of shots fired, but the basic description of events hardly varied. They surrendered, were detained for a day and then sent packing back to Progress City on foot. The two guards had been allowed to keep their sidearms but with the proviso that they'd pocket just one magazine containing a single bullet–just in case they ran into any predators along the way. Dirkson also realized that walk allowed time to get their story mostly together. The consistent bottom line was that they were taken by surprise and overwhelmed.

There was an anomaly with the last tech worker's rendition. It came almost as an afterthought, a coda tacked onto the end of his interview. He asked, "Did you see the text messages from someone named 'Ceci' or 'Celi'–something like that?"

The room was silent. The lead interviewer prodded. "Well, go on. What about these messages?"

The techie's nervous demeanor was eclipsed by a look of surprise. "Oh my! For the past several months, our relay tower has been receiving very weak but decipherable transmissions of some girl writing on a tablet or other device. It's like a diary. I don't know how the thing transmitted. Judging by the data signature, and the processing program, the device is antiquated. I'm surprised it still worked, much less, was able to transmit a signal. Barely ten megahertz and on a side banded freq that we just happened to pick up."

Silence.

He cleared his throat, as the tension returned. "I, well, we, my co-workers forwarded these messages along as attachments to our monthly reports. I, uh we, presumed they were being read and filed somewhere in the system."

"Goddammit! Sonofabitch!" Dirkson exploded loudly at the screen. He'd been watching the interviews and up to this point, there'd been no real surprises, just a parade of plebes trying ineffectively to save their ass from prosecution. He slammed the top of his desk with his right hand, then pounded it with his closed fist. "What the hell is going on here? Goddam incompetent shit-for-brains staffers!"

He jabbed the intercom button. A timid woman's voice on the other end responded, "Yes sir?"

"Get Jones in here! Oh, and call that piss ant

Greaves up here too. I'll see him after Jones."

"Sorry, sir. My locator indicates an appointment block on Mr. Jones schedule–he must be in a meeting. Shall I–"

"Override! I want him here, in my office, in ten minutes or less. Got that?"

"Yes, sir. Right away, sir. I'm on it, sir!"

"And if he asks you about the reason he's being called up, tell him if he's not here ASAP, he won't need a reason."

"Yes, sir!"

"And get me Intel on the line. Whoever heads the records division, archives, whatever the hell they call it! Patch me in as soon as they pick up!"

"Yes, sir! Anything else, sir?"

"Just do it!" Dirkson switched off and stood up. He reeled with the urge to strike out and crush something.

His rage was fueled by trepidation that this incident would derail his long-awaited promotion to the global council. He'd presumed by now he'd be living the life in Lucerne or Rio or Shanghai. One didn't rise through the ranks by sitting on the sidelines. He'd thought taking on the most challenging region in the system and bringing its populace to heel would be a giant step in his ascension to the top tier. Now, that giant step threatened to be into a trap door. He could see the dark abyss of failure and ignominy yawning below him. He could feel the scaffolding that he'd so carefully built falling apart piece by piece.

The intercom beeped, "I have the IO Officer on the line, sir."

"Well, patch me in!" Three seconds of silence ensued. "Didn't I say patch me in?"

"Yes, sir. Just wanted you to know who—"

"I don't give a flying fuck who. . . Miss Harris! Will you just make the connection and leave us to talk? Wait! Wait! What about Jones and Greaves?"

"Both on the way, sir. Here's Officer Lockhart. Sheila Lockhart." If he detected a rebellious note in his secretary's voice, he let it slide.

In a tense but brief conversation with the head of archives, Dirkson was dismayed to learn that there had been a complete communication breakdown. Reports from the Tug River facility were routinely sent to Operations Central, scanned by mid-level energy controllers and then filed away. It was all in the routine—the mind-numbing day-to-day that lulls one into missing little nuances or, in this case, little icon-sized attachments.

"We never laid eyes on the reports, sir." Lockhart's tone was unrepentant, tinged with umbrage that the mistake would be laid in her lap.

"I want those reports sent to me now. I don't want excuses, Miss Lockley; I want to see those reports. Now!"

"I'm in the OpCen database now. I see the files and will have those to you in less than a minute. And there's also an envelope that one of the detained techies carried back from Tug River. He didn't know what to do with it, as it was addressed to you, by name, RM Dirkson."

He immediately sensed a threat. "Have you scanned the envelope? Have you made sure it's not rigged? Examined the contents, dusted for prints, traced any DNA? You understand this: once cleared, all of these materials go to me, no copies, no reports until I say so. Is that clear, Miss Lockley?"

"Yes sir, that's what we've been doing prior to sending it to you. We've run the envelope and its contents–nothing more than paper and ink, sir. There were prints all over it, but most match those of the techie. It's still sealed. The techie said they'd threatened to come after him if he opened it, that somehow they'd know. We took a sample of the seal and found a trace of DNA–running it now."

Dirkson huffed. "I want those results in front of me the second they come back! And send over that envelope. Anything else to report?"

"That's it sir. Well. Just one more item. It's Lockhart, sir. My name."

Dirkson clicked offline. He was in no mood to

be polite. *What a little bitch! Correcting me! Lockley,
Lockland, whatever! Intelligence should have been all over this.
She and her sort will be on a farm shoveling chicken shit by next
week.*

Soon after that, his desk pad chimed the arrival
of the digitized reports.

He opened the most recent transcript and
scanned through the technical gibberish then he clicked
the red square at the bottom and commenced to read
the actual contents. *What the hell **is** this?*

He read through several more pages and then
stopped. *What the hell **is** this? "The Story of MY LIFE-So
Far, By Celi Pierce." Some childish prattle, some kind of coded
communiqué? Why hasn't IO offered some analysis?* Then, he
remembered he'd overridden the SOP himself by
demanding to be at the head of the line in reviewing
the materials.

His attention focused on the screen until the
intercom noise interrupted. "Sir, a runner from IO just
delivered an envelope. It has your name on it."

"Bring it in, Harris," he said with an edge of
exasperation. Madeline Harris was a hand-me-down
from his predecessor and somehow had attained a kind
of tenure as the staff receptionist for the director. He
would have preferred a younger, more attractive
person, and obviously, someone who was not as dull-
witted; but his predecessor, a prepossessed dolt intent
on spending the remainder of his retirement days fly
fishing, had insisted Harris remain onboard. "She has
some interesting connections, y'know." The subtext of

which implied that to let her go would be a serious misstep. *Whatever! I'll be done with that crone soon enough.*

Harris entered his office quietly and slipped the letter onto Dirkson's desk. He didn't look up or offer any thanks–he merely sniffed. She eggshell-walked back to the door and quietly closed it behind her.

He looked over at the envelope on his desk. Block letters identified the recipient as "REGIONAL MINISTER JH DIRKSON." *I'm amazed to see the idiots can spell with that many letters.* As if to avoid being contaminated, he flipped the envelope over with a letter opener drawn from an antique desk set. The flap on the back had been partly removed for DNA analysis just in case, by some stroke of dumb luck, whoever licked the seal had their DNA registered in the system. The harvesting and logging of DNA had gone on long before chipping.

There were many who'd unwittingly had their DNA registered. Decades prior, a genealogical research breakthrough widely promoted a DNA-based search for one's ancestry. There were also programs aimed at garnering DNA from children for their so-called safety. All military and nearly everyone in law enforcement were fingerprinted and genetic samples drawn. Of course, the same went for high clearance government staff, and anyone who'd had a brush with the law or landed in prison. Most often, the current database could identify the person, or at the very least, their close kin.

He gingerly opened the flap using only his manicured fingernails and extracted several sheets of yellowed paper. They were legal size sheets, folded in thirds. When he unfolded them to reveal the first page, he saw a note had been appended at the top. It read:

> DNA taken from saliva samples on the seal correlates 92% with Johnson, James Lee; b. 1994 d. 2047. Records indicate most likely a positive match– elder brother, Johnson, Virgil Robert b.1989 current status: unknown. Former special ops, covert action in N. Africa, S. America, M. East. Medals: PH (3 times), MV, DS (2 times). Charged with insubordination–charges later dismissed; demoted; honors revoked. Served last year (2021). Received Other than Honorable Conditions Discharge. Employed by Private Security Firms G4S 2021-2023, DYNCORP 2024-2027. After 2027, no further records found.   J P Lockhart, IO #212

"Got you, you slope-headed fuck! I'll have the IO follow up and will trace every little bud on your family tree. If we can't find you, we'll make you beg to find us!"

He unclipped the attachment and set it aside. Doing so revealed the full title of the handwritten document.

A DECLARATION OF FREEDOM
Well, well, he thought. *What have we here? A puny rebellion?* He read what followed, all the while sneering and chafing at the audacious fools who, in his mind,

had issued their own death warrants.

> *WE, the men and women, former citizens of the states of West Virginia, Kentucky, Virginia, recently known to form part of the greater United States of America, do hereby reinstate the declaration of freedom first made on July 4, 1776 and known as the Declaration of Independence. We declare this tri-state region and its citizenry free from the tyranny of the Global Environmental Ethics Organization, its governors and the United Nations Environmental Program Administration World Council.*

> *Over the past decades, we have been subjects of tyranny. We have seen our rights as they were prescribed by the United States Constitution and the Bill of Rights abrogated, subordinated, consumed, and subsumed by a body of self-appointed global governors who have overtaken our proud nation, deprived the people of liberty, and subjected us to:*

> *Laws without the consent of the people for the so-called sake of "the greater good" and "planetary sustainability;"*

> *Taxation without representation and regulations that have destroyed our industries and livelihoods, deprived us of our property;*

> *Obstruction and over-riddance of Justice by curtailment and refutation of*

the US legal code and the adjudication
of laws related to fair trial by judge or
jury, due process, private property,
freedom of speech, the right to have
and bear arms, the right to a speedy
trial, and fair sentencing.

Dirkson's intercom beeped. "DM Jones is here, sir."

"Have him wait!" Dirkson snapped back and he continued reading the last two pages. It was more of the same ridiculous drivel. A closing message written in very concise print appeared as a postscript:

By now, no doubt you are aware that we have commandeered the power plant on the Tug River. Our objective is to redirect the power feed to our own communities. We have a right to access the same utilities as the people in your city. We will supply any surplus power to your city. But know this: We have set explosive devices in and around the station. Any attempt to retake the plant will result in immediate power cuts and permanent disabling of the facility. We have survived without power for years; we can go on without it. Can your people do the same?

Montani Semper Liberi

At first, Dirkson furiously wondered who the hell this Montani person was. He had not studied Latin in school. When he tapped in the entire name and hit search, the result did nothing but enrage him further.

Montani Semper Liberi – Mountaineers are always free.

"We'll fucking see about that!" He grabbed the letter opener and viciously stabbed the pages on his desk.

Chapter 25

RM Dirkson Ponders the Future
April 4, 2053

RM Dirkson had raged and ranted enough. He consciously chose the theatrics as both his way of dealing and keeping his subordinates in a state of apprehension. He never liked surprises, especially unpleasant ones that occurred on his watch. *I've got to think! How can this work for me? How can I come out of this looking like a prince, the man who saved the day?*

He needed allies. He needed scapegoats and fall guys. He needed to keep things tight and tidy. A plan began to form in his mind. The more he thought about it, the better he liked it. The better he liked himself pulling the strings.

He would keep the takeover at Tug River and the rebels' declaration quiet. There'd been rolling blackouts and brownouts already because of the decimation and take over. He'd find a pawn; Greaves would do. I'll send him to Madison to test the resistance. An alert signal sounded from his desktop. He saw it was from that Lockhart bitch. He touched the icon and another report file, based on the letter's DNA scan, opened.

ADDENDUM
Extrapolating DNA from James Lee Johnson, b. 1994 d. 2043, court records show marriage on May 10, 2020 to Rosalyn Ann Pierce, b. 1994 status

unknown. Records show adoption of Rosalyn Ann Pierce's son, Benjamin Robert Pierce (b. 2013) on June 12, 2020. None of aforementioned have been registered. Marriage certificate filed on June 27, 2039 to B. R. Pierce and E. F. Boone.

Intake file of Estelle Boone Pierce (b. 2018) and son Jordan Webster Pierce (b. 2043).
Registered August 6, 2049. RFD #'s 96498310 and 96498314 respectively. Estelle Boone Pierce works at Fabric Sort Facility, Sector 11. Son, Jordan is in Creche 020, Sector 14. Intake officer on site: Candler S. Greaves, agent #37.

Indication from intake agent #37, Candler S. Greaves, noted incident on September 8, 2051, Benjamin Robert Pierce may also have a daughter (no further information available).
<u>Recommend interview with Estelle Boone Pierce and Jordan Webster Pierce.</u>
Note: Jordan Webster Pierce under treatment for severe asthma, production actuarials border on failure to achieve a net gain. Assessment indicates Life Status: Provisional. J P Lockhart, IO #212

Well, he thought, *I may have to commend that impertinent hag, after all. We have some very interesting relationships here. I'll have Jones handle the woman and the boy, and get Greaves to reel in the Celi girl.* He smiled. *Now, didn't the report say her last name was Pierce? Well, well. So this is a family affair. Family means leverage, and leverage means ways to bait the trap.*

At the center of his scheming, his artful machinations, his winning formula, there was one central objective: catapult himself into the stratosphere of world governance and bestow upon himself his rightful destiny. He would seize this engine that this Celi person had described that could draw power from nearly nothing. He would present it to the Global Council. What they would actually do with such an invention, who knew? Harness it to power the world? Smash it into oblivion to retain their power? Who cared? What mattered was that they would accord him praise, accolades and a permanent seat on their bench. Nothing more powerful than to command boundless power itself!

Yet the elixir of power flowed even deeper in him now. Meanwhile, he would retain copies of the design. The military applications of such a device were not lost on him. Neither were the profits that would be derived from a bidding war between rivals. Finally, the opportunity he'd long sought had practically landed in his lap.

First, he had to dispatch these Montani vermin and seize their prize. He pressed a button. "Send Jones in."

Chapter 26

Strange Happenings
April 8, 2053

The raiding party, consisting of fourteen riders and three pack mules, was halfway to Madison when a messenger appeared. It was their scout, Von, who'd just come up from Madison. He was on foot, having run the distance of a marathon to make contact with his unit. He stood by a rocky outcrop on the upside of the trail. For some reason, he didn't approach.

As usual, Virgil was riding point. He raised his hand to halt the riders strung behind him. He then dismounted and, handing the reins to the second rider, walked toward the scout.

"It's Madison. Just came from there. Something's up, boss," the scout spoke softly. Virgil figured he'd been waiting here for them, heading them off by the cliff before his party could be spotted from the town. He also noticed that his dark featured face clouded with worry—something he'd hardly seen in the usually dauntless young man.

"I can see that. Hold on a sec." He turned to catch Ben's attention and motioned for him to come. He knew the scout's background and understood how the boy had chosen to "go native." For all the world, Von appeared to have just stepped out of the early nineteenth century. He was clothed entirely in deerskin and sported a broad-brimmed hat made of oiled hide. His feet were booted in high-topped moccasins. A long knife was belted to his hip and he carried his favorite rifle, a bolt-action Ruger 308 with iron sights, slung diagonally across his back upside down to foil the rain. He was known to be a consummately skilled woodsman, tracker, guide and marksman.

After Ben joined them, Virgil raised his eyebrows. "So?"

"It looks like things are heating up in Madison. A Green Hat convoy has just arrived and set up shop at the town center. Looks like a recruiter team, but they also have security and techies. Three armored vans altogether. Trackers most likely."

"Do you think they were called out to deal with the situation at Tug River?"

Von pressed his lips together and shook his head slightly. "Not sure about that. You think they'd muster up more force than just a light security team and some techies."

Virgil puzzled over the situation. Surely, by now the head honcho had received information about the Tug River Power Plant takeover. Surely, the declaration they had drawn up had made it all the way to the top. The promise to blow up the plant was no ruse. They could level the facility in a heartbeat. What kind of game were the authorities playing? This question made Virgil very edgy.

"I'm thinking it best we continue toward Madison. Make camp above Crossroads Creek. What'd you think, Von?"

"Sounds good. I'll see about finding a good place to set up." He turned to go, but then Ben touched him on the arm.

"You have any intel on who that recruiter is?"

"Yeah, the guy's name is Greaves. He's been here a number of times before, but never with a team of trackers."

Ben immediately recognized the name. The agent that he and Celi had run up against nearly two years before, the one in the Post Office who wanted a closer look at her wore a badge that read "C. Greaves." He didn't say it, but he sensed this went beyond mere coincidence. He wanted to rush back home and warn them but knew he needed to remain with the riders.

Von regarded Ben with interest. "Would that be someone you know?"

Ben had the thought that nothing much got past this keenly observant young man. "Yeah. We do have something of a history." Ben's response was guarded.

Von picked up on this as well, but didn't push for a straight answer. He nodded and said, "Okay. I best be off now. I'll meet you before you get to the crossroads. Reckon that'll be around dusk." He gave a curt nod to them both, spun on his heels and sped back down the trail. His feet made no noise whatsoever–they barely touched the ground, or so it seemed.

Virgil watched as the scout disappeared around

a curve. "Damn! That boy's gotta have some Indian in him."

Ben nodded. "Part bloodhound, too." He looked at his uncle who seemed to be transfixed on something far away. "Hey, Virge. Think we oughta' get movin' so we can set up before dark. Virge? Hey!"

Whatever realm Virgil's mind had occupied dissolved into the moment and he was back with Ben. He still seemed occupied but not as distracted. "Yeah, I'm thinking we need to camp on the back side of Bate's Knob, y'know, above Old Sixty. Set up sentries and wait. Just wait."

"What about Von saying he'd meet us?"

"Oh, he'll find us. I have no doubt. What's worrying me is what those Green Hats are up to. I thought our debut performance woulda stirred up a bigger nest of vipers. Something ain't right."

Ben agreed. He thought back to the encounter he and Celi had with Greaves at the Post Office, and then the situation with the spotters back in the fall. It seemed all the commotion had come to nothing. Not likely. Not likely at all.

They'd heard someone had done away with the surviving spotter, found the burned up rail cart some twenty miles south of Fyco with a body tied to the pump handle. Wintertime hardships had loomed before them at that time, but Virgil had been adamant about setting off on what he called their "mission."

Chapter 27

The Mission
(Back in the fall) November 20, 2052

Winter was upon them. The snows had come early and never melted completely. Travel from one district to another was treacherous. Snowshoes and draft horses were the order of the season. Folks who'd not prepared for a harsh winter and hadn't laid up stores of food and heating wood would die. Not to say neighbors didn't check in on one another. They did and special attention was accorded to the old-timers living alone who couldn't do much for themselves. Yet, times were hard and charity only went so far. Blizzards could sock everyone in for days at a time. Every year, people would be missed in the spring—this year more than most.

Virgil and Ben spent endless hours of planning their next steps. The early onslaught of winter and the import of the game-changing power generator gave impetus to hasten their mission. They mapped out an itinerary and identified whom they would visit in each enclave. They would go on foot to their first destination, Virgil's place near Rupert. They'd stock up more supplies and arrange to borrow a couple of horses from a neighbor.

From there, they'd go north to Coalburg in what Virgil called injun territory, not that there were any native hostiles, but a bunch of rough and wild mountaineers were up that way. Virgil hoped an old soldier buddy would put them up and help coordinate a meet-up. They were hard pressed to keep the travel distance down to what they could cover in a day. They didn't relish camping along the way. The Wildlands had really gone back to being wild. If the wild cats, wolves, coyotes, and feral dogs didn't come around, there was always the biting–ass cold. Their itinerary was a circuit through four different districts. They saved the lowest and flattest Monroe District for last since winter would be full on them by then.

They met with clan and community leaders in churches, at people's home's, in abandoned factories–just about anywhere and everywhere a number of people could safely congregate. Once gathered, Virgil and Ben gave a rundown on the general conditions of life in their area–the hand-to-mouth subsistence that most everyone could recognize in their own community. Having established rapport, they'd commenced listing a series of "what-ifs."

"What if there was a way for us to create our own energy?" Usually, this would set the listeners to thinking why the hell they had wasted their time to come listen to snake-oil salesmen.

"What if it were cheap and freely available and we could use it any time of day or night to heat our homes, to light the night, to run those appliances that some of us fondly remember as the good old days?" The cynical and taciturn would start planning their exit and rustling in their overcoats.

"What if we had a way of making electricity independently, even exclusively within our own communities—no need for any power company monopoly or GEEO control?"

They'd continue on this track—noting that eventually nearly everyone's interest had been piqued. Naturally, there'd be a few who snickered, made cynical remarks about "pie in the sky" and "bullshit," or just stood up and walked, but most attendees were willing, even if cynical, to learn more.

"Would you care to see the very thing that could make this all possible?" Enough nods and voiced affirmations indicated a majority would. The doubting Thomas's poised to debunk any such claims as they dialed in their BS detectors.

Then the magic show would begin. Using an old time incandescent light bulb, an old countertop appliance, or whatever was handy that could be supplied by one of the townspeople, they'd have a volunteer start the little wheel spinning and allow the machine to rev up just enough to light the bulb or enliven the antiquated blender or play the old CD player. At an old meat processing plant in Webster, the demo got nearly out of hand when every intact light in the place began flickering and the conveyer belt kicked on. The generator was revved so high, they barely got it stopped. One old timer, a preacher, loudly declared it was the work of Satan and that Ben and Virgil were Satan's acolytes. Luckily, this notion didn't catch on with anyone else, all too thrilled to see the place alight, and the preacher left in a self-righteous huff.

After the impressive demo, Ben would show them diagrams and detailed drawings, making clear that the little machine was not a perpetual motion energy engine, but a super-efficient mechanism requiring very little combustible material to produce a huge amount of ready-to-use AC electricity.

In general, the import of this discovery wasn't lost on the community and clan leaders, especially when it was explained how it could be replicated by scavenging parts from junkyards and deserted factories. "Heck," Ben said, "my grandpa built this one in his work shed mostly outta old tractor parts, a busted up washing machine and an alternator from a '74 Chevy truck! I'm sure we could do just as well or even better."

The impact of presenting the little dynamo around the region was sensational. Being able to utilize such an energy source for wells, washing machines, hot water heaters, power equipment, lighting and such was a prospect around which the people could rally. Older folks could remember the days when electricity flowed into their homes, when they didn't concern themselves with chopping wood, hauling water, burning oil or kerosene for meager light, hand washing, line drying–all the things needing done to get by on the basics. Life for them had become very hard and, in some cases, almost unbearable.

Inside of three weeks, Ben and his uncle had covered most venues of the region except for the town centers. These centers were in former county seats and administration officials often made use of the political infrastructure like courthouses, town halls and sometimes privately-owned buildings; they were where GEEO stationed what they called "outreach programs." Local folks would come to make application for government services and shop for essentials. This harkened back to the bad old days when coal companies printed their own script and no other form of payment, even cash dollars, was accepted at the company store.

Given the presence of GEEO agents and contract workers, Virgil and Ben thought it best to steer clear of these locales. There was too much risk of GEEO officials finding out about the device and contriving some way of appropriating it and, likely, apprehending anyone involved in its development and promotion.

They also steered clear of lower Putnam all the way down the line to Fyco. The Burkharts ran things there. Even though Burkhart country was near to Ben and his family's cabin home, no effort was made to gather those locals. Plus, rumor was Sade Burkhart had it in for Virgil. Besides that, being all for themselves, the Burkharts liked running things as they were.

For the leaders who came forward to see how they could reenergize their community, arrangements were made to meet privately. The quid pro quo was that in order to participate in the "program," they had to have skin in the game and that skin was to join what Virgil called the rangers. The official name was the Mountain Rangers.

Leaders were tasked with choosing up to a dozen members of their respective community whom they would classify as the kind of people you can count on. They'd then need to qualify.

The qualifications to join up with a special unit

dubbed The Mountain Brigade were tough. First, you had to have horseman skills and provide your own horse. Second, you had to qualify as a marksman and bring your own gun(s) and ammo. The test for being a marksman was to hit a four-inch target from standing or kneeling position at a distance of fifty yards. They got one shot. Those who hunted for a living had no trouble. Even some of the older huntsmen who had to wear spectacles made the target. It was no surprise since bringing in game was vital to living the life of an outsider.

Those who missed the shot were able to participate as regulars (versus marksmen) and take on supportive roles such as supply procurement, horse tending, smithing, message running and the like. They could always hone their shooting skills and test up later. Much support came from those back home. They'd provide food, water, clothing, reloaded ammo and other necessities for the rangers.

An elderly lady over in the Monroe District volunteered to sew them a banner. She showed them a sketch drawn on a piece of old cardboard. The most obvious feature was a mountain rattler in the shape of a lightning bolt. It bisected a shield. She'd done the silhouette of a mountain range in the background. Above the mountain range was their motto Semper Liberi.

"They'll see you comin' fer miles!" She laughed and slapped Ben on the back. Her joviality seemed to drain away from her as her voice turned somber. "They got my Nellie and the grand young 'uns. She went in for kerosene. They told her no more credit lessen she came to the city and worked up some more. Come spring, that'll be two years ago. Haven't heard a word from her or when she'd be comin' back."

Her face flushed crimson and her eyes glinted with pain and passion. "You boys get them bastards and show 'em we're done with being treated like animals. Y'hear? I'll have this flag ready in justa coupla weeks." How could they refuse her offer?

By mid-spring, the Mountain Rangers had been training and practicing maneuvers for two months as weather permitted. They weren't all seasoned veterans, not by a long shot. Given their strong streak of independence, it was difficult at times to keep order. They needed to be tested and proven. Taking over the Tug River Power Plant would be their first objective.

Chapter 28

Setting the Snare
April 9. 2053

It was still dark when Candler resolved to get up. A quick glance at his portable PD showed the time as 0430. He had barely slept. The cot was cramped and hard and the old military surplus blanket that reeked of mothballs offered barely enough warmth to keep him from shivering. Apart from all the physical discomforts, an internal clamor of misgivings kept dodging about his brain. He couldn't escape the impression that something was wrong with this mission from the get-go.

Days before, he had sat outside Dirkson's office, listening. Whoever was inside there was getting a major dress-down. He had no idea who was on the receiving end until the door opened and Art Jones emerged. Jones looked shocked to see Greaves but recovered quickly. "Why Greaves, what are you doing here? Don't you have work to do?"

Candler responded coolly, "As a matter of fact, I do. RM Dirkson called me, saying he had a special assignment for me."

Jones appeared to bristle with anger and resentment. He sneered. "Well, if I were you, I would not put much stock in your abilities to accomplish any special assignment. Everyone has their limits, Greaves, and it would be such a shame to see you exceed yours. Again." He punctuated his faux concern with a short derisive laugh. As he turned to go, he advised, "Be careful. He's a bit edgy today. Your little retros up in Madison seem to be making trouble."

RM Dirkson greeted him cordially, asking him if he cared for anything to drink from his selection of juices, exotic coffee or teas. Candler politely declined. "Very well then, let's get down to business." He motioned to a chair directly in front of his desk as he himself took a much taller chair behind the desk. As he sat down, Candler realized he had never been in Dirksen's office. It gave him pause to consider the real reason he had been called up. The atmosphere around Dirkson crackled with foreboding intensity. Pale adamantine eyes bored into him. On the desktop between them lay several typewritten pages. It was odd to see paper lying about these days, given that paper was a rare commodity. Paper production had been proscribed for decades due to its obscene impact on the environment. Dirkson noticed Candler's gaze and commented. "We'll get to these in a moment, Agent Greaves.

"Now, I understand you have an upcoming foray into Madison District?" Candler nodded. "And that you have a certain acquired familiarity with the inhabitants of that district?"

"Yes sir. I have served several functions in that district on perhaps a dozen or more assignments. I have also done extensive background readings on the area and its culture. All that said, I really wouldn't consider myself—"

"I will do the considering here, Agent Greaves.

I've read your files and believe you have the skills, the knowledge and the motivation necessary to take on this vital mission successfully and swiftly. Of course, such a performance would redound to your prospects for an upgrade. Perhaps a double or triple."

Candler reigned in a rush of excitement. The prospect of having it all and then some was titillating to say the least, but he knew in the corporate world such prospects did not come freely. The bigger the prospect, the bigger the catch. He had to wonder what, specifically, did this special assignment entail?

As if reading his thoughts, Dirkson broke in, "Now, regarding the assignment, I want you to have a look at this." He shoved one of the pages across the desk to Candler. "This is the first page. I want you to read it."

Candler leaned forward and picked up the single sheet. He began reading aloud "'The Story of My Life-So Far'" by—"

Dirkson raised his hands, his face wincing as if in pain. "No, no, Greaves. Read it silently!"

Candler felt his own face flush with embarrassment. "Of course, RM. I am so sorry." He continued to read the page, picking up where he left off.

"The Story of MY LIFE-So Far"
By Celi Pierce
First of all, it's so very VERY COLD. And we
don't see the sun anymore. The skies are as gray

*as ashes. It even tried to snow last night, just
enough to stick white on the ground. It is still
September. . . .*

He quickly read through the page. The last few
paragraphs caught his attention–defiantly boasting of
poaching and black market activities.

*It's so cold most of the time now. It's all we can
do some days just to keep from freezing to
death. The ones who go around wearing Green
Hats tell us it's not safe to burn wood or coal.
We could buy these special made energy pellets
they sell for creds in town, but My Gram says
they can go to hell. PA too. Only he says it
more.*

Candler looked up at Dirkson, who was leaning
forward with both hands on his desk. "Well, Greaves,
do you appreciate the gravity of this. . . piece of
perfidy? Do you?" Greaves thought, *No, but I think I'm
about to hear about it.*

Dirkson jabbed his finger at the pages on his
desk. "Somehow, this tripe is being broadcast all over
Madison District and most likely beyond. Our sources
tell us that the retros have found some way of sending
this out in order to foment widespread resistance
which, as a matter of course, leads to violent rebellion
against our global initiatives." Candler ascribed
Dirksen's reference to "our sources" as newly inducted
citizens who'd been incentivized to cooperate.

Candler looked back at the first page and the
unread stack underneath, what appeared to be at least

ten more pages. "I see, sir."

Dirkson edged into a tirade. "Do you? Do you see? This is completely unacceptable, completely!" He slapped the desktop with his right hand and then pointed at Candler.

"I'm aware that, in a few days, you are scheduled to foray into Anthony District to tag reprobates, but I want you to focus first and foremost on finding this Celi person, and chances are it's not a real girl, but some fabrication by a hardcore rebel faction looking to stir things up but whoever this is, I want you to find them and shut them down. It doesn't matter how; just shut them down. Do you understand me?" Dirkson's handsome face flushed crimson, a matrix of bulging veins laced from his neck up to his temples. The stony eyes were those of an apex predator scanning for any weakness or challenge to his authority.

In spite of feeling tyrannized, Candler replied evenly, "Yes, sir!"

"You will be assigned an extra contingent of armed enforcers, Special Patrols. Commander Echols will be the SP team leader, but you will be in charge of this operation and have full responsibility for resolving this issue. Is that clear?"

"Yes, sir." Candler snapped his answer with a nod, careful not to display even a hint of hesitation. "I'll get it done, sir." However, inwardly he cringed and considered how much he hated surprises, especially those that demanded immediate responses.

He held out a small digital data capsule. "Here's my report from the last mission, sir."

Dirkson relaxed his posture and leaned back in his leather chair. He even smiled slightly, but it was a sly, intrusive expression. "Never mind that, Greaves. That was just a ruse to get you up here. This mission of yours is on a need-to-know basis and you are to say nothing about the content of these transmissions to anyone. Do you understand? No one but you and I are to discuss this."

"Yes, sir!" With that, the assignment to "shut down" the Celi communiqués became his mission. His team would be briefed, but not fully. So, there they were, their first day in Madison.

Sitting on the edge of his cot, he yawned, stretched and flinched as his bare feet touched the cold floorboards. He flipped on his penlight and could see his exhaled breath. The town centers had suffered massive cutbacks even on basics like heating fuel. Bedding down indoors was hardly better than being outside. Yet, the surrounding walls and the fifteen-foot high-security fencing around the entire compound gave some comfort. No one came or went but by the guarded gate.

Having slept in his long underwear, he pulled on the rest of his clothes, socks and boots, and clumped down a hallway to the bathroom carrying his dopp kit. After his bathroom routine, he came back to his bed and briefly considered another go at sleeping. He reminded himself that he was the team leader and, like a good lieutenant, he needed to serve the example.

First to lead, last to eat and sleep, or something like that.

He made for the commissary where they served the meals, thinking to find some semblance of coffee or tea. On his way, he passed the dormitory room noting that his enforcers and techies had not stirred from their cots, except for one. As he rounded the corner, he nearly collided with Technical Operator Renick. TO Renick stood five feet four inches, the best techie he'd ever led, and quite adept at meeting every challenge.

He'd specifically requested she be on his team. He never knew when she ate or slept, but she was always "on." Her dark brown eyes shone with a keen intelligence, and her dark complexion appeared nearly flawless. Her full lips, high cheekbones and luminous raven hair hanging straight to her broad shoulders gave the impression of a diminutive Amazon warrior princess. She moved her lithe body like a gymnast, perfectly poised and fluid. None of these attractive qualities went unnoticed. Least of all by Candler, who'd formed a nascent infatuation for her but had so far kept their association "professional." In his more self-reflective moments, he had to admit he enjoyed having her as a team member for a host of reasons beyond the utilitarian. Whether she reciprocated any romantic notions toward him remained a complete mystery.

They both had stopped inches apart from each other. She'd reflexively brought her arms up, her right palm facing him. Candler's reaction was to freeze and self-consciously utter an inane expression of surprise. "Oh!" Then, "Sorry." Her smile caught him as she relaxed her arms and deftly sidestepped so he could pass. "My fault, sir. I should know better than to cut corners."

He managed a nod, a smile and an innocuous greeting. "Well, good morning, Renick. Nice to see you up and at it this morning. We've a big day ahead."

She sounded cheerful. "Yes, sir. We sure do. I'll be going over the equipment and mapping out coordinates. Is there anything else you need done?"

Her fragrance momentarily captured his entire attention. Whatever she was wearing was alluring and intoxicating but he recovered quickly and put on a face he hoped would convey careful thought. "Ah, no. I think that should do, for now. Thank you."

They went their separate ways. As he absently looked around the commissary for something caffeinated, Candler was thinking, or rather rethinking, his decision to bring in TO Katrelle Renick. He needed to focus on the task and if just this one little run-in looped him, what would it take to throw him off completely? He had to admit: *Not much, but then again, she is the best at what she does. I'll have to ask her to lay off the perfume—or not.* He smiled at his own equivocation.

Chapter 29

"The best-laid schemes o' mice an' men
Gang aft agley,
An' lea'e us nought but grief an' pain,
For promis'd joy!"

~*Robert Burns*

April 9, 2053

As a dull seep of morning light filtered into the valley, they loaded up the three vans and headed for the northern hill country where the directional RFAD had flagged the source of the subversive transmission. The crew knew the coordinates and the mission to confiscate any and all electronics.

Candler believed he had exclusive knowledge of the details and that it would likely involve more than confiscation. The core mission was to shut them down and though he was averse to violence, he would meet force with force.

The road they traveled was little more than a cart path. The vans' wheels were locked in four-while drive and forward progress was slow and jolting. They ascended into a fog bank that shrouded the higher elevations. Soon, the driver of the third vehicle could barely make out the taillights of the first van.

The lead van towed a trailer loaded with three side-by-side ATVs, which they'd requisitioned from the center's transportation pool. Each one had a storage box strapped down on the back end and black ABS scabbards attached to the right side that secured their high-powered rifles. Several Special Patrol guards sat in their assigned vans, one assigned to each as a driver. Additional security men occupied the shotgun seats of the lead and rear vans.

The euphemistically dubbed survey crew, consisting of Candler and his two techies, rode in the middle van where a battery of stacked electronics were bolted on either side of the interior. TO Renick sat before one panel and her assistant TO Simms, a newbie on his first foray, sat beside her looking opposite at his own monitors. They both wore miked headsets that linked to each other.

"Agent Greaves?" the techie behind him called out. Candler turned his head to see a pasty-faced young man with late blooming zits, incongruously, wearing dark wraparound sunglasses in the dim light. The shades added no luster to his geeky aspect.

"Agent Greaves, is there anything different about this field trip?" He motioned with his thumb to his companion beside him. "TO Renick here says we've got some RFT equipment aboard, the kind for homing unauthorized transmissions. Does this mean we'll be making direct field contact with the retros?" His voice cracked, betraying his anxiety.

Candler gave an honest answer. "I don't know for sure, Simms. We are tracking signals coming from the upper regions, but how far we'll need to foray, I've no idea."

Soon they reached an impasse. The convoy was

descending a curvy section with a high bank on their left and a steep drop to the right, when they encountered a huge fallen tree. It was too big for the van's winch to manage and it would take at least a half hour to cut up to clear. Candler and the guards recognized they were in a dangerous choke point that could easily be a trap. The metallic slither and clank of rifle bolt carriers being drawn and released jarred the stillness.

After cautiously surveying their surroundings from inside the van and spotting no immediate threat, the two SPs stepped out to assess the situation—one exiting from the side, the other from the rear door. Candler joined them. The SPs in the lead and back vans had also emerged. They hung close to their vehicles with guns at the ready.

Just ahead, the road was somewhat broadened by a foot trail on the high side of the fallen tree trunk where travelers had detoured around the exposed plate of twisted roots. The dirt trail showed faint evidence of horse tracks and several sets of lugged boot prints. *Not good*, Candler thought. *We gotta move outta here!*

Peering through their rifle scopes, the guards scanned the hillside. Every sound was amplified over the low idle of the vans, the flutter of a bird wing, branches moving against each other. It was an extremely long five minutes before the guards lowered their weapons and motioned all was clear.

Candler gave the order. "Okay. We're going with the ATVs. Let's saddle up! We're nearly eight miles from our waypoint and timing is crucial if we want to finish by nightfall." The techies got busy pulling together their portable equipment stowed in hard shell cases and stuffed in sacks. The SPs busied themselves with packing their own gear. No one wanted to be stuck in the outlands past dark.

While two SPs stood watch, a third SP dropped the trailer ramp and the offloading commenced. He inspected each ATV's fuel tank and tires. Satisfied, he cranked each one in turn and soon all three were at low idle ready to be loaded and mounted. The van drivers were tasked with turning their vehicles around and remaining behind as a rear guard. They were in a hollow, so radio comms were dicey. If the forward teams hadn't returned by 0530, they would backtrack to a spot where they could signal for reinforcements.

All of the ATVs were loaded. Extra rifles fit into side-mounted scabbards for quick access. Sergeant Echols, the lead SP, told the team to mount up. Candler followed the protocol for the civvies, like himself, to be the driver and the guard to be seated to the side riding shotgun. He could tell the newbie tech Simms was unsettled by the task of operating the ATV. As part of their training, all field techies were supposedly trained to drive a variety of gas mobiles including the two-seater ATVs, but lately, due to shortages and budgeting, trainees received only vicarious instruction on computer programmed simulators—not exactly the real thing. *Well*, Candler thought, *no time like the present for hands-on.*

They made their way around the fallen oak and proceeded upward on the battered highway. Landslides and washouts had to be carefully negotiated. Each of

the ATV side-by-sides was equipped with a steel cable
winch and an assortment of nylon tow straps with
hooks on either end. Candler's extensive field
experience included hundreds of hours on ATV
vehicles, so he was quick to take the lead and pick the
safer routes. The SP sitting next to him was constantly
scanning the forest terrain for any would-be attackers,
occasionally signaling for Candler to stop and throttle
the engine to idle.

As they passed through the forest, the canopy
on either side began to grow closer and formed a kind
of living tunnel through which the small group passed.
Had it been a different time and a different climate,
Candler thought, this would have been a beautiful
scene with sunlight filtering down through the
crisscrossed tangle above and light dappling the
ground. Instead, what meager light leaked through did
little to assuage the fear that they were burrowing
deeper and deeper into a black hole, a spider's lair that
twisted and turned. As they climbed the mountain, the
canopy opened and blackened trunks of large trees
revealed traces of a forest fire. Candler knew that
natural fires were rare, but that the locals would
occasionally set fires to clear out dead wood and
underbrush allowing young shoots to flourish, the kind
of vegetation that attracted game. The Native
Americans had done the same years before any
European showed his pale face.

They reached a tight turn where a jumble of
logs blocked the path upward, leaving only a narrow
side trail on the downhill side that detoured around the
blockade. The three ATVs came to a stop. The SPs
immediately recognized this as a choke point where

they would be most vulnerable to ambush. They racked their ARs, thumbed off the safeties and began scanning with their scopes in both light and infrared mode. They had to be careful not to fire their weapons unless there was a clear threat. The sound of a gunshot would alert every retro for miles and whatever militia was up in the hills would soon descend on them. The SPs were all former military, well trained in tactical maneuvers.

Sergeant Echols stood up next to Candler as he scanned the area around them. He gave a slashing sign across his throat for all drivers to cut engines and the idling sound of the ATVs was snuffed out. Immediately, a shrill cry from above made everyone jerk their heads upward. A red-shouldered hawk circled overhead, its cries unmasked by the silence. The shrill cries were soon joined by churling sounds from the treetops.

The techie, Simms, anxiously asked, "What's that sound?" The SP beside him smirked and half whispered, "Don't get your panties in a knot, plebo. It's just squirrels warning each other about the hawk." The techie looked dubious but seemed to relax a little.

As the minutes passed, other woodland sounds drifted around them. The staccato rap rap rap of a woodpecker some distance away, the flutter of wings in the low growth nearby, a cawing of crows passing overhead, the sound of dead leaves gently wafting to the ground—the last remnants even winter could not dislodge. The woods were pulsing with life. There was a kind of rhythm, a subtle cacophony that was at once random and yet somehow measured and meaningful.

After fifteen minutes of tense observation, Echols gave the signal to proceed. Candler was reaching forward to turn the ignition key when suddenly he heard a shooooop and felt a blast of air in front of his face as a silvery object whizzed by and thudded into the trunk of a tree beside his ATV. The missile had also barely missed Echols. He'd reacted by ducking down as low as possible from his seated position, pulling Candler down with him. Candler surmised the others were taking cover as best they could. They stayed in that position while the SPs scanned the hillside area that straight-lined with the trajectory of the missile.

The SPs held their fire. It was always a catch-22 whether to lay down a barrage of defensive fire and risk half a legion of hostiles with illegal weapons being drawn to their location, or just wait and take a quick shot at a definite target. What worried the SPs and Candler was how close the arrow had come to spiking Candler through the temple if he'd been leaning just slightly forward. Was it their luck or the archer's skill? From his semi-prone position, Candler could barely see the short metal arrow stuck in the tree trunk. A rivulet of amber sap was oozing from the wound. He shuddered. Then he noticed that along the length of the silver shaft were fine black markings.

They waited a half minute. The lead SP barked, "Everybody out! Stay down! This side!" He was pointing to the downhill side of their ATVs, which afforded some cover.

The newbie Simms noisily clambered from his ATV, comically scrambling over his assigned SP to gain refuge to the other side. The female in the third ATV deftly slinked over the passenger seat and down beside the rear guard SP. She was wide-eyed, alert and had armed herself with a rifle.

They waited and waited; the sounds of the woodland began to dominate all else. The rhythmic undulations no longer seemed so friendly.

After what seemed forever, Echols tentatively raised up from his defensive crouch. He still kept his one eye on the scope, fanning the hillside above as he back walked the short distance to the stricken tree. With a few quick twists, he broke the bolt off leaving the deadly point lodged in the trunk. He came back to his defensive position next to the lead ATV and handed the shaft to Candler.

As Candler had thought, there was some kind of writing scrawled along the length of the metal tube. Echols read the crudely written message along with Candler and flatly offered his uninvited opinion, "We're in a heap of shit."

The message read, "Proceed at your peril. Turn back and live."

Candler assessed the situation. He had to drive back the intense panic brought on by the deadly projectile that had whizzed within an inch of his head. He had to focus on the mission. If they retreated, then it would be a tactical victory for the retros. If they proceeded, it would mean putting the entire unit at risk. He'd about decided to go it alone when TO Renick appeared crouched at his side.

"I'll go with you, sir. I'm the highest rated TO here and I've acquired a number of tactical skills as well." He wondered how she knew his inclinations. Was he that predictable?

Candler looked at her confident poise and radiant enthusiasm to plummet into danger. He was familiar with her file. She'd arrived at Progress City as a child of ten with her mother and two brothers. They were from these very same hills. Her aptitude tests steered her to the Security and Enforcement Academy where she excelled. Later, she branched into the Technical Corps graduating at the top of her class. They'd served together on several prior missions and she was a top notch Technical Operator. That's why he chose her to be on his team—well, mostly.

"All right Renick, you do realize the risks. I have to advise you that anything could happen and there are no guarantees we'll make it back."

Damn! He thought. *I'm scaring myself.*

TO Renick cracked a roguish smile and said, "Yes, Agent Greaves. I'm totally aware and ready to roll!"

Echols took exception. "Sir, as lead security officer, I strongly advise we retreat and reassess with drones and IR image scans. We don't know who or what we're up against, sir. All due respect, if anyone were to accompany you further, that should be me. I have seen a lot more action than Miss Renick and know how to deal with these people."

Positioned between Renick and Echols, Candler could feel the sparks flying past him, but he quickly asserted his authority. "Sergeant, I see your point, but in addition to her tactical training, Renick is a fine technical officer and a native to the region. I want you to take TO Simms and your men back to the vans and await our signal as to your next action."

He caught the sergeant's glaring resentment at being ordered about by a civilian and could see a storm of protest brewing. "We have limited time, sergeant. Need I remind you that RM Dirkson has placed me in charge of this operation? You will follow my instructions, will you not?"

Echols drew in a loud breath and exhaled a desultory, "Yes, sir. I will."

In a flurry of activity, personnel and gear were shifted around. Candler took over driving the ATV while TO Renick took the shotgun position. As an afterthought, Candler got out of his seat, extracted a white handkerchief from his pocket and tied it onto the six-foot radio antennae attached to the back bumper.

They were equipped with a homing device, a GPS, and a two-way radio but no weapons. TO Renick plotted in a course on a handheld. After giving a few final instructions to Echols, Candler admonished everyone to take care, then slowly drove the lone ATV up the steep hill and out of sight. The little white flag sank as they crested the top of a hill and that was the last they saw of them.

"Damned fools!" Echols said.

#

They'd proceeded some seven miles without incident but were quite certain of being watched and expected to be confronted at any moment. TO Renick was reading signals from her lap desk securely clipped to the dash that indicated the last known point source of the "Celi" transmissions. She announced, "It's in a deep cove some thirty-three miles northeast of this location."

The trail had broadened into a track; there were traces of horse prints and wagon wheels and an occasional tire print. "Odd," thought Candler puzzled that any sort of motorized vehicle would be driven in this zone—other than a GEEO unit, which he knew had not been through there for years. Rails and old railroad beds had become the key routes into the mountains.

They proceeded slowly to demonstrate their non-bellicose intent. "We come in peace," was the hoped for message. It wasn't long before they met their welcoming committee.

They'd stopped at a stream crossing where the steep bank had to be carefully negotiated on the diagonal. Candler carefully coaxed the ATV down the steep bank and into the stream. They quickly realized the water was too deep for the rover and they'd need to cross elsewhere. Candler backed up and swung around to renegotiate the steep bank. That was when they looked up to see a line of retros, about twelve men, standing above them with an assortment of weaponry aimed in their general direction.

"Raise your hands. Don't move," a gravelly voiced man nearest them shouted. This was punctuated by a motion with the end of his weapon alternatively aimed at Candler and then Katrelle. A younger man with a long-barreled Colt revolver in hand sidled past the speaker and skittered down the bank, keeping a sharp eye on the pair all the time. He was slight in build and just barely taller than TO Renick. He approached the ATV and deftly reached in to shut off the engine. The gurgling flow of the stream became the ambient sound.

The man on the hill shouted, "Keep your hands up and slowly step out of the buggy." The young man near them stepped back a few paces taking point blank aim at Candler's torso. Katrelle moved first, slowly emerging from her seat. Candler did the same, realizing there was nothing to be done but surrender and hope for some kind of rescue or opportunity to escape. That is, if they weren't murdered.

The young man backed away from Candler and came around to TO Renick. He was angling his head from side to side as if peering at some oddity of nature. He approached her directly, keeping the gun trained on her torso.

"Hey now, don't I know you from somewheres?" She said nothing. "Might you be Kay Renick from over Neola way?" Katrelle's eyes flashed, but she remained silent. "Sure. I remember now. You and your family used to barter stuff at the town center before the goddamned GEEO's made it illegal for public bartering." He looked her over. "I'll be! You really are that pigtailed runt all grown up." He leered at her and came closer.

Katrelle raised her chin in defiance and countered the insult. "Yeah, Hardy. I'm her. All grown up and so glad to kick your ass into the next county if you touch me."

Hardy smirked, showing bad teeth along with disregard for her threat and stepped within arm's reach. Gun still aimed at her center mass, his left hand grabbed a strand of her dark, sable hair. He raised it to his nose saying, "Awww, my my, you sure smell—"

The heel of her hand struck his nose with such force it sounded a crack loud enough to be heard by even the men up the hill and sprayed blood instantly. She whirled him around like a rag doll and, in a blur, plucked the gun from his grasp, breaking his trigger finger in the process. With his right arm twisted behind him, using his body as a shield, she held the barrel to his temple. Blood gushed from what remained of the youth's nose as he moaned pitifully. Her blood-splattered face punctuated a dead earnest resolve. She addressed the leader.

"Now captain, commander, whoever you are. I suggest you order everyone to lower their weapons or this boy of yours will be permanently ventilated." No one on the hill moved. "If you decide otherwise, well, for me, it's as good a day to die as any and I'll take as many with me as possible." She smiled without a trace of pretense and cocked back the revolver's hammer for emphasis.

Candler was agape, still standing by the vehicle with his hands raised. He, for one, was not ready to go out in a blaze of glory like his gung-ho sidekick. He felt almost giddy and fought a strong impulse to laugh aloud as if this were some scene being played before him. He knew Katrelle had expertise but had no idea she possessed such prowess, and he couldn't avoid the chauvinistic coda by thinking, "a diminutive female at that." He eyed Katrelle with a newfound regard and wondered what other skills she had yet to display.

The apparent leader gave the order to his party to lower their weapons.

"That's not good enough!" Katrelle yelled and jammed the muzzle under her quaking captive's jawbone.

"On the ground, sidearms too! Real slow, now." The leader nodded and slowly laid down his weapon. The others followed suit.

"Sidearms, too!" she shouted. This was tricky because everyone had coats and many of the weapons could be concealed.

She regarded the leader, noting a rough-looking character with a gray beard wearing a wide-brimmed fedora. Yet, there was a certain sophistication and charm with which he addressed her. "Miss, with all due respect. You have to concede we have the high ground and, thus, the advantage. You can't hold Hardy there and drive off at the same time without at least one of us plugging you and your friend. Besides that, Hardy knows we're all expendable. Matter of fact, he's a real

MOUNTAIN WHISPERS – DAYS WITHOUT SUN

pain in the ass—pardon my expression, Miss, but it is so. He just happened to pick the short straw today. Some of us wouldn't mind being shed of him." The man's voice was gritty but sounded calm, well-reasoned. He'd even touched the brim of his hat like a gentleman greeting a lady on the street in bygone days. "Sooo, whadyasay, Miss? How 'bout we parlay so everyone gets to live another day and part company with the same number of holes we begun the day with?"

Katrelle assessed her situation and couldn't figure if the fedora-capped man was bluffing or deadly serious. Surely, they wouldn't gun down GEEO field agents, including a high-level green like Candler. They might take them hostage and hold them for some kind of ransom. Then again, GEEO central had a policy to never deal with extremists. Agents had disappeared and were never seen or heard from again. She began to second-guess her reactions. Her professional persona prevailed. She'd parlay.

She replied to the apparent leader, "All right! What's your game?"

"How 'bout, letting go of Hardy, dropping that six-shooter and then you and your sidekick turn around and hightail it back to your beehive. On foot, you take only yourselves."

Candler had recovered his senses somewhat. All this had occurred in a matter of seconds but seemed much longer. He spoke in a shaky warble, "We come here on official business and are empowered by the Regional Council of Governments to enter any zone, place of business, factory, or domicile under Section

Forty of the UN Code and you, sir, ALL of you, will be brought up on charges and prosecuted un—"

"Does your compadre there ever shut up?" the man at the top interrupted, looking only at Katrelle. "He's gotta know we don't abide by his rules or jurisdiction or UN claptrap. We're free citizens and unless your so-called council has declared war on its own citizens, we have every right to defend ourselves against your intrusion—with our lives if need be. As far as we're concerned, miss, *you're* the trespassing party."

Candler felt his blood percolating. He'd shifted internally from fear to outrage. "What you are not understanding, is that all of you are squatters living on borrowed time and it's by our council's humanitarian concern with social justice that you've been allowed to remain in this territory and subsist on your own. We have the public good as our prime concern and you are not legally sanctioned to carry firearms, much less threaten government representatives on government property. By decree of the Global Council, we have every right to pursue our assigned mission and you are in flagrant violation of Section Forty—"

Katrelle glared at Candler for an instant and shook her head. She spoke so that only Candler could hear, "Will you shut up? Are you trying to get us killed?" She could tell Candler was only incensed by her warnings and he'd likely write her up as a traitor if they ever got back.

The man on the hill seemed amused. "Well, I see we have a little lover's spat going on down there. That fella of yours is as full of shit as a Christmas turkey. So, I'm talking to you, miss. Are we gonna work this out or are you really serious about the good day to die thing?"

She spoke again to Candler in an even tone. "We have to parlay. These men mean to kill us if we don't. It's your call, Candler. I'm willing to go either way." He seemed to bridle at the familiar use of his first name.

She wasn't sure if what she said was true but wanted to shock Candler back to some semblance of reality and make sure he knew it was his decision–that he was the lead agent. Meanwhile, the young man in her armlock was getting heavier, mouth breathing loudly and moaning about losing so much blood. "I'm dyink, beedink, beedink."

She gave his bent arm a hard jerk and rasped, "Shut up, dirt bag! Or I'll bite off your ear." This seemed to have the desired effect and his timorous rambling subsided into soft, dog-like whimpers.

Candler hissed, "I pressed the ELT as we got out. So base can send a team, maybe a drone. Nothing else we can do. We'll have to go along. . . ."

"Great!" Katrelle said barely moving her lips. In actual truth, sending a distress signal was pointless. A drone might arrive in twenty minutes, an extraction team in an hour. Whatever was going to go down was going to do so in the next few minutes. She considered the options of escaping with their hostage on foot, trying to drive the ATV across the swift water that looked way too deep or giving up for now and escaping at the next opportunity.

"Pardon me, miss, but we can't be here all day, especially since your driver there has engaged the ELT and is hoping for an ER crew to show up—which, by the way, isn't that likely—but we don't need any more complications. So what will it be?"

In answer, she shoved Hardy to the ground and tossed his gun into the stream. It plopped like a heavy stone. Then she raised her arms indicating surrender. Candler, who'd already raised his arms, heard himself saying, "We are your prisoners according to Convention Seven Ninety-six of the UN Code, and as such you are required by said convention to treat us—"

The pack leader looked at Katrelle. "Will you shut him up? As far as we're concerned, you're on our land and there ain't a sovereign soul here that abides by any bullshit UN code." His voice turned hard and flat. "And, young lady. . . try any more smooth moves and your fellow agent there will be fit only for the buzzards and you won't be so lucky as him. Do you understand me?"

She managed a subtle nod. Her clenched teeth and corded jaw muscles betrayed her inner urges to fight to the finish.

The leader pointed toward two taller men who took his meaning and after retrieving their rifles, skittered down the steep bank. They approached Katrelle with caution. The one to her right instructed, "Kneel down, hands behind your back." They produced several lengths of nylon cord and proceeded to bind her hands.

Still moaning and bleeding, Hardy was lifted by the nearest man and pushed toward the steep bank. He was still yammering, "My node ib boken, beedink, my node. . ." His demonstrations seemed not to impress his fellow riders a whit. When he reached the top, someone handed him a sooty bandana with which he began gingerly dabbing his face, flinching and crying out with each dab.

As Candler was being tied up, he couldn't resist saying, "Now, wait a minute, you said we'd be released to walk out of here. You won't hear the end of this. Abduction of GEEO agents is a federal—"

"Y'know," one of the approaching men quipped, "I think we got us a fence pisser." Everyone seemed to get it but Candler; even Katrelle cracked a slight smile or maybe a grimace. It was the last thing he saw before the butt of a rifle slammed into the back of his head and all semblance of consciousness vanished.

Chapter 30

Celi's Diary
April 3, 2053

The men are still gone from our lives. Pa and Uncle Virgil are off somewhere making trouble for the Green Hats. Ever since they took off with that little sparky machine, it's been just Gram and me here all alone. Well, except for each other, which, don't get me wrong, I love Gram but I miss having Pa here and seeing Uncle Virgil. Before they left back in the fall, they laid up a lot of firewood and Pa brought home several bushels of lump coal. He and Uncle hunted enough game to carry us through the winter. Gram and me did most of the curing and canning.

We used to eat just only veggies, but my folks decided that to grow up healthy and strong we kids needed more protein. We tried raising rabbits, but at the table, I would gag and throw up whenever I remembered hearing them scream, as they were being what they call harvested.

Chickens are a bit easier. I try not to name them. That helps.

I think fish work the best. They don't scream or squawk. It makes me sad though to whack a beautiful colored trout on the head and feel it shiver its life out and then see the colors fade almost right away. Turtles are okay too, but they're chewy and taste real strong. I keep burping the taste for days.

Gram is the only one of us who has stuck to veggies. She says her system just can't take the meat. Something having to do with her believing in karma. "If I eat that animal, it comes back to bite me," she says, but I seen her pop a chicken's neck in half a second. Pa and Uncle Virgil showed us how to dress out wild game like deer and squirrel. If we had to we'd likely eat our goats, do them up like the deer, though it's better when we get their milk. I don't think I could bear to hurt either of them and it would be impossible to eat them. Ugggggghhhh!

Speaking of uggghhh, there were these two men who came up to the door one day, soon after Pa and Uncle Virgil had set off. One old man acted real polite. He stood on the porch with his hat in hand and smiled. Another man had come up with him, looking to me like they were related. He kept staring at me. Reminded me of some hungry animal.

Gram came up behind me, toting her shotgun, and asked them their business. The old man said they'd come by to pay their respects and to let Uncle Virgil know they'd done so. The old man, he was bigger than our doorframe, asked when we might expect to see Virgil Johnson, and Gram said she had no clue but that he could show up anytime.

I started to say they'd be gone a while but Gram interrupted by asking them who they were. The old guy said they were Burkharts, Sade and Carter Burkhart from over in Putnam. Gram seemed to tighten up at hearing this and she stepped between me and the old guy. He smiled and said they'd best be on their way. His son just stood there looking at us. He said something that only his Pa understood. The old man shook his head, and I thought he spoke something like "No. Now's not the time." Then the old man kind of bowed, thanking Gram for her hospitality, which seemed odd since she'd not offered any, and they left. They took their time looking around the yard as if they were curious about something. Finally, they were out of sight.

Gram kept eyeing them the whole time. I asked her about them and she said those two were the meanest devils that had ever walked the earth. I wondered at that. The old man seemed real polite, but there was something in his rough face, in his eyes that looked sly. Reminded me of that coyote that took our hen Stacey. And the way the younger man kept looking me up and down gave me creepers. I didn't care for either one of them.

When Pa and Uncle Virgil returned a few weeks later, I figure Gram told him about those two, but I can't say for sure she did. When I asked her about it, she told me to never mind and that the topic was closed. We never seen them devils since.

It has been a mean winter. Back late December the pipes from the spring froze up and we've been out of piped-in water since then. We had to bring the animals inside sometimes just to keep them from freezing to death.

Our men would pass through now and then to check in on us. They showed up in early March and stayed only a couple of days and then they went off again. Said they had business down the river.

So, it's been just Gram and me. I for one am about to go nuts just hanging around. I think I might just grab Pa's crossbow and see if there's any game out there, something fresh.

Chapter 31

Perchance to Dream
April 13, 2053

When Candler awoke, pain was his first sensation. With every pulse, the back of his head throbbed. It was a symphony of pain. His eyes blurred and his sense of orientation was topsy-turvy—like being on a tiny boat in stormy seas complimented by waves of nausea. He eventually noticed he was lying on his back staring up at the bottom of a wobbly wooden platform. A dim yellow light flickered.

His memory of how he got there was fragmentary. He tentatively tried to fit pieces together but there were huge gaps, and the pulses of pain only seemed to widen them. All he really wanted was to escape the pain. He reflexively reached his hand to the back of his head, felt a huge lump, which rewarded his exploratory venture with a blinding stab of agony. He jerked his hand away and held it in front of his face, half-expecting to see bloody gore on his fingers. There was no trace save for a few crumbs of dried blood. *Okay, I'm gonna be okay.*

He summoned all his strength trying to rise up from a prone position. He made it to the point of sitting up but had to close his eyes as they watered with pain and his gut lurched with the tilting, whirling scene before him. A foul-tasting bile rose into his throat and mouth. It burned. He twisted to his left, bracing his torso with his arm, and spat off to the side.

He groaned plaintively. It was too much. He felt any vestiges of strength leave him with each dry heave. He curled into a fetal position on his side and for the first time, through bleary eyes, realized he was in a room or chamber laying on a cot, totally alone. His wakefulness unreeled and the last tether of reality slipped away into the depths.

When he came to next, there was someone with him. An icy cool sensation surrounded the back of his head. His eyes fluttered open and he vaguely saw the outline of a person in front of him. He lay on his side breathing shallowly and let the images resolve into a semblance of reality.

The person in front of him was TO Renick. She leaned closer to Candler's face and smiled.

"Welcome back to the land of the living, Agent Greaves. You got a nasty bump on your head there and a moderate concussion that likely scrambled your brains a bit."

He reached his right hand back to the sorest spot and felt where a cool compress had been placed against it.

Renick gently grasped the back of his hand and laid it on his left arm. "So, let's let this poultice do its job and I'll try to tell you what's happening. So all you have to do is listen, okay?"

Candler tentatively nodded.

"So, where are you? Well, that's easy. You're at

the Madison Town Center Infirmary where you've been treated for a traumatic concussion. We cannot do X-rays, but we're fairly certain you'll make a full recovery, over time, that is.

"How long have you been out of it—unconscious? Well, we think about three days, but there was one time two days ago when you apparently woke up and puked, which was right during a brief absence of your assigned caregiver." She gestured to herself. "A girl has to relieve herself every now and then, and it was only for a few minutes. Sorry about that." She smiled slightly without parting her lips.

She continued her debrief as if reading from a printed status report. Her voice was pleasant but not given to anything more than factual recitation.

"Anyway, you're probably wondering what happened up in the valley with those men who accosted us. They took our equipment, our weapons, our communication and surveillance devices and stripped down our UTV to its bare essentials leaving just enough gas to get us back to Anthony. We were cuffed to make sure there'd be no shenanigans. They were going to release us to walk out, but I convinced them to consider how you were rendered non-ambulatory due to a failure on your part to communicate in a, shall we say, 'sensitive' manner."

"They did honor their word to release us. I think they are, for the most part, honorable, though there are always exceptions like Hardy Wickline who I look forward to meeting up with again someday, but the leader, whom locals refer to as the Captain or Boss, is known to keep his word. Of course, that can cut positive and negative. If he says it, he means it. He said if we or anyone from GEEO came back to the high valley again we'll be apprehended and, how did he phrase it?" Her deep brown eyes darted upward. "Oh yes! Terminated with extreme prejudice, which I take to mean executed on the spot." There was a strange, incongruous lilt to her voice as if she was proud of herself for getting the man's words just right given their dire import.

"Once back here, I did some research on this 'Captain-Boss' fellow and it's quite interesting studying the man behind the legend. He has apparently been able to cobble together an alliance of clan leaders. They have the common goal of driving GEEO from what they claim is their territory. I did some research, cross-referencing the archives and discovered that this leader is a former special ops veteran named Virgil Henry Johnson, and. . . " She paused. "So sorry, sir, I can see you're fading a bit. Just a couple of things before you go." She produced a penlight from her pocket and shone it back and forth a few times into each of his pupils. She seemed satisfied, muttering a barely audible, "Okay."

She picked up a pitcher of water on the bedside table and poured it into a glass. A straw was inserted and she lifted the glass toward Candler's head, coaxing the straw between his parched lips. "Here. You really need to hydrate. Good thing you woke up or we'd have to figure out a way to get fluids into you—there's not much here for doing IVs. So take as much as you can. Okay?"

As he was slowing sipping the water, she mused, "You know, sir. I've never actually met anyone with heterochromia before. You know, with your two different colored eyes?

"Back when I was a child living in the hills of Neola, I heard it has to do with being marked as special. Like you can see things from different points of view. Some say it's a gift really, and a rare one at that. So you may not feel up to the notion of being lucky or even blessed, but I think you could be, given the fact you have one green eye and one blue eye."

Eventually, he was able to down the full glass, feeling his scaly mouth and throat soften with saturation. He was even able to hold the second glass in hand. As the shrunken cells were drenched and revitalized, pressure built in his bladder, and he realized that somehow he had to get himself to a bathroom. He only had on boxers.

As if in answer to his unspoken plight, TO Renick touched his arm and, as before, her tone was solicitous but somewhat distant. "We'll see to your bathroom necessities just like we have all along. Just like with the IVs, they're short on catheters. They did have a quantity of blue pads and we've been able to keep you cleaned up. Lucky you!"

He flinched with the prospect of having been so exposed and could feel a flush of embarrassment.

"Oh, not to worry, sir. Taking care of the cleanup was done by one of the male attendants. Though I am well trained and adept at doing whatever, it seemed best to outsource the basic services." She smiled a half-crooked smile and patted his bare arm.

He felt a sudden urge to reach up and kiss her full on the lips, as his loins came to life and began pulsing with heat. He felt the urge but lacked any strength and could only manage a feeble wave of his topmost hand.

She gave his arm another little pat, while still smiling beatifically, and he noticed her other hand burrowing under his bedcovers. His nether region flared higher in anticipation until he felt a cold metal object being pressed against his thigh.

Here you are, sir, you've now graduated to your very own bedpan. Congratulations! I'll be checking back in just a while. Take your time." She briskly rose and disappeared. A door clicked shut. His heated libido diminished as quickly as it'd appeared. He was, however, able to muster enough focus to urinate. Afterward, he tried using his knee to push the partly filled bedpan away when it tilted over the edge of the bed and landed with a clatter on the hardwood floor.

Seeing the yellow puddle spreading across the floor, Candler tried to raise up on one elbow but once again his body faltered and he had to resume his supine position. The ceiling spun like a cartwheel. He could only grumble aloud, "Sonofabitch! Can't do a damned thing!"

In a few seconds, TO Renick appeared and calmly surveyed the mess. Amazingly, she sounded chipper. "Oh well, not to worry, sir. This is just temporary, and soon you'll be back to taking care of yourself." She quickly grabbed several dingy white towels and was on her knees mopping. "And don't worry about reports, sir. I filed the preliminaries with the admin. I've also drafted the detailed reports and, when you're able to, you can check them over."

Out of nowhere, Candler felt tears welling in his eyes and his throat tighten. This feeling of being so dependent and childlike had compromised his sense of rank and dignity. Yet, he was also humbled by the kindness of a woman he definitely admired but barely knew.

Rivulets of tears ran down his cheeks. He'd not cried in years, always the reserved one, the analytic one, the rock of reason, and now here he was reduced to bedpans and tears. He would have easily succumbed to self-pity, but he felt the comforting caress of a cool hand on his forehead and the brush of soft fabric wiping away his tears. "It's okay, sir. You'll be fine. You'll see. It will be okay."

He saw her hovering over him, her face just inches from his, almost floating there, floating like an angel. The visage began to ripple and fade but the feeling of being comforted by an angelic being persisted. All he could manage before slipping back into the deep abyss was a frail but heartfelt, "Thank you."

Chapter 32

All too Familiar
Morning, April 15, 2053

His next waking vision was by no means
heavenly. He awoke to a voice, a familiar voice, telling
him something about a mission. He squinted open an
eye to see who it was and saw the scarecrow face of
Art Jones just inches away. "Well, Greaves. Looks like
you really blew it this time. Yes sirree, you are definitely
out of the running for that upgrade. Now, didn't I warn
you about going beyond your limitations?"

Candler felt a flush of anger rising to his face as
his expression tightened into a scowl.

Jones seemed to take pleasure in this reaction.
"Oh, I see you might actually be understanding what I
am saying. Going by TO Renick's report, you got a very
nasty knock on the head. Really, Greaves, how could
you let those hooligan retros get the drop on you like
that?"

"Why are you here?" Candler croaked. His
throat was cotton dry and something like sandpaper
coated his tongue.

He glanced at a glass of water on the bedside
table but felt too weak to reach for it. Jones didn't seem
to notice. "Actually, Greaves, your little escapade has
cost us quite a bit in carbon units, not to mention the
loss of some very expensive electronic equipment. I'm
certain you'll be wanting to make up for this. TO

Renick says you should be on your feet in the next day or so. You'll have a huge mess to clean up here before you can return to Progress City, but don't worry, Greaves. RM Dirkson wants you to report to him immediately upon your return. For some reason, he has taken a shine to you. I'm sure he'll understand why you failed so miserably."

Jones sighed as if in sympathy. "Oh, well. . . In the meantime, I've been tasked with completing your failed mission in this backwater hellhole. We have different ways of getting the job done, you and I. You're very quick to offer the carrot and I, well. . . I find that the stick is more persuasive. Soooo, we've seen how your modus operandi has failed, haven't we? It's now my turn to demonstrate how to actually get things done in, well, let's just say, it's a more practical way. I'm sure you don't mind if I borrow Ms. Renick; she and I go back a long way, a long way."

Candler winced and Jones leaned closer as if in confidence. "You see, Greaves, I know how people work. I know what makes them come to terms. It won't be long before whoever is sending these seditious transmissions will be brought in, tagged and bagged. Oh yes, I know all about them and that Celi whoever who's putting them out. Soon as I'm done here, I'll be upgraded to living at Evergreen. And where will you be, Greaves?" Jones slowly wagged his head in mock pity.

He started to leave the room and was almost beyond the door when he turned to say. "Oh, Greaves, you have a water glass just beside the bed. I really think you should try to stay hydrated."

Then Jones was gone.

Chapter 33

Into the Wildlands
April 4, 2053

She'd gotten nearly all the way to the river
before realizing how turned around she was. *Lost! Hush
up, Celi, not lost, just a bit confused. I can always head for the
river and then backtrack up to Odyssey Creek where I know our
trail leaves off. Not lost!*

She felt the extra weight in her satchel from the
two squirrels she'd shot. Just one more, and then head
home, but she'd continued hunting for over an hour
and it seemed they'd all disappeared. The drizzle would
occasionally intensify and the sound of drops
drumming her broad-brimmed hat made it hard to pick
up any limb rat sounds. That's what Uncle Virgil called
squirrels.

Her hat and wet-shined rain slicker had kept
her dry and warm. She wore fingerless gloves for clean
handling of the crossbow and bolts. She'd started out
with six bolts and had busted one against a tree trunk
when her shot missed by a hair, clipped a branch and
hit the tree sideways. Her Pa would be mad, but she'd
find a way to explain. She tried to avoid the tangled
thickets of laurel—a course that put her on trails scuffed
by the deer and other creatures. After a few twists and
turns, everything looked the same. *Not lost! Just a little bit
confused.* She spied a great oak at the rim of a sink. She
thought the tree looked familiar. As she approached, a
noxious rancor invaded her nostrils. Though her
instincts told her to take flight, her curiosity led her to

the edge of the sink. Latching onto the oak with one hand and holding her breath, she peeked over the edge.

The head, or what remained of it, appeared first. Most of the skull was exposed but oddly, one ear was intact and lifelike. The antlers were huge so that Celi immediately knew this was no deer but an elk. She'd heard about the elk coming back but had never seen one or part of one, dead or alive. How had it been killed? A chill corkscrewed up her spine as she realized whatever had taken this huge creature might still be lurking about. Drawing back, she leaned against the tree trunk feeling its solidity, its long abiding strength. She set a bolt in the groove of her crossbow and switched off the safety. Her heart beat madly as she became hypersensitive to everything around her. She would sit and wait until it felt safe, all the while trying to ignore the offal of death that pooled the pit and censed the air around her.

Presently, there came a soft, nearly inaudible, rustling of leaves, a krisshhhh, too measured to be the effects of a random breeze or flurry of rain. The sound grew louder and she determined it came from above and behind her. A random thought, *Maybe the stench will drive it away. It? What is it?*

The pattering noise stopped. All was still. Then, it resumed again, louder, closer. Either it was a four-legged animal of unknown magnitude or two persons. Either way, she didn't want to be discovered. Again, the noise stopped as if whatever it was had caught her scent. *I'm being tracked. Hunted. How stupid can I be coming out here? Stupid!* She took as deep a breath as she dared and readied to fend off whatever or whoever was approaching. She'd wait until the last moment before it rounded the tree, then she'd swing around and face whatever was after her.

Finally, she couldn't stand it. She had to see what or who it might be. She slunk low as Uncle Virgil had taught her when spotting nearby game. The sounds stopped again. She waited. Silence. Not even a breeze or leaf drop. She wanted to scream, she wanted to run, she wanted. . . The noise picked up and drew closer. *Okay, now!*

She pivoted around the base of the tree with the crossbow raised and ready. As she did so, she bumped it against the tree trunk so hard that the bolt became unnotched, forward of the bowstring—a critical mishap. Worse than that, hardly a stone's toss away, she faced two grown men who immediately stopped and grinned at her. The grins were feral in nature, instinctive, not well meaning. The one on the right was a short mottle-faced fireplug-shaped male dressed in coveralls. Both he and his attire had seen better days. He regarded her with his head slung down and his milky eyes rolled forward reminding her of an old basset hound she'd seen once. Most unfortunately, she had seen the other man before. Dark features, coal-eyed, a sizable version (though not as broad) as his father. It was Carter Burkhart, leering at her and once again looking at her as if she'd make a fine meal.

He'd pulled out a long-barreled Colt revolver and aimed it at her almost playfully. He spit something brown onto the ground and grinned wider. "Say, Grady, looky, looky. What do we have us here?" He then acted spooked and widened his eyes. "Oh, look out, Grady.

She's aiming to shoot us." The stout little man cackled as he casually lifted his rifle so that it rested in the inside crook of his elbow. The barrel pointed toward Celi's midsection, even though she was partially obscured by the tree, she was exposed.

"Awww, now a little girl like you shouldna be out here in the wild all alone. And I doubt you're gonna get that arrow gun to shoot right since your little arrow's just lying in the groove." He took a step forward and his partner did the same. "Now, I do remember you. You live up in the third holler over, doncha? Kin to Virgil Johnson, right? Do you remember me, sweet thing?"

Celi pressed the stock into her shoulder and aimed for the younger Burkhart's center mass. She was shaking inside but managed to hold the weapon steady. "Stop or I'll shoot!" she tried to sound convincing.

Carter raised his hands up in mock surrender. "Hold on there, sweet pie. Even if that thing gets a shot off, do you really think you can nail both of us?" His voice changed to a syrupy tenor that made her skin crawl. "C'mon now, we can be real, real nice if you just put the bow down and be nice back to us. Ummmmm. Yes, that's it." He took several more steps forward and his pal, Grady, stepped off to the left and slowly began to arc his way to flank her. She'd have nowhere to go but over into the pit some thirty feet straight down.

The big man came to within spitting range. He smiled and in a falsetto sing-songed the words. "Here now, little kitty, little pussy, here now, put your little toy gun down and let's just be real nice." His eyes showed nothing but fiendish hunger and a twisted pleasure of having someone at his mercy—nearly.

Celi saw the short man still coming toward her from the side. Neither of them seemed intent on shooting her outright, right away. Carter also moved closer; his stink ranked so bad it overcame that of the dead elk. Death was in the air. Her future caved away. She pictured Gram worried sick, her Pa desperately trying to find her, Uncle Virgil too. They might never know what god-awful things happened to her.

No! Her finger moved. The cord slid along the grooved rail of her crossbow at blinding speed, catching the nock of the bolt along the way and slinging it forward in a straight trajectory toward Carter Burkhart's trachea where it collided with the soft cartilage, glanced slightly to the side, then severed the right carotid artery. A brilliant spray of oxygen-rich blood spewed forth, as the crow feather fletchings sank deep into the flesh.

Carter's knees buckled and he slumped down, sitting on his heels at first with an incredible look at Celi. Then his eyes rolled white and he toppled face-long into the soggy leaf fodder. The spurts of blood decreased as his heart failed.

Celi held her hand up to her mouth in horror. She'd never even thought to kill anyone. She spied the short man, Grady, hoping he might turn heel and run, but he watched his partner crumble and bleed with an odd air of curiosity. He just stood there watching. Finally, he turned his hangdog face toward her. "Well, I'll be. Ain't you a fuckin' wonder?" He regarded Celi with amusement. "You fuckin' kilt Carter Burkhart!" He even laughed a little.

"Well, missy, hats off to ya! I'm sure he never saw that comin'." He laughed again. "But you know what? I got this gun here . . . and this, too."

He drew a long knife and showed it to her. Leaning the gun against a tree, he came toward her with the knife. "Still looks like this ain't gonna be your day. Betcha I can get to you quicker than you can reload. Betcha I can. And now I'll have you all to myself." He crept closer, grinning with his rotten teeth.

Celi backed around the tree and crouched low. She had to think quickly. He was right. No way could she reload the bow. She could barely manage cocking it under ideal conditions. She grabbed a bolt anyway and held it tight in her fist. The first thing she saw of the man was his foot. She took the bolt in both hands and drove the point into the tongue of his boot.

The man yelled at the pain and thrust his knife forward barely missing her as she ducked out of the way. He yanked the arrow out of his foot with another yell and a string of curses. He stumbled slightly over the terrain. This gave her a notion.

"Hey! Come back around here, you little bitch!" She was agiler than he was, especially sporting a punctured foot. She kept circling around the tree without him catching her. It was definitely cat and mouse, and he only had to get it right once. At one point, she circled near the precipice. She let him catch sight of her, but this time she ducked just out of view leaving a bit of her sleeve showing. Sensing he was near to claiming his prize, he said, "I gotcha now. I gotcha!"

As he strode quickly around to catch her, she thrust her bow between his feet causing him to stumble forward near the very edge of the drop-off. He'd almost recovered when she came behind him and shoved with all her might. He tipped forward and toppled headlong, screaming, into the pit. She leaned over to see him fall directly upon the elk's antlers impaling himself through both legs and lower torso. He screamed horribly. He called for help and screamed some more.

An hour later, she'd found the familiar track and half-ran, half-jogged in desperate haste to get home before dark and before Gram got too sick with worry. She'd left a note on the mantle about going out to forage, but it said she'd be back before lunch. Gram might even come looking for her. *Oh God! Please stay home Gram. I'm coming. Coming!* She kept reliving the terrible events that hung fresh in her mind. It all happened pretty quickly, but her memory played it back in agonizingly slow motion. Carter Burkhart's black marbled eyes, the other man's voice, "I gotcha, now. I gotcha!" Then the man's screams as he lay twisting on the headdress of a once proud bull. She had neither the pluck nor the physical reserves to arm the crossbow and put the wretch out of his misery. It would be an easy shot. She could have used his gun or the other man's, but all she could do was run. Run away as fast and far as she could go.

In her life, she'd never dreamed of inflicting serious injury on anyone. There were scuffles with

Jordy and occasional male classmates; she'd given as well as she got, due to her tomboy nature. Now. . .she paused by a tree and braced herself as she heaved over to throw up for the third, maybe the fourth time. Hardly anything came. She wiped her lips and noted the bile on the back of her glove. *I didn't even bring the game home.* In her haste, she'd left the gunnysack of dead squirrels laying on the ground. Now, she had just two crossbow bolts and nothing food-wise to show for it but a trove of God-awful recollections she could never ever reveal, except maybe to one person. *You're a fool, Celi Pierce! A stupid, stupid fool for setting out into the wild on your own. Now, you see? You see what it got you?*

She felt the cold press of metal against her waist where the revolver she'd grabbed had rubbed her flesh raw. She tightened her grip on the stock of the short-barreled scattergun that the other man had left by the tree. *Well, I guess I got something to show, but I can't tell anyone about this either. I'll have to hide them somewhere safe, maybe in the root cellar or under the cabin.*

Chapter 34

Jones Does It His Way

As he left the building, Art Jones congratulated himself on how well things were working out. Dirkson had picked right. Greaves was just the kind of shill needed to make the operation, Jones' operation, succeed. Greaves' humiliating failure to penetrate into the nether regions of the hill country in pursuit of the Pierce girl along with the predictable reactions of the retro ruffians had worked out even better than planned.

Now, those slope-headed infidels have me to deal with, and they have no idea what's coming. It's the only thing they'll understand.

Jones strode outside to the courtyard where a convoy of vehicles awaited. He'd commandeered part of Greaves' crew and added in his own security unit–a strike force known for their deadly cleanup operations.

It was the same strike force who'd been involved in putting down the Swain County food rebellion. Local retros had taken over the food distribution center to protest the dwindling food distributions. After negotiators failed to end the occupation, the SFs were sent in to restore order. Jones was their commanding officer. One ultimatum was issued. When the occupiers refused to comply, an all-out assault occurred. The building was hit from all sides with incendiary missiles. No one escaped, the structure burned to the ground. The result was fourteen dead retros, all unarmed. Collateral casualties also included several women and children. As a kicker, all future food distributions were redirected to more cooperative regions.

The news of this event never came out in the GEEO-sponsored media outlets. Rumors had circulated among the various departments about the Swain County Massacre but no inquest was held, and there were no follow-up investigations.

Other similar incidents seemed to follow the course of Jones and his specialized unit. It came to a point that, if Jones and his unit even appeared in a troubled district, their presence alone would quell almost any protest or uprising. In the rare instance where the retros persisted, it always ended the same—with total annihilation and destruction. He would fly the black flag once again.

Jones reviewed his convoy. A large framed man dressed in battle fatigues stepped forward and saluted. "Ready to deploy, sir!"

Jones nodded. "Do we have the tracking units up and running?"

"Yes, sir! TO Renick is on board and has plotted our track."

"Ahhhh, yes, Ms. Renick." He pursed his lips and nodded.

The sergeant noted a certain familiarity in Jones' voice. "Is that a problem, sir?"

Jones' face cracked a slight smile. "Not at all, sergeant. Not at all. And our first waypoint is?"

"Where Agent Greaves first encountered the retros, er. . . the insurgents, sir."

"Very well. Then let's get moving!" Jones had begun to clamber aboard the second vehicle–the one with the most armor plating. He abruptly turned around and called after the sergeant. "Are the prisoners in place, sergeant?"

"Yes, sir! In the back of the third van, sir."

"Then let's move–we need to make the first waypoint by mid-morning. This will be a day of reckoning, sergeant!" Jones headed for the van.

His sergeant didn't know what "a day of reckoning" meant, but he was looking forward to the hunt, and most of all, the kill.

Chapter 35

The Ultimatum

The convoy arrived at the waypoint just prior to 0950. The spot was just as TO Renick had reported, a choke point where vehicles were obliged to slow to a crawl in order to negotiate the obstacles in the roadway.

The convoy slowed to a stop. Jones barked into his earpiece mike for everyone to remain seated in their respective vehicles. After a five minute wait, he instructed the driver of the lead van and the sergeant to deploy and start surveying the densely covered hillside above them with IR binoculars, marking locations of any warm signatures.

After another five minutes, an arrow sped past the two men and lodged in a nearby tree. It had the same warning message as the one mentioned in TO Renick's report—a warning to turn around and leave.

Jones keyed his headpiece. "Sergeant, do you have anyone on your scope?" He was referring to the heat detection optics as well as visual.

"Yes, sir! At least four, perhaps another two thermal, positioned from our bearing at about eight and nine o'clock."

"Well, well!" Jones was excited. He grabbed a megaphone from the console and opened the door to step onto the running board. He faced the hillside and keyed the megaphone.

"We have received your warning. We have come here to issue you our own warning. First, if you make any move to attack this convoy, we will take immediate countermeasures." Jones motioned to the soldiers in the third van. The van's backdoor opened and a soldier emerged with two hand-bound and hooded figures. One was slight in frame—likely a woman; the other had the stature of a child.

Jones stepped onto the ground and walked to the back of the van. He nodded and the hoods were ripped off to reveal a tousled dark-haired woman, and a dirty-faced lad who seemed to be having a very hard time breathing. Jones regarded the woman with malevolent glee. "All right, if you want to live, I want you to shout out your name, your full name." The woman looked around in helpless bewilderment, appearing as if she'd just stepped out of a cave into the sun.

Jones approached and grabbed her lower jaw, wrenching it toward his own menacing face. He breathed words into her face. "Like we agreed, if you don't cooperate you'll see your son go first, slowly begging for mommy to save him. Then it will be your turn. You'll be begging too. Begging to *die*!" He shoved her head back and painfully grabbed a hank of her hair. "Now, are you going to do as I say? Or not?" She attempted to nod.

"Then, say it!" Jones commanded as he thrust the megaphone in front of her face.

The woman spoke in a high-pitched warble. "My name is Estelle Pierce."

"Say it again, louder!" Jones spurred.

"Estelle Pierce."

Jones leaned into her ear. "And who is your husband. Say who your husband is."

"My husband is Ben Pierce." Her voice echoed up through the folds of the hollow.

"And tell them what you told me, who is your daughter?" She seemed to waver until Jones jerked hard on her hair. He prompted "My daughter is. . . "

"My daughter is Cecilia Pierce."

"And where are you from? Say it!"

"I am from Clay County, near Meadowbridge."

While this was going on, the boy continued gasping for air and crying for his mommy.

Jones shouted at him. "Shut up, you little shit, or I'll shut you up." TO Katrelle Renick appeared at the backdoor. She'd been riding shotgun in the third van.

She flashed Jones a hard look and said, "I'll handle him, sir." Her voice carried a distinct tone of sarcasm that didn't get past Jones. She placed her arms around the lad. He began to calm down.

I'll handle her later, he thought. He returned his attention to the task.

He aimed the megaphone toward the hillside. "We know you're up there, you hill jacks, you bogs and bohunks. Your lame attempts to disrupt this district are over. Do you understand? We tried to offer a simple solution a few days ago, but you attacked our envoy. Make one move toward us and you'll see this woman executed on the spot along with her air-sucking brat.

"That's our first warning. Our next order of business is an ultimatum." His voice became condescending, pedantic. "That means you pig fuckers have to do something. If you don't, then we teach you a lesson, a very painful lesson."

He gestured toward the captives. The woman was wide-eyed with terror and confusion. The boy had settled down as Katrelle stroked his hair. "You see these two former members of your community? You know them? Relatives of yours? Fruits of your family tree that doesn't fork?" He laughed at his own attempt at humor.

"Well, you have until noon tomorrow to send Ben Pierce and his undocumented daughter, Cecilia Pierce, into Madison, the town center, or else the blood of these two will be on your heads. Do you understand? On your heads!"

He scanned the hillside, looking for any hostile reaction. It was dead quiet. He spoke again. "We're leaving now! You have barely twenty-four hours to comply. . . or else! And if you try anything between now and then, these two are finished." He lowered the megaphone and spoke into his earpiece radio. "Sergeant, let's leave them with something extra to chew on."

Sergeant Mitchell replied with gusto. "At the ready, sir!"

Jones was making his way back to his van as he caught the soldier's attention and waved him over for a private word. "Sergeant, wait until we're all turned around. I'll give the signal."

"Sir!"

Mitchell grabbed a long container from the back of the van and told the driver to turn the van around. He set the case on his lap and unlatched the lid that was marked, SCHEDULE 1 SENFAS. He extracted a large-bored gun with a laser-mounted scope. He removed one of the magazines clipped to the inner lid, tore off the protective red cap and shoved it into the breech. There was a loud clack as the bolt carriage was racked and released. He closed the case and set it down between the front seats.

All of the vans had turned around by then. He heard Jones say, "Whenever you're ready, sergeant, light 'em up!"

Mitchell opened his door, placed the bulk of the weapon on the top of the doorframe and quickly acquired his first target. "Fire in the hole!" he shouted and immediately fired off a series of rounds approximating the locations where the infrared scope had indicated warm bodies. The rifle blasted out ten rounds in a matter of seconds, each round tracing its trajectory onto the hillside where it exploded on impact into a small yellowish cloud.

He thought he heard someone on the hill shout, "Gas!" By that time, they were already putting a good distance between themselves and the target area.

"Any hits, sergeant?" Jones' voice came through his earpiece.

"The hillside was covered, sir. I'm sure we got some contact." What they'd just deployed was a derivation of sulfur mustard, a lightly calibrated dose actually, but immediately effective in producing massive painful skin blisters. Anyone breathing in the material would potentially choke to death from the internal swelling of their esophageal tissue. If they got an eyeful, it resulted in a searing pain followed by blindness.

"Excellent!" Jones effused. Visions of grimy hill jacks falling to the ground choking and writhing in pain tokened deep, nearly erotic, satisfaction. He slapped his knee and gloated, "Hah! That'll teach those retros who's boss around here! Right?" Jones looked over at his driver.

The driver, a member of Candler's original crew, spoke stoically, "Well, sir, I'm sure they learned something."

Chapter 36

Willing but Weak

Around midday, Candler was able to weave his way to the john and back to bed. The vertigo seemed to be lessening and he could sit up without the room spinning. An attendant appeared, and he was disappointed it wasn't Katrelle, TO Renick. Instead, it was another tech on his team, J.D. Simms.

"Where's TO Renick?" Candler inquired.

"She's on patrol with Agent Jones, sir," said J.D. flatly. "They left early this morning with the boy and his mother."

He looked sharply at Simms. "What boy, what mother?"

"Sorry sir, I thought you knew since Jones had been here and. . ." he stammered, "Well, it is a need-to-know situation, sir."

"Well, TO Simms," Candler countered, "I NEED to know. What boy and woman are you referring to?"

There was a brief silence. Simms was weighing the matter. After all, Candler was his original team leader and they'd been together on numerous field missions. Besides, he never much cared for Jones. No one did.

"It was the Pierce woman and her son."

Candler couldn't recollect the name, "Who?"

"Agent Jones had triangulated the source of the seditious transmits and found the most likely persons involved. Jones tracked their family background and the mother and son are relatives who had come to PC several years ago."

"But why did he bring them out here?" As soon as he'd asked the question, Candler knew the answer. "For bait!" He swung his legs over and his bare feet met the cold floor. "That's a violation of Citizens' Precept Fourteen—there's no way Jones can get away with that!"

"Apparently, he can, sir. Agent Jones claimed he had a warrant, signed by RM Dirkson himself giving him authority to take any and all necessary measures to resolve the crisis. He cited the EPA."

The Emergency Powers Act had been invoked. Candler was stunned. According to code, the EPA was used only in the direst of situations. How could this situation have risen to such an extreme level of concern? It didn't make sense. His head began to throb in tandem with each heartbeat. He felt a wash of nausea pass through his gut.

"Where did Jones go?" he asked Simms.

"Back up the way we went, a couple days ago." Simms seemed to struggle. "Sir?"

Candler looked at him. There was a catch in the TO's voice.

"I think you should know, sir. Along with Agent Jones and TO Renick, there's an SF Unit."

Not good, not good at all. The Strike Force was reserved for combatting violent aggressors, terrorists and heavily armed insurgents. The riders that he and TO Renick had encountered were at best lightly armed and certainly not barbaric enough to justify calling forth an SF unit. These units were made up of hardened soldiers, shock troops really, who were armed with devastating weaponry including shoulder-fired missiles, fifty caliber canon, and incendiary thermite grenades.

Candler rallied his energies and made his body stand. He was still in his t-shirt and briefs. "I need my clothes, Simms! We have to get to Jones before. . . before. . ."

Simms observed his boss's eyes rolling upward to where only the whites appeared, his body swayed and knees began to fold. He grabbed Candler under both arms and felt him become dead weight. He struggled to get him back down on the cot.

"Sorry, sir. I don't think you're going anywhere anytime soon."

It was the oddest sensation. Candler felt separated from his body. He saw himself collapsing, saw Simms lifting the body and heaving it like a sack of flour back on the cot.

He tried to make himself wake up by mentally screaming "Get up! You have to get up!"

Instead, he felt the weight of his body wrap around his consciousness like a chain and drag him down into a dark abyss. His last thought popped to the surface–*Katrelle.*

Then nothing.

Chapter 37

Katrelle Shakes Loose

As the convoy rolled away, Katrelle thought she heard several rapid-fire explosions. *Surely, they wouldn't just fire randomly into the hillside.* She looked back to see yellow smoke clouds drifting down the slope. *Oh no! They've used some kind of gas!*

She closed her eyes and tried not to imagine the effects. Yet, images arose of bared skin boiling with blisters, eyes dissolving into bloody sockets, lungs cauterized with each intake of breath. She'd seen these horrific injuries in training films taken from vintage war documentaries. Never would she imagine such weapons would be sanctioned for use by any civilized society. Those people on the hillside were *her* people. She likely knew some of them or their kin. In fact, it could *be* her kin up there writhing on the ground, screaming in agony. Cousins Dan Paul, Cassie Mae or Uncle Elvert, how could she know they weren't part of the resistance? *God knows what Jones has planned for the woman and the boy. What have I become a part of here? This is madness. Evil!* She caught sight of her reflection in the blacked out screen of her monitor. It stared back at her and shook its head as if to say, "Is *this* what you have become, Katrelle Renick? Is *this* your new normal?"

Nothing seemed real–Jones holding hostages, his threats, his ultimatum and his use of the Strike Force thugs. Now, blasting the hillside with gas? *I trained to protect and serve the global community not to seek and destroy resistant primitives!* Our mission guidelines say we are to use positive incentives. She'd heard rumors about how Jones preferred coercion to persuasion, but for the sake of Gaia, this wasn't right. She would do some digging once they returned to base. For now, she needed to reorient. *Focus, Katrelle!*

Her van had become the lead vehicle. Seated at her station in the back section, she kept dividing her attention between the tracking scopes and the two hostages. She'd come aboard as a techie—not for security. Yet, her situational awareness sounded internal alarms. Having just witnessed an awful scene, she maintained a close watch on the boy in particular. Their hoods had not been replaced. *Jones just needed them for shock value.* They were both still hand-bound with flexi cuffs. Katrelle debated whether to cut their cuffs or not. She decided it best to leave them on and not have to explain to a raving, make that *raging*, lunatic Jones why the cuffs were removed, but her main concern was with the boy.

The mother looked dazed with shock and her face shone bone white. The boy was beginning to wheeze and gulp air like a landed fish. The mother seemed totally oblivious to her son's condition. Katrelle called out, "Miss Pierce, Hey! Miss Pierce!"

The woman began mumbling about her hair and being hungry, and cold. Katrelle reached over and shook the woman's knee while shouting, "Miss Pierce!" Then finally, "Estelle!" This barely got her attention. The woman's eyes wavered as if looking for a distant object. Katrelle leaned in close. "Your son, Estelle, he's not breathing like he should."

"My son?" She sounded surprised. "Ohhhhh, Jordy. . ." Katrelle saw the woman lapsing back into insensibility. She grabbed the woman's head so they met eye to eye. "Your son, Jordy, is sick. He can't breathe! He's dying!" Katrelle was about to shake the woman's head like a maraca. The woman blinked several times. Her brown eyes widened with a semblance of awareness. "Jordy has asthma. Pocket. . . puffer in his pocket."

Katrelle released the woman's head, which sagged as soon as she let go. No matter. There was a bulge in the boy's left front pocket. He was actually fumbling for it himself; his flex-cuffed hands seemed to have gone numb. He was now really struggling for air. Katrelle reached in the pocket and extracted a small metal canister. She flipped the hinged cover off with her thumb and inserted the nozzle into the child's open mouth. His lips were turning a bluish cast. Though panicked and fading in consciousness, the boy's mouth reflexively locked onto the nozzle. She depressed the top plunger three times then waited for a few seconds. Nothing. She repeated, hazarding the chance that he would overdose. Finally, he was able to suck in a shallow breath and then gradually began breathing deeper and deeper.

Meanwhile, the mother, her head still drooping and bobbing as they jostled down the road, was alternating between jags of crying, mumbling about her hair and being either cold or hungry. She never looked over to see what was happening with her son. *Hmmmm. That's odd. Well, it must be the shock or Jones drugged her with something. I'd put nothing past that sick bastard. Nothing!*

The boy was back to breathing in and out in a normal cadence. The onrush of oxygen had the effect of loosening his tense body. He slumped toward Katrelle. His eyes were closing and he was about to tip forward. She removed her field jacket, knelt toward him and laid him back against the corner where the seat met the side panel. As she did so, she placed her wadded jacket under his head and covered him with a poncho from her rucksack. His lips were losing their blue tinge. The little veins in his pale face were receding. He was a lovely child, so young and innocent.

\#

I was innocent once. Just a little older than Jordy when we came to the town center and applied to become citizens. My brothers, mother and me.

Her mother held out as long as she could after her father's fatal accident at the Cooper Mine. They'd quickly become destitute and dependent on government credits. Finally, Nelle Renick decided it best for all of them to live in the population settlement of Progress City. The entire family became "wards of the state" and it took only a few days to approve their applications and transport them to the Assessment and Placement Center. The boys were young and, thus, relegated to their mother's care. Nelle had skills ranging from quilt making, hooking rugs, mending clothes and animal husbandry. She was sent to one of the GEEO farms along with Katrelle's siblings, who were to be laborers at the farm as well. Little hands and fingers were highly prized in organic farming.

Ten-year-old Katrelle remained behind to train

at the Institute for Global Security.

IGS had two major divisions: cyber network security and enforcement. They needed to keep their forces diversified and reflect the ideals of a socially just society. She was intelligent and impressionable, as well as petite at that age but quick and strong. She tested exceptionally well for both cyber security and enforcement. Due to her tomboyish proclivities, she excelled at martial arts (the more robust the better), and weaponry of all sorts. She earned expert marksman at age twelve. It was no surprise since she'd been handling a twenty-two rifle since age eight, and shooting still targets was nothing compared with pegging squirrels on the run and birds on the fly. She was also able to cross-train in cyber security and, as a result, graduated with high honors in both categories.

Her sadness and anger at the losses in her life were channeled by her handlers into a belief that she'd been saved and was now responsible for a whole community of people and beyond that, to the wellbeing of a beleaguered planet. People who cared for the Earth were the ones who really mattered. She owed them her loyalty. In turn, she was occasionally sent to classrooms where she presented herself as an example of what a former outlander could accomplish in serving the order. If she performed well, she'd have the privilege of occasional visits with her mother and siblings.

Over the years at the academy, Katrelle had learned to survive by locking others out. She'd hardened herself into a monk-like resolution that attachment to others only brought pain. Consequently, she'd resolved to keep her distance and pour all of her energy into being the best soldier and cyber tech she could be. If the authority had plans for her to be matched and mated, as it did for some she'd known, she never heard it. Her goal was to become so damned good they'd never consider shifting such a useful asset into producing offspring. She'd just turned twenty-five, was in her physical prime, and at the top of her game. Her service record was not just spotless; it was outstanding!

Oh, yes. There'd been compromises. She hadn't escaped the fact that she was a female in a mostly all-male corps. She'd been taken at an early age in more ways than one. She went back to her first encounter with Jones. Art Jones was a field agent, a Green Level. She'd just come online as an intern. Jones spotted her and brought her along on several forays into the hill country, forays that included perverted and sadistic liaisons. Jones had his way with her.

Katrelle had heard rumors of Jones' proclivities. On their first encounter, she learned of them directly. Her psychological armor insulated her from being totally victimized. It was ironic that even at the supposedly tender age of eighteen, she could have crushed Jones in so many ways physically and psychologically, but knew that would derail her intended career and likely end with her execution or a lifelong sentence to a penal colony. The admin were quick to protect their own.

Even so, she wondered how Jones had made it so far without someone higher up seeing at least a hint of his sick and evil character. He covered well to a point, but his foaming fits of rage were like seizures, and could be triggered by the least little thing. He seemed to manage them in public, but not so in private. Katrelle determined that these fits were the chinks in Jones' armor, and she set out to exploit them, to free herself from his sadistic bondage.

She'd not been with a man until Jones. It was awful and all too frequent. These intimate encounters revealed his violently abusive traits, the kind that would cause him to fly off into fits of foaming mad dog rage. One learned to make themselves scarce any time his left eyelid began to twitch—a sure signal that an episode was about to erupt. Jones got his jollies from inflicting pain–not exclusively the physical sort. He'd become adept at delving into his victim's psyche, finding the weak points in their personality and watching them squirm as he gnawed away at their inner foibles like a jackal seeking marrow.

On what would be their last liaison, Katrelle deployed a scheme that she hoped would free her from such hellish encounters. During these encounters, her keen eyes had spotted several cameras, likely wireless, dotted about the office. The large sofa, where she'd first been taken, was the focal point. *That perverted SOB; he must get off replaying his conquests. It's like being virtually raped over and over.*

Then she realized an opportunity to turn the tables. It would be easy to intercept the recordings and then transmit to her personal lap desk, which she further programmed for an array of contingencies. It was the contingencies that would make Jones come to heel. At least, she hoped his sense of self-preservation would trump his rabid insanity. Dealing with psychopaths was tricky business.

She went to Central Cyber Distribution and procured an array of electronics including a signal scanner, a code reader/repeater and a relay box. On the requisition form, under intended use, she wrote, "Security Analysis—Bug Scan." *That should be generic enough–but not too vague.*

During their next encounter, she recorded one of his most outrageous episodes. As anticipated, it began with another brutal bout of foreplay and Jones, true to form, initiated their encounter by roughly grabbing her, shaking her tiny frame, and painful squeezes of her unbared breasts. He practically threw her onto the large sofa, but before he got himself excited enough to completely ravage her, she managed to put him in a carotid restraint hold otherwise known as a sleeper. She let him fall back on the sofa.

She dressed quickly, scanned Jones' microchipped neck with the repeater device, then using the code unlocked the entry door, and left the office. It was after hours. The secretary had left. *Time for me to head home, too!* On the way, she was expecting a call back any moment after Jones came to, but it never happened.

The next day, Katrelle spent the morning in Data Central. Her level of certification allowed her access to several major feeds. After causing a brief downtime in the system and as the system rebooted, she uploaded a chain of protocols and scheduled events. Redundancy was key. It was like hacking in and strategically placing viruses and Trojans that would only multiply if deleted. She even named her mini-Trojan Hydra. Upon leaving the secure area, she noted Jones had delivered several urgent messages on her lap desk– the final one demanding she report to his office immediately.

As she entered Jones' office, she heard the door lock behind her. He was standing behind his desk with both hands pressed flat on the surface as if just completing some form of modified push–up. He'd stripped off his shirt to expose what he fancied as his taut torso. Actually, his scrawny physical frame was underdeveloped in all areas. If he'd expected some swooning reaction from her, it was not forthcoming. She only stared blankly as if to say, "Well, what do you want this time?"

He cocked a deferential smile. "You really shouldn't keep your boss waiting. I've been trying to reach you all morning, and what, by the way, have you been up to that was so important that you ignored my messages?" He stood erect placing his bony hands on his narrow hips as if he were posing for her benefit.

She felt no need to apologize. She told him flatly, "I was in the research unit, when the power surge zapped my hand desk. Everyone there had the same issue. It took time to bring it back online and recover the data, and I assisted others in doing the same."

She knew he knew where she'd been. The research unit was where she spent a lot of her time, and his tracking of her embedded RFD chip would confirm what she'd said. The only variance from the truth was that she'd cause the surge herself to allow her private access to the records and to insert a series of links and automated protocols.

"Well, my dear, you need to be careful about your priorities. After our rendezvous last evening, I was most disappointed that I'd awakened to find you absent."

She felt a pang of anxiety. *Did he know? Had he somehow anticipated her actions and brought in a team of techies to thwart her plan?*

"Well, can you explain yourself? And also explain how my office security system, my own minicams, had a gap of missing data, specifically, during the time of our last appointment?"

She noted it odd that Jones seemed to have no memory of the actual episode of her rendering him unconscious. At least, he acted as such, perhaps to preserve a very warped sense of superiority in all things.

Jones had rounded the desk and was advancing toward her. She then saw he was dressed only in his boxer shorts. He'd grabbed something from his desk drawer and held it in his right hand. She could tell from the two metal prongs protruding from the device and a faint humming sound that it was some kind of Taser.

"Well? Are you going to answer me or do you need a little prod? Hey, now, don't look so shocked. Ha! Get it? Shocked? This could be fun!" He'd come closer. She had to fight the urge to lash out and render him insensate—or worse. Instead, she held her position and spoke.

"I have the recording. It's completely embedded in the main system and coded with automated protocols. Would you like to see it?"

Jones froze in place as Katrelle drew forth her hand desk and held it before him. It played out all the sick lurid details, including the audio of Jones' vociferous attack and Katrelle's pleading for him to stop. It was damning evidence of a violent rape. She'd edited out the final part where she'd neutralized him with the sleeper hold–one didn't need to see Jones carry through his attack–it was all too obvious what got him excited.

As she showed him the recording, it triggered his left eye to twitch, the first wave of vitriol to spew in her direction, with his face reddening every second. He came at her with the Taser. She deftly swept it out of his hand with an inside crescent kick. He then tried to snatch her lap desk away. She leaped sideways and grabbed his boney hand, twisting it back toward the wrist. He howled in pain. She forced him to kneel. Releasing the hold, she stepped back and sat down on top of his desk, a gesture she hoped would impart her total disdain and superior advantage.

"Now, you listen to me, you sick fuck. You know I have high-level training in cyber security. If anything happens to me, if you even make another threat, the video will go viral in an instant and not only hit everybody's desk pads and hand desks, but the public jumbo screens as well. If you try to take me out or make me your captive, an auto-drive program will release the video automatically. Once again, your vile habits will be made public. I'm sure your enemies, and you do have them, would love to see you go down in flames."

She explained this to him in such a dead serious tone that his reddened face paled, his shaking turned to trembling. His hands, poised to throttle her, instead raised in mock surrender and he said, "Okay, my dear, you've got me. I always knew you were a smart girl. So what's next? A raise in pay? Something nice for your family?"

In fact, she felt very comfortable blackmailing this pig bastard. She actually relished the situation. Her extortive demand was two-fold.

First, he would release her for immediate transfer and second, she'd never be assigned as his subordinate ever again. He actually laughed sardonically and then agreed to the terms. She sensed he was formulating some trickery.

She closed the distance between them so rapidly that he actually flinched. Leaning over him, she spoke into his ear as if sharing an intimate secret. "And, asshole. If I even get a hint that you're pulling strings to mess with me or my kin, you're so done. Get that? Done."

Jones grimaced and gnashed his teeth into a semblance of a smile. "Of course, my dear, but you know how I'll miss you." His breath smelled like rotten fish.

She pondered how an elbow strike at just the right angle would send his teeth to the back of his throat, but recognized that Jones was goading her to make just such a move. She did move. It was a quick turn and seven steps to the door. It unlocked as she approached. She'd programmed his office security system to operate on her RFD signal. "In case you were wondering, I've sequenced the system to respond to my code as well. So much for your lock-tight security!" She swept out of the door and just as it was about to close, she stuck her head back in and added another perquisite.

"Oh, one more thing. If I get even a snippet of a rumor that you're still out there trolling for victims to molest, you are finished! Clear on that? Finished!"

Jones had managed to stand himself straight, his good hand cradling the injured one. Teeth appeared between his lips forming a death's–head smile. "So sensitive! You know, dear little Kay, you were my favorite toy. I will so miss you."

Once again, Jones was fishing for a reaction. Katrelle's parting shot as she slipped out the door was, "You better *keep* missing me or it's all over for you, you sick bastard!"

As she closed the door and walked past the secretary's desk, the middle-aged woman was staring at her in amazement. She must've overheard the bits of conversation that flitted out the partially open door including the "you sick bastard" part. Katrelle supposed she'd been deeply offended by such flagrant derogatory epithets hurled at her boss, but as she

walked past the desk she heard the secretary whisper–
as if speaking only to herself–the word, "Finally!"

It had been seven years since she and Jones had
any interaction. She kept the incriminating video on
permanent standby realizing that, as Jones climbed the
ladder, the evidence in the video might be diminished
as he attained enough power and influence to override
its impact. Several months back there'd been a brief
prelude of Jones flexing his prowess at the Springs
resort where one evening he'd drunkenly started to
accost her, but his intentions were thwarted by
extenuating circumstances.

She'd not had any further dealings with him
until he'd unexpectedly burst into the Madison Town
Center and commandeered her services. It was his way
of letting her know she had nothing on him he couldn't
contravene. He was nearly at the apogee of power and
influence. There were rumors that he was next in line
to become a regional manager once RM Dirkson was
promoted. She knew the day would likely come when
he would be bulletproof. Knowing Jones, his first move
would be to beat and ravage her for old time's sake.
Then having recollected her, he'd go after her family,
bit by bit, tearing her life to shreds. The pain she
suffered would be the pain he enjoyed best.

The instant Jones laid hands on her, she'd kill
him. Suffocation, a blow to the heart that an examiner
might miss, an extended arm lock closing off the
carotid arteries, a lot of options there. Then she'd need
to find a way to take herself out because the
defamatory evidence on Jones would be automatically
unleashed as promised, and the images of Jones'

lathered lunacy would be released for all to see, which would result in such scandal that the admin would try to brush the entire incident under the carpet, no doubt necessitating her death. She could only hope taking herself out of the picture first would save her mother and brothers from any retaliation.

Was it a perfect plan? No. So many variables. *Hey*, she remembered one of her favorite trainer's frequent quips, *a good plan today beats a perfect plan tomorrow.* She surveyed the scene before her–the young boy asleep on her jacket, the babbling mess of a woman across from her, and images on the tracking screen showing mass movement of blips in their direction. *Whatever happens, I'll not likely even have a tomorrow.*

She recalled her statement at the Cross Creek standoff just days before—that it was as good a day to die as any. *Well, today might be even better. So be it!*

Chapter 38

Escape and Pursuit
Evening, April 14, 2053

According to her makeshift plans, a rapid-fire series of tasks needed doing. After she returned the cellblock key to the sec sarge, Katrelle called Jones on his private channel. "Art Jones here. What is it?" he snapped.

"TO Renick, just now getting done with the two detainees and need more time to prep a report and get washed up."

Jones' tone shifted from irritated to oozy. "We have the entire evening, my dear. Take your sweet time." As an afterthought, he threw in, "Just know that if you decide to carry through with your previous little plan to release the recordings, it will have no effect. Blackmail is a very serious crime, you know, and I'd hate to hear of something happening to your mother and her bumpkins."

She purposefully hesitated, then spoke quietly. "I understand. I'll be at your door by 1900."

"Ahhhhhh yes, it's been so, so long since our last rendezvous. We've got a lot of catching up to do, my dear." He clicked off.

Yes. There is that. She shuddered. Then she thought of her mother and her nearly full-grown brothers, still at the work farm. *The only real solution is to kill him. Then me. Then the tapes will surface and if the admin has any integrity left, they'll leave my family out of this.*

Another stream of thought eddied into her conscience. *What about the Pierce woman and her son? You can't very well help them if you've offed yourself. Right now, no one has checked on them and begun to stand guard. No one's discovered the half-latched door I'd left for them. Now's the time!*

Right! Think, Kay! She began to formulate and assess. Her solution was to get the mother and son out ASAP, find the renegades, turn the captives over to them and persuade them to let her return. If the timing were right, she'd then present herself to Jones and go from there, but she had to do some digging first and, if possible, inform Candler about what was really going on. She had the feeling all along they'd been set up. Jones had shown up way too quickly. The entire so-called mission stank.

She allotted herself twenty minutes. After locating a vacant terminal in the records room, she began digging and sifting. The access codes allowed her to burrow deep into the encrypted archives and inter-office communiqués. Within five minutes, she had the answer to the real purpose of Jones' mission. *Candler has to be told about this. After all, he's been kept as much in the dark as anyone. He deserves to know we were just expendable pawns. They expected us to fail. In fact, wanted us to.*

She posted a coded message to Greaves, then cleared and shut down the screen. After sneaking down the hall to Candler's room, she discovered him soundly asleep. *Probably best, there's no time for explaining all this.* She scribbled a note and stuffed it under his pillow. He never stirred. She noticed his face was not as pallid as before. *Looks like he's gonna be okay.*

She spied the black case containing his lap desk on the top shelf of the open door locker. *Too easy to steal.* Then remembering that the table beside Candler's bed had a particularly fussy drawer, which was hard to open and close, she patiently worked the drawer out, inserted the lap desk and gradually pushed it shut. As she made to leave, she paused a moment looking down at her boss. She'd come to respect, even admire, Candler Greaves. He'd always been kind, awkward and bureaucratic, by the book, but he still looked out for his people. As she left, she silently wished him a good life.

Nearing the stockroom, she caught sight of First Sergeant Mitchell. He was heading down the hall just ahead of her but then sidetracked off to a room they called the armory. Fortunately, he did not hear her. She sidled past the door to the armory and quickly slipped down the hall to the stockroom.

A few moments and a hallway later, she entered the vaulted chamber and immediately spied Jordy kneeling by his mother who lay on her side in a quasi-fetal position. As she came near the enclosed cell, she heard him saying, "Mommy, wake up. Please wake up. That lady left the door open and we gotta get out of here." He gently jostled her shoulder. "Please, Mommy!"

This little guy doesn't miss much. He saw how I left the doors and thinks it's up to him to get them out of here. He's not just tough; he's a smart one.

Sensing her approach, the boy turned around, his face at first fearful but then seeing Katrelle, he half-smiled in relief, "It's you! Are you gonna help Mommy and me?"

"Shhhh. I'm going to try, Jordy. We don't have much time. Here, put these on." She had purloined the smallest camo coats she could find from the makeshift ready room along with two sidearms and some ammo.

He pointed toward the mattress. "She won't wake up. If we could just get her to stand, she might come out of it." He shook her shoulder more forcefully. "Mommy, we have to get out of here. Get up, please!"

Estelle Pierce roused enough to open her eyes and survey her situation. There was Jordy, dirty-faced and pleading with her to do something, to wake up. Yes, she needed to wake up. It was all a bad dream. In just a moment, she'd wake up and be back in her own clean bed. In just a moment. . . her eyes started to close when hands shook her. Then, another person in the dream hovered over her, a dark-haired girl who looked vaguely familiar.

"Ms. Pierce, we need to get you up. You and Jordy have to get out of here. Please, Ms. Pierce, try to clear your mind. We need to move now!" She felt the girl's hands slipping under her arms. It all seemed so real. She shook her head trying to wake up to a new reality. Nothing changed.

She felt herself being stood up, something being slid over her arms and fastened around her body.

Oh God. This is it. This is it. Memories of the past thirty-six hours came flooding back. Their apprehension, being locked in a room, a scary man asking them questions, then he stuck her with a needle, a long ride in the back of a van, the hood over her head and what she'd heard the scary man say.

The shock of realization helped bring her around. She felt herself being led through several doors and then into a cold rain. "Where are you taking me?" She'd found her voice and repeated louder. "Where are you taking me?"

A hand covered her mouth and a voice whispered. "Shhhhh. Please, Ms. Pierce. You have to be quiet. We're going to the woods right now. We're getting away from the bad men, Ms. Pierce. They intend to hurt you and Jordy. We have to keep moving. Please be quiet. Let's move!" She felt the hand move from her mouth to just behind her elbow pressing her forward.

"But I don't like the woods. I wanna be home. Home back in the city. Home." Again, the hand came over her mouth. "Ms. Pierce, Estelle, please be quiet. If we're caught out here, we'll all be killed. Killed, Estelle. You, Jordy, me, Killed. Will you please, please, be quiet?"

Estelle nodded. They passed through a service gate and into the dark streets furtively picking their way toward the edge of what remained of the town. Katrelle hoped she could quickly locate the renegade locals, turn the escapees over and then hustle back to the compound before her absence was discovered.

Instead, she heard a bustle of activity coming from the town center compound. Men shouting, engines revving and movement of vehicles in all directions, including toward them.

Once again, Katrelle needed to reassess. *Well, so much for a good plan. Likely, Mitchell discovered the missing hostages and me gone. It won't take a second for Jones to figure it out. Nothing to do now but head north and hope we connect with some friendlies.*

The rumble of several approaching ATVs was growing louder. Worst of all, Katrelle heard the shouts of men and dogs tracking them through the streets.

It couldn't have happened at a more inopportune time. Estelle started making noise again. "I'm tired. I need to rest. I'm tired. Let's stop." The searchers were already at the bottom of the hill. Katrelle realized they'd also be homing in on their chip implants. Then Estelle started up again with, "I just want to sit for a while. What? Why are you dragging me up this hill? Let go of me!" Then she shouted. "Help! Somebody help us!" At the same time, Estelle's body went limp so that it became nearly impossible for her to be dragged farther up the hill.

There'd been no instance in Katrelle's relatively short life where she had to make so many difficult decisions and do it so quickly. It was that time again. Her spurious plan had completely disintegrated. Jordy was in a panic now, pleading with his mother to stand up. They had only seconds before the dogs would be on them. Then capture, then Jones, then torture, death, retribution on her own family. The mother and son were short-timers. They'd be killed. Jones would have won it all, especially if he were to break up the local resistance in the process and come back to Progress City with the prize he sought.

You gotta execute, Kay! Now or never!

Chapter 39

Prodigal Coming Home
Early Evening, April 4, 2053

She eased the backdoor open quietly, hoping to gain entry into the washroom where she could clean up before Gram saw her. She'd found a safe place to stash the guns she'd taken from the woods, a secret place. As she stepped into the washroom, a floorboard creaked. She froze.

"Is that you, Celi? Celi? Answer me! Is that you?" As she heard footsteps approaching, it was plain that she was about to get an earful and maybe a switching as well. Her grandmother appeared in the doorway, barehanded but flushed red in her face. Her blue eyes stood out as they shot fire in her direction.

"Celi Pierce! Where in the world have you been? Do you have any idea how much I have worried about you? Do you know how many bad things I imagined had happened to you out there? Well, *do* you?" She would've kept going but she needed to pause for a breath.

Celi stood there looking like she'd been living in the woods for a week. Her face was smeared with dirt; though braided, her hair was festooned with clingers of moss, beggar burrs and tiny thorns; her hands were scratched up and grimy; and her clothing caked in mud and debris. She was a sore sight. She began to say something about being sorry but try as she might, she couldn't hold back. The dam broke and she rushed into her grandmother's arms wailing, shivering, suffering pangs of torment that made her moan like a feral creature deeply wounded.

Rosie gasped as she felt the child shudder from head to toe in her arms, heard her tortured cries. Something terrible *had* happened! Instantly, Rosie's blood ran cold, but she quickly shook off her mind-numbing fears that the worst had happened, and simply held Celi close to her heart with all the tenderness and balm she could gather. Her granddaughter was here, the worst had *not* come to be. Wave upon wave passed through the child, and Rosie felt all she could do was hang on and ride it out with her. "There, there." Another wave. "There, there, it's all right." The pangs of anguish gradually waned until they just stood there in the silence holding each other. Breathing together.

PART 3

Chapter 40

"The Evil that Men Do. . ."
April 15, 2053

Just before noon, Estelle Pierce, her hands cuffed behind her, was prominently paraded outside and around the inner courtyard of the town center compound. She shuffled along, head hanging as she murmured insensibly. Her presence would be obvious to any observers on the nearby hillsides. Jones figured they'd be up there and had planned it to finish the job he'd commenced the day before, only this time instead of gas, deploying deadly incendiary projectiles. He considered the weaponry his own special version of Greek Fire. There would be no escaping this time.

Just behind the interior wall, SF troops were ready to loose hell upon the surrounding slopes. They were just visible below a sandbagged perimeter ready to fire on his command. Inside the only private office, Jones faced a wall mirror preening and adjusting the uniform he wore for special events. It was crisp and clean, solid black with just enough padding in the shoulders to compensate for his skeletal frame. He'd chosen a black beret with the SF insignia blazoned in red on the wide side. He liked the hollowed look of his face and minded not the resemblance it bore to a skull with skin tautly stretched, the sharp nose giving him the look of a patrician hawk. Indeed, this was a big day, and yet, he brooded.

Things hadn't quite gone as he had planned. That bitch Renick had taken off with his hostages.

Fortunately, the Pierce woman's shouts had led the search team right to her. However, Renick remained at large with the boy, but not for long. He had dispatched his best man, Mitchell, and his unit. *Oh, how I'm going to have my way with her! She'll be getting it all six ways to Sunday!* He felt excitement in his loins at the prospect. A knock sounded on his door and someone said, "We're ready sir." He wrested his attention back to the immediate task. *All right, it's show time!*

The black-clad trooper had brought the Pierce woman to the center of the courtyard. It was seconds before noon. A tall, lone figure clad in a dirty nylon windbreaker and ragged pants appeared at the gate. From a perch up high, a voice sounded, "Halt! State your name and business."

The man raised his face and spoke in a flat, clear voice. "Ben Pierce, here for my wife and son."

There was a brief pause as the sentry radioed in. Then the voice spoke again. "Approach the gatehouse and stand there with your arms raised." Several red laser dots painted the center mass of his chest. The man complied.

A guard stepped out of the gatehouse and scanned all areas with a heat signature device. Then he drew forth a wand scanner and passed it over Pierce's entire body. The gate guard pressed his comm unit. "There's no RFD detected. Cannot make positive ID but he's clean." Somebody squawked on the other end. "Copy that." The gate opened and two burly, black-clad SFs came forward, flex cuffed the man's wrists in front of him, then roughly escorted him through the gate into the open courtyard.

Ben Pierce immediately saw Estelle in the center of the courtyard. She was on her knees beside an SF trooper. Her hands were cuffed behind her. Her once carefully coiffed dark tresses were matted and splayed in all directions. Her head hung forward so that her face was obscured. She was moaning softly and shivering.

He was escorted to a spot several yards away from Estelle and forced down hard on the pavement into a kneeling position facing her.

"Estelle?" He felt an odd mixture of familiarity and estrangement saying her name. "Are you okay? Where's Jordy? Estelle?" One of the guards gave him a solid back-fisted rap on the side of his head.

"Shut the fuck up. No talking!" Another hard knock was delivered on the other side of his head. The scene before him careened and tilted, then righted itself as the initial pain and shock diminished.

Estelle raised her head and looked at him, trying to focus out of her self-pitying stupor. "Ben? Is that you, Ben? Help me, Ben. You have to help me. If you love me, Ben, you have to. . ." Her pleadings were cut short by a gloved hand grasping her throat. An angry face appeared close to hers.

"You, too. Shut your fucking yap or I'll snap that pretty neck like a frigging twig. Got that?"

The woman's eyes widened and she made a

compliant motion with her head. The guard released her and she began coughing and sputtering. She then returned to her former state of numbed stupefaction, moaning and babbling. The guard took a rag from his pocket and stuffed it partly into her mouth to muffle the woman's pitiful whimpering.

"So touching! A family reunion!" Jones' voice brayed as he stepped out of the main building and down the stairs. He strode toward the kneeling captives. His arms raised to indicate his exasperation. "But what's this? There seem to be at least two other members missing. I distinctly recall sending them an invitation. Mr. Pierce, would you care to explain why you would dare show up here without them? Did you lose them along the way? It's twelve noon and only you have come."

Jones approached Ben from the side and edged up so close that his hot noxious breath collided with his prisoner's face. "I'm asking you a question!" With that, Jones kicked Ben hard in the side with the toe of his boot.

Ben absorbed the blow by falling sideways. He was immediately jerked upright. He thought a rib might have been broken but managed to suppress the pain and speak. "My uncle is dead. My daughter is caring for her sick grandmother. It's just me. I'm here to exchange myself for my wife and son."

Jones leaned in. "Oh, I see. You think you are in a position to change the terms of our little family get together. How noble of you, Mr. Pierce, but, apparently you didn't get the memo, that is, if you can read. Do you think you carry enough importance to make up for two other retros, especially when one of them has been fomenting rebellion and disunity? Do you?"

Ben turned his head toward Jones. His cold, gray eyes and hard facial features gave Jones the distinct and uncomfortable impression he was being sized up the way a hunter seeks the a vital area to target. "You only brought my wife out. Where's my son? Where's Jordy?"

Jones launched another swift kick into Pierce's ribcage. Once again, Ben rolled with the force onto his side. "I'll be asking the questions here." Jones' left eye was seized with some kind of tick and started to rove around in its socket. He then let loose a string of frothing profanities and a series of kicks to all the exposed parts of Pierce's body.

Ben protected his organs as best he could but was now sure he had at least two broken ribs. Every intake of breath was brutally painful. After Jones had spent his manic energy and was breathing heavily, Ben was again raised up back onto his knees. Jones spoke. "We're keeping the boy inside for added insurance. He was desperately hoping to see his old uncle and his sister. Celi, is it? Ahhh, but that's right. They didn't come in. That's really unfortunate for all concerned, Mr. Pierce."

Art Jones' pocket desk started to beep. "Oh my, my, my, it seems the conditions I so carefully laid out for this little family get together have fallen short of being met. You understand, Mr. Pierce, that what happens next is not my fault. It wasn't my choice you see. It's all on you. You are a stupid slope-headed retro who has made a very bad choice. A very bad choice!"

Jones cocked a smile. "I know there are those who say I am ruthless, a monster of sorts. It's really hard to live up to such a reputation. Really it is, but to show you I'm not as hard as people claim, I will make an allowance. You may have a few moments to speak with your estranged wife. I don't understand what you might see in her. Pretty, yes, but not so much now. She'll do anything now for a shot of lodaine—anything." Jones leered at Ben just to make certain he knew what "anything" meant then gave a signal to the guard in charge of the woman. The gag was removed.

She took in several deep, unsteady breaths and raised her head and eyes toward Ben.

It was the look in her eyes that made Ben suffer most. Those eyes that'd once sparkled with beauty and life were now hollowed and dull. Her face was gaunt and ashen, livened only by a wide-eyed look of desperation. This was only a shade of the woman he'd known and loved, but it was, nonetheless, Estelle.

"Ben," her voice quavered, "they're going, they're going to kill me. I know it, Ben. Tell him you'll bring Virgil and Celi in. Tell him you'll do that. Just tell him, Ben. Ben, Jordy's gone. He's gone with. . ." She was cuffed hard from behind and the gag was stuffed back in her mouth. Her eyes grew wider as she began to scream through the cloth.

"Well, you see, Mr. Pierce," Jones sounded injured, "I try to be gracious and kind and look how my considerations are received?" He heaved a dramatic sigh of faux resignation. Then his voice hardened, "You people are a scourge. You're a plague to this region; you're a pox on this planet. We really have tried to rehabilitate your kind into the global community, into our population centers, but your inbred genetics, your clinging to a past that is no more, make it impossible!"

"I ask you, Mr. Pierce, rhetorically, of course, if you even know what rhetorical means, what more can we do with you people other than to throw up our hands and say, 'well, we tried'? It's become obvious we have need of a final solution."

Jones reached for the man's chin and wrenched it upward. Pierce's eyes still had the cold steely look of a predator, but Jones persisted. "You made a very bad choice, Mr. Pierce, to think I am a man to be trifled with." Jones nodded to the guard beside Ben, and then over at the guard by Estelle. "Do 'em both. Her first. Now!" He spun on his heels and dismissively turned his back on the tragic scene about to unfold as he strode toward the main building.

The guard stood behind Estelle, unholstered his sidearm, and in one swift and practiced motion, drew back the slide, released it and fired a single round into the back of Estelle Pierce's head. She collapsed forward, slowly, silently, her head coming to rest sideways on the ground. Her teary eyes clouded over. Blood pooled then ran in rivulets along the cracks in the dirty pavement.

Ben looked on in stunned horror. He heard the

guard behind readying his firearm for the fatal shot. He
felt the pressure of the muzzle against the back of his
head and braced for the impact. His last thought was,
They didn't make it. He could feel the gun trembling
slightly in his executioner's hand. He even felt
movement of the trigger. *Here it comes.* His eyes never
stopped tracking Jones.

There was a sudden thwack sound from behind
them. Then the report of a long gun off to his right.
The gun muzzle pressed to his head slipped off
sideways. The guard crumpled on top of Ben and
rolled to the ground. He saw the man's face, slightly
deformed from the projectile that had just penetrated
behind his ear and out the other side. Though rendered
completely brainless, the man was trying to suck air and
his eyes were reflexively blinking.

The sound of gunfire erupted all around taking
down the guard who'd just shot Estelle and all those
stationed within the courtyard and visible to the hills
including every trooper on the perimeter who was
poised to set the hills ablaze. One incendiary projectile
was fired, but it shot off toward the river. It exploded
onto the bank; fire flared along the bank and even onto
the river itself where it floated downstream for a
distance.

Ben lay as flat on the ground as he could using
the body of the dying guard as cover. Several guards
hunkered behind an armored vehicle, but a carefully
aimed RPG dispatched them readily. Except for the
search party headed by Sergeant Mitchell, the entire SF
force had been taken out in a matter of seconds.

Jones had momentarily frozen in shock and amazement at the scene unfolding before him. Then panic set in and he began to run toward the main building. He was ten feet from the front steps when his right leg was shot out from under him and his left ribcage received a stunning blow from behind. Now, he was kneeling on the ground but still struggling to make it to the safety of the main building. Somehow, he got to his feet placing most of his weight on the good leg and began hobbling closer to the stairs.

Jones shouted toward the building for aid. "Somebody, help me! Get me inside. Somebody, goddamit! Help me!" The front door opened, but instead of rescuers, three men emerged–one of them carrying a white flag–all with their hands held high. They stood on the porch ignoring Jones' orders. These were not soldiers; they were just techies and town center staff.

Jones began screaming at them, "You fucking cowards. You goddamned traitors, wait until I get back. I will nail every one of you to the wall!"

Behind him, Jones heard someone say, "Not if I can help it." Jones turned to see that it was Ben Pierce who'd spoken. He'd somehow gotten to his feet, retrieved his executioner's weapon and had fired the two crippling rounds at Jones. Pierce's gray eyes never wavered. "There's a special kinda hell waiting for you, you cold-blooded son of a bitch."

Jones touched the wound on his side and raised a bloody hand to examine it.

Although quaking with pain and shock, he retorted, "Hell? I don't believe in your mindless hick superstitions."

Ben Pierce came closer and said with dead certain finality even as he breathed through the pain of two broken ribs, "Oh, you will. You will. Fact is, I believe you're going to beg for it."

Chapter 41

On the Run

Dawn was slow coming. Katrelle hiked westward toward the fringes of Anthony District. It was dark at first and the deep woods made it even darker and slow going. Jordy kept asking about his mother and all Katrelle could think to say was that his mommy was right behind them and would catch up soon, but they had to keep moving so the bad men wouldn't catch them. Jordy at least knew about the bad men who had dragged them from their cube back in Progress City three days before.

It had been a very long night and this early morning they'd spent dodging and hiding from the search teams. Estelle Pierce's wails and cries for help had likely been a decoy, probably a recording, but she'd effectively kept the boy focused on escape, which bought Katrelle and Jordy time to make the river where they found an overhang of greenbrier under which they could hunker. After several close calls, they moved upstream to a tributary and clambered up its western slope, stopping every few moments to listen for approaching sounds.

At one point, Jordy stopped. "But what if they catch Mommy?" his little voice insisted, full of panic and concern—and very loud.

"Shhh!" Katrelle spoke in a whisper offering more hope than truth saying, "She's very smart and knows the area very well, so she'll know how to get away from them."

He picked up on her bend of the truth. His hope was that his mother would be rescued by his father who conjured the image of a hero in his mind.

Later that day, they heard gunfire coming from the direction of the center. "We gotta go back and get her," he announced. In an instant, he'd turned around and was running back down the trail. He was surprisingly fast and it wasn't until he had made it down to the creek and up the opposite bank that she finally caught up with him. By this time, he'd started wheezing and was struggling to breathe. Katrelle recognized the symptoms of an oncoming asthma attack. He sounded like a wounded piglet. She fretted about all the noise attracting would-be trackers' attention. She caught him from behind and deftly picked him up as he feebly kicked and labored to breathe.

Poor little guy, she thought. *Who am I to take him away from his mom like this?* She knew the most likely reason for the gunfire. One shot followed by a fusillade had echoed through the hollows sounding like a crack of lightning, then a rumble of thunder. He tried to wrestle out of her arms. She held on, careful not to squeeze his chest. His energy was failing as his difficulty to breathe increased. He pointed to a bulge in his pants pocket and mouthed the word, "Puffer."

She extracted the small cylinder and placed the nozzle to his mouth. Together, they both pressed down as the medicine gassed into his lungs. He took several ragged breaths and then pressed the nozzle again. It took three pumps before his breathing began to even.

She kissed the top of his head and then leaned back to look at his pale face specked with sweat and dirt. She tried to say it confidently. "It's okay. You'll be with your mommy soon but we have to keep going or the bad men will catch us. She wouldn't want that."

Jordy was in no shape to stand, much less walk. She sat down on the bank, with her back against a large poplar and feet braced on the downhill slope and let the boy lay in her lap. She cradled his head and noted by his increasing weight that he'd exhausted himself. The sunlight slanted through the woods, yet there was still enough daylight left for travel.

If they were going to continue their escape, she'd need to carry him, about fifty or sixty pounds. She put the puffer back in his pocket and noted that he was dropping off to sleep, his eyes flickered closed and his breathing deepened. "God," she sighed. "How's this kid gonna make it in the outlands without medication?" She couldn't remember if there was any herbal remedy or some other alternative treatment for asthma.

Katrelle felt the boy's weight increase as his frantic state subsided and his corded muscles unwound. She resolved they'd have to pause here for him to regain his strength and if need be, she'd hoist him over her shoulders and carry him. She gazed down at the boy's face and brushed his matted hair away from his brow. He'd descended into a light sleep. Well, she thought, at least he was quiet.

She flashed back to occasions of herself, as the older sister, having to soothe her little brothers through their minor bumps and scrapes. A pang of grief caught

her unprepared as she remembered the last day she'd
seen her mother and little brothers, standing there by
the farm gate. Waving goodbye to her, her mother in
tears, little Tad and Lee looking baleful, and then the
green clad farm boss herding them like wayward sheep
back toward a compound of metal-roofed buildings.

Reliving the experience brought on tears. She
used the back of her free hand to wipe them off her
cheek. *Dammit, Kay! Get a grip! Nothing you can do but move
on.*

She didn't know Madison District as well as her
own native region, but she figured they were headed in
the general direction of Tommy's Crossing—not far
from where she and Candler were ambushed by the
men on horseback. Poor Candler, she thought, he was a
wimp and at times a typical bureaucratic dolt but he
seemed genuine in his belief that he was rescuing folks
from the wilds as opposed to hunting them down like
Jones. He was, in his own way, gallant. That was the
term; he was gallant, sort of. She wondered what would
become of him and felt a tinge of guilt in leaving him
at the center at the mercy of Art Jones and company.

She covered the child with the flaps of her
coat, felt his warmth, the soothing sounds of the creek
water. It had been a long time since she'd actually been
in the woods. More or less alone. She started to take a
deep breath; it turned out to be a yawn. She relaxed a
bit more and drifted.

Her repose was interrupted by the sound of a
footstep just behind her. She had no time to react as a
gloved hand clasped over her mouth.

Chapter 42

Awake in a Nightmare
April 15, 2015

Candler Greave's first waking moments floated
up before him like a smoky dream. He saw the dingy
ceiling, mottled grainy wood that ran in long strips.
Once in focus, he felt like the ceiling had become the
floor and that somehow he'd been plastered against the
real ceiling behind him. The illusion wavered back and
forth until his brain righted itself and his bearings
returned as well as his memory. He was in a room, at
the town center, lying on his back, recovering from a
nasty blow to the back of his head. For the first time,
he felt hungry without the accompanying flush of
nausea and thirsty.

"Hello," he croaked just barely above a whisper.
"Hello?" A little louder. "Anybody?"

No answer. "TO Renick? Katrelle?" His voice
was a bit louder and sounded increasingly desperate.
"Simms? Somebody! I need help! Hello, somebody!"
No sound of footsteps. He was alone.

Rather than despair, he determined he would
get up on his own. He rolled to his side. His vision
blurred a second, then snapped into focus again. Okay,
now for the feet. With a groan, he lifted his blanket,
swung his feet to the floor and felt the cold wood on
the soles of his feet. A cold shiver also met his bare
legs and his upper body. Apart from his boxers, he was
naked. He took the blanket off his cot and wrapped it

around his shoulders. There was a nearly full glass of water on his bedside table. He grabbed it and took a few sips to sooth his cottonmouth and parched throat. He could practically feel his body's cells reviving with each sip. His bladder also came to life and insisted on relief. *Okay,* he thought, *been here long enough.*

Using his arms, he pushed up to a standing position. The blanket slipped away as he stood up, but he got himself covered up again. *Just a little woozy.* A few buggy black spots danced before his eyes. He let the room settle then moved in stiff-legged, short steps toward the closet that contained the chem toilet. A short distance and a half turn. Success. He sighed as he sat, able to relieve himself.

Why was there no one responding to his calls? There should be at least three workers on duty at all times. Why was it so quiet? He pushed off his knees and with a groan, stood up letting the blanket drape over him. He slowly shuffled across the room heading for the door to the hallway. As he was opening the door, he heard voices—voices on the outside, then a gunshot, then someone shouting. It was that hyena Jones' voice, cawing and cloying with menace.

"Oh, no, no, no," Candler whispered to himself. He increased his pace, careening from wall to wall down the hallway toward the front room that looked out on the courtyard. He saw Simms standing beside the window peering out. Simms caught sight of Candler and made a shushing motion with his index finger, followed by a get down motion with the flat of his hand.

Candler ignored both gestures and in his stilted gait, came over to Simms and stood in full view of the steel-grated window. He got a brief glimpse of what was unfolding in the courtyard. A woman was collapsed at the feet of a black-clad enforcer—one of Jones's elite SF squad. The figure with a smoking pistol in hand stood like a dark shadow above the woman. She was not moving as a lagoon of red formed around her.

A hand reached out and jerked Candler to the side of the window. "Sir!" It was Simms. "It's gone to shit, sir. DM Jones just ordered a summary execution and he's about to do it again!" Simms pointed to the left where a black guard stood over a pale-faced man kneeling on the ground. Candler thought he recognized him. *Benjamin. . . somebody.* The guard had a gun in hand pointed at the back of the man's head. Jones said something indecipherable as he strode toward the building. His eyes betrayed a wicked pleasure as his lips formed a vicious grin.

The guard pressed the pistol against the back of the kneeling man's head. Candler reacted. Heedless of his feeble condition, he made a move for the outside door. *This could not happen. Jones was going to touch off a war. It had to stop!*

He'd almost reached the door, when a volley of gunshots sounded all around them. Peering through the door's window, what Candler saw next appeared surreal. All, not one or two, but every single one of Jones's elite Strike Force thugs were on the ground dead or dying. The man Jones had intended to execute was still on his knees, head bowed. Jones himself was fast walking toward the front doors, his face a contorted mix of rage, terror and snarling defiance. He was almost to the front steps when two gunshots erupted with a double tap. Jones' scarecrow frame jerked to the right then to the left and he collapsed to one knee.

His right shinbone looked shattered, and his right side was bleeding through a perforation in his leather coat. He reached down to swipe the blood from his side and held the reddened hand up to examine it. His expression was incredulous as if he'd thought himself bulletproof, immortal. He turned his head to see all of his henchmen had been taken down. Eyes wide, his head swiveled forward and he shouted toward the building "Help! Help me!"

The three center workers who'd remained inside hiding behind a partition near Simms reached an unspoken consensus. They were neither field personnel nor trained soldiers. They dropped whatever weapons they had onto the floor with a clatter. Unarmed, they regarded each other and moved toward the door, past Candler. One of the three extracted a white kerchief from his pocket and opening the door just a crack, dangled the token of surrender outside. Then very slowly, they emerged to stand on the porch with their hands held up in surrender.

With the front door open, Candler could hear Jones erupt in a frothing fit of deprecations, curses and dire threats directed at the three. The vile words were spat out of his mouth like snake venom.

Candler also got a wider look at the devastation spread out in the courtyard. He was amazed to see that the shooter was the man Jones had just ordered to be executed. What surprised Candler most of all was that the man had shown restraint and not peppered Jones with a full magazine. The man was standing, holding his would-be executioner's black gun, still smoking, in his flex-cuffed hands.

He approached Jones from behind. They exchanged words, which Candler couldn't make out, but he could tell that Jones was attempting his faux bravado and likely threatening all manner of retribution. Even in his decrepit condition, he looked like a vicious jackal that'd been wounded and cornered.

For his part, the shooter's rasping voice was deliberate and tempered. Candler couldn't make out the words but divined their meaning. His face betrayed no outrage. It was the face of a hunter closing in on his intended prey. Candler was certain the coup de grace was only seconds away.

"Sir, we have to get out of here. Sir!" It was TO Simms just behind him urging him to make their escape. He was pulling Candler toward the back of the room so forcefully that given his weak condition, he nearly toppled over headlong. His blanket fell to the floor exposing his state of undress. Simms righted him and offered his apologies.

"Sir! Can we move, please? At least hide ourselves somewhere. I have a girl back home and we're going to be paired next month and I don't want to have it end here." Candler recalled that, unlike TO Renick who'd been cross-trained, Simms was just a TO and had no combat skills. "There's a safe room toward the back and down the stairs." Candler knew about this room also, but it seemed kilometers away as his legs swayed under him.

He heard the clopping sounds of boots climbing the steps and moving onto the porch. They were coming inside.

"You go, Simms. Take the passage through the cellar! I'll talk to these men and try to keep them here. Go!"

Simms seemed to hesitate, his loyalties divided. Candler pushed him toward the rear door. "Simms, I ORDER you to go! If you make it out of here, then you can report to admin and tell them all that has happened. GO!"

Simms gave a respectful nod and slipped out of the room into the back hallway just as a tall, gray-cloaked old man strode through the open doorway. He was dangling a bleeding, mewling Jones by the scruff of his neck. Doing a visual sweep of the room, the gray man saw the weapons lying on the floor amid a clutter of overturned tables and chairs, a backdoor leading to some hallway and a bedraggled Candler still standing by the front wall and shivering in his blanket.

It was the leader of the ruffian horsemen who'd clobbered him and taken him and Katrelle hostage. The gray man looked at him. "You armed?"

Candler shook his head.

"Thought so." Another two men came through

the open door, their guns sweeping the room as they entered. Their leader regarded them and motioned toward Candler. "Would you gentlemen escort Agent Greaves back to where he can be tended to in comfort? He's not been par-tee to the evil deeds we've witnessed." They nodded and slung their weapons over their shoulders.

Candler thought, *How did this man know what I've done and not done?* As the two men came up to him, he involuntarily shrunk toward the corner clutching the blanket protectively around his neck. They stopped their approach and spoke to him calmly. "It's okay, Agent Greaves. We just want to get you to a safe place is all. There may be some more shooting and 'sides that, you look like you need to rest."

One of the men, with red hair and beard, looked vaguely familiar. The man stepped slightly closer to Candler and with an earnest expression said, "Agent Greaves, I didn't mean to give you such a hard blow back there at Cross Creek. Vince here will tell you, I don't abide by unnecessary violence. So, I'm sorry. I hope to see you make a strong recovery."

Meanwhile, Art Jones had dropped his head and neck in a posture that made him look like a vulture. His eyes skewered Candler. His lips contorted into a hateful sneer. "You fucking coward, Greaves. I'll have your head for this. I'll see to it. This was *your* assignment Greaves. You'll never. . ." Jones' arm was jerked nearly out of its socket as he screamed "Aiyeeee!"

The leader leaned into Jones' face and spoke

through clenched teeth. "You've no cause to threaten Agent Jones. I just witnessed the execution of a kinsman, as ordered by you. You're in our world now. The most you might be allowed is a quick execution–that is, after we're done with you."

A rider came into the building. "The Pierce woman is confirmed; the major is seeing to the body. All of Jones' men are done. We've captured the town center crew and what remains of the field personnel. We saw one man escape into the woods. He looked like a techie. No casualties on our side. All are accounted for, except. . ." the man hesitated seeing the penetrating intensity in the gray man's eyes, "except for the boy, sir. Nowhere to be found and neither is there sign of that woman who we met up with at Cross Creek."

The old man gave a nearly imperceptible nod and his gaze fell to the floor as he assessed the report. He then turned toward the men assigned to escort Candler. "What are you two waiting for? Get him out of here!" There was a spall of anger that Candler hadn't heard before. It did not bode well for Katrelle, or him for that matter.

Sensing a possible opportunity, Jones struggled to free himself and was violently thrust into a chair. He was bleeding some, but the blood was dark red. No major arteries had been severed. The leader said, "Rope him. Get Patches. Have him fix the wounds best he can. Call me when you're done."

These were the last words Candler heard as he was being led toward the back hall. Unbeknownst to him, it was the last time he'd ever see Art Jones, dead or alive.

What was now known to Candler was the dead woman's name and her relation to the man who'd just shot Jones—Pierce, Estelle Pierce. She had a son, Jordan. He'd done the intake personally. Her son had a medical condition. They'd received provisional care at the free clinic in exchange for the mother's conscription to the fabric sector, a factory job. The woman had seemed quite grateful. Candler remembered thinking how he'd done such a fine thing.

Her husband, the man who'd just shot Jones, was Benjamin Pierce. He was an unregistered retro. Reports were they had a daughter. The daughter had never been registered either. Could this daughter be the one called Celi? Cecilia? She was off the books– probably a home birth. The retros still practiced the crudities of midwifery. There were likely thousands of births that were off the books.

Jones had apparently determined the source of the seditious transmits–or at least, he was willing to discover the culprits by a process of elimination. So, he used the wife as hostage to lure the rest of the family into town. Ben Pierce's aged mother and his daughter had not "come in."

Jones was not one to make idle threats. After all, he had a reputation for using cruel measures to get whatever he wanted. So, true to his legacy of atrocities, he had the woman executed and had been moving on to the next of kin, when the retros attacked.

What about the boy and Katrelle? She would

not be one to kowtow to Jones' harsh tactics or concede to the summary execution of a mother and child. Would she endanger her own family members by going against Jones' orders? Candler's brain was on process overload. His focus started to kaleidoscope and waver as he tipped over sideways. Seeing him falter, his escorts came up to either side and helped him back to his room.

He was nearly dead weight by the time they reached his cot, but rather than being slung down like a wet sack of flour, he was placed with care onto his back. A pillow was propped under his head. Someone murmured, "Rest easy there, pard."

The beaded board ceiling above slowly ceased its drunken motions and resolved momentarily into straight lines. He felt himself being drawn down into the dark recesses of slumber. Instead of struggling to retain his consciousness, he relaxed and welcomed his blackout like an old friend. The last physical sensation was that of a blanket being drawn over him up to his shoulders. He hoped to wake up from what his mind could only construe as a very, very bad dream.

MOUNTAIN WHISPERS – DAYS WITHOUT SUN

Chapter 43

The Encounter
Early Morning, April 16, 2053

In disbelieving horror, Katrelle realized she and the boy had slept through the night. The hand pressed hard over her mouth.

"Now, missie. I want you to be real quiet and still. No fancy moves, now." A man's gritty voice was in her ear. She smelled horse scent and tobacco. One of the mounted marauders, she thought. With the delicate child cradled in her lap, she had no immediate way to defend or strike. *Best wait.*

"I know you and your kinfolk," he said in a raspy but not unpleasant voice. "It's Renick. Your Momma was a Claymore. And I know you just did a very brave thing to rescue this boy. You are now more wanted than any of us retros for turning renegade and you probably have a sizable bounty on your head by now." His other hand clasped the back of her neck so that his thumb pressed into her carotid artery. "Missie, you're not the only one with combat skills. I can knock you out in a second with just a little more pressure and leave you here for the Green Hats or you can agree to come along to a place where you'll be fairly received and kindly treated. We have little time and need to take advantage of their confusion. Are you with me?"

It felt like her brain was ballooning inside her skull as spots began to dance before her eyes. She was all too familiar with vulnerable spots of the human anatomy. She'd be out in seconds if his grip intensified. She'd yet to see the man's face but knew who it belonged to and had no doubt he meant every word. She nodded. The man released his neck hold, but not the hand over her mouth.

"So, you're gonna make this easy, right? It's been a long day and I don't care for any more complications. So, nice and easy, right?"

She nodded and he uncovered her mouth. She could still smell, almost taste, the tang of horse sweat and leather on her lips. A tall figure stood up behind her. She turned her head to look up at him. Sure enough, she and the boy were now in the company of the legendary Gray Ghost, known to his men as "Boss" or just as often referred to as "the Captain." During her rapid-fire data research the day before, she'd discovered a secret dossier highlighting his exploits from decades ago. He'd been fingered as the rebels' leader and the one who'd masterminded the takeover of the Tug River Power Plant. So it was he who'd presided over her and Candler's capture at Cross Creek. The admin alleged he'd been killed by a drone. So any future sightings were ascribed to be mythical, but seeing him still alive, and obviously in charge of this current operation, shot a tingle of awe mixed with fear along her spine. Why or how he'd come to find her, or rather, them, remained a mystery.

He offered to take the boy, but she instinctively held him closer and stood up with him still cradled in her arms, half-sleeping. The captain gave heed to her maternal nature and indicated they were to walk down the bank toward the creek. She realized it was probably the creek's gurgling sounds that'd masked her captor's approach. She should have known. Nodding off didn't help either. How stupid! By the looks of the dim gray light filtering down through the canopy, she and the boy had been sleeping nearly all night. As they descended the slope and walked a ways downstream along a deer track beside the creek, the boy began to rouse.

Katrelle was carrying him upright with his head over her left shoulder. He blinked his eyes open and they focused on the wraith-like figure walking behind them. His eyes widened as he gasped, then smiled wanly and said, "Uncle Virgil!"

Chapter 44

Waypoint Rendezvous
April 16, 2053

The sky had lightened its silvery sheen through the early morning fog as they arrived at a familiar creek crossing where a cluster of riders sat astride their mounts looking expectantly in their direction.

A pall of somber weariness hung in the air.

She observed with a hint of pride that Hardy, the boy she'd incapacitated days earlier, was not among them. She also noted there was no sign of the boy's mother, Estelle. She'd hoped against hope that the gunfire she'd heard earlier was the sound of liberators fighting to gain freedom for the captive hostages, but from the looks on the men's faces, she could tell something had gone terribly wrong.

Then, she saw the riderless horse, a makeshift travois lashed behind it. An oblong bundle lay strapped to the travois. A blotch of something dark had saturated the cloth at the lower end.

She knew then, as her intuition painted the dark and bloody scenario, that Jones had followed through with his threat. She gave Virgil Johnson a sidelong glance. He pointedly glanced at the boy in her arms, then back at her giving his head a slight shake. The message was conveyed. "Not now."

A tall hatless man clad in a duster and square-toed boots handed the reins to the rider beside him and then stiffly dismounted. He never took his eyes off Kay and whom she was holding. He came toward them in long even strides. The boy had been tightly clutching Katrelle's neck as if she were a rock in the middle of a madly rushing torrent. He sensed someone approaching and turned his head. "Mommy?

"Mommy?" he repeated as he looked past the approaching man and scanned the group of horsemen. Then his eyes focused ahead and he began to twist and turn in an attempt to escape Katrelle's protective hold. Not wishing to hurt the boy, she relaxed and let him go. The man picked up his pace as the boy raised his arms and rushed forward. "Daddy! Daddy!" They closed the distance between and the man sank to his knees, arms extended and enfolded the boy in a tight embrace. The boy sank his face into the crook of the man's arm; his cries mingled joy with sorrow and relief.

Katrelle felt a surge of gladness. Seeing father and son reunited like this felt so right—she'd done the right thing, after all. Then she glanced at the travois. *Maybe I could've done more. I should've done more.*

The kneeling man had his head over the boy's shoulder. His face was ashen and drawn, his eyes squeezed tight with unspoken intensity, but his features softened as he looked up at Katrelle and mouthed the word "Thank you." He blinked as tears fell from his cheek onto the boy's back. After a long moment, the boy shifted his head to look up in his dad's face. "Where's Mommy? Daddy, where's Mommy?" He began making moves to escape his father's embrace, his mood becoming frantic. "Daddy? That lady said

Mommy would be meeting us. Where is she?"

His father held him at arm's length by the shoulders and regarded his son through a curtain of pain and tears. He began to speak softly. Katrelle couldn't make out the words but knew what was being said. She felt the embattlements around her heart–the ones she'd walled up herself as a matter of survival– give way.

Her attention was diverted by the approach of a stocky man with a balding crown and red beard. He was carrying what an average person would presume to be an oversized ink pen with blinking red and green diodes running along its length.

She recognized the device and its function. It was a portable electromagnetic pulsator designed to eradicate RFIDs, tags, with a concentrated burst of energy similar to the way ultrasound was used in non-invasive surgeries.

She was surprised to see such a sophisticated device in the possession of the retros. She'd never used one herself, but had observed it being applied to a man whose chip had malfunctioned and needed replacement. She guessed they must've procured it from a lockbox at the town center. Given its potential misuse, it wasn't something one would leave lying about, so there was high probability they'd already gotten into the medical lockout closet, which meant they'd taken things over.

The red-haired man addressed the commander. "Shall I cut their cords, sir?" His eyes shifted to

Katrelle and then to Jordy. She felt her body stiffen
with resistance and fear as the Captain said, "Do her
first."

The burly man pressed a button on the backend
of the device and she could hear it cycling up into a
high-pitched whine. He approached her warily saying in
a conciliatory tone, "All right, Miss Renick, this will
only take a second. You won't hardly feel it. Okay?" She
heard a tinge of fear in his voice. He'd either witnessed
her formidable skills in action at Cross Creek and
feared approaching her or knew as well as she did that
the PEP would be painful—or both.

She felt her muscles coiling to strike and was
ready to let go a flurry of blows when the Captain said,
"Missy, you didn't come all this way to start a fight and
get us tracked down and killed, right?" The voice of
reason began to override her reactive state. All her
adolescent and adult life she'd been told and had, in
fact, been comforted by this tether that connected her
to a higher authority. It made her feel like she was never
alone.

The Captain continued, "You and the boy have
likely been tracked all the way from Madison, and now
they know where you're standing, among us. Them
finding you and us would kinda sabotage your
charitable intentions to save the boy, wouldn't it?"

She had to concede to his logic. She shrugged
slightly and gave the red-haired man a slight nod of
submission. He approached and asked her to hold her
hair up from the nape of her neck. She braced herself,
clamped her teeth tight, for the inevitable pain that

would follow. She felt the tip of the PEP pressing in and a slight vibration. The PEP emitted a high-pitched squeal, then she felt a kind of pop sensation—like when the ears adjust to altitude—only this was in her neck.

As the device was cycling down, she thought, *Is that it?* She'd heard horror stories about how dangerous and painful removing a tag could be. *More crap from on high.*

The man stepped back and looked at her face with genuine concern. "Miss Renick, are you okay?"

She nodded.

He pointed to her right hand. "Okay, the standard tag is done. You have one more in your hand. It may be tricky."

She'd forgotten about the second tag. It was installed just before her graduation from the academy. Nothing more than a pinprick in the fleshy part between her thumb and forefinger. They'd said it was a programmable security device that would allow her to incorporate pass codes, breeze through checkpoints and be scanned for positive ID. No one mentioned it was a tracking device as well.

The man gestured again at her hand. "May I?" She nodded consent and watched as he placed the PEP's tip between forefinger and thumb and booted its cycle. This time it felt like she'd been stung by a hornet. A dark red spot appeared where the probe had made contact.

The man was most apologetic. "Sorry about that. We've not done security tags much. I tried to get as close to the critical frequency as possible, but I had to fish around a bit. You should be fine in a coupla days. Cold water compress, or ice if you can get it, would help." Katrelle rubbed the area with her left hand as the throbbing began to diminish.

"Much obliged for your cooperation, Miss Renick." She noted the rough-hewn man's courtly mannerisms. *Yes, Kay. Appearances can be quite deceiving.* Then, it struck her.

The realization that she, TO Katrelle Renick, Special Operations Coordinator First Class, had just willingly become a total off-the-map retro.

Meanwhile, Jordy and his father remained wrapped around each other. Having heard about the fate of his mother, the boy stubbornly refused the tragic news. "No, no, no, Daddy. She's coming. That lady over there said Mommy's coming to meet us." He turned his head toward Katrelle to indicate who "she" was. His face flushed and angry words hurled at her. He pushed away from his father to turn toward her. "You said she'd meet us. You took me away from her. You said she was coming! Coming!"

The boy was in such a state that he started to wheeze and his breathing became more and more labored. Again, Katrelle had the dire thought of how the boy would make it in the Spartan conditions of the district. She felt responsible, guilty, even though she'd actually thought the boy's mother might somehow make it. *Really, Kay? Would Art Jones ever yield mercy?* She stepped toward the father and son, saying through her own tears, "I'm so sorry, Jordy. I thought. . ."

"You lied! You. . . You. . . You. . ." He took a tattered wheezing breath and then froze wide-eyed. He was going into anaerobic shock again. She rushed toward him and kneeled close enough to pull the puffer from his pocket and plunge the mist into his mouth several times. The father, who was still on his knees, watched the scene unfold. Once the boy regained a semi-normal cadence of breathing, he was worn out and his body's posture wavered. Jordy practically collapsed forward into her arms.

She met the father's eyes, close up for the first time. She thought of her own father and a longing sense of loss began to close in on her. He said nothing but gave her a slight bow of his head. Holding the boy in her arms, she could feel his body growing more relaxed. *Why would he ever trust me again? Yet. . .*

The red-haired man approached with the PEP in hand. "Pardon me, miss, but now's as good a time as any." He pressed the device against the slight dimple in Jordy's neck and toggled the on switch. The boy barely moved when the pulse popped and his connection to the central authority was permanently severed.

"We gotta move." The leader was taking swift long strides toward his dappled horse. "Mount up!" He swung up into the saddle and immediately started forward in the lead.

Katrelle handed the boy back to his father. He was semi-conscious and as she brushed his bangs away from his forehead, his skin felt clammy. "He's a good, strong, brave boy.

He did his best to save his mother. . . but she. . ." How could it be said tactfully that Estelle Pierce was a walking basket case?

Ben looked up from his son's face and locked eyes with her. "I know. She's always been fragile." He quickly changed topics. "You're welcome to come with us, y'know." It was more a statement of fact than a cordial invitation.

She smiled. Then a dark veil masked her face. "I have some loose ends to tie up back in Madison and we're being tracked." She thought of saying something cordial or nonchalant but "Nice meeting you" or "See ya later" just didn't fit. She took a deep breath and gave a quick smile with a nod. It was on to business. She, the hunted, was now the predator. The boy was safe and thanks to the removal of her tags, she had stealth on her side. She started to turn, but Ben's voice stopped her.

"No need to worry about Jones. He's our prisoner now. We'll exact justice." His voice sounded hollow as if reciting lines from a textbook of civilian protocol.

Katrelle clenched her fists, an audible groan accompanying her disappointment. She wanted the honor of impaling Jones—of being there right in his face to deliver all the backload of karma that was his due, then, taking leave of this life herself.

Recognizing the pain and anger etched in her face, Ben lightly touched her shoulder and said, "I, too, would cherish sending that evil bastard back to hell." He paused to look down at Jordy, fast asleep. Then, his clear gray eyes returned to hers. "You've done a great deal of good, miss, and I can see there's more good left in you, that is, if you choose to remain here."

Remain here? A flood of memories flowed through her mind of her father's booming laugh, her mother's lively voice at breakfast, she and her brothers romping in the fresh mown hay, flying off the rope swing and landing in the chill waters of Howard's Creek. Seeing herself at some future time stepping onto a front porch wearing a colorful plaid skirt swirling about her bare feet as children ran carefree in a white fenced yard fronting their little cabin on the hill.

Yes. Even the sun shone warmly on her face. She blinked away the visions and turned her face toward Jordy. She touched his head lightly as if to feather away all the evil that had come his way. She heard herself say, "Perhaps."

Suddenly, the leader called out again. "Let's move!"

With that, she turned back toward the track they'd just come down and broke into a run.

Perhaps, she'd not be able to exact her deep-seated vengeance on Jones but she could at least put a roadblock or two in front of the trackers. That is, if she hurried to take advantage of her newly acquired invisibility.

Ben watched her disappear into the morning mist. He took a deep breath and as he exhaled, he said aloud, "Perhaps."

He walked back to his horse and gently placed his boy in the saddle in front while he seated himself wincing at the pain in his taped up ribs. He brought his long coat around and fastened it across Jordy's chest. They had become as one body bound by the cloth, and two souls now bound by tragedy, going home.

As he rode up next to Virgil, he saw his uncle's gaze lingering on him and the boy. He nodded. Ben returned the nod with his own. "All set." Virgil nudged his horse into a canter and they rode out apace down a narrowed trail that, in an earlier life, easily conveyed motor cars and tandem trucks.

They soon arrived at a three-way crossroads. The Captain took the red-bearded fellow along with a tall, thin rider and turned back south toward Madison. He had unfinished business back in town. The rest of the party headed in the opposite direction in a slow-paced somber procession toward the old Johnson farm, to the family plot where Estelle's body would be interred. Ben Pierce and his newfound son would be in attendance.

Chapter 45

The Fog Lifts
April 16, 2053

When he woke, the room was dark and cold. He could feel the tiny pricks of frigid air on his face and see his breath fog as he exhaled. He was on his side with the blanket drawn up tight around his head. He sorely needed to relieve himself, but dreaded the shock of the cold floor on his feet and the exposure of his bared body. He did what had to be done anyway and returned to his warm nest directly afterward, shivering under the covers until warmth slowly seeped from his core into his extremities.

The hallway door opened and one of the retro riders poked their head inside. Seeing that Candler was awake, he chimed. "Ah, Agent Greaves!" Then, with a sudden shiver as he entered the room, said, "Sorry about the cold. I'll get the heat going and then you can get dressed and join us for a meal in the main room." The man then bustled about whistling quietly as he fired up the gas heater box and adjusted the settings. The flames made the room brighten. "There!" he said cheerfully. "That should do it! Your duds are here at the foot of your bed and your boots are right here on the floor. See you in a bit!" The door closed and the man was gone.

Candler had to collect his thoughts and bearings. He flashed back to a panoply of memories– his assigned mission, RD Dirkson's admonition not to fail, the incident by the creek, Katrelle, the bloody awful scene in the courtyard, Art Jones, and the tall gray commander. He knew the game had changed. He was likely a prisoner—a hostage too, maybe, maybe not. He was being treated with civility–something unexpected given the bloodshed his cohorts had wrought. What must he do? What could he do to salvage the mission? It had all gone to shit. There was nothing he could think of that would save his hide and place him back on his former trajectory to attain level blue status. He would be lucky to just live through whatever was to come.

He resolved that, no matter, he would try to make an escape and meanwhile gather all the info-intel—he could about his captors, their plans, Jones, and the others. He observed a rather unseemly rush of satisfaction about Jones' capture. He chastised himself for being so callous about a fellow agent's plight. He smiled. *But satisfying nonetheless.*

When Candler appeared at the threshold of the main room, he immediately smelled coffee and the sweet aroma of fresh baked bread. Having subsisted mainly on dry crackers and mystery broth, his appetite was returning with a vengeance. There were two men and a woman in the room, garbed in hill fashion, cleaning the floors and wiping counter surfaces. The woman noticed him first as she looked up from swiping a table with her damp rag.

"Ah, Mr. Greaves, you're up!" She had the same cordial tone as the man who'd come to his room earlier. She even smiled as she eyed his scrawny, pale, unshaven appearance. She was a middle-aged matron, with her hair tucked back beneath a pale green kerchief. Her brown eyes were friendly, even motherly.

"Here, young man." She patted a chair by the table. "Sit yourself down and we'll fix you up with some real food, not that junk they keep in storage here. Baked the bread myself in the Dutch oven. Coffee's made, too.

"Clarence, will you get Mr. Greaves here a hot cuppa and a plate of cornbread and beans?" A younger man who'd been kneeling while he scrubbed red stains off the floor with a stiff brush, tossed the brush in a bucket, stood up and walked toward the back galley area.

Candler noted a family resemblance between the young man and the woman. "Well, come on. Don't be shy!" The woman smiled and waved him over and he surprised himself by the speed with which he complied. *Hmmmm*, he thought, *I'm getting my legs back.*

As she set utensils and a clean cloth napkin in front of him, he could smell wood smoke and it alarmed him that the rule about burning wood had been violated so flagrantly. He was disarmed though by the woman's friendliness. "Oh dear, Mr. Greaves," she chimed, "I am forgetting my manners. I'm Sheila Nestor, and that over there is my middle boy Torrence, Tory for short."

The young man with the broom gave a curt nod as he continued to sweep. "And the young'un who's bringing your breakfast is Clarence." She had an air of pride, but it was the pride of accomplishment, not the put-on hubris of social position. In all of this mess, she made Candler feel at home—even though it clearly bore no resemblance to his own tidy cubicle and food dispensary.

If there was anything positive Candler had gained from the major clunk on his head, it was to take more care with his words. Obviously, he was no longer in charge here. He asked the woman an innocuous question. "What's happening here?"

She took a deep breath and smiling indulgently said, "Oh, quite a lot. Quite a lot." She pointed to the empty chair across from him. "Do you mind if I sit a spell? I gotta tell ya, my feet are just hurting like the dickens."

Candler waved her toward the chair, and as she sat, she sighed with relief. "I tell ya, I am not the young gal anymore. These bunions are just a nuisance," she paused, "but you don't want to hear all about my little problems. You've had your own troubles from what I understand. How are you feeling?"

Candler reflexively reached for the back of his head where the rifle butt had connected. The swelling had gone down and there was no longer any pain at the touch. "I am getting better every day."

"Well, that's a good thing, Mr. Greaves." She looked past his shoulder to see her son bringing a platter of food and coffee from the larder. It was hard to procure coffee and it was so expensive the vast majority couldn't afford it and settled for substitutes. Evidently, they'd broken into someone's special stash. "Here's Clarence with your breakfast. I imagine you're ready to eat some real food by now."

Indeed, Candler was ravenous. He had no idea what the gray sauce and round bread contained, but the taste was incredible. The eggs were fresh and the coffee, it was strong but not bitter like some he'd had before. He noticed it had a light color and sweeter taste. As Sheila sat across from him, telling him what was going on, he never stopped forking food into his mouth and washing it down with the coffee.

"Well, sir, let's see. I guess you can tell there've been some changes around here. In town, I mean. We locals have reclaimed Madison and this town center. Your people have all left—well with a few exceptions, you being one of 'em." She smiled and then her face darkened. "And that Jones fella, your boss, he's under heavy security and will answer for his evil doings."

"What about me? Am I also a prisoner?"

"Well, that depends on how you declare someone a prisoner. Y'see, we've got you here but once our Doc Patches figures you've pretty well recovered then you'll be free to return to your city. Mind you, there's some of our folks that don't feel very charitable toward you—they see all the Green Hats, pardon the expression, GEEOs as jackbooted thugs." She raised her eyebrows and, like a doting schoolmarm, warned Candler not to step outside the building for his own personal safety.

"Anyway, Patches will have a look at you. He's also called Doc Davis, a veterinarian by trade, but he has a lot of skills from doctoring animals, y'see, that pertain to us people as well."

"And who is your leader? Is it the tall one with the gray cloak?"

"Well, y'see, that fellow is like a commander of the militia. He don't deal much in the running of towns and such. He just kinda paves the way for us to reclaim what's ours.

So, you'll be meeting with the mayor of Madison, who's also been appointed sheriff, and also," she gave a little grin, "happens to be Doc Davis, Patches, y'see."

"Where is RM Jones? Is he still alive?" The image of Jones' cursing countenance loomed before him, snarling, "You fucking coward, Greaves! I'll have your head for this! You'll see!"

Sheila pressed her lips tightly as she seemed to resist the temptation to hurl epithets. She heaved a breath and said, "That snake of a devil, he's over at the old mill there on the edge of town. Y'see, I wasn't around for all the shooting and what happened directly afterward, but I hear Patches got him doctored and he's been interrogated. May still be. After all that evil bastard has done, I'm surprised they didn't just string him up and gut him on the spot."

The latch on the front door clicked and it swung open. A burly man with graying red hair strode into the makeshift dining room. He spotted the pair at the table and made his way over to them. Candler recognized him as one of the riders he and Katrelle had encountered at the creek crossing. His stature was stout and muscular though considerably shortened not being mounted on a steed. He wore a battered, black, watch cap and sported a large handlebar mustache, sideburns, a sidearm strapped on his right side just visible under his open leather jacket. He reminded Candler of some old cartoon character he'd seen as a child except for the hat.

He approached Candler and offered his hand. They shook and without invitation, the man sat down and asked for real coffee. Sheila yelled over at her boy Clarence, and he disappeared into the back. She stood up and excused herself saying, "I've got too much to do around here without sitting down. Clarence will see to you," she nodded at the man. "And, Mr. Greaves, don't be shy about asking for seconds. Gentlemen." With that, she returned to her tasks of cleaning and straightening.

The man addressed Candler casually. "So, how're you doin'?"

"Improved, but I'd feel much better if I knew more about what was happening," he earnestly replied. "Am I a prisoner or a hostage?"

The man appraised Candler for a few seconds. "Naw. You're free to go once you're able to travel. By the looks of ya, 'pears to be at least a day or two more in sickbay."

"Sickbay?"

"Ah, yeah. It's an old sailor term. Used to be in

the Navy. . . years ago, that is."

"When do I see the doctor?" Candler tried not
to sound too anxious.

The man huffed and smiled. "You're lookin' at
'im! Pardon me for not properly introducing myself.
I'm Arnell Davis, AKA Doc, AKA Patches. I'm also
the interim mayor of Madison—well, what's left of it
anyways. And also the sheriff, now that we've liberated
the town and the surrounding community."

Candler bristled at the notion of a district being
overrun by retros and "liberated." "Mr. Davis, uh
Doctor Davis, you do realize that you are in violation
of regional authority and that you and your cohorts will
be brought up on severe criminal charges?"

"No problem, Mr. Greaves. I understand you
are in a delicate position here. I don't envy you that."
He smiled sympathetically. "We've gone easy on you.
Word is, you've always treated our folks with respect.
You appear to believe your social engineering work has
helped others and maybe it has to some extent for a
few, but as an old folk singer used to sing, the times
they are a changin', Mr. Greaves. We've made great
strides in becoming more independent. Your programs
of bringing folks in to live in your beehives is no longer
needed. In fact, your grand experiment is failing and if
you're really honest with yourself, you'll see my point.

"As for retribution and charges and such, from
what we've derived from Jones, your leaders are
becoming more desperate. Jones' real mission wasn't
what he said it was. I'm not at liberty to divulge the

specifics. Things are still up in the air.

"You, my friend, might see yourself as our captive or even an enemy combatant but that's not the case in our eyes. The only thing keeping you here is that rather nasty knock on the noggin. You're welcome to return to Progress City, file your reports and get back to your day-to-day life, but. . ." he raised his index finger for emphasis, "after what happened here yesterday, we've justly declared any GEEO agent, security personnel, administrator or district entity as persona non gratis. You understand? Madison District is now off limits to you people and anyone crossing into it will be dealt with as an intruder. Whether taken into custody or shot on sight will be up to our discretion. You understand?"

Candler pursed his lips and nodded once. He felt offended and stunned by Davis' declaration. Madison was essentially seceding from the regional government and de facto from the global council of governments. This could start a trend, a cascade of similar secessions. Madison District would have to be nipped in the bud and dealt with severely to serve as the example of how renegade districts would be treated.

Yet, even "dealt with severely" in no way reflected the brutal acts under Jones' orders. He could see why the people of Madison would be so incensed by Jones' horrific measures, which were not at all in accord with the basic precepts. Jones had gone rogue— no way would his superiors have sanctioned such extreme tactics. To Candler's knowledge, no one had ever been summarily executed, especially a bona fide citizen of Progress City like Estelle Pierce. For that matter, he'd never seen citizens used as hostages to draw in retros. Totally out of line and unprecedented. Jones!

"What about Agent Jones? What are your intentions?"

The man's face went from amiable to fierce as he leveled his eyes at Candler. "Our intentions? Intentions?" He drew a deep breath to contain his fury. "Mr. Greaves, I can assure you that DM Jones will be accorded justice, the same as any monster you can name with a history like his."

Candler frowned.

"Oh, so you're not aware of the history of DM Jones? AKA the Black Fiend, the Butcher of Caldwell, the Dread of Darrow, the Beast, the Demon? Hmmm, apparently not.

"Well, Mr. Greaves, I'm frankly surprised you really don't know about your compatriot's black-hearted doings. I reckon to take your blank expression as one of ignorance."

Candler blinked under Davis' harsh gaze. He flashed through memories of rumors, sidebar conversations, water fountain chatter and admitted to himself, Jones was known as a bête noire as it related to the districts under his authority. He was described by some as a hardliner that had garnered him a phenomenal bag and tag rate, which, in turn, propelled him up to ever-higher rankings. His tactics were said to be draconian but obviously quite effective. Whispers of something called the Swain County Massacre, orchestrated by Jones, had been dismissed by gossipers once the allegations were officially labeled unsubstantiated. In response to Davis, Candler equivocated, "We agents at the lower levels are on a need-to-know basis with what goes on in other districts and at higher levels."

"Well, son," Davis said in a less strident tone, "I think I believe you, but if you've spent any time around that bastard you'd have to know he's a shit poor excuse of a human being."

Candler considered what he'd known about Jones apart from the rumors. Jones was for sure a jerk, braggart, a bully, a sleaze and all, but never had he featured him as an all-out sadistic monster. Then he thought about the tragic scene that had unfolded in the courtyard the day before: the execution, Jones' fiendish, sated countenance and his frothing manic beast-like behavior when shot and held captive. "Greaves, you fucking coward! I'll have your head for this! You'll see!" The hatred fairly bilging from Jones' twisted face hovered for a moment in Candler's memory. *Yes, a monster indeed. The creature with that face would be capable of anything; murder, torture, genocide–anything.*

Candler looked down at the pattern of scratch marks etched into the tabletop and sighed.

Davis nodded, then spoke evenly. "Soooooo. . . maybe now y'see why whatever we do with Jones or to him won't compare hardly to the atrocities and hardship he's inflicted on masses of folks. He has no remorse. He only feels trapped and like any card-carrying psychopath–unappreciated.

"Oh, and by the by," Davis gave Candler the hint of a smile, "he's mainly blaming you."

Chapter 46

Round One
Midday, April 16, 2053

TO Renick stopped just below a ridge to
hydrate and eat a crumbly protein bar. She could hear
the ATVs approaching and as they grew louder, she
thought she heard Sergeant Mitchell shouting.

Hearing from the riders that her intended
target, Art Jones, was now in custody, gave her no
satisfaction. Even though she knew his fate was one of
pain and suffering, she realized that he could also be a
hostage and a high-level bargaining chip. She had no
bearing on all the politics of either side of these
factions, the trading back and forth between hostile
entities, but she was bound to make certain Jones
would get his due and if the Rangers didn't see to it, or
worse, negotiated releasing Jones for some pittance of
a concession, well, she'd already determined her self-
appointed mission and was bound to achieve it at all
costs.

"First thing's first, K," she murmured to
herself. She knew where the search party was headed–
the point last known, the PLK. That would be below
the next ridge down by the creek where their tags were
demolished. She was going to meet them halfway and
somehow take measures to defeat them by herself. She
knew Mitchell was an arrogant, ruthless pig–the kind
that would never miss a blood party and would rabidly
exact his own satisfying revenge on her for escaping
with the boy. On ATVs, they had the advantage going

uphill but if she made for the rock outcroppings, the terrain would be too rough and they'd have to pursue on foot. She figured the search team consisted of five, including Mitchell.

They needed some incentive to take the route to the rocks so she made her way to a stack of boulders where she drew a small round disk from her satchel, placed it on the lowest downhill rock and engaged the timer. *Two minutes should do.* She scrambled off to the side and downhill where she could conceal herself beneath a thick patch of laurels.

She listened as the ATVs rumbled closer hoping her timing was such that they'd be some distance away from her hide when the stones came down. From a prone position, she had a partial view of the old trail they were riding. Just as she spied the top edge of one of the ATVs, suddenly, their motors changed pitch as they slowed for some reason. "Come on, come on!" she whispered.

She heard one of the men call out, "Tree down!" Then someone farther away shouted, "To the right, you friggin' fobbit, go around it to the right!"

That'd be Mitchell. So, we meet again, sergeant.

She saw the ATV of the point man roll back as he cut a detour. He was headed straight toward her! Mitchell shouted something from behind and he stopped. *So close.* She could make out the man's face. Pale, unshaven, about her age. He was glancing down at a handheld tracking device and peering up at the ridge. He then looked in her direction, right at her.

She immediately thought that he'd spotted her or that she still had some kind of tag that had not been zapped. *Oh, shit!*

She slowly turned her face away and tried to flatten herself into the moldy wet leaves. Her right hand clutched a forty-five caliber pistol and there was a nine millimeter holstered in the small of her back. *That's thirty rounds altogether—not much to bring to the party if things break loose.*

The lead rider turned and shouted, "Sergeant, sir! I'd say we need to proceed along the intended route. Looks like we can break around those bushes and get back to the trail."

The sergeant shouted back saying something about daylight and moving on. The young soldier revved his ATV and began moving closer. Katrelle was kicking herself. She didn't see how he could miss seeing her as he approached. *Well, K., looks like plan B, whatever that is.* Instinctively she felt her body tense like a panther fixing to spring on its prey.

Then a muffled explosion above them shook the ground, and the sergeant swung his head around at the clacking rumbling sound. Katrelle looked up: *Oh no!* Rocks, some as big as their ATVs, came rolling down the slope at incredible speed with such force they were taking down the smaller trees and, in some instances, becoming airborne as they bounced. A massive rockslide was not what she'd intended.

The front rider's gaze transfixed on the scene above them. He sat there astride his machine with his mouth agape. She felt an urge to abandon her hide and drag him off the machine to safety, but she knew it would be impossible to close the distance and then make it to a safe spot. *A safe spot? Now where would* **that** *be?* The ground quaked, as the embankment gave way to the hurtling and growing wall of stone and debris.

Amid the din, Sergeant Mitchell must have shouted for his unit to take cover. She saw them dismount and dash toward the fallen tree to crouch behind its large trunk. Most of the rocks and boulders slipped off to the far side, but several large ones had pin–balled off the trees and terrain and, bouncing high, caught three of the ATVs dead on, smashing and dragging them downhill. Smaller rocks followed suit and the fallen tree where Mitchell and his men were taking cover was soon stacked and overflowing with stones on all sides.

As the barrage of falling rock passed by, the sounds of destruction receded down the slope into the valley. A few smaller slides above them still tumbled an occasional ripple of stones toward them. The old logging trail had acted as a channel creating a path of least resistance down which a slew of boulders had streamed. She'd had no idea. *Well, K, they didn't exactly cover DIY avalanches in training.*

Katrelle had been lucky. A massive boulder had lodged against a double-trunked tree just above her. Had that tree not been there, neither would she. She chanced a look through the foliage at the area where Mitchell's men had hunkered; they were not so lucky. She heard one man, maybe two, cough and another groaning in agony. She hoped Mitchell was among the casualties– if not dead, at least, severely injured.

The young soldier near her had apparently been struck with enough force to knock him off the ATV and carry him some distance down the hill. His body lay motionless and sprawled across the limbs of a rhododendron. His face was turned toward her, still transfixed in surprise, but the eyes no longer looked outward.

She slowly slipped out of her cover while holding her forty-five in ready position and cautiously approached the nearby ATV. Not only was it still upright, it was still idling! She kept the body of the vehicle between herself and the others, just in case someone over there had survived more or less intact. She peeked around and saw rocks being shifted and heard noises, then grunts, then words. Arms and legs began to emerge from the rubble.

Then she heard his voice. She had to admire Mitchell for his toughness and his ability to string together so many profanities in one breath. She steeled herself for either taking on Mitchell or making a break for it. If it became a shootout, she'd likely lose. He trumped her on marksmanship, range and armaments.

There also remained an ATV on the blocked trail that appeared to be in one piece. The one right next to her sat purring away. This was not at all like she'd planned it, but she was more than willing to seize this opportune moment. She slung herself up on the seat, positioning herself backward and lay prone on the tail end taking careful aim. No one had noticed her yet, but they did when she squeezed off three quick rounds in their direction. All three rounds hit her target: the only functional ATV. To her amazement, it actually caught fire. She spun and reseated herself in forward position and leaned as low as possible.

A flurry of cursing shouts and scrabbling rose up behind her. Her path led down and around trees and boulders. If she moved quickly, but not too carelessly, she might avoid the obstacles and flipping. She figured if she kept her back to them, they'd have to second-guess whether the boy was with her or not.

She couldn't help herself. She pumped her fist as she shot down the hill and let out a kind of warrior's yell, a cross between a rebel yell and what Custer might've heard a lot of at Little Big Horn. That was just before a swarm of projectiles shot past her; she could feel the wake of their trajectory as they whizzed by. *Close! Too Close!*

A hot spike of searing pain penetrated her right hip. The impact nearly knocked her off the seat. She whipped the ATV around a copse of evergreens and drove more sideways than downhill, hoping the maneuver would give more cover, but the bullets kept whistling past. Another one nearly creased her scalp. *They must be using IR scopes.* She was tempted to reach up and feel her head for blood but checking herself out was not a priority. She could feel seepage just below her right buttock and hoped it wasn't a main artery.

Just ahead, she saw the logging trail. It was clotted with rocks that she'd have to slalom around and over. She saw a break in the rubble and crossed over the trail just as she heard the first kawonk sound coming from the hill above her. More sounds followed. She'd just come beside a large boulder when the cluster of small incendiaries broke up and started exploding all around her. It was the same weapon Mitchell's team had deployed against the locals on the hillside. Only instead of gas ammo, they'd loaded incendiaries. She felt the stinging phosphoric heat about to envelop her.

There was nothing to lose. She crouched low, leaned forward, gunned the machine and careened downhill at high speed. Control gave way to momentum as she barely missed several large trees. The obstacles rushed toward her. Fast! Too fast! The rock ledge appeared just in front of her and in a flash, she and the machine became airborne. She felt momentarily suspended. Weightless and free, the wind whipping against her face, all sounds a distant roar. The machine sank below her like a rocket booster while she continued her trajectory above the canopy of bare branches.

Time stretched. The scene before her gained a beautiful clarity at treetop level. She spied tiny water droplets on a hemlock frond and a spider writing a secret glyph on its web while little bombs exploded in the distance. Pop! Pop! Scents of rain and luxurious woodland perfumes filled her nostrils. Eternity seemed to stretch out forever. *Perfect*, she thought.

A branch slapped her face and tore at her cheek. Another jabbed into her shoulder, spun her body sideways where she struck another tree and another. She began grabbing at branches to control the rate of her descent, but she'd become a ragdoll, and the forces of inertia and gravity dragged her mercilessly toward death. Nevertheless, she fought for control all the way down.

Chapter 47

Doc

Doc Davis' words echoed in his mind: "He's mainly blaming you. You. You. You."

That son of a bitch would write him up for this one and Candler could kiss his vaunted aspirations goodbye. *Probably put me on a farm somewhere or worse.* His reverie of misery to come was interrupted by Davis.

"Hey, Mr. Greaves, I wouldn't pay it any mind. You're a different sort. We have our own profile on you and while you've seen to your assigned tasks dutifully as a Green Hat, er um, agent that is, we know of no instance where you used physical force or blackmail. Well, except that little episode last week by Cross Creek when your gal pal put the hammer down on Hardy Wickline." Davis smiled, "but Hardy actually had it coming. The little twerp was on thin ice to begin with. The commander let him go right after that. I patched him up, packed his nose in a poultice and sent him home. Good riddance, I say. That boy needs to learn some respect. Maybe that little gal of yours taught him some." Davis laughed and shook his head.

Katrelle? She's no gal of mine. Although. . .

"Now, as I was sayin', we know what kind of game your agency is playing. We've seen you decrease the various public services, put out more land restrictions, cut the availability of this and that, especially medical treatments. We know you mean to entice, some would say sucker, us into living in your population centers, work in your factories, on your farms. You let on about how we'll be fed and taken care of in exchange for us doing our fair share as citizens. Many of us couldn't hardly wait to leave these parts and move into your beehives, but some were desperate, at the end of their rope and made the choice out of dire necessity—y'see? To a certain extent, Mr. Greaves, you really did rescue folks—and it seems you really believe how you're helping out. I'll warrant that.

"But, I'll say this one more time," Davis' voice was grave, "when you return to Progress City, let it be known that you and your GEEO folks had best not set foot in the district. We've reclaimed it and will fight to the last man, woman and child to keep it. Do you understand?"

Candler nodded. To his surprise, he found himself wondering if he had a choice not to return. *Then what?* He thought of Katrelle, remembering she'd disappeared along with the boy. She was a dedicated agent; she must have taken the boy as hostage, planned to use him somehow as a bargaining chip to save the mission or. . . *could it be she's turned renegade herself and has taken the boy to safety? Maybe I should ask this guy if he knows anything, but it might be a touchy subject if it looks like she's taken the boy hostage.* He decided not to ask.

"All this aside, Mr. Greaves, we hear you city folks are having your own troubles with your food, your power supplies and infrastructure. Hard to get new parts if the factories have shut down or you can't find the fuel to ship 'em, right? By the way, while we've appropriated a couple of power plants here in the district, you can't lay the problems you're having at our feet. No sir. Now, if you were to go back in history and make a study of what all went on with the collapse of Rome, Greece, Soviet Russia, Venezuela and the like, you'd see a common pattern. Top down, big intrusive government ruling in league with crony interests like banks and corporations just doesn't work.

"Your leaders are corrupt as any that've ever been. They are sucking their citizens dry. Why do you think them upper crusts are flocking in droves to their so-called resorts? Why is it, given all the food, water and energy shortages, your leaders are diverting huge lots of provisions to those very same resorts? Oh, Mr. Greaves, please don't look so incredulous. We have our sources that've reported and confirmed this.

"There's a sayin' an old African shipmate told me back in the day: 'When the waterhole gets smaller, the animals turn meaner.' What do you think your fearless and faithful leaders are going to do when the fan dips down in the shit?"

Candler had no answer. He was internally resistant to what he'd heard. Yet, he was having a hard time steering around the truth he'd seen and realized himself. Things were falling apart. Rations had decreased in proportion and increased in cost, but the leadership seemed to be thriving in spite of it all.

Yet, his lifelong ambition was to be a part of the very leadership Davis was decrying. He wanted to help guide humanity toward a harmonious existence with the planet. From his childhood readings of the revised "Rescue Mission: Planet Earth" to the lessons on green ethics, he'd always thought such a massive undertaking absolutely required the uber guidance of a global entity, and his region, his city, was a part of that entity. They were making progress and he was helping them. Wasn't he?

He could only muster a lame question. "How do you know all this–being isolated like you are?"

"Like I say, we have our sources. There're more people bailing out of the city than you might think. I'm sure your leaders wouldn't want it known. There's some showin' up here. We don't just take 'em back, y'see. Our resources are limited too. They have to have a skill or something to contribute. We interview each and every one. Ones that we turn away go elsewhere. There's a number of refugee settlements in the foothills. I guess they're scraping by but, uh, back to the question: We come by information in other ways too. Ways I'm neither allowed or inclined to speak of. Let's just say we've got eyes and ears in high-powered places."

There was a momentary lapse in the conversation. Candler mentally sorted through the possible moles within his administrative realm. The sounds of the cleanup crew were accompanied by the tapping of light rain on the tin roof.

Davis absently twirled one end of his handlebar mustache then broke the silence. "Okay, enough jabber. Let's get a look at ya."

The doctor's demeanor changed as he took on a professional air. Grabbing a black zippered bag, he opened it up and began fishing out the tools of his part-time trade, an old otoscope, several tongue depressors, a stethoscope and some kind of wooden mallet.

Candler looked at the implements then glanced around the room where Sheila and her sons were still busily engaged.

Doc answered his unspoken question, "Aww. Don't worry. There's more light here and no one will pay us any mind. Just take off your shirt."

Chapter 48

Celi's Diary
April 15, 2053

It's dark and middle of the night. I'm afraid to sleep. I do but then I see the faces of them. I see the dead elk rise up and shake the man from its antlers and the man, all bloody, swings up and rides on the skeleton of the elk and comes at me hollering "I gotcha now!" And I jump up out of bed shaking like a leaf.

Gram has even taken me to her bed for comfort, but it hardly helps or I might see the big man with those empty eyes right in my face. They pop out and blood covers me. I drown in blood and I scream myself awake or I think I'm awake and I look out my window and see the men standing right outside, grinning. Oh, God, I hate even writing about this. I hate it!

Gram is there. She holds me and rocks me. I still haven't told her everything. She thinks it was animals that got after me. Well, it was like animals, but I don't know if animals could hold so much evil inside. I stay awake until the day comes on and then I can sort of sleep on the couch with the window curtains open.

Gram, she worries enough about Pa and likely Uncle. I don't need her to worry about me. I just want to go back to being the way I was before, but I'm so jumpy inside, at the least little thing. Gram keeps saying this too shall pass or to just give it time. I think she knows something more about being attacked. The coyotes attacked her for sure, but she's made out like there were other times. I just want to have a normal life. I am afraid to go outside alone. I don't like being this way. Fact is, I HATE IT!

Chapter 49

A Message Found
April 16, 2053

While returning to his quarters, Candler noticed the hallway remained perfectly stable. The floor didn't move in waves under his feet and he felt nearly one hundred percent. The Doc had indicated the same. Looking at Candler's eyes one by one and then flashing the bright light from one eye to the other, Doc had seemed pleased with the results. He had Candler do a few balance postures, several rapid head swivels with eyes open, then with eyes shut.

"Well, son, looks like you're making a fine recovery. I still advise you stay another day or two–for observation. I'll check in on ya tomorrow. Just take it easy; drink a lot of water. They've got good spring water here. Let Sheila know if you have any problems or need anything. All right?"

Back in his room, Candler realized it had been days since he'd seen his lap desk or his closed cell earphone. *Man, I've been so out of it. Anybody could've taken them.* He started looking in the lockers across the room and to his relief, he spied his earphone on a shelf just above his jacket and cargo pants but his lap desk was nowhere to be found.

He wandered over to his cot and peered underneath. Nothing but a scrap of folded notepaper. *Hmmm. That's odd to see paper just laying around. Hardly anyone uses paper notes anymore.* He picked it up and unfolded it. He was surprised to see it had been written to him, and scanning to the end, he saw Katrelle's initials penned at the bottom.

It began without any formal salutation or introduction and appeared to be written in haste though legible.

Agent Greaves
I can no longer abide with the tactics and increasingly violent attacks on the people of my homeland. I am resigning immediately with the full knowledge and expectation that this will mark me for life as a traitor and deserter in the eyes of the authorities. But before you join in the hunt for me, have a look at the encrypted file I put on your PM board. Use your personal key. It reveals that our mission was a set-up, a lie!
One last request: When you return to PC, please do all you can to see that my mother and brothers are not punished on my account. They are innocent.

Respectfully, KR
PS: Taking Pierce boy and mother
PPS: Destroy this note

Respectfully? Candler was crestfallen. He'd no chance to thank her for getting him back to Madison, basically saving his life. She'd watched over him as he phased in and out of consciousness, and although not really hovering, at least he'd felt she was always nearby, and he'd hoped it was more than just loyalty. *Perhaps...*

Her message seemed only personal when mentioning her family. She wanted him to give special attention to them and he would certainly see to it, but his heart sank every time he read the sign off, "Respectfully." *Well, buddy,* he thought to himself, *you really got yourself going for nothing.*

He heaved a deep sigh and slumped down on his cot. His thoughts turned to finding his lap desk. A spike of panic shot through him as he tendered the dark possibility that Jones had taken it. This only made his search more desperate. He stood up and began searching every area of the room, the lockers, his field satchel, even behind the chem toilet. Nothing!

He looked at the table beside his bed. He walked over to it and tried to open its skinny drawer, but the wood had warped and the drawer was jammed tight. *Nearly impossible to open. Nearly,* he thought, *but not impossible.* He placed a hand on the top and tugged at the drawer's knob as forcefully as he could. It barely budged. In doing so, the table shifted and he heard something rattling inside. *Maybe.* He managed to grab the lip of the drawer on either side and gradually, by wiggling it side to side, gained access. When he squeezed his hand in and his fingers made contact, he knew what it was immediately. *Gotcha!*

Someone, likely Katrelle, had stashed his lap desk in there knowing how hard it would be to extract.

When he switched on, he was glad to see it was over halfway charged.

Just as Katrelle had said, there was an encrypted file in his PM folder. He keyed in his code and chose the custom decryption format. It took a few seconds before the jumbled script blinked and the contents became readable.

At the top of the page was a note. This time, there was no salutation at all.

> *Deep searched all files pertaining to the Celi Pierce writings and transmissions. We received only partial. Much more reveals true nature of our mission. Also, discovered time stamps had been changed. A. Jones was assigned to do cleanup and acting under EPA to obtain a certain device (see docs). Our mission was set up from the get-go; intended to fail. KR*

The main document contained excerpts from the girl Celi's diary. What RM Dirkson had handed over to him evidently had been altered. There were additional entries that had been culled out. One in particular was devoted to her uncle and father's discovery of some kind of generator. Someone, he presumed Katrelle, had underlined and highlighted sections of the entry.

In the margin, she'd written:

T
H
I
S
I
S
W
H
A
T
T
H
E
Y
,
R
E
A
F
T
E
R
!!
!
N
O
T
A
P
E
R

S
O
N
B
U
T
T
H
I
S
M
A
C
H
I
N
E
!!
!
K
R
P
S
B
E
T
I
T
I
S
N
,
T
F
O

R
P
R
O
G
R
E
S
S
C
I
T
Y
C
I
T
I
Z
E
N
S
E
I
T
H
E
R
!

Chapter 50

When the Man Comes Around
Late Afternoon April 16, 2053

Virgil and Stokes split up when they rode into town. Stokes went to the town center to check on things while Virgil had business to attend to at the old mill. Jones was being held at the mill awaiting what Virgil liked to think of as an interview. The ultimate disposition of the captives, particularly Jones, invoked heated and often conflict-laden opinions from just about everyone. Suggestions like, "We oughta skin that Jones like a catfish, and let the buzzards have him while he's still breathin'" or, "Let's scalp him, then cut off his fingers, one at a time, and then his toes, keep him alive while we draw out his guts" and other imaginative modes of horrendously painful dispensations.

The blood lust ran hot among his men and Virgil understood its vengeful basis. The gas attack on the hillside had congealed a hatred among the clans that would be hard to control—now and later. Once the ego-driven Jones had started his loudspeaker tirade of demands, a shiver of caution had made Virgil motion his men to scatter from the hillside where Jones aimed his words. Even at that, two of his men, still too close to the detonation of the gas, had suffered dreadful deaths, writhing in pain within view of their comrades. Virgil had to hold back those who wanted to help the two—the gas would have killed them as well. By the time the agony of those men had ended and the gas dissipated, a burning hatred for Jones and all the Green Hats had been permanently seared into the hearts of his men.

Now, Virgil found it no easy task to turn the tide of that hatred and counsel more circumspect treatment. He played the trump card that it was his niece whom Jones executed and that her husband, Ben Pierce, had more right to declare Jones' fate than any of them. He admired how Ben had restrained the urge to kill Jones outright. Actually, the orders to capture Jones alive had been issued by Virgil prior to the men taking up their positions, and Ben knew that Jones was more of an asset alive than dead. Yet, Virgil wondered if he himself could have held back from terminating the perp who killed his own wife. He knew the answer to that one—oh, hell no!

The protests among the men got so boisterous that Virgil had to issue an ultimatum. "If there's any among you not willing to abide by this decision, then you aughta leave this outfit. In fact, I insist. You can take what you brought with you–nothing else." No one rode away, and that pretty much solved the issue for the time being. The exception was Sid.

Sid kept on about hanging the "scrawny sonofabitch."

"Damn, son. He killed your nephew's wife. He gassed your men, for Chrissake! I'd sure as shit make him pay! A slow, painful, lingerin'. . ."

"I get it, Sid! Just know, I got plans for that sick bastard but we have to think strategically. It's pretty obvious what they came looking for, isn't it?"

"Ya mean that little Celi and them?"

"C'mon Sid! I thought since you were in my head you'd know what I was thinking. Hmmmm. Guess not." Virgil felt a wash of relief at this notion that Sid had his blind spots. "It's not the who. It's the what."

For a long moment, Sid was silent. Virgil thought maybe he'd run off somewhere to wherever disembodied pests retreat. Then: "Ohhhhhh!" Sid had it. "The machine. Somehow they know about the little dynamo, and they want it bad!"

"Yep." Virgil was riding up to the front door of the old mill. It was in pretty good shape. Though the waterwheel and the sluice had fallen down long before, the warped gray clapboards still held firm and the metal roof, orangish with rust, remained mostly intact. Virgil continued his back-and-forth. "And that's why we need to do this little interview, find out what they're aiming to do, and make them believe they have the upper hand.

"As Sun Tzu said, 'It is better to crush your opponent's spirit and to crush his will to fight than to face him head to head in battle.'"

"What's this Sunny Zoo fella got to do with anything? Damn son, you got some pretty strange ways of thinking."

Virgil had to smile. His hand was reaching for the door latch. "Well, Sid, maybe that's how I've come to live this long; whereas you cashed in at, what?" Sid did not answer. "Oh, that's right. Twenty-eight." Funny, whenever the subject of his early demise was brought up, Sid would turn peevish and stop conversing. This suited Virgil just fine. He had work to do.

Chapter 51

The Interview
April 16, 2053

The day before, Art Jones had a violent fit laced with claustrophobic terror from being gagged and strapped to a chair. After that, he'd been taken to some kind of rundown plant. The guards' instructions were, "Do your best not to kill him. If he starts bleeding bad, call it in. He'll be interviewed in the morning, Oh-nine-hundred."

When the guards closed the door, once again, panic hit. The walls closed in on him; he trembled all over, gasping for breath and he rocked the oak wood chair so violently it fell over and both his wounds started bleeding. Lying on his side, Jones watched as the white bandages reddened with fresh blood. He felt weakened so much that he ceased his hysterics.

A guard came into the room and roughly set him upright. Seeing the fresh blood, the guard warned Jones, "Look here, you sonofabitch, I gotta call someone to get you fixed back up. Next time, I swear I'll let your sorry ass bleed out." He cuffed Jones on the back of his head. "Are you hearing me?" Jones gave a jerk of his head and said something unintelligible through his gag. "I'll take that as a 'Yes.'"

Their assistant medic came in and redressed the wounds. He, too, warned Jones that they had limited supplies and better things to do than to keep doctoring him.

Jones had remained in the old plant all night under guard. He had drowsed off and on through the night, exhausted by his violent outbreaks and loss of blood. He experienced cycles when his wounds throbbed with pain. Then, endorphins would kick in and the pain would subside enough for him to doze. How many cycles? He'd lost count.

At oh-eight-fifty, a man appeared with a jug of water and a towel. Jones' head cocked to the side as he heard the sound of someone approaching. Seeing the jug and the towel jolted him with fear. He was certain that he was about to be water–boarded, a terrifying interrogation procedure he himself had employed on many occasions.

Instead, the man set the jug down and produced a glass that he sat on the floor. He filled the glass halfway and left it on the floor. His demeanor was collected, cursory, and, unlike the other guards, he was deferential in his tone of voice. "Mr. Jones, I've brought water for you to drink. You'll not be receiving any other sustenance as long as you persist in screaming and yelling. We don't want you gagged and choking on your own vomit.

"So, I'm gonna offer you this water, but you need to keep quiet and not make a ruckus? Nod if you agree."

Upon the mention of water, Jones became aware of an extreme thirst. His throat was raw and his tongue dry as lizard skin. He nodded. The man removed the gag and helped Jones drink a couple glasses of water. "I need to piss, now." Jones said this, but his goal was to get out of his constraints and possibly escape. Surely, they'd allow him an opportunity to relieve himself.

The man tending him gave a slight smile and said, "Go ahead. What's stopping ya?"

A torrent of rage enveloped Jones. This time, ungagged, he could vocalize it. He yelled, "Don't you realize who I am? I'm a Blue Level Admin, you hokey shithead! You inbred backwater pig! Do you even know what that means? I am a high-ranking officer of the Global Energy Enforcement Organization. My office will have dispatched a squad of SFs that will be here at any moment and wipe out every single one of you. Then they'll spread out and find your miserable shitholes where you live and leave nothing, not a single one of you stinking retros, not one. All of you! Dead! You hear me? Dead!"

By this time, veins were popping out of Jones' rage-reddened face and neck. Fresh patterns of red were filling in the white of his bandages. He saw the man casually pick up the gag.

"Oh no, you don't! You friggin' dog-faced piss ant. The only way you get anyone out of here alive—anyone!—is you let me go! I am a high-level officer of the GEEO. If you want your families, your ragged little urchins, to live out their miserable lives in this cesspool of a district, you let me go, now! Let me go or you're all dead!"

Instead of responding to Jones' vociferous diatribe, the man drew a pocket watch from his vest and clicked it open. "Well," he said as if to himself, "I don't reckon we'll need the gag anyways. Boss'll be here soon."

"Well, you can tell your goddamned boss he better let me go. . . or. . ." Something in Jones' peripheral vision caught his attention. A tall figure shadowing the doorway. It spoke low but with a clear excoriating intensity.

"Oh, we'll release you all right. Right outside the gates of your city. We'll release you. Alive. Free as a bird."

Jones twisted his head around to see who'd spoken. The figure in the doorway moved toward him, silent as smoke. A long gray coat opened at the front, a dark gray fedora atop his head made him look taller. His boots were laceless and mud-stained, but left no trace in their wake as he came closer.

The man's face was like stone; his countenance was that of a man who'd seen lifetimes of hardship, each deeply furrowed line on his unshaven face carved by tragedy. The cold gray eyes regarded him with unblinking intensity and Jones had to admit they betrayed a fierce intelligence. Jones knew this was the same man who had dragged him into the town center. If he'd ever feared anyone, it would have to be this man but he was loath to admit it.

Virgil Johnson motioned for the attendant to leave, then drew up another chair and sat down nearly knee to knee with the prisoner. His eyes leveled intently at Jones. The man repeated, "You'll be returned in due time, Agent Jones, but first we have some questions to—"

"Who are you to question me?" Jones interrupted in as haughty a voice as he could muster.

The interrogator silently deliberated. Then he spoke, "Let's just say I'm the one standing between you and an angry, vengeful mob just outside this building who'd love to tear out your black heart, rip your head off and stick it on a pike."

Jones reacted. "Bullshit! I'm not some simpering low-level plebe you can intimidate into spilling their guts. I insist that you release me immediately or face total annihilation. Do you understand? If you're the lead rabble-rouser, I demand that you release me this instant! Or we'll see whose head ends up on a pike!"

"I see. . ." Virgil's left hand flashed as it struck with a side motion to the left side of Jones' neck. A bag of glass shards burst open in his head. The pain was instantaneous and excruciating; he nearly blacked out.

When the room came back into focus, the stone face loomed before him. Gray eyes were steady and bore a resemblance to that of a predatory raptor.

"Welcome back, Agent Jones. Let's do a quick reality check. There's nobody coming for you. We've been in communication with your home base sending updates on the great progress you're making in your mission to bring in the rebellious retros of Madison District. Your forces were taken completely by surprise and had no time to report anything on their own. Do *you* understand?"

Jones' head was still wobbly, but he managed to nod. *He's bullshitting. No way.*

"We need information and how that is obtained is entirely up to you, Agent Jones. That little tap on your neck was just a prelude to what could be a symphony of pain, but should you choose to cooperate, there is no need for such intensive measures. Do *you* understand?"

AJ sagged in his chair. His desire for self-preservation was paramount, so he began to recalibrate a new strategy. He would play their game, feed them all kinds of misinformation, maybe do some damage to his rivals, and then, when he was returned to Progress City, he'd unleash a firestorm of vengeance. This would be the turning point for his agency, what he had hoped for all these years—the extermination of all retros. He, Alexander Jones, would be at the vanguard! His ambitions reached far beyond being just the regional director. He could definitely envision his rightful place among those in the Global Directive.

Yes, indeed. This situation could actually work well into my dossier: brave agent wounded in battle, taken as prisoner by violent savages who realize his value and cash in on some kind of ransom. Yet, he's able to sabotage the efforts of his captors in the process, and upon his return is hailed as a hero. Through the haze of pain and looming defeat, Jones saw himself as the fabled phoenix rising from the ashes to great heights of glory.

After the first few deceptive answers, the man in gray became ominously silent and regarded Jones like a general would survey the arena of battle—distant, calculating. "Agent Jones, you must have done enough of these types of interviews yourself to know we'd be asking an occasional question for which the answer's known or some question that was purposely baseless and had no answer. So far, you've failed to convince us of your sincerity and willingness to cooperate."

Odd. Why is he saying "us" when he's the only one here?

"So, Agent Jones, you have one last chance to answer fully and in truth. Or. . ." A hand slipped forward cupping Jones' chin while a single finger on the other hand pressed into a point just behind his ear. His head lit up in a panoply of flashing light and excruciating pain. Jones squealed like a piglet caught in barbed wire. After an interminable period–actually about twenty seconds–the pressure eased and the throbbing pain lessened with each pulse. "Last chance, Art." A frozen smile was fixed on the old man's lips as he emphasized his first name.

At this juncture, Jones reassessed his strategy and began to sing like the proverbial canary. It was in this stream of revelations that Virgil learned of the Regional Administration's grand scheme. Jones left a few bits out pertaining to his personal agenda, but only he knew about those. He still had Greaves to blame when he got back to Progress City, and now that little bitch Renick who'd apparently gone retro could provide cover too. Plenty of room to operate and spin his own version of how the retros came to know of their true mission. *These stupid ass retros will do what they call the honorable thing, release me, and then. . .* He savored the bloody, burnt imagery of his surprise comeback. *Then it will be* my *turn!*

Chapter 52

Round Two
Afternoon April 16, 2053

How she'd been able to climb the tree so badly wounded, with a head concussion that kept throwing her off balance, and in bare feet, made her question the sincerity of her death wish. *Just get outta this mess, Kay. Then terminate Jones, and then we'll do what we gotta do.* She laid down lengthwise on a thick horizontal tree limb, hoping she'd not be spotted from the ground. She could hear men coming down the hillside. A jolt of rage coursed through her. *Dammit, Kay! You should've just taken them out one by one. I'm like a treed raccoon. If they spot me, I'm dead but not without a fight.* Instinctively, she went to grab her pistol from its side holster and then remembered it and the rifle had been lost during her rapid descent through the tree limbs. She barely touched the wounded area of her right thigh. A flash of pain riveted her attention for a moment, then subsided. The endorphins had worn off and she knew she'd soon be dealing with effects of shock.

They came closer. They'd split up and were doing a sweep. She turned her head and gazed down at the rock ledge a short way downhill. Her boots were just barely visible protruding from the shelter of the rock overhang. For extra effect, she'd smeared blood on them. The diversion might work if the search party kept their eyes to the ground. As she lay there, listening to the sounds, she tracked back to her moments of heightened consciousness just before crashing into the trees. Never had she felt so aware, so connected. *What* was *that?* Her question hung in the air for a moment and quickly faded as she saw two men approaching her position. *Well, Kay, game on! Time to show 'em what we got left.* She pressed her body down wanting to merge with the tree as much as she could and lay dead still.

The blotches of blood were fresh on the ground. The lead man signaled the other one to approach from the far side while he edged farther around the nearside of the rock. They'd spied her bloody boots. Apparently, there were just two of them, Mitchell and a slug named Dumwalt. She'd heard some shots earlier and thought they were aimed at her. Maybe not. Another jab of pain shot through her leg sending her body into a series of convulsions. *Shit! Shit! Shit! Not now!* She focused on her breathing. *Breathe!* She pulled in a lung full of mountain air, a cooling balm to the shivers that threatened to overtake her. *Easy, easy.*

Alerted by the exposed boots, the men below her had both raised their weapons and now came toward the ledge from opposite sides. Dumwalt broke the silence. "Hey sarge, why don't we just shoot her feet off? Huh?" Mitchell made a hand motion for Dumwalt to STFU.

Mitchell hated everyone but based on her prior observations, Dumwalt occupied a special place on Mitchell's beat-down shit list. He often referred to Dumwalt by the handle "Dumb shit." Obviously, Dumwalt hated it. No one would be surprised to hear of a friendly fire incident between these two men.

After seeing Mitchell's gestures, Dumwalt glared back, eyes seething with malice. Mitchell missed the look, as he crept closer to the rock. "All right, doll, you make it easy for us and come out showing us your hands. No weapons, understand? Do you hear me?" His voice was beguilingly soft and disarming. He saw Dumwalt coming around from the other side and motioned him to stop. Mitchell stood almost directly below her perch. *They've taken the bait! Now what?*

She'd need to take both of them down almost simultaneously, but how? Mitchell would be no problem, but Dumwalt could duck behind the rock for cover.

Mitchell's voice switched over to a harsher, foreboding tone. "Do ya hear me, Renick? You come out right now and show yourself or I'm gonna shoot your fuckin' feet off one at a time and leave you to the coyotes and vultures. I'm counting to three. Show yourself, bitch!"

Still. Nothing.

He raised his AR10; a bright green dot danced like a firefly on her left boot. "One. . . two. . ."

"Three!" she called out from above and behind him. He spun around, caught the blur of her as she dropped from the tree just before the violent force of her bare heel slammed into his temple, and he dropped hard on his side. He rose to one knee and fired off a splatter of rounds at his attacker, but she'd already rolled to the side as gunshots flew above her. Suddenly, Mitchell groaned as a bullet slammed into his left shoulder. They both snapped their heads toward the source. Mitchell instantly fired off more rounds but now in that direction. Direct hit! Dumwalt yelled just as he was hit, then staggered over the edge of the rock, and fell out of sight. "Dumb shit!" Mitchell cursed. Then he stood up, ignoring the pain and blood flow coming from his shoulder, and whirled around gunning for Renick. "Right. Now it's your turn, you little—"

"Hey sarge!" He twisted in the direction of the voice. "Mission accomplished, asshole. You found me!" She sprung from his blind spot. A hard object crashed into the side of his head. He fell hard to the ground and did not move.

Chapter 53

The Tracker
April 16, 2053

The tracker followed the signs to the first body. It had been there for a time, its skin white as alabaster. Something had pierced the neck, cut the artery clean. Then he noted the projectile's fletching barely poking out of the neck.

He soon spied the splotches of blood at the base of a big tree. All around it, in fact. What would create such a design? He discovered a black-feathered arrow a hand's toss away. Actually, it was a crossbow bolt. Had a kinda distinct notching. He wondered if it was the one that killed the man lying stiff on the ground.

He'd been smelling something rank the whole time, but it seemed a lot stronger than what just one mouldering body would make. In fact, it seemed stronger by the tree. Even more so as he approached the sinkhole. There it was, some thirty feet down, a body laid out like an old discarded scarecrow stretched over a bare-limbed hawthorn. Only not a tree, but a rack of considerable size.

Had they gone down together? Did the man crucified on the antlers kill the white-skin? Did the elk run down and gore the scarecrow only to fall to its death?

All a mystery, except for two things. He knew

the scarecrow's name was Grady McDowell and the man sucked white on the ground was a certain Carter Burkhart, son of Sade.

He spoke to himself. "I'll figure this out, but the hardest thing to figure will be breakin' the news to Sade."

Chapter 54

At the Edge of Town
Evening April 16, 2053

Crawly Mayfield was on guard duty that night. He was posted at a choke point just outside of town. It was where the road into town narrowed as it was bounded by a nearly sheer rock cut-in on one side and a very deep drop off on the other.

By Crawley's stem-winder, it was nearly three a.m. and the weather was miserable. He had a slicker to stop the rain but the cold was seeping into his bones from the ground up and he had to piss something awful. Something about Sheila's coffee just set his bladder on edge. He'd already gone three or four times—walking over to the edge of the road, slinging his rifle behind him, undoing his slicker, digging into his trousers and eventually achieving some relief. It just made him wetter every time. It also left him very vulnerable.

"Well, hell's bells!" he murmured. "One more time. Damn that coffee!" He proceeded with the ritual of pissing over the bank. Before he was finished, a very light sound came from behind him. Suddenly, a hand clamped over his mouth and a five-inch blade pressed flat against his throat.

"Surprise!" It was a woman's voice, right in his ear. He was in a fix and an embarrassing one at that. He'd forgotten all about peeing, but his hands were still frozen in place.

A gruff whisper demanded, "Who are you and who are you with?" She jerked his head back just a little. "And no bullshit, mister or you'll wind up singing soprano. Do you understand?" He thought he detected a bit of desperation in her voice, but sure as hell wasn't going to be a hero.

She slid her hand from his mouth to grab a hank of his hair.

"I'm, I'm . . . I'm Crawley Mayfield. Serve with the Mountain Rangers."

She didn't let up. "So, Crawley, who's your commanding officer?"

"CCCCCap'n Johnson. Virgil Johnson." He felt the blade slip and the hand release.

"All right, you finish up there." After a moment, Crawley buttoned his slicker and started to turn around. He caught just a glimpse of a diminutive wild-haired creature before the muzzle of a handgun pressed against his back. "Whoa! Stay turned around. You got a radio? Good! Call in and say Art Jones has a visitor and that visitor needs an escort."

He complied. The base station operator apparently forwarded the request and got a quick answer. "We're sending an escort now."

"Not to worry, Crawley. You did just as I asked. I had to come on pretty strong 'cause I'm actually feeling a little. . . a little. . ." He turned his head and saw her swaying slightly. Her face was white and her eyes were aflutter and unfocused. He looked at her pants; they were soaked, but the right pant leg was several shades darker than the left. She was wearing a tactical jacket that had been shredded and torn. He'd not seen anyone in this bad shape still standing. The woman seemed to recover slightly and shoved her pistol back in its holster.

She smiled and said wanly, "You tell 'em TO, that is, Katrelle Renick is here." Crawley edged up closer and taking her right arm, slung it over his neck. He had to crouch down since she was so short. She didn't resist or complain. He knew he was busting protocol to leave his post, but the little gal half draped across his back was in a very bad way and wasn't going to make it for long. Something about her, or maybe the way the dispatch answered so quickly, made him think it was worth the breach of duty. If they at least met the escort team halfway, she'd maybe have a chance. He gallantly offered to carry her, but damned if she didn't insist on walking.

Chapter 55

Parting Ways
April 17, 2053

She vaguely recalled being drunk-walked down an avenue and through a gate that looked somewhat familiar. What happened after that was a wash of bits and pieces: A man's face, then words, "You've lost a great deal of blood." What deal? What blood? Lying on a hard surface. A smell of turpentine, and the sensation of her body being turned, rolled, lifted. She drifted into a delirious mantra. "Jones, gotta get Jones, gotta. . ." She flailed as one does in a dream and connected with something solid.

"Dammit! Somebody get a hold of her!" A slight prick on her exposed arm and soon she blanked out completely.

In her next wakeful moment, she found herself lying on her side with a pillow between her bare knees covered with a sheet and a blanket. She scanned the dim room for something familiar, something that would let her know where they'd taken her. As she shifted her body, a sharp pain erupted in her thigh and she wondered why it hurt so badly. She reached down to touch the area and felt something like a tube had been shoved into her thigh. The slightest movement of the tube made her flinch. *Damn, what have they done to me?*

A hand came onto her forehead, a gentle stroke back toward the hairline. She heard a chair scoot forward and there, looking worry-faced, sat Candler

Greaves.

She managed to say "Hey."

His smile eclipsed his look of concern. "Hey. You made it back. You've been mostly out of it for twelve hours. The locals have taken over; they have killed nearly all of Jones' men and have taken Jones prisoner. They've been quite kind to me and say they'll allow us to return to Progress City."

Hearing Jones still lived stirred her resolve to get up. The pain stabbed her again and she slipped back into her side position. Candler grabbed a glass of water and a small pill bottle. "The most they can dig up around here is this Tylenol. No guarantee how old it is. It might help you rest. The doctor says you have to let your wound drain for some time before he can do anything else."

"Could I see the bottle?" He handed it toward her, label side out to read it, and let her take it. She quickly removed the cap and tilted the bottle toward her mouth. Half a dozen tablets landed on her tongue before Candler restrained her from downing the entire bottle. He grabbed it out of her hand. "Whoa, Kay. That's enough. You trying to kill yourself won't solve anything."

She rolled her eyes and pointed at the glass of water and he let her wash down the pills in her mouth. Then she shook her head at him. "I'm trying to kill the *pain* so I can get up and outta here. Something I need to do."

"Oh. Well, if it's something to do with Art Jones, I believe you'll have to stand in line. He killed a woman two days ago, a local woman. I never saw it coming. It was awful." He looked away as his eyes rimmed with tears and she saw the shuddering horror in his face.

She realized that she wasn't the only damaged goods Jones left in his wake. She softened. "Kinda funny, isn't it?"

He turned smearing his wet eyes with the back of his hand. He looked perplexed. "Funny? What do you mean? I don't see anything that is in any—"

She held up her hand. "No, no, not what we were just talking about. Just saying, it seems funny that only a few days ago, we were in the exact opposite places—you lying in bed all messed up and me coming in to check in on ya and. . ." His expression had hardly changed. He wasn't following. "Oh well, I guess maybe not so funny, huh?"

He dropped his shoulders and sighed. Then he smiled. "Y'know, you're right, but from what I've heard you actually did heroic things to get where you are. Me, I just mouthed off and wham! Out of commission for days, still having headaches, but a million times better thanks to you and the others. The locals who took over have been very kind and say I'm free to return to PC anytime. I had planned to leave today but when they brought you in like you were last night, well, uh, I just thought it best to stay and see if, uh. . ."

"If I was going to pull through?" He looked at

his feet and gave a nod. She reached out and offered her hand. He gently closed his own hand around hers and looked up at her, a little surprised blink at her gesture and personal touch. "But you know I resigned and after all I've done and all. . ." She continued in her mind, *and all I'm going to do.* "You've been a fine boss, a great agent, and a good friend, Candler Greaves." This time, tears welled in her eyes. She drew back her hand. *Stay on track, Kay. Watch yourself. Cover!* "Wow, this leg really hurts. Could I have just one more of those tabs, just one?"

He made a smile, but she saw his shoulders slump when she'd pulled back her hand. He grabbed the pill bottle and opened it. "Well, okay, here's one more tablet—and some water." He watched her swallow. He cleared his throat. "I can fix this. No one has to know what you've done. If Jones is let go, I'll make it his word against mine. I can make this work out so that we. . . that you. . . can return to the city with a clean account."

She saw the expectant look in his face and wished things were different. "Candler, I have seen too much and I have done a lot of damage. I've killed our soldiers and aided the enemy. As long as Jones is alive, I can never be. . . " She hesitated. It was a brush off and by Candler's sullen expression, his inability to look her in the eye, she knew he was feeling the effects. He stepped back and grabbed the empty water carafe from the bedside table.

"Well, okay then. I'll bring you more water." He didn't wait for her to say anything more. He turned around quickly and left.

Candler walked briskly down the empty hall, past the kitchen and never went back with the water. In his room, he fought the tears, the disappointment, the surety that they were set on different paths—maybe always had been—and there was nothing to do about it. What was now just diverging footpaths would soon enough be a canyon. Yet, her scent and the tone of her voice lingered through the night for him.

The locals had made it clear that he was free to leave anytime. So the following morning, he set out alone, driving a vintage Mazda compact, a one-way loaner salvaged from the motor pool that chugged away on its last wheels toward the lower valley and on to Progress City. He had become a kind of emissary to the GEEO leadership, tasked with relaying that the local area was, so to speak, under new management and not to be encroached. He would seek to broker some truce between the locals and the regional ministry. Dirkson was a snake in a suit, but Candler would do his utmost to keep an all-out war from breaking like bloody waves across the foothills and into the high country. Forget the upgrade to level blue, to hell with the mission to save the planet, to conserve the population. He would do it for her, even if he never set eyes on her again.

Chapter 56

An Ignominious End: Phase One

Three days had passed since the initial interview. A side-by-side ATV rolled up to the main road about two miles from the gates of Progress City with two people in its seats. They stopped, got out and lifted a lone figure out of the back cargo bed, setting it on its feet pointed in the direction of Progress City.

From a distance, one might describe the figure as some kind of phantasmagorical giant bird, covered with white feathers with black patches showing through random spots. Odd calling sounds, like elongated vowels echoed from it. Very guttural sounds too. Its head was black and bald and yet, on closer inspection, human eyes peered out from the black. The nose stuck out thin and pointy, yet it wasn't a beak. The pink and red lining of the open mouth contrasted with the blackened lips, displaying a ghoulish image.

The ATV turned and sped up a hill to a promontory that gave vantage toward the high walls of the city and the road leading to it. The two figures raised binoculars and sat watching the scene unfold as the strange bird-like thing shambled forward. The figure had a distinct limp and would occasionally throw out what appeared to be its left arm to compensate. What made this creature all the stranger was that it cradled in the crook of its right arm what appeared to be an old carbine rifle–the kind the hill folk still used. Only on close inspection would one be able to see that the rifle stock was attached to the man's inner arm with wrappings of twine that had been tarred over and feathered like the rest of him.

The guards posted at the city's gate had watched all this transpire and sited their weapons on the creature, alert to the possibility that some sort of attack might be underway. They called up an SP unit and dispatched them to intercept the lone figure. The unit rode out in three separate ATVs. One vehicle was a slightly larger side-by-side. It stopped fifty yards short of head-on. The two other vehicles flanked the intruder.

All the men had their weapons trained on the figure except for one SP, the command sergeant major, who held a megaphone up to his mouth. "Lay down your weapon and identify yourself or be fired on. Repeat. Lay down your weapon. Identify yourself! Or we will fire." Red dots flitted over the creature's white plumage.

The creature increased its strange vocalizations. "A om omm a om om. Eeeeeeee ommm ee aaaa oooo." The SPs were confused. They'd never heard of the old time punishment of being tarred and feathered.

They'd no suspicion that the creature's tongue might have been cauterized with a burning bit of coal and that the weapon being waved in their direction was firmly affixed and impossible to drop. For all they knew, this was a lunatic retro all done up in some weird camo outfit coming into the city zone on a suicide mission. They kept their distance and crouched behind their vehicles.

The sergeant turned the megaphone toward the ground and spoke into his headset. "Uh, captain, we gotta situation here. Looks like some kinda weird-ass retro, decked out in white feathers, coming in solo, making weird noises and refusing to disarm." As he spoke, his head cam captured the scene on magnification and was transmitting the image to the command control at security. "Right, sir. No sir. No shots fired. We only presume he may have an IED. Right sir, understood."

The SP keyed the megaphone. "Okay birdman, whoever the hell you are, this is the last time. Put down your weapon or you will be shot. You have ten seconds to disarm."

The countdown commenced. "Ten, nine, eight..."

By the time the countdown reached five, Art Jones had gone berserk, not with fear so much as with outrage. His angular arms waved and jerked like some animated demon from a Bosch painting. His words were garbled, but he screamed them nonetheless. He shook like a demon possessed by another demon. He cursed, he spat, his mouth spewed blood and vile imprecations at the soldiers, the retros, his circumstances, his thwarted machinations, the world of bastards. The last two things he heard through his tar-encased aureoles was "one" and the surprisingly robust thwack of bullets smashing into him from three directions.

The air cleared as the gunshots echoed away down the valley. The sergeant shouted to his men. "Bag 'im!"

The two observers on the distant promontory lowered their binoculars. Neither of them spoke. After the shots were fired, what was left of Jones was loaded into the larger ATV. If any of the soldiers had spotted them way up on the knob, none seemed too interested.

The tall one spoke, "Satisfied?"

His diminutive passenger replied, "Barely," then she smiled, "but worth getting out of bed for."

Chapter 57

An Ignominious End: Phase Two

The chief medical examiner rang up RM Dirkson saying he'd made a positive ID relying mostly on dental records. Jones' demise had an upside for Dirkson. He wouldn't need to be looking over his shoulder wondering if and when Jones would knife him. *Besides that, there's always a backup plan. Friends in high places.* He smiled at his own cunning.

What the ME had said about Jones no longer being tagged bothered him most. He'd been issued an advanced RFD CLASS 3 chip, but it had been removed–skillfully. After mulling over these findings, ever cautious, Dirkson advised the ME to eradicate all traces and admonished him to keep the matter under wraps. The ME was made aware as to how much the accidental termination of a high-level official at the hands of their own SP would negatively affect the populace—who were already roiling under the food and energy shortages. He swore he'd keep everything on the down-low.

To preserve this secrecy, Dirkson ordered that Art Jones' history, his data and, in effect, his entire life, were to be thoroughly swiped. There certainly could be no memorial services since the man officially had never existed. Not that anyone cared; Dirkson knew Jones had no surviving relations, and his co-workers and subordinates universally detested the man. His position could be filled by any number of rivals glad to do so and, of course, say nothing. Perhaps, he could wave the open position in front of the recently returned Agent Greaves. Greaves had yet to be completely shaken down by the interrogators. He'd handle Greaves.

The one conundrum Dirkson hadn't counted on surfaced when the ME called him, wrestling with what to do with the body. Jones' entire form had been covered in bituminous material, tainted by hydrocarbons that prevented it from being cremated–though it would have lit up like a candle. The usual green method of dealing with dead bodies was by dissolving the remains in a tank of corrosive lye, then recycling the sludge into fertilizer. It made for the penultimate "giving back to the Earth" but the ME's tank operators said they would not accept the tar-encased John Doe because of contamination concerns. Being a profligate, Jones had no credits in his account, but moreover, he was deeply in debt. There would be no monetary incentive to allay the concerns of the tank operators. RM Dirkson saw this sticky ending to the situation as emblematic of the failed mission. It wasn't his fault this mission had turned into such a mess but others might see it that way. He angrily informed the ME in no uncertain terms that he wanted no further involvement in the matter or manner of disposal.

So it was that Art Jones' remains were sealed within a recycled wooden crate and placed in the back of an old factory storeroom. The man, so convinced of his destiny to rule, might indeed have yet to incur a legacy. Perhaps, some future archeologists would decipher the oddity of his death rites and they'd conjure a very plausible theory about how certain deceased members of this ancient society received very special treatment like the pharaohs of old.

Chapter 58

Sid Confesses
April 17, 2053

They'd made camp on a high rise above the river valley. The night sky was diffused with the light of the full moon above the clouds. On occasion, the clouds would thin into a veil where one could barely make out that there was a cosmic realm. Virgil Johnson had just stepped away from the encampment and stood on the rock promontory gazing down into the coves laced with gossamers of ground fog.

His mind was tormented by images of Estelle Pierce in her final moments. He'd spied her through his scope seconds before her sudden execution. The memory dragged up similar hellish visions of his own wife and unborn child, the images wheeled past, then cratered. If only. If only he'd acted more quickly. *Just like I should've done with Stancie. Too late. Never should have left in the first place.* His thoughts rebounded to the scene in Madison. *Should have known that son-of-a-bitch was psycho. Goddammit! I need a shot of something!* He settled for a home-grown smoke. *It helped, a little.*

There was no consolation for either incident. It was all on him. Except perhaps that, just as he'd done in the past, he would don the black wings of an avenging angel and find a shred of solace in exacting retribution, what some might call justice, but he knew that, no matter what passed for justice, there was nothing to do for the pain. He started in again dredging up his failures to act or react and retching up fresh self-accusations. Sid's voice broke in as calm and even-handed as it had ever been.

"Hey there, amigo, you are salting over open wounds right thickly. It's doin' you no good."

Virgil closed his eyes and flung out his arms as if shedding on old serape. *Go on! Get out of my head. I don't need anybody advising or moralizing. By the way, where the hell were you, Sid Hatfield, when Jones gave the order? Huh, Mr. All-Seeing High and Mighty?"*

A gap of silence ensued. Then Sid came on in a fury. "What? The hell, you say? You tell me to quit and then you ask me a question like that? You think I know the future? You think I'm here to save you, Virgo? Jeezus H. Christ!

"You ever think maybe what happens is just supposed to happen? I'll warrant it's so. Bigger things to consider than how it affects just *your sorry ass*. We all play a part, Virgo. That Jones feller, your people, those riders, everybody has a part to play. It ain't what happens that's so monumental. It's how we deal with it. You get me?"

Virgil opened his eyes on the vista below and saw the tendrils of fog reaching upward toward the backlit screed of vapors skying the earth. "Well, it's easy to be so philosophical if you don't have to contend with this world."

"Really!" Sid sounded put out, even tired. He seemed to be chewing on something. Then, out of the blue, came, "They shat on my grave."

Virgil drew back. "What? Sat on your grave?"

"No. I said they shat. They dumped their bowels on my grave. Pissed on it too."

Virgil remained baffled. "Who? What are you saying, Sid?"

"The townsfolk, some would come up at night, drop their drawers and shit onto my grave. Just sayin'."

Virgil shook his head as if to shake sense into the voice that spoke something illogical. "But you were a hero! You fought off the company thugs. People went to war on Blair Mountain over your assassination!"

"That were the union's doing–not mine. I had me a number of enemies and they weren't hardly just the coal company men. I weren't no lily-white flower, y'see. At one point, they's callin' me the "Terror of Tug River." No way was I any sorta model citizen."

"Well, who is? But you were a police chief, a defender of the people, a protector of the working man."

"Well, that's the way the union organizers spelled it. I was also in it for myself, Virgo. A lot comes from being treated like a hero."

"Well, sure, but what you said about being defiled just doesn't fit."

Sid's tone rendered somber reflection as he

continued, "It does if you know that I grew into being a thug, a hit man, an intimidator and a thief. It didn't start out that way. I never knew my real parents, but was taken in by the Hatfields and raised as their own. I worked the Red Jacket mine. Couldn't stand it. So I learned blacksmithing as a youth and got skilled pretty good. A girl I cared for got beat to death and I went for the man who'd done it and after that, I took up being what they called a thug. A lot of it I did for the union people, but most of all for just me. I was a gang leader. I s'pose my earlier reputation never changed and that, for all the hero claptrap, I never redeemed myself among some of those townsfolk."

They both kept silent a moment. Then Virgil asked, "So why are you telling me all this, Sid? What's the point?"

"Well, Virgo, maybe I'm just tired of your bellyaching. Thought you might get over yourself if I explain some things. Truth is, I never was any kind of hero. Sure, I shot them Baldwin-Felts, and they sure as hell shot me—me and Ed, but it weren't nothing but one gang a fightin' another. I'd worked for the union for years, and they were just as greedy as them coal company fellers. We'd waylay payrolls, set fires and rob company offices. Fact is, they called in the Baldwin-Felts fuckers 'cause of men like me and we was layin' in wait for 'em to come. Was a set up from the get go.

"Being Two-Gun Sid, I got drinks, slaps on the back, admirin' looks from the women, and special considerations when it came to court hearins. When me an the boys got acquitted, my wife and I came back to a big hullaballoo in Matewan. Took us two hours to go two hundred feet from the station to the house, that crowd was so hepped up wantin' to thank me and all. Yes, sir. That was some receivin' we got." He paused as if to savor the experience. "Well, it weren't nothin' compared to my funeral when they say thousands turned out. Covered the hillsides they did. In the rain, no less."

Virgil cleared his throat. Once again, he caught himself starting to talk aloud. "Y'mean. You tended to your own funeral?"

"Why's that a surprise? Hell yeah! I wanted to see how'd it turn out." He sounded offended.

"Is that a common thing, dead coming to their own funeral?"

"More common than you might think, specially if you get kilt sudden like, and I'd linger now and then. That's how I knew those sons-a-bitches were shitting on my grave." He then turned stoic. "Yeah, them days was wild and loose. We did things. I did things that kinda made for them to act that way. "

"Like what?"

"No need to go into all that. 'Sides, I'm here to make up for it, maybe. Maybe come to terms with that hero bullshit them unions told."

"Earning your wings?" Virgil sounded sarcastic. He used it to ward off a feeling the rabbit hole he was tumbling down had no bottom.

"Wings? Naw. It's like I woke up into a dream. You ain't any more real to me than I am to you, Virgo, but from somewhere, I know, if'n I'm gonna find peace, it'll be when I reckon all the bad shit I done by doing something good. Nobody told me so. It's just in me to know that. Your cause is as good as any."

"So," Virgil was still doubtful, "you're here to square up to your hero legend?"

"And to light a fire under you ass, Virgo." It got quiet for a moment. "And, another thing. She's okay."

"Who's okay?"

"You know. She did her best to love you, to be a good person. Her soul is exalted."

"What the f–"

"Just know it! Same goes for that little gal of your nephew's. She'll be all right."

"How the h-"

"If you're gonna dote, do so for the living, Virgo 'cause it ain't over just by putting that scum bastard Jones outta commission. You have your own reckoning in your world and you're wasting time getting on with it. No amount of drink or slobberin' self-pity's gonna help. Point is, neither of us can amount to much until we see it through. I ain't no fuckin' hero, but we both could do what needs to be done. Let the cards fall where they may."

At Sid's sudden silence, his presence seemed to evaporate. Virgil had a million questions. The most troublesome concerned Sid's comment: "You ain't any more real to me than I am to you, Virgo." For an instant, Virgil felt like he was about to vaporize himself, to rise up into the cloud ceiling. Sid's words careened through his head: "She's okay." Virgil found himself looking up—at the sky, the clouds, whatever was above. *She's okay.*

He closed his eyes and took in a huge breath then slowly exhaled as if to release what remained of his life into the firmament. Yet when he opened his eyes, he found himself still firmly rooted on the earth. His thoughts turned to Ben, his estranged wife's body lying dead on a travois, awaiting burial. His nephew Jordy clenched in Ben's arms after they desperately tracked him down. Hearing revelations from the young woman who'd rescued Jordy and who then polished off the search team. From what Jones had told him, Rosie and Celi had wound up on the Green Hat's hit list. Likely the whole of Anthony District had been placed on that same list. Indeed, Sid was right. They would be coming after the little generator, coming after all who knew about it, coming after Celi and Rosie, and now Jordy.

Damn sure enough, there remained much to be done

Chapter 59

April (don't know date)
CELI'S DIARY

I don't know if I can write about this. I can
hear others in the front room. Speaking softly or not at
all. Gram pulled out her old collection of incense sticks
and has set them burning in all four corners of the
room. Jordy, my brother, is lying on my bed with his
eyes closed. I've been lying next to him for a long time.
He has not said anything about what happened. I have
not asked.

I know she left us. Her choice, but it was to live
somewhere safe, not die, and though Pa hasn't told it,
she didn't just die. I just know this is so. When I first
saw them out the window, I blew out the front door
and ran toward them, shouting, happy. I ran up to hug
them home but when I saw Pa's face I knew something
was bad wrong. I stopped and stood there trying to
figure what. Where's Mom?

Pa was carrying Jordy who kept his face turned
into Pa's coat. I looked behind them to see Mom. I
looked at Pa. He'd never looked so sad and gray. Mom?
He looked up at me and just that look told me she
wasn't coming. "Mom" I said, but Pa just came up
close, reached down and pulled me into him and Jordy.
I wrapped my arms around them both and squeezed
real hard. Pa groaned. I felt Jordy move a little.

"Let's get inside" was all he said and he let go
of me, but I kept my arms around them. I felt Jordy's

skinny shoulder bones poking out. He got really still. Then he started shaking and making this moan like a wounded creature, and he shook some more. I kept saying 'It's okay Jordy' but he would not stop. He made almost the same sound that came out of me after my time in the woods. Mom was gone. I just didn't know how gone she was.

Pa reached down and put his arm around me. I could feel his strength but could also tell he was shaky too. When I gave him another big hug, he groaned again. Pa, I said, are you hurt? He whispered in my ear that he was just a bit sore and we needed to get inside where Jordy could rest. We walked into the yard and up the porch steps.

Gram met us on the porch. She'd been watching us. She looked at Pa and he looked at her and shook his head just a little. I could see her little body sag down and she said something like, "Oh no," real soft and sad. Then she swung open the door and grabbed onto Jordy and took him into her arms. His head was laid across her shoulder. He was over half as tall as she was, but she cradled him in her arms as if he were a baby and then he went from wailing to crying. She carried him inside the cabin, sat down with him in her lap and pressed his head close to her chest. Tears ran down her face, but she never made a crying sound. She kept stroking his hair saying things like he was home, everything was all right, he was safe and all, but he never stopped crying until he started the wailing thing again.

I don't know why but I thought food might help, so I got to the kitchen and threw some wood into the stove and put the pot of soup on the top to heat. Pa came to the kitchen and began telling me about Mom in a quiet voice, I guess so Jordy couldn't hear. His words kind of bounced off me. I felt hard and like all this was some kind of bad dream. Mostly, I couldn't understand why they'd come to Madison, why didn't she and Jordy come back together. What happened?

I knew Pa was not saying everything. He had dirt and scratches on his face and red angry looking rings around his wrists. When I asked him about them, he said it was from carrying Jordy part the way home and getting caught up in some greenbrier. I was not fooled.

He wanted me to know that Mom was a good person who always wanted the best for everyone and that she wanted us all to be together but had had an accident on the way home. She hadn't suffered and was now up in heaven with Grandpa Jim, and they were watching over us. He tried looking me in the eyes as he said these things, even tried to smile. She was with the Lord.

Why did this have to happen? If God takes people to live with him like that, he has to be what Gram calls a bastard. Instead of saying this, I say to Pa that God is one mean sonofabitch. Pa looks at me and asks me where I got such a trash mouth and I say I hear Uncle Virgil saying it now and then. Pa says not to pay any mind to Uncle Virgil; I need to act like a young lady.

Then his eyes get kinda softer. He's getting those dark things under his eyes that make him look tired all the time. He hugs me and says something that I hear a lot about understanding when I get older. Older? I remember that he knows nothing about me in the woods and nearly being killed but instead me killing those devils. Skip it. Doesn't help to go back there. At least I am sleeping at night, mostly.

Well, we do have our secrets don't we? Some scars are obvious, but I believe the ones that hurt worst are those below the surface. I look at Pa with his scratched up face and his red wrists to make it clear I know there is more to the story. I say I am older than he thinks and what I understand is that people aren't telling me everything. He hugs me and I feel like he's trying his best to protect me, but it doesn't help the hurting inside.

Now, I look over at Jordy, finally sleeping next to me. He has come back to us and that is good. I will be his guard and protect him. I figure he has been through a lot. I want him to feel safe now. He is my little brother and I do so love him all the more. I am so very grateful. We are back to being a family once again and I won't let anyone change that ever again.

Epilogue

They'd rendezvoused at the old depot near the foot of Keller Mountain. Dirkson arrived in an armored train used for troop transport but containing just his own luxury Pullman. The two men sat in the salon section smoking cigars. Dirkson raised his glass of fine brandy. "Here's to the future and allies richly rewarded."

The burly man sitting opposite cranked up a crooked smile, raised his meaty hand and replied, "Here's to them that wish us well. All the rest, can go to hell!" Sade Burkhart then downed the entire portion in one swallow.

End of Book One

Afterword

Q. Why write this story?

A. Short answer "No system which implies control by privilege seekers has ever ended in any other way than collapse." Erik Larson

A. Several years back, when the high priests and (can I say?) priestesses of the global warming tsunami were rallying for an end to fossil fuels, pushing for green sustainable development (or rather cessation of capitalist industry) and a self-enriching carbon tax scheme, I began tracking down the promoters, the wizards behind the curtain, who stood to gain the most. They were found but there's nothing anyone can effectively do about them. Or is there?

The fact is, humanity has advanced this far on the basis of cheap, available, abundant fuel from carbonaceous material-coal, natural gas and, did I mention coal? The call for an immediate end to burning fossil fuels, if achieved, would be an unmitigated disaster. It's a future begging for dystopia. Yet, these do good planetary redeemers insist that disaster hangs like the Sword of Damocles, tethered by a thin hope that we can save this planet if only we can shut down all carbon intensive activities and bring on climate justice.

Seeing this anthropogenic global warming meme snowball into what is now a tenant of the politically correct uber status quo, I started toying with the idea: Well, what if the self-anointed planetary saviors achieved their ambitions and put all of our energy dependence on renewables? What if the same well-meaning coterie reigned supreme as a global greenocracy able to dictate their long-standing agenda verbatim?

Who would rule?

Who would be ruled, most willingly?

Who would be ruled, grudgingly?

More interestingly, who would NOT be ruled?

Five Hundred Days

Midstream while writing Mountain Whispers, French Foreign Minister Laurent Fabius stated, "We have five hundred days to avoid climate chaos." That was on June 16, 2014. It grabbed headlines. Nuanced further, he was actually referring to the 21st session of the Conference of the Parties to the United Nations Framework Convention on Climate Change, which was five hundred days away.

As of this writing, we've crossed the halfway mark to climate chaos and we're still counting. . . tick tock!

Six years ago, I approached a fellow attendee at a mineral property owners' meeting with a concept I'd been noodling for some time.

My question was, "With all of these regulations, expenditures and rulings related to the coal industry, why are we addressing this barrage of environmental fallout when the premise of carbon-based manmade global warming is at least questionable and likely bogus? Why not spend more time going after the premise?"

The gentleman, an attorney, was quick to reply. "It's too late. The premise has been accepted and now the best we can do is deal with these issues at hand." That was six years ago. A lot has come down the pike to deal with since then. Anyone reading this with their blinkers open must know what travesties have been visited upon our industry, our pocketbooks and our local economies here in coal country.

So, why not take these well-meaning posers at their word? Drink down their green Kool-Aid and let them have their way. What then? That's what fired my imagination and inspired the writing of this saga. The lawyer guy was right—no way can we pull the deep-rooted underpinnings of global warming from under that which is "settled" as science. By consensus. By order of the UN. Apocalyptic predictions upheld with religious fervor and damned be those who would dare to question.

So let them have everything they want. The land, the people, the resources, whatever they need to achieve their vision. Do what the captains of industry did in *Atlas Shrugged*—abandon ship! Let them have it all! Give them all the rope they need.

By way of surrender, we discover many things. For one, we see who's really running the show, to what end and how far they will go. History offers many dark examples of Utopic visions gone awry. Whoever holds the reins of energy (power) rules the world. Will it be with a green scepter or an iron fist? Is there a difference when every rule and regulation that comes to pass is ultimately enforced at the point of a gun?

My heroes are born of the Appalachians, the Alleghenies, the Cumberlands and the elevated plateaus of Virginia, West Virginia and Kentucky. Many of these rugged highlanders still bear the tough-minded independence of their Scotch-Irish forefathers. The region where *Mountain Whispers* unfolds has been a hotbed of family feuds, coal wars and violent resistance to heavy-handed intrusion by federal agencies. They are among the first and last to stand against confiscation, subjugation and intrusion by outsiders.

So the stage has been set. Big global green government versus a rag-tag bunch of daringly heroic mountaineers. The main characters of *Mountain Whispers* have their own lessons to learn and shadows to conquer even as they take on the colossal powers that be. They are all at the whipsawed end of what can happen when an ideology is hijacked by what CS Lewis deigned "a tyranny sincerely exercised for the good of its victim." The worst kind.

Mountain Whispers is a trilogy, a saga of two cultures, of two divergent ways of life, and ultimately, two paths leading into our future. One way leads to empowerment and living close to the land; the other promotes safety, security, and a global technocracy prescribed to minimize human impact on the environment.

So, I sincerely hope you have enjoyed reading this first book, *Days without Sun*. In the next two books, more character history will be revealed, the constant overcast of sky explained and the powers that be will put our mountain heroes to the test. Book II is ostensibly titled *Mountain Whispers: Echoes* and Book III concludes this series with *Mountain Whispers: Legacy*.

***

Acknowledgments

My thanks go out to everyone who offered encouragement and interest in seeing this first book completed. Reid Lance Rosenthal, a good friend and great author, gave guidance and inspiration. To my angel editor, Sandra Haven at Bristol Services, who patiently waded through the months of my grindings while deftly deploying her soulful understanding and commentary to the story. We never met in person, but I feel we met on a higher plane. You understood the gist of the saga straight away and kept me on track.

I was privileged to have an extended conversation with Robert "Bob" Buskirk who filled me in on Sid Hatfield's checkered career and true incidents related to Sid's burial site. If I say much more, it will be a spoiler.

Two other guys I need to thank have no idea about me, this novel, or how much their mentorship (albeit virtual) has helped. Kudos to Steve Pressfield and his pal Robert McKee. I recommend them to any aspiring or practicing writer. They kick writer butt!

Writing is a lonely affair. I began this work in 2011. My family has provided the necessary means and understanding that enabled me to sequester for untold hours of writing. How fortunate can a man be to have such support in pursuing his passion? To top it off, my son, Nikolai, has offered many ideas on weaponry and battle maneuvers (his province) and my daughter, a blossoming writer herself, has been a fount of fresh ideas. Devani is also a cyber-media-marketing-maven whose assistance with all phases of this work has been ginormous.

I would not be where I am without the constant support and inspiration that I've received from my wife, LeAura. It was Franz Schubert who said it best – *"Happy is the man who finds a true friend, and far happier is he who finds that true friend in his wife."* I am indeed that most happy man!